Close Your Eyes

Tales from the Blinkspace

Edward Martin III

Published by **Hellbender Media**

rare and voracious entertainment

hellbender.net

This book is a work of fiction. Any resemblance between the characters, events, and places herein and real persons, events, and places is purely coincidental, except for such cases where they specifically requested themselves be in the story. In stories in which historical figures are used, it is for purely fictional reasons, humorous reasons, or some unholy combination of the two.

Fear at your own risk.

The stories and images in this collection are © 2012 Hellbender Media and Edward Martin III.

All rights reserved. No part of this book may be used, reproduced, or transmitted in any manner whatsoever without the written permission of the publisher, except in the case of brief quotations embodied in critical articles or reviews.

Cover photography by Edward Martin III

Cover design by Leslie Herzfeld

First edition, released January 2012

This book is dedicated to:

Mia gepatroj,

because of their belief,

mia elekt gefamilio,

because of their support,

mia geamikoj,

because they laughed nervously at the right parts,

kaj mia gemodeloj,

who put up with my crazy requests.

Dankon!

(Vi estas preta por alia libro?)

Table of Contents

Introduction 1

Bodiless 2

February Eighth.. 10

Scales 16

Best Intentions 26

I Saw a Pony.. 31

The Knot 35

Watching 45

Eventuality 49

Cursed 54

X.. 61

Bugs 68

Devotion... 73

Shock Troops 80

The Collector, Part 1: Appetizer 86

The Collector, Part 2: Entree... 92

The Collector, Part 3: Dessert... 96

Adventure... 101

For Space is Deep and Hungry 103

True Love.. 106

Lady Ghost.. 110

The Club 115

The Dance 125

The Theory of String 127

The Gift 132

The Carnival... 138

The Measure of a Man 148

The Score 154

Hearing 162

Vows 165

The Silver in the Dark 171

Love, She is Blind 175

Moonsong 181

Inside Out 185

Underbelly 190

Appetite 196

Making the Deal 202

The Trail 217

The Picture of Myself 223

A Cycle of Echoes 227

Lowercase "g," But Still Worth Keeping an Eye On 233

Sometimes They Know What They're Talking About 239

Songs of Freedom, Songs of Loss 240

Curtains 245

Acclimatization 249

Cryptozoology 254

His Great Power 258

The Circle 262

Freedom's Cost 266

There was Record of its Passing 270

The Fine Print 275

The Dream House 277

No Trouble 282

Maturation 284

A Progression of Eyes 291

Blood of my Blood 297

The Publisher 299

The Author 300

The Last Word 301

Close Your Eyes – Tales from the Blinkspace

Introduction

Behind six million eyeblinks lies another world

A human being blinks about ten times a minute. In that fraction of a second the brain shuts itself down during the blink, so there is no perception of the darkness, or even the passage of time. Everyone's existence appears seamless, but is constantly punctuated by periods of unseen dark existence. At any moment, there is a hole in perception, a cognitive-blind place where someone is mid-blink.

In this place, this ephemeral web of existence spread across the human experience, there are things, places, and life. Hidden from eyes, it is the shadows within the shadows, the teeth in the dark, the true secrets of the world, and usually, it can only be found in the space of an eyeblink.

Usually.

Close Your Eyes: Tales from the Blinkspace explores that Secret World, and brings it out into the open, to properly drive you mad. Read, enjoy, and share with others.

Close Your Eyes: Tales from the Blinkspace is the result of a year's dedication to writing at least one story per week. Sometimes there were more. Most of these stories appeared in the Blinkspace online blog: *hellbender.net/activities/blinkspace/*.

Many of the stories were written as part of a writing marathon at the *H. P. Lovecraft Film Festival*. During that marathon, participants would offer their names, their preferred fates, their favorite settings, and – if they wanted – a story they wanted to parallel. The stories were then written from scratch during the dead zones in the movie schedules. It was an insane combination of improvisation and writing and period-level performance.

And it was wickedly fun!

May you enjoy reading the stories as much as I enjoyed writing them. May you visit the Blinkspace again, for the latest stories. There are always more, it seems...

Bodiless

Part of a writing marathon at the H. P. Lovecraft Film Festival, "Bodiless" is inspired by Travis's request for something "messy."

Travis couldn't sleep. He tried, of course. Every night. But still, no sleep. On the plus side, he was used to it. Travis had not slept in more than two weeks.

After a few days of insomnia, things start to look very different. After a week, they start to look the same. After two weeks, it's most accurate to not refer to experiencing Life as "looking" anymore.

Walking is the best thing you can manage sometimes when you're completely dragged out and tired. Even calling it "tired" seemed a bit of a misnomer. Travis was long past being "tired," but he was not past walking. Even at three in the morning.

"Hey, how ya doin'?" asked the bum.

He stopped. Normally, no one talked to him, especially after the one-week mark. When you look like a zombie, but not as attractive, people leave you alone.

"I seen you around," said the bum. "You walk around."

"Can't sleep," said Travis.

The bum nodded. "Same here." He pulled a pack of cigarettes out of a grimy breast pocket and offered one to Travis. "Smoke?"

"I quit. It was fuckin' up my body."

Again the bum nodded. "That it does," he said. "One of the many inconveniences about bodies – they get fucked up. Well, whatever works for you, my man. Catch you later."

He lit his own cigarette and walked on.

Only after he had gone around the corner had Travis realized all of this had been performed with only one hand – the man's left hand had stayed in his coat pocket during the entire encounter.

Later that night, once he returned home, Travis tried drinking warm milk. It wasn't his idea, but one of his co-workers suggested it. An hour later, while staring at the mixture of warm milk and toilet water, he swore to never listen to that co-worker again. Warm milk. Stupid idea. Stupid co-worker.

The next night, walking again.

"Hey, I knew you would be back," said the voice.

He turned, and the bum was there with another bum. Second bum was in a wheelchair and had no legs. First bum introduced them: "This is the guy I met last night. He's not sleeping." First bum's left hand was missing, the bandage somewhat new.

The second bum nodded sagely. "That's how I got it," he said. He looked up at Travis and waved a hand. Waved a stump, actually.

"How you got it?" asked Travis.

"How I started seeing what really mattered," said the second bum. "How I started realizing what was right with life and what wasn't right with life. It's not always easy, but I found out that the more you sleep, the harder it is to see. Not sleeping – that's the key. You'll find out."

The first bum beamed. "Is that cool or what?" he asked.

Travis nodded.

"He's almost ready to move on," said the first bum.

"Okay," said Travis. Then, to the second bum, "I wish you luck."

"Oh hey, for you, too," said the second bum. "I can't always tell, but with you I can. You're close, man. Really close. You'll start seeing soon what I've been seeing. You'll start knowing what really matters."

Travis moved on into the night. He settled on a park bench and watched the dawn come, thinking about bums without hands.

He saw a woman lead her child to some early appointment, probably some School for Children Who Can Get Up Early. Her fingers were wrapped around his and they

Close Your Eyes – Tales from the Blinkspace

looked like obscene sausages making fingery love. He thought about that and queasiness came over him. Thankfully she moved around the corner.

That day he called in sick. He couldn't call in tired so he called in sick. No one allows you to call in tired, more's the pity.

He got his hair cut. Better. He cut his fingernails down. Better. He looked at himself in the mirror and decided that he could easily stand to lose a little bit of what he saw. Well, eventually, better.

That night, more walking, but a different part of town. Business lights flickered as he walked by, alleys yawned, darkness whispered.

"Hey," said a voice.

He stopped, turned.

"You dropped this." Another bum, missing an entire arm, held out Travis' wallet. Gingerly, he accepted it back.

"Thanks."

"Oh hey, I know you," said the bum.

"I don't think so."

"Yeah, yeah. You're the guy who walks. Who doesn't sleep."

Travis stared hard at the man.

"It's okay," the bum assured him. "We all know. It's cool." His smile, in the grease and grime, was winning, even beatific, and Travis found himself nodding and smiling back.

"Well, you have a good night. Be careful of your wallet – it's part of your identity."

The bum turned and walked on, whistling.

Travis stared, then continued on his walk.

The next day, he tried working again.

"You look like shit," he was informed by his Supervisor.

"I haven't slept in two weeks," he said. "I'm seeing colors that don't exist. I'm hearing sounds that don't exist. I'm apparently famous in the bum community."

His Supervisor nodded absentmindedly and advised "Well, you should get some sleep."

"Well, maybe you should go pound sand up your ass," replied Travis, although it sounded a bit more like "yeah, that would be good, thanks" by the time it actually came out of his mouth.

4

Close Your Eyes – Tales from the Blinkspace

More walking the next night.

"You know how to play?" the voice asked.

Travis stopped. Two bums playing some game, shifting marbles around on a board with holes scooped in it.

Each was missing their legs and an arm.

He stopped and watched.

"It's all about subtraction," said one of them. "It's not a matter of just taking stuff off," he said, as he collected marbles from the board, "but being able to do it in a way that keeps you in the game. You want to stay in the game as long as you can."

His partner nodded and ran his hand across the board, picking marbles up and dropping them off in a pattern that made no sense at all.

"No one respects subtraction," was his addition to the conversation. He looked up at Travis. "Lemme ask you something – have you ever added anything to your life that really truly made you happy?"

"Sure," said Travis, but for a moment, he was silent. Everything he could think of that was supposed to bring him happiness, a new car, a new place to live, a better stereo, whatever – they all ended up having a cloud to mar their silver lining.

One of the bums nodded. "That's what I thought. Now think about subtraction. What has been good to lose lately?"

"Uh… my hair."

"Yeah, good one," said the bum. "Easy one, though."

"My nails. Some weight, I guess."

"Sure," said the other bum. "I read you on that!"

"But there's been a big one," said the first bum. "What've you lost lately?"

The answer came absurdly fast to Travis. "Sleep."

Both bums nodded.

"I'll bet you've been seeing some things, huh?"

"You know it," replied Travis.

"Subtraction," said the other bum.

The first bum made another play, rearranged the marbles on the board. "I think you might find," he said, almost absentmindedly, "that in some cases, more of a good thing is even better."

5

Close Your Eyes – Tales from the Blinkspace

The other bum glanced up. "Are you sure that's a good thing to say?"

The first bum shrugged. "I don't think it's ever a bad thing to say, and I think our walking fella here is starting to see the difference between lies and truths. I think he's starting to see the beauty."

They turned to Travis, a mild bit of amused expectation playing on their faces.

"I don't–" started Travis, but then he thought more. He remembered his days and nights, his walks, the oddly beautiful things and the oddly horrific things. He remembered sausage fingers, and the feeling of touching some peculiar web of happy bums.

One of the bums smiled broadly.

"You should come back tomorrow night," he said. "Downtown. It'll be great."

"What'll be great?" asked Travis.

"You'll see."

"Or you won't, but I'd be surprised if you didn't," said the other.

The next day at work, all Travis could think about was late-night bums. Amputee bums.

"Hey, you're really spacey today," said a co-worker. "What are you thinking about?"

Travis looked up, and without blinking, replied "Hallucinations and midnight bums with not the right number of arms and legs, inviting me to oddly comforting meetings while everyone else I know sleeps and dreams."

His co-worker looked at him, and said "Okay, well, maybe you should get some sleep, then." Then we waved a hand. Travis looked at it. It seemed like a horrible thing, that hand, like some sort of fleshy useless tube with fleshy tubes attached to it. The tubes wiggled. He watched it and felt like vomiting.

That would be a subtractive process, he thought to himself, and that would also be better.

The co-worker kept talking, but suddenly, Travis noticed the man's tongue, also waggling around. Air passed back and forth over his lips, and the tongue moved, and some sort of wet wheezy disgusting sound came out.

"You would be better if you had no arms," Travis said, "and I think maybe your lips and tongue could be torn out and that would be okay," but it came out sounding like "Uh-huh" by the time he said it.

He stepped out that evening, and went downtown.

He walked and waited, and eventually heard "Hey buddy, you made it!"

Close Your Eyes – Tales from the Blinkspace

It was the first bum, a young man with short curly blonde hair. Travis thought he looked surprisingly angelic. Except for the wheelchair, which he operated with his one remaining arm.

"You're in a wheelchair now," he said.

"On my way, on my way," said the man. "Come on, the others are waiting. It's gonna be a great night."

He rolled away and Travis followed. It made sense.

They followed an alley, dropped down a ramp, entered a building.

"It gets harder the farther along you go," said the bum, "but we manage. I think it's close to all working out."

They passed a trio of dirty people, playing some sort of game with bits of broken rocks on the floor. Travis looked more closely and saw that they weren't rocks, but bones. And the people had no legs.

But somehow, that too made sense.

At a downward stair, the bum in front paused. "I'm a little slow going down," he said, "but we'll get there. This next level's where it's really happening."

Expertly, he step-by-stepped his wheelchair down the stairs. It seemed miraculous he never lost control and went careening.

At the bottom, they passed a couple talking softly. They were both bald, and had no legs. The man was bandaged heavily around his midsection, and seemed thinner. They looked up and smiled and Travis found himself grinning back. They just seemed so happy, it was infectious.

His escort leaned back after they had passed.

"It gets serious after this," he said. "I'm happy to bring you down, but I want to make sure you're okay with it."

Travis thought, but realized that he was, in fact, okay with it. The deeper they went, the happier he felt.

"It's always been a process of subtraction," his escort said, as they went deeper. "There isn't a religion that doesn't embrace it, there isn't a god that doesn't respect it. Sometimes it's symbolic, such as fasting. But in other cases, in our case, the symbolism made less sense than actually manifesting."

They passed a small cluster of people, all resting against the wall on raised benches. Legs removed, most arms removed. Other signs of surgery.

"Even medicine recognizes the act of subtraction as an attempt to achieve perfection," he said.

Close Your Eyes – Tales from the Blinkspace

Another cluster of people, and Travis could hear some sort of commotion ahead. In this cluster, there were more things missing. In some cases, eyes.

"People have a lot of trouble with the eyes, until they realize how imperfect vision is, as opposed to spiritual vision. Spiritual vision is perfect. What we visualize can never be as horribly awry as what we actually see. So, eventually, even vision goes. But the senses are always tricky. We're so addicted to them."

The murmuring ahead grew louder, and rhythmic. Travis could feel a subsonic component thrumming through him.

"We never expected anything to come of it, though," his escort said. "We never expected the kind of enlightenment we've had, the kinds of visions we've seen, and the kinds of responses we've had. It's almost a miracle. No, not almost. It is a miracle."

They turned the corner and the hall opened up into a room. The room was a series of progressively higher platforms, and was covered in bodies. All were partial, missing legs, arms, eyes, ears. The higher the platform went, the less each person had.

Travis stopped.

His escort nudged him.

"It's okay," said. "New folks are encouraged to go to the top. To meet Him."

Travis raised an eyebrow.

"We trust you."

He stepped between the people who had removed their flesh, who had removed their imperfect senses, who had removed their connections to a world of pain and fury and frustration. He stepped past them carefully, and noticed that each one hummed and murmured, and it was this music that filled him.

He stepped to the top of the platforms, and saw before him a pile of blankets.

And lying on the blankets, Travis saw Him.

He was hardly physical. He was a brain, kept moist by a soft spray, and an impossibly thin string of muscles and nerves that dangled and coiled from beneath. He was almost entirely subtracted.

And He spoke.

In Travis' brain, He spoke. He said words that only Travis could understand, whispered of great vistas and scenes and abilities. He spoke of the power and the vision. He shared with Travis all the pain, and all the joy of a life, and showed him how it could be placed in a context, how it could still be a memory without twisting and contorting the flesh.

8

Close Your Eyes – Tales from the Blinkspace

He showed Travis how imperfect the flesh was.

They spoke for what seemed like years, and then He brought Travis back. There was a direction now.

Quietly, Travis moved back down to the floor. Only moments had passed and he had seen more in those moments – those insomniac prophetic moments – than most people saw in a lifetime.

He knelt by his escort, and took the man's head in his hands. Tears streamed down his face. "Now I know," he whispered.

"Kinda figured," said his angel. "He has that effect on us all. Here."

From a pocket in his wheelchair, he produced a brilliant reflective item, a polished scalpel. He handed it Travis, who accepted it as his tool to move further. Its cleanliness was its consecration.

He looked at his angel, and his angel looked back.

"It's okay," he said. "We all have to start somewhere on the Path."

Travis nodded, and raised the scalpel to his face.

END

February Eighth

I'm sure nothing this bad can happen on a domestic flight...

Every day is February eighth. She crouches over pretzels and orange juice, pressed against her seat by the deceptively flimsy unfolded tray table. Every day is February eighth.

Out the window, clouds slide by, thin wispy high altitude clouds. More like streaks or rips. Far, far below, the black ocean glitters, reflecting the full moon in a million instant flashes. She looks up and sees the moon swollen high in the sky.

She breathes deeply, and the dry air scrapes her lungs. February eighth. She wipes the last of the pretzel salt from the bag, licks her finger, polishes off the rest of the orange juice, and quietly curses the combination of flavors. She leans back, eyes closed.

"Where are we going?" she asks, in that special way. The voice beside her answers immediately: "Reykjavik," in a deep and confident tone. "Reykjavik," she whispers. She sighs.

She remembers.

This is her job, remembering.

"Sybil Drake," she says.

"Excuse me?" a voice to her left asks.

She opens her eyes and sees a pretty young woman next to her in the middle seat. She smiles and extends a hand. "I'm Sybil Drake," she says. The woman smiles back, takes

Close Your Eyes – Tales from the Blinkspace

the offered hand. "Julie. Julie Tayback." The man next to Julie waves. "My husband Anthony," she adds. "We just got married. We're going to visit Anthony's grandparents."

Sybil smiles. They reek of being in love, these two, and it reminds her of her own life, her wonderful, wonderful life. "Congratulations," she says, and she means it. "I've been married fifteen years and I can't recommend it enough."

"Really?" asks Julie.

"Really," says Sybil.

"Where's your husband now?" asks Anthony. "He's home," says Sybil. "Home with our boys. Two of them. Five and nine."

"And you left them alone?" Julie asks in mock horror. Sybil smiles and remembers the peculiar uncertainty that always accompanies New Love. "Is this really real?" it seems to ask. Impossible to answer, of course, without time. With time, the question becomes foolish. "Hardest thing I've ever done," she says. "No kidding," says Julie. "You'll get back home and they'll be running around in their underwear eating nothing but Pop-Tarts: morning, noon, and night."

Sybil laughs at the image of her three angels doing this. It's funny because she can totally imagine it, totally imagine them losing control and running around the house whooping it up like a bunch of savages. Then she misses them and her heart bounces.

It's February eighth. The date tickles an almost-memory, something like a memory, but not, exactly. She feels hollow.

"What?" asks Julie, seeing the shift. Sybil smiles again. "It's not that," she says. "It's not that at all. It's just that… just that I've never left them alone before." Julie is shocked "Never?" Sybil shakes her head. "I'm a homebody."

She gestures at herself, at the crisp business suit, at the professional hairstyle. "This isn't really me," she says. "I've never been away from my family."

Anthony's interested now. "Never?"

"I was married right out of high school, moved into our place from home. I was a housekeeper. And then, a mother. Never did anything else."

"What about now?" he asks.

Sybil smiles again, and leans forward, conspiratorial. "Now I'm terrified," she admits. They're confused. "I'm a writer," Sybil explains. "Have been all my life. Never sold anything, never published anything. Never even sent manuscripts out to publishers. The boys saw it as my one eccentricity, until last summer, when my husband read my book."

"You wrote a book and never sent it to anyone?" Tony asks.

11

Close Your Eyes – Tales from the Blinkspace

"Nope, no one," she says. "I wrote three mystery novels, actually, and then Craig – that's my husband – saw the third manuscript. He read it and loved it. He read the other two and loved them."

"He better!" says Julie. She favors Anthony with a defiant sort of glance that warns him he better like her books, too, should she also decide to take this path.

"He insisted that I send all three to a publisher immediately. He insisted! He found an address, brought me the envelopes, and helped me write out a cover letter and everything. The boys helped too, talking me up, telling me that they believed in me."

"What happened?" asks Anthony.

"I sold it," says Sybil. "I sold all three. I sold all three to the same publisher and they want more."

"That's great!"

Sybil nods. "So, they're sending me to Iceland for a photo shoot, because the novels all take place in Iceland."

Julie raises an eyebrow. "They're sending you just for pictures?"

Sybil nods. "It's crazy, I know. Just pictures."

"But that's great," says Anthony. "Why would you be terrified of that?"

Because they're taking the pictures tomorrow, Sybil thinks, and feels hollow again. She looks at them, not sure how to explain what she feels. There's nothing wrong, she thinks. It's scary because I've never done this before, never thought I could do this before and here I am, first time out the gate, and I'm doing it. How could that be anything but terrifying?

That's what she wants to tell them, and that's what's probably true, but that's not what feels true. That's not what's haunting her secretly from behind her brain. Behind her brain, it's February eighth and she feels hollowed out, stretched thin, impossibly twisted.

Sybil shakes her head. "I don't know," she says, and it's the truth.

The stewardess breaks the spell. "Can I take that from you?" She holds a bag and gestures toward Sybil's cup. Sybil drops the cup and the pretzel wrapper into the bag and looks up to thank the stewardess. She looks into the woman's eyes, and they are hollowed out as well. A weary sadness hovers over them, painfully visible behind the smile, behind the perky cock of the head. Sybil holds those eyes in hers, and the stewardess holds the gaze for a second longer than normal, instinctively reciprocating.

"I'm so sorry," whispers Sybil. The rumbling roar of the engines masks any sound that might have come out, but her lips move, and her heart stretches out, and this empathy breaks through the cloud around the stewardess for the briefest moment, like a needle through thick cloth. The stewardess stares, caught, exposed, puzzled, and then her

Close Your Eyes – Tales from the Blinkspace

mask clamps back down. Her face becomes professional again, and her smile practiced perfect. "Thank you," she says, shaking the bag slightly to emphasize that this is the only reality she will acknowledge, that she is rejecting whatever it is that just happened.

She moves on.

Sybil turns back to the window, her mind racing.

Anthony asks "Are you okay?" but she doesn't hear his voice. His words are only vibrations, air shaking against membranes in her ears. She's not listening. Something's going wrong.

Her hands shake and her heart rate increases. Whatever it is, it's behind her brain, back where her terror comes from. What is it?

She stares outside.

It's February eighth.

The wing of the plane moves slightly, the running light bobbing up and down. She knows this motion. She's seen it before. It's normal. This isn't the problem.

The ocean below shimmers silently, beautifully. It could be an ocean of black mercury, it's so surreal. This is normal as well. This isn't the problem, but as she says that, she feels the thing behind her brain stirring. It's close, she thinks.

She sees the distant line of lights of the coast of Iceland, coming closer with every second, but seeming so far away. No, she thinks, that's normal, too.

It's all beautiful, but it's all as it should be. She feels this. This is not the problem. But something is. Something is.

She looks up. The moon is full and brilliant and the stars are gone from the sky because of its light.

The thing behind her brain lunges forward, racing, charging blindly to a place where she can tell what it is.

"The moon," Sybil says. "It's the moon."

Julie looks out the window, too, and Sybil stares at the moon, at the perfect silver disc. She hears Julie say something, but she can't stop to even understand what the words are. She stares at the moon. She stares at it and she is afraid.

There is a wobble, and she wants to think it's the aircraft, but it's not.

It's the moon.

It billows, stretches, impossibly, distending.

The moon shatters.

Close Your Eyes – Tales from the Blinkspace

The light flickers out over the ocean, and she cannot take her eyes from the place. Stars spring out. She hears a few gasps from elsewhere in the plane, other people who happened to be looking out, who don't know what just happened, or who don't understand, or who simply don't believe.

But she knows. She watched it, and her eyes are not blinking. Her eyes are not blinking because where the moon used to be, where the glittering spread of stars now shines, there is a circle. A black circle.

Now the plane does buck slightly, and Sybil's stomach lurches, but she ignores this. She watches the circle as it grows.

You couldn't just tell us, she thinks. You couldn't just let us find our own peace with it. You had to hide it from everyone else, had to hide this intruder, this monster of a planet, dark and solid, hurtling through space. In one instant, she hates every astronomer on the planet – every astronomer and their terrible secret. In the same instant, she feels a great sadness for them, knowing the burden they carried in secret. For how long, she wondered? The answer comes to her as instantly. For only a week.

The circle grows and there are red glowing veins on it, friction rips from the death of the moon, spreading to reveal the intruder's mantle. The sun, on the other side of Earth, lights a ring around the planet as it comes closer.

Her heart stops and her stomach lurches again. She feels light and buoyant, as if cresting a hill. The plane bucks again, the engines pitch high, and the scene shifts, but not enough to block it. Not enough to block her view of the intruder.

It fills the sky, and, dimly, she hears screams around her, people making their last seconds as noisy as possible, calling out, wishing for help, pleading.

Buoyancy increases, and the plane bucks a third time, and this time there is no recovery. It's gravity, she thinks. Inverse square of the distance. As the intruder gets closer, we are pulled away. Her eyes flicker down, but the ocean is not visible. The ground is not visible. She looks back to the sky.

The stars are gone and the sky burns violet, cracking open. She feels herself, the airplane, the world, falling upward, and then there is a noise that no living creature should ever hear, a stretching, tearing, unbelievable ripping.

It's February eighth when Earth shatters.

And there was Nothing.

"Please stop it," she whispers in that special way. The voice beside her, deep and confident, speaks. "You always do that," it tells her, "but it's exactly what you asked for."

She knows this.

Sybil Drake is gone, and she remains.

Close Your Eyes – Tales from the Blinkspace

"How many?" she asks.

"Seven hundred fifty-two thousand, eighty-six down…"

In Nothing, she would weep, if she could.

"Not again," she begs, but she knows the words will be ignored.

"Six billion, nine hundred forty-four thousand, five hundred and sixty-four remaining."

"No. Please."

"You were very specific with the Wish."

"No."

"'Longer than everyone else,' you said."

"You–" she starts to say.

There is a flash.

She opens her eyes. Today is February eighth. She stares at the strange woman in 19C, the woman with the compelling eyes. For a moment, she is not thinking of her boyfriend – of her ex boyfriend. For a moment, she is not thinking about the brand new infection tearing the hell out of her body thanks to that total bastard. The woman seems to see right through her and for a moment, she is soft, but that moment passes.

She remembers. She clamps the Happy Face of Servitude on, thanks the woman in 19C and moves on, remembering. That's her job, remembering.

Her life unfolds, the past unfolds, and she remembers.

Today is February eighth. Every day is February eighth.

END

Scales

"Scales" is a story that took a long time to cook. I'm not sure I can wish you to enjoy it per se, but on the other hand, I do hope it stays with you as much as it's staying with me.

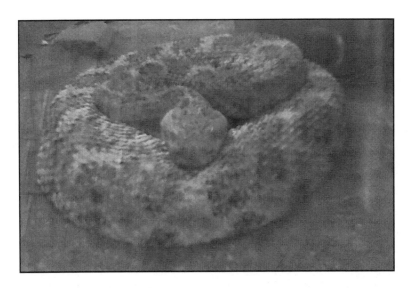

It was hot. Damn hot. The road ahead wiggled and buckled from the heat, and in the Dart's rearview mirror, Petra could see the road behind her doing the same thing.

The wind buffeted her from the open windows, letting in the Sonoran heat. The Dart had switches that claimed to be air conditioning, but she had long ago concluded they were simple decoration. The only thing worse than the hot wind blasting through the car's cabin was the soul-smelter it turned into when she closed the windows. At seventy miles an hour, this wind was a hurricane.

She looked through the rearview, and the road – still twisting like a snake in mirage – spread out empty behind her. Empty! She slowed down and turned her head. The road was empty for at least five or ten miles. Then – a flicker. The little flame of hope puffed out as the flicker resolved enough for her to recognize the green Challenger coming over the hill. Still, ten miles behind is better than here.

She floored the accelerator pedal, hoping to coax a few more miles per hour out of the Dart's engine, but it was clear the only way she was going to go faster was to suddenly discover downhill, a tailwind, and an impossible patch of luck. "The Dart's a great car!" he told her. "I can keep it in tune for you and work on it for you," he said. "It'll never let you down," he said.

She glanced back into the rearview mirror. "I've been let down," she muttered.

Close Your Eyes – Tales from the Blinkspace

She pressed the pedal harder against the floor, mostly because it felt a little better, as if she could push the car a tiny bit faster with the pressure. Ten miles was a ten minute lead, and that was better than nothing. She rubbed the back of her head carefully, and her hand came back with a little blood on it. "Bastard," she said.

It shouldn't have caught her by surprise. She was smarter than that.

*

Over the past three years, Cory's mind had started fraying, and his responses became unpredictable and sometimes violent. Everything had seemed fine, had seemed hunky-dory up until that point, but by the time things got really bad, Petra could review her entire history with this man and see every little cascade of pebbles that led to the eventual avalanche.

She nodded grimly to herself in answer to the question that always followed – yes, it was true she ignored a few signs. But love, ah, love does strange things, and you always hope it turns out better than it would, that the mountainside would settle down and the shifts mellow out and everything would return to normal.

No such thing had happened, however. Things simply grew worse and worse, and she started to understand better the entire picture. She started seeing the pattern the way she ought to have seen it from the beginning. She started seeing the monster he had been hiding.

She should have been ready for the first blow.

It caught her just behind her right ear. Had she not suddenly turned her head as she came into the motel room, it would have been on the side of her head, maybe even right in the face. She wasn't even sure what it was that struck her – a lamp or a piece of chair, or whatever – but it rang her bells bad and she fell to the floor.

His face came in above her, the face of the man she loved, the man she married, the man who asked her out on a surprise weekend vacation to the middle of the Mexican desert. His face wavered like a heat mirage, and his words came out like soup, and she knew it was something in her brain that made it that way, that jumbled his face and words. She knew he had hit something important.

She raised her arm as he swung the thing again, and a detonation of pain numbed her arm.

He roared inarticulately (or maybe she couldn't understand him), and raised it again, but then the room was flooded with sunlight, and she heard voices shouting in Spanish and saw other people at the door. The man who ran the place, the maid, and someone else. They also wavered in her vision. One of them seemed to have a baseball bat.

Cory lunged at them, and all four dissolved in her mind into a mass of screaming blows.

Close Your Eyes – Tales from the Blinkspace

Somehow she rolled onto all fours, and crawled past them, out into the sunlight, and pulled herself into the Dart. Her arm was no longer numb, and for that she was glad, but only a little, as the whole thing throbbed and pulsed in pain. It didn't feel broken, but at this level of pain, there was hardly a difference. Most importantly, she had managed to start it and drive away, her arm screaming, her brain thick and garbled, and blood seeping down her neck and into her shirt.

*

At least the blood flow had slowed. It was only oozing. Still, she knew she would have to do something about it, as soon as she had time. She'd been driving for nearly two hours.

She looked back again. About ten miles of desert road spanned the space between she and Cory's Challenger.

She kept the pedal pressed against the floorboard, and tried to not think about what must have happened back at the motel.

Ahead, in the dance of the heat mirage, she saw a break, a dark smudge, something in the road. Maybe a town? Maybe something else?

It was a house.

It rose above the desert, alone and dark, like an ancient hand, with towers and high windows. It didn't belong here, she knew. It was an anachronism, something from the turn of the century, a gothic and forbidding import from a time and place that no longer existed. As it grew closer, she could see that it was huge, four stories at least.

She looked at the fuel gauge and decided this had to be the place. A quarter tank wasn't going to take her much further anyway.

She swerved from the road, fishtailing into the courtyard, wheels skidding over gravel. The house loomed above her as she tumbled out of the Dart and slammed the door.

"Anyone home?" she called out. "Help!" She ran to the door and pounded on it, but only silence and echoes replied. She tried the lever. Although it was rusted stiff, it cracked free, clanged down, and the door swung open.

"Hello?" she called out as she stepped into the gloom. "Hello, are you here? Is anybody here?"

There was still no answer.

Dust lay thick on every surface and the air was still, dry, and dead.

Ten minutes. Probably less.

She ran through the house, calling out, and searching for anything, to help her. Maybe she would find an old hunting rifle, or pistols, or maybe something else.

18

Close Your Eyes – Tales from the Blinkspace

Petra raced through every room, pulled open drawers, shuffled through ancient papers, objects, and artifacts. She touched everything, looked everywhere, and finally, she saw the stairs leading down.

It was absurd to think of a house with a deep basement in the middle of the Mexican desert. It made no sense. She was about to turn away when she heard the revving growl of the Challenger's engine as it pulled up in the courtyard.

She hissed and ran down the stairs.

The stairs went deep.

The walls changed as she descended, becoming more rocky, and she realized the house had been built over whatever this was, a cave or cavern or something.

Streaks of phosphorescent material lined the walls and ceiling above her and by the time she reached floor level and stumbled out across the dirt floor, the room around her was light enough to read by.

She stepped through the hall, avoiding a couple of stones on the floor, around a corner and into a temple.

It had to be a temple – it couldn't be anything else.

Grooves and designs in the floor radiated from the altar at the lowest end of the room, and even the phosphorescent material followed those rows. Chairs and benches and old church pews had been dragged down here and situated around the altar, in a semicircle.

Petra walked past the pews, drawn toward the altar, eyes wide in wonder and fear.

Her head twinged again and she reached up and felt it. Her fingers came back wet with blood, but still no more than in the car.

The altar was wide and formed a shallow bowl. It was carved all over, some in fine script she couldn't read, and also in pictures she could. One in particular, a central image, was a snake rising hypnotically from a spiral of flame. It held her eyes and she gazed long at the carving. It seemed to be the oldest, most worn carving on the altar.

She trailed a finger up the snake's carved body to the head, and her finger moved perfectly in the groove. Then she saw the streaks of blood left over from her head.

"Oh no!" she whispered. She scrubbed it off with her shirt sleeve. "I'm sorry," she whispered to the snake. "I know no one's been down here for a long time, but I didn't mean to make a mess. Sorry."

She looked at it and it looked clean, and smoothed out her sleeve.

There was no blood on it.

19

Close Your Eyes – Tales from the Blinkspace

She looked back at the sculpture, and at her sleeve. No blood on either. Maybe it was just moisture, not blood? Maybe–

"Petra! Goddammit!"

She jumped as if bit as Cory's deep voice bellowed from the top of the stairs.

She stood up, searching for a way out, but the temple was a dead end, was a cavern that the stairs led to. There was nowhere she could run.

Against the wall at the back of the temple were cupboards – also random furniture that must have been brought down to hold supplies, clothes, food, whatever.

She dashed over and tried the knobs, and nearly laughed in joy when she found one that was empty and practically her size. She squeezed in and closed the door behind her.

Just as the latch clicked, she heard his heavy footsteps coming down the stairs.

A slivered crack above the hinge offered her a view of the temple, only a few degrees, but she could see the altar, could even see the snake on it, which must have been a trick of light and shadows, as the carving seemed weirdly in motion.

"I wish you were alive," she whispered. "I need your help – anybody's help – so much."

"Petra!"

He was in the room.

She froze, staring at the snake, wishing herself tiny and invisible.

He stomped past her field of vision, carrying the baseball bat, which was now dark-stained.

He walked up to the front of the room, to the altar, and looked around it.

"I know you're down here," he muttered. "I can smell that fuckin' perfume."

He bounced the bat against the top of the altar, emphasizing each word.

"You and I need to have a little talk, Petra. A little talk, y'know. Just a little talk."

He walked over to one side, out of her field of view.

"That's all I wanted," he said. "Just to talk. You didn't have to drive away. You didn't have to leave me. It was a mess, baby. A real mess. All I wanted was to talk!"

He slammed the bat against something she couldn't see, probably one of the pews or chairs.

She jumped a little. Not much, but a little, and he was silent. She knew this silence. It was his crafty silence.

20

Close Your Eyes – Tales from the Blinkspace

Her eyes locked onto the snake, pleaded, begged, and then the cabinet door whipped open.

She screamed and flailed out, tried to ward him away, but he reached in and grabbed her. His fingers closed around the hair at the back of her head, and he yanked hard and she tumbled out onto the floor.

"Knock it off!" he said, and she felt her head jerk sideways as the bat connected.

She tried to twist, tried to turn, but it wasn't quite working. Her eyes darted around the room, and his shadow fell over her.

He swung the bat again, twice, and her ribs burst in a flower of pain. She heaved and felt the grating of broken bone. She screamed, and it was deep and guttural. She tasted blood.

"Shut up!" he screamed, and stomped on her chest, cutting the scream off with a whoosh. The pain was stars and rays of light and a bomb of unbelievable agony. Her eyes focused briefly on the altar, briefly on the snake, and she knew she could see it moving, could see it looking at her.

"Pluh- pluh-" she tried to beg. Nothing came out but blood.

Cory hefted the bat. "I only wanted to talk!" he swung the bat down and she stopped trying to speak.

"I only just wanted to talk." He swung it again. "I'm no different than anyone else." He swung it again. "I have needs, and I need to be heard." He swung it again. "It's not that hard, is it?" He swung again. "Just, just fucking listen to me once in a while, bitch!" He swung the bat again.

Then he stopped. He stopped and looked at her. At what was left of her.

He knelt down, poking at her with the bat, which had splintered as much as she had.

Slowly, he started to nod. "Good," he said. "You needed to listen. I'm your husband. You, you, you gotta obey me."

He stood up. Sniffed. Wiped the sweat out of his eyes with his sleeve. A bright red streak crossed his forehead.

"Well, okay," he said. He pointed the bat at her one last time, just in case, but she was never going to get up. He stared at her. "Okay, then. Fuck this." He threw the bat to the other end of the room. It bounced off the rock wall and fell at the foot of the altar.

"Bye Petra," he said. "It's been real."

He stomped across the room and up the stairs.

*

Close Your Eyes – Tales from the Blinkspace

At the top of the stairs, he stopped, puffing from exertion. The room seemed bright after the dim light of the cavern, and he blinked away a few stars before stepping out.

He looked around for a minute. Maybe there was something here of value, something that he could take that would make up for this fucking mess. He spent a whole minute squinting through the dusty air, just letting his breath catch back up with him. Some of this shit looked like antiques, but it was all run down, all dusty and faded and cracked.

He shook his head – the best thing he could get from this place would be distance.

He walked across the room and opened the door, but the lever slipped through his fingers and the door closed, blown by a brief wind. He reached again, but this time, the lever, having rusted for years, finally broke off, leaving only a jagged stump of red metal in the door.

"..the fuck?" he said. He knelt and looked at the knob. He poked at it with a fingernail, but it wouldn't move. It was completely fused by rust.

"Okay, fine." He looked around, and picked up a vase. He walked over to the window and heaved the vase through.

Except it didn't go through – it bounced off the ancient glass, and shattered on the floor at his feet.

He stared at the uncracked, unmarked window.

Next to the fireplace, he found a poker, and came back to the window. He swung the poker, but it also bounced off the glass, skidding off his shoulder in the process. The other three ground floor windows similarly resisted his attempts to break them.

Then he heard it.

It was a whisper in the air, a whisper just outside of his own brain, a whisper that felt like the whole house coming alive.

He heard a voice in it.

"Who's there?" he called out. "Who's in here? Look, I'm done. Just let me out and I'm done."

The whispering continued, intensified, became soft voices he could just not quite hear.

"I'm serious – you let me outta here or I'll fuck you up!" He brandished the poker. "You don't think I will, you better check your basement, assholes."

He spun, and tripped on a fold of rug, and fell. He scrambled back to his feet and waved the poker around some more. Where the hell where they?

Then he heard voices, distinct voices in the whispering, and one voice in particular. A voice that sounded soft, yet precise. A voice that was in the whole house, and in his own ears.

22

Close Your Eyes – Tales from the Blinkspace

"Imbalance," it said. "There is imbalance. You are imbalance." He looked around, because it sure sounded like someone right behind him, but there was no one there.

"Where the fuck are you?!"

The voices whispered to him, and he heard a few words distinctly. He heard "we" and "here" and some other word that his mind couldn't understand, some syllable he couldn't grasp.

The soft deep voice spoke.

"My children," it said. "My hunger, my children, my… arms. Balance," it said.

Damn – it sounded exactly in his ear, like someone was right there. Cory swung blindly behind him, but hit nothing.

He crouched and turned, and again, he tripped on a fold of carpet. This time, the poker skittered across the floor.

He clambered to his feet and stepped over to collect his weapon, but fell again.

His foot was wrapped up with a length of diamond-patterned carpet runner from the hallway. He reached to untangle his foot and stopped, frozen. Another loop of carpet runner swung lazily over his leg. It settled like a broad hand, gripping his calf.

"Balance," whispered the voice, and the runner started moving.

He beat at it with his hands, but it heaved and buckled and twitched and lifted itself into the air.

He was jerked flat, and then raised up by his foot, suspended in the air. He screamed, and it was a hoarse, girlish scream.

The carpet runner swung him about, and he saw the entire length of it, slithering through and filling the hallway.

It moved him through the air, and toward the basement door.

He kicked and screamed and tried to bend upwards to stop it, but it was steel cable as far as he was concerned.

It weaved and slithered and brought him down into the basement. Into the temple.

*

He had not left her on the altar. He was sure of that. But when the runner lifted him high into the air, even upside down, he saw that her body was cradled on the altar, which he had not done. She was naked and he could see other marks on her from other times she had been trouble.

His mind started to fragment even more.

Close Your Eyes – Tales from the Blinkspace

"No," the voice whispered, and this time, in its silent strength it shook the room. "You are not leaving yet," it said. "There is an imbalance."

"What imbalance?!" he screamed, and spittle flew out and into his eye.

The runner dropped him to the floor and he tried to roll, to stand up, but it wrapped itself around his waist, held him upright and in place. He struggled, clawed at it, but it wouldn't budge.

"My children and I," said the voice, "need our hands, need her. She is our hands. She is our..." it searched for the word. "...our priestess. You took our hands just when she came. You took them and now there is an imbalance. I need my hands. My children need their hands. We need our priestess."

"What? She's never been here before. She's not your priestess. She's my fucking wife!"

"She gave the promise," the voice said. "She gave her blood. She gave herself."

On the altar, there was a twisting winding glowing thread, a finger-wide tracing in the form of a snake. The other lines on the altar lit up, a dark rich red.

On the altar, Petra sat up.

Cory giggled, because there wasn't enough of her to know how to stand up – she looked like a doll without a head. His mind cracked more deeply.

She stepped from the altar, and stood behind it. She reached down and picked up the bat. It was splintered and broken and soaked in blood. Chunks of bone and hair clung to it. She held the bat to her body, ran it over the surface, poked at the exposed shattered ribs. Where she touched, the bones knit. Where the bat passed, the flesh sealed and healed. Even bruises disappeared.

He watched as the bat replaced brain and blood and snot, rebuilt her skull, and replaced skin and hair. She was beautiful again, more beautiful than he had seen her in years. She practically glowed.

"Petra?" he said. "Honey?"

Slowly, her eyes rose to meet his. She shook her head softly.

"I promised," she said, and her voice was the softest steel he'd ever heard. "I gave myself, body and soul. I was accepted."

She held the bat out in front of her. It was no longer splintered – it looked new.

"You had no right to take me back," she said.

"You're my wife!"

"No. I am not yours any more. I am his."

24

Close Your Eyes – Tales from the Blinkspace

She touched the altar and the symbols flared. In the room around him, he heard the voices again and now he could see where they came from. Now he could see the floor and walls of the temple constantly moving with a layer of snakes, of black snakes and red snakes and white snakes and yellow snakes. Of snakes with stripes, of snakes with spots and rings and patterns. They all whispered as they watched him.

"I belong to him and I belong to his children. You made an imbalance. I am whole, and now there is an imbalance. Now there is something needed. You are needed to rebalance it all. Your flesh. Your blood."

She stepped back and the muscular bands of diamond-patterned carpet runner lifted him in the air and lay him atop the altar.

"No," he whispered, not believing.

"I'm sorry," she said. "I'm not as strong as you, so I'm afraid it will take longer."

She swung the bat and he screamed.

END

Best Intentions

Part of a writing marathon at the H. P. Lovecraft Film Festival, "Best Intentions" is inspired by Emily's request for a story for a couple of friends. One must perish and the other not. And it must take place in a library.

"I hate working Friday nights," grumbled Danny. He had an apple and he stared at it. The library was utterly silent except for the faint echoes of Danny's voice coming back at him.

His own voice sounded terrible, so he opted for a different sound. He slid open a desk drawer, pulled out a sharp pencil and tossed it dart-like at the apple. The first three times, the pencil missed and skittered across the desk and fell on the floor. Each time, Danny struggled, trying to decide if he actually wanted to stand up and retrieve it and each time being so overcome by boredom that the sound of pencil skittering overrode the effort of collecting the pencil.

Finally, he struck the apple dead-on. The pencil wavered, the point buried deep. He leaned closer. Staring.

"Fascinating."

"Excuse me," said the voice.

Close Your Eyes – Tales from the Blinkspace

At first, Danny thought it was a voice in his head, so he dutifully ignored it, as was his habit when the voices in his head tried interrupting an otherwise fascinating activity.

"Excuse me," the voice persisted, and this time he looked up. His ears had clearly heard the voice.

One of the students stood in front of the desk, as if needing help. "Am I interrupting your apple experience?" he asked.

"It's Friday," said Danny, by way of explanation.

This was sufficiently opaque to the student that it took him a few seconds to form a response.

"I'm looking for a book," he said.

Danny nodded. "Are you a student?" he asked. It was, unfortunately, not uncommon for non-students to try renting books. You would figure they could steal books from MIT or Harvard, but apparently those fine institutions didn't attract thieves nearly as well as Miskatonic. Apparently, Miskatonic's library was a sweet, sweet honeypot of some kind.

"Yes," the man said, and handed a card over.

Danny examined it, as if it were a hundred-dollar bill. As if it was possibly a clever fake.

"You are Barry Ginsburg?" he asked.

"I look enough like him, don't I?" the man asked.

Danny narrowed an eye. Smart-alecks didn't last very long at this school.

Warily, he handed the card back.

"How can I help you?" he asked.

"I'm looking for a book."

"Yes, I got that. But the shelves are open. Do you need help searching? We don't have everything in the computer yet, but the card catalog–"

"I'm looking for a copy of *The Necronomicon*," said the man.

"Oh."

There was a silence between them.

Danny kept hoping that the student would understand that "silence" was the equivalent of "please don't repeat your request and in fact, go home."

Barry leaned closer.

27

Close Your Eyes – Tales from the Blinkspace

"Are you okay?" he asked.

"Yeah," said Danny. "Okay, are you sure? That's a rare book."

"Yeah, I'm working with Dr. MacLaren."

Danny nodded slowly. "Be right back," he said and stood up.

The Rare Books Room always smelled dank, a little bit like feet. Danny hated it.

He came back.

"Here," he said, and handed the book to Barry.

Barry stared at the title.

"You're joking, right?"

"You don't want it?"

"This isn't the book I asked for." Barry held the book up. It was a copy of *Wee Tommy Schnizzlefritz*.

"It's not?" asked Danny.

"I don't even know what this is. What is this, German?"

Danny peered at the book. "Probably," he said.

Barry set it down. "I want a copy of *The Necronomicon*."

Danny stared. "Are you sure?" he asked.

"Yes. I'm sure."

"Okay, I'll be right back."

A few minutes later, he came back and handed Barry a book.

"This should work," he said.

Barry's eyes narrowed.

"Why are you doing this to me?" he asked. He held the book up, accusingly. "This is Italian erotica."

"Yes," said Danny. "I think you'll get more out of that than the other book."

"Are you... is there something wrong with you?" Barry asked.

"Why?"

"These are not the books I'm looking for. Why can't you bring me the book I'm looking for?"

28

"The Necronomicon is a very serious book," said Danny. "A very dangerous book. I don't think it's such a good thing to be carrying around willy-nilly."

"Willy-nilly…? I need it for class!"

Danny rested his head in his hand. "Yes, I know, you told me. But it's very dangerous."

Barry took a deep breath. "Look, I'm a student, right?"

"Yes."

"And you're the librarian, right?"

"I am."

"So why can't you just bring me the goddamn book?"

Danny said "I can tell that we're not going to come to an agreement on this."

He turned and left.

Five minutes later, he returned, a large misshapen manuscript in his hands.

"Is that *The Necronomicon*?" asked Barry.

"I don't think you're going to like it," said Danny.

"It's not some book of Rumi poetry, or some other crap."

Danny looked offended. "I told you it is," he said, "but I really recommend against this."

"Just give me the book."

Danny set the book on the counter and slid it across. Barry rested his hand against it.

"Feels weird," he said.

"I told you – I don't think this is a good idea. I do have a copy of some really nice Rumi poetry if you prefer."

Barry stared at him. "Check me out, please."

Danny swiped Barry's card and the computer beeped obediently.

"Thank you." Barry started opening the book.

"I'd rather you not do that," said Danny.

Barry glared at him and flipped the cover open.

It was like a tornado. It was brilliant and sparkly and there was a sound coming from it that was like a scream, but a scream that could never come from the throat of a man.

Close Your Eyes – Tales from the Blinkspace

Danny shaded his eyes.

The book jumped and skipped and the maelstrom of energy, barely contained, spun furiously around the room.

Barry tried backing away, but a thread of energy, like a hooked finger, wrapped itself around him. He screamed, but another thread reached into his mouth, grabbing his tongue. His eyes sparked, his hair stood up, and his body lifted from the ground.

Everything that was Barry was twisted and turned inside out, was thrown into the air, was tossed and spun and, eventually, once the book had extracted everything it could, slowly spiraled back down through the air, back down into the open pages, back deep into the book.

The final impact shook the counter, flipping the book's cover closed.

Danny uncovered his eyes and stared.

He shook his head, picked the book up, and walked it back to the Rare Book Room.

A minute later, he sat back at his seat, pulled the pencil from the apple, aimed, and threw again. The pencil missed and flew to the floor.

He glared at the pencil.

"I *really* hate Fridays."

END

I Saw a Pony

"I Saw a Pony" is inspired by lonesome morning walks and the fact that My Little Pony dolls just stare and stare and stare at you...

I have seen the Future. I am terrified, and I am at peace with that.

I can't show anyone else the Future. I'll certainly never see it again. I do, however, with an internal compass confidence, know that this is it. I don't have to see it again. I just know.

I knew it as soon as I saw the pony.

The paths between my house and my work run through a wetlands area. All the developments within three miles drain into this area, into the sullen creek threading through it. A couple times a year, the whole thing floods from upland rain, then drains

Close Your Eyes – Tales from the Blinkspace

again, reeking of moist rot and leaving silty slicks that Summer and the passage of feet eventually destroy. It's harmless, and no one will ever build here.

Paths sliver this wetland into long strips, sometimes disappearing into housing developments, sometimes dead-ending at lonely park benches, sometimes looping back on themselves like a duck-infested Klein bottle. The asphalt of the paths is old, cracked, and humped up from underlying tree roots doing the thing that underlying tree roots have done since the beginning of Time. Sometimes the paths are in the open. Sometimes the paths twist under thick trees.

Four different kinds of people use these paths.

First are the Day People, with their oh-so-bright clothes, their mp3 players strapped to their biceps, or their pert little bluetooth sets. They huff and puff and jog and shout out their cheerful mating calls: "Morning! Good morning!" to each other and to anyone so hapless as to cross their paths. I've seen them greet dogs. Unaccompanied dogs. Day People are like the Sun – they're everywhere and you can't get away from them.

The second are the Night People. They brood and pace and smoke. They grind up their daily life debris, sucking down cigarettes, weeping over breakups, fuming over personal transgressions. Sometimes they perch in the playground swings, squeaking back and forth while they formulate random plans. You see the cherries of their cigarettes, or you sometimes hear them, but there is no talking with the Night People.

The third are people like me and I can tell you we are few in number. We use the paths for business, going to or from, and at ungodly hours. We watch the sun rise in the morning and we watch the sun set in the evening. In the evening, we watch the Day People drift away, and the Night People slouch in. In the morning, we watch the Night People slink away, and the Day People bounce in. I'm neither, and as far as I'm concerned, that's a good thing. People like me don't really like people very much, including other people like me. We don't talk to each other.

The fourth kind of people, though? I didn't even know they existed until I saw the pony.

Of all the habits I've acquired in my life, none has been so peculiar as my quietness. I can't remember when I thought that would be a neat thing to learn, but it was early grade school. All the other kids were noisy, and I wanted to be quiet. I wanted to be so quiet they didn't know I was there. After years of practice, I've become pretty good at it. I can creep on practically any surface. I don't shuffle or hitch my feet unless I want people to hear me, and I pay a lot of attention to where I'm walking. Being quiet isn't just footsteps, either. This took a while to learn and understand. It's everything else you do. It's how you breathe, how you move your body, how you dress, everything. All these things contribute and if you do them all right, nobody will ever know you're there. My neighbors probably think my apartment is empty. I'm fine with that – I can't imagine getting on well with them, based on what I hear through my walls.

Everyone else is noisy. You don't realize how noisy other people are until you're quiet. I suppose that's obvious, but you really have to experience it to understand it.

Close Your Eyes – Tales from the Blinkspace

Being quiet has a lot of benefits. You learn more when you're quiet. Some of those things are things other people might not have said if they knew you were around, so that can be a mixed blessing. Also, it's fun. Try and see how complicated a day you can have and still be completely silent. It's like always playing a personal game in your head. And, of course, if I weren't so quiet I would never have seen the pony.

A particular section of my morning path is even less frequented than the rest. Roots heave through the asphalt, completing the cycle begun by the tangled tree crowns overhead. The creek is only a few yards away and the draft is very shallow, so this section floods often, coating the trees with mud and flotsam. Most people avoid this part of the path because there is a much more civilized one parallel to it, that runs in front of a housing development, with lots of people visible and lots of social interaction. I prefer the path for exactly the same reason – because everyone else is somewhere else. If that's not a good reason, I don't know what is.

It was on that particular piece of the path, while I was walking without noise, just before I emerged from the dark canopy of trees, that I saw the pony.

I heard it before I saw it, a soft pat-pat of feet on the asphalt. At first, I had no idea what would be causing that sound, and then I saw it, and it saw me. In that instant, I knew the Future.

I'm sure that at some time in the distant past, a hundred million years ago or so, a huge dinosaur was tearing up the vegetation, or chowing down on some other huge (probably dead) dinosaur, and noticed – barely – the tiny furry things skittering off in the bushes, or at the edge of the kill. Too small to screw with, and they certainly don't eat enough to even be noticed, so no sense in paying attention to them. Is it possible, I wonder, for that dinosaur, somewhere deep in its brain, to recognize that this insignificant little furry thing was a precursor to the Rise of Mammals? Is it possible that somewhere, a dinosaur saw these creatures and recognized them for what they were, that this was their own Future, staring them right squarely in the face. I wonder if it shocked them. I wonder if they felt, in their minds, the whispered knell of their own end?

I know I did.

It stood, at most, three inches tall. Its skin was smooth, hairless, and translucent. In the moment we stared at each other, I could have sworn it was a toy, a detailed, delicate toy. A mad creation from a line of mad creations, creatures as different from us as a vole might be from a dinosaur.

Its four legs ended in slender paws, each splitting into thin fingers that gripped the rocks of the asphalt. Its head narrowed into a glass bulb, like a child's drawing of a seahorse, and two black dots marked eyes.

Across its tiny haunches draped lacy bags, woven of forest silk and stuffed with sweet maple helicopter seeds and one enormous blackberry, early for the season. Food for days.

Close Your Eyes – Tales from the Blinkspace

I stared at the pony, this creature that was at once so common and at the same time so alien. I stared at it for long seconds, my eyes watering, because staring at this creature was infinitely easier for my stunned mind than to try and take in its rider.

It balanced on the pony, boneless legs curled underneath, thin skin pulsing with blue and pink fluid. I forced myself to look at it, to see it. With inky pinprick eyes, it stared back at me. It blinked once, a thin flashing film.

Softly, and without a sound, I inhaled. My world fell apart.

I saw the Future. I saw the giants of the world, consuming food and themselves in a manner nothing less than obscene. Mountains of food, chewed, swallowed, excreted. And reproducing, mating, sweating, seething, and spreading across the planet in a desperate gamble for immortality, but ultimately like all of Nature's large-scale experiments, doomed. Doomed and knowing it.

This was the Future. The Future was tiny and small and quiet and could live for weeks on three seeds and a berry. The Future's feast was the crumbs of our leaving. We will eat, consume and, eventually destroy ourselves, but the Future will enter a world that is an unimaginable bounty.

It leaned forward, nudging the pony, and reluctantly, the pony continued across the path. I did not move.

Pat-pat-pat…

Just as it drifted into the salal at the edge of the path, it spared one last look at me. I lost myself in the eyes of the Future.

I don't take that path anymore. I don't know anyone who does. I take different routes. I walk with others. I drive sometimes, playing my music loud. I prefer the company of people whenever I can get it, the chatter and buzz of common life. I am noisy.

I avoid the quiet. When it's quiet, when I can hear nothing else outside my skull, I still hear the footfalls of the pony, the soft pat-pat-pat of the Future.

I am terrified of this sound. I am terrified, but I am at peace with it.

END

The Knot

"The Knot" started out as a brief moment in watching the results of one of my buddy's 48-hour Film Festival entries. While I'm disinclined to participate in the 48HFF, nevertheless, I'm glad I watched their entry, as it started the seed for "The Knot".

She quietly watched him.

She was expected to take notes, but she always spent a little time first, just watching. It often revealed more than any pile of notes.

His hands shook as he tied the knots. The rope was a green hempish kind of rope, with lots of chaos in the weave. She imagined how rough it would feel running through her fingers. His hands were old, sporting wrinkles and dark brown patches. She watched as the knot grew in complexity. His shaking fingers slid rope in and out of loops, twisting and tugging.

After an intense twenty minutes, he seemed done. He held the ball of string in the air, staring at it.

Nothing happened, but Elizabeth found herself leaning inward, also looking at the knot.

He stopped staring and set it on the floor. His face was filled with disappointment. After a long sigh, he started untying the knot, unraveling his sculpture.

Once he had nothing but loose rope in his hand, he stared off into the distance a moment and then started tying the rope into a knot again.

"He'll do that all day," said a voice behind her.

Close Your Eyes – Tales from the Blinkspace

She jumped.

The intern was a young man and he smiled at her. "Sorry," he said. "I didn't mean to scare you."

"You didn't," she said, "I was just..." she pointed back at the old man. "That's what he does?"

"That's all he does. All day. Every day." He offered a hand. "I'm Jefferson. Jefferson Carver. But everyone calls me 'Bug'."

She shook it. "Elizabeth," she said. "Elizabeth MacLaren. I don't have a nickname. Sorry."

This time, he jumped. "Wait – you're Doctor MacLaren?"

When she nodded, he asked "Why didn't you let us know you were here? We've been waiting for you."

She shrugged and smiled. "I don't like making a big fuss."

"It's not a fuss, Doctor MacLaren, it's just that we had an orientation planned and everything." He stepped away. "Is now a good time?"

She glanced back at the man in the white room, alone with his piece of string.

"I suppose," she said.

They left.

He finished another knot and stared at the new one. When nothing happened, he wept, then started untying it.

*

"Hello, Douglas," said Doctor MacLaren.

He spared her a glance and then went back to work.

She watched a moment, and then asked, "Can you tell me what you're trying to do?"

He shook his head, and continued knotting the rope.

"It's okay," she said. "I just want to know. I'm not here for any other reason than to understand."

He glanced up again, a little longer, focused on her, and then bent back to his work. "Not right now," he muttered.

When she was sure he was done, she tapped on the door and it opened.

Close Your Eyes – Tales from the Blinkspace

"Not bad," whispered Bug, as he relocked the door. "Doctor Finch worked with him for six months before he even spoke to her, and you're getting a verbal response after three weeks."

Elizabeth watched Douglas through the observation window. His old fingers unwound the latest knot as he shook his head in frustration.

"There's something about him," she said. "I can't put my finger on it, but there's something just past what we can see."

Bug nodded. "Everybody's got a pet project," he said. "Douglas isn't too bad. Pretty quiet. At first we were worried about the rope thing, so we only gave him little pieces, but we figured out he wasn't being trouble, so the docs've pretty much let him have what he asked for, ropewise." He watched the old man through the glass. "He's still dangerous, I guess, but he's content with his rope."

"No," said Doctor MacLaren, shaking her head. "He's a lot of things, but he's not content."

*

"I can't remember," muttered Douglas. "Sometimes I come close, but then it's gone. So far, it never works anyway."

He held up his finished knot, turned it in his hands, staring, and then sighed.

"I keep trying," he said. "I have to get it right eventually."

"What happens if you get it right?" asked Doctor MacLaren.

"You'll see," he replied, and bent his head to concentrate.

*

"You're not tired of him, yet?" asked Bug.

"No. Not yet," said Doctor MacLaren. "I think it's a sort of game. I think he's waiting to see if I'm still willing to play."

"A game?"

She nodded, watching the old man weave rope through the glass.

"I think he wants me to know – I think he even wants me to help, but I have to unwrap the layers of meaning first. I get the feeling that the things he says and does are several layers of abstraction from what he thinks he's really doing in there."

"Living a secret life?"

"In his head, yes. Maybe not secret so much as veiled. Maybe he can't quite peel it open alone, and he wants help."

37

Close Your Eyes – Tales from the Blinkspace

"Doctor Finch tried for quite a while before you."

"I know, but I think she approached it wrong. Or maybe he wasn't so close to giving up."

Bug cocked his head. "Giving up?" he asked.

Elizabeth crossed her arms. "I think Douglas is getting desperate," she said. "The way he moves seems jerkier and more frightened than when I came here."

Bug stared at the old man's hands.

"You figured all this out in three months?" he asked.

"I figured it out in six weeks," she said. "The rest has been filling in the details."

"Well, don't forget one detail," said Bug.

"Which is that?"

"He's a murderer."

*

She watched him for ten minutes before speaking.

"Douglas."

He glanced up at her, then back to his rope. That was his way of greeting her.

"Do you know why you're here?" she asked.

"It's a pause," he said. "It's between breaths. I'm here because no one's sure if I'm mad or not. If I am, then one thing. If I'm not, then another."

She thought about it. "Pretty much," she said.

"It's important to be mad for a little while," he said, "until being not mad isn't a problem."

"Do you think you're mad?" she asked.

"The question means a different thing to you than it does to me."

"Why?"

"Because when you ask it, you know what the answers will mean. When I answer it, I'll know what the answers mean. But your meaning and my meaning are different."

"How are they different?"

"You'll think my answer means I'm a murderer, Doctor MacLaren."

"What will your answer mean to you?" she asked.

38

Close Your Eyes – Tales from the Blinkspace

"My answer will mean I've shown you I'm not a murderer," he replied.

"I'm not here on a legal basis," she said. "I'm just a doctor interested in you."

"That's why I talk with you and not that other gal. The one that was here before you. With the horse face."

Elizabeth stifled a grin.

"I've seen pictures of her," she said. "She's not that bad."

"Try being locked up with her," he replied. "She was here because the State wanted her here. The State wanted to know if I was mad or not, so they put her here; assigned me to her."

"What do you suppose she thought?" asked Elizabeth.

"I'm still here, so I expect she decided I was mad."

She nodded.

"Are you?"

He smiled a little, but kept working the rope.

"When I do this right, you'll see. When you see what I see, you'll know the question has no meaning."

*

"Do you think you'll ever find it, Douglas?" she asked.

"I need to."

"To prove your innocence?"

"We've all done terrible things," he said, "and I'm not an innocent, but at least to prove I'm not a murderer."

"I've read the police report," she said.

He hesitated, uncertain, and then continued.

"Then you already know what you need to know, I guess," he said. "I'm sure I appear quite mad."

"I'm not so sure I can make that conclusion," she said. "There are some… irregularities. Some things I wanted to ask you about."

His only reply was the scratchy hiss of rope sliding through his dry fingers.

"How did you know they were sick?" she asked.

Close Your Eyes – Tales from the Blinkspace

He stopped and stared hard at her. "How were they sick?"

"They were anemic," she said. "Not even their doctors knew."

He sighed, and renewed his knotting.

"They weren't," he muttered.

"I talked to the M.E.," she said. "He remembers it like it was yesterday. It was the one thing that didn't make any sense. Six completely unrelated children, severely anemic. No one else on the playground that day, and no medical history suggesting it, but you knew. How did you know?"

"They weren't anemic," he repeated. He put his knot down and his voice rose. "I'm not being stubborn – I'm being factual. Nobody knew they were anemic because they weren't anemic. They–"

He stopped. His face turned pale. He looked down at his knot.

"I... I have to start this again. I've lost track of where I was."

"Douglas," she started to say.

"I have to get this right, Doctor. Could you please leave me alone."

He began to unweave the cord, but his fingers were shaking more than usual.

*

It was late. Past eleven. She wasn't wearing her suit – just jeans, a turtleneck, and a jacket. A purse.

She didn't close the door behind her as she entered the cell.

Douglas woke up when she flicked on the lights.

"What are– Doctor MacLaren?" he asked, blinking back the stars.

"Not right now," she said. "Just Elizabeth. We've been talking for nearly six Months, Douglas, I think we can be on a first-name basis."

He sat up. "How can I help you... Elizabeth?"

"No more games, Douglas. No more layers or tricks or riddles. I've learned more. I've talked to people. People you've never heard of. Some of them even know what you're trying to do, with your rope."

His eyes flickered to the edge of the bed. The length of rope was never far.

"I want to know," she said. "No more games – I want you to tell me everything. I want to hear it from you. I want to know what you saw, Douglas. I want to know everything."

40

Close Your Eyes – Tales from the Blinkspace

He waited a long time before speaking.

*

"I used to make animals," he said. "Out of rope. When you're retired, you drift away and I didn't want to drift away, so I went to the park and made animals. Gave them away to anyone. It was fun, and once in a while, someone else who knew about it would come and teach me a new animal. The kids loved 'em and the moms knew I was harmless."

"I've seen some," she said. "People showed them to me. You realize that a lot of them still can't believe what you did."

"They don't know what I did."

"They know what it looked like," she said. "Unless you explain, that's going to be what they come to believe."

"Why do you think I do this?" he asked, and waved the rope at her.

She waited until he continued.

"I wasn't paying attention one day, just tying, and it got bigger. It wasn't an animal, but there was something to it, something compelling, and I kept going. I was almost out of rope, but I had to keep going."

He shook his head, disbelieving his own words.

"Time and space are weird," he said. "We think of travel and we think of boxes and cylinders and things like that, but I think there's other ways to travel, other ways to connect places, and I think I found one. I think I found it in the knot."

Elizabeth nodded. "What happened?"

"As soon as I finished it, I knew something was different. I knew something had happened to me. The world tilted, but not really tilting, if that makes sense. I could see things differently. I could smell and hear things differently. It even felt different. The air was electric, the sky was brown and yellow, and the land was a plain of smoking craters and ancient death.

"But I wasn't gone from here. I could still feel the bench beneath me, still hear the birds, still hear the laughter of the children in the park. I could even see them, ghostly and faded.

"In my hands the knot felt like a living thing, throbbing and pulsing. I was in two places at once. One was my world – our world – and the other was this horrible place that stank of sulphur and hurt my eyes to see and my soul to consider."

"I know what you did," she said. "I talked to a man who told me. You built what he called a treph. The word means a sort of path or route. It's pretty rare."

Close Your Eyes – Tales from the Blinkspace

"A 'treph'? You mean someone knows about this?" His breathing rate increased. "Maybe they can talk to the police!"

"Someone was willing to speculate," she said. "A treph is more than just an object, it's a part of the person, too. I couldn't build the same one you did – only you can, and usually, a person can build only one, and it only goes to one place. What did you see, Douglas? It's important."

"I told you what I saw," he said.

"You told me what the area looked like. You didn't tell me what you saw. You didn't tell me why you did what you did."

He glared at her.

"I think you can rest assured that I'll believe you," she said. "You've already told me more than you've told anyone and I'm still here. And I've told you something you didn't know. But I need to know what happened next. I need to know what you saw."

He took a deep breath and fingered the string in his lap.

"I don't know what it was," he said, "but it was huge. It was like a football field. No, more like two or three. Huge."

He closed his eyes and she saw the pain in his face as he remembered.

"I thought at first it was just smoke, you know? A big cloud of black smoke. But I guess I also knew it wasn't. It was moving. It was galloping. It had legs and a body, but it was all made of smoke. And it was coming toward me. I knew that. It wasn't just out running; it was coming toward me. Toward us. It shook the Earth. Well, maybe it was Earth. I don't think it was, but it shook the ground, anyway. And it shook me. It shook my soul. Every footstep I could feel in the ground, but I could also feel in my heart, like each step was another beat lost. It was… was so dark.

"I should have stopped, should have torn the rope apart, but I was mesmerized. I kept watching it as it came closer. It moved like air but moved like an animal, too. Then, it arrived. It came here and stood high above us, high above the park and the plain in front of me. I could hear something – I'm not sure I can call it 'breathing' but it was air moving through, it was a sound of life. Maybe it was some sort of vocalization, but it was deeper than that, and all around us.

"I saw tendrils of smoke come from its sides and drop down, down to the plain, and strike the ground. I saw those tendrils spinning and pulsing. I saw it drawing something from the ground, and I saw it pushing something back down through.

"I looked up to its body and then I saw its eyes. Its eyes were so deep, so dark, like stars without stars, like space forever, like hellish nothing. Its eyes were forever and empty. I stared into them and knew we were lost.

Close Your Eyes – Tales from the Blinkspace

"And then I heard a scream. Not a scream, but more like a squeal. I looked back down to the ground, to the blasted plain at my feet, and I also saw the playground in front of me, and I saw where the tendrils had landed. I saw what it was doing. I saw that each tendril had touched the plain where, on my end of the Universe, there was a child. I saw children sitting and playing games, I saw children standing, puzzled, and some just caught mid-step, pausing.

"I saw the tendrils pulling light out of the children, pulling them out of their own shells. I saw them darkening as something else came in from the tendril, something cloudy, something not of this world, and barely of this Universe.

"I realized then what the plain was, what this hell was I had tied us to. It used to be a place a lot like Earth, filled with life and growth and joy, and then this thing had come to it and had eaten it. Had eaten everything. This one thing had destroyed an entire world, and now it was here, and reaching through to ours.

"Now I saw why it had waited. I had thought that it was trapped on that planet, and I was right, but it wasn't quite trapped – it had a path, and it was waiting, and now it was doing what all things do after they eat.

"It was reproducing."

He looked up at her.

"I'm not a murderer," he said. "Those children were already dead the moment it touched them – they were just husks and it was hollowing them out, feeding on them one last time to fuel its... reproduction. It was making them into another one of its kind."

"I know," she said.

"Does it have a name, too?" he asked.

"No, Douglas. It has no name, but you described it right. You described it how I was told it looked. It's the closest thing to death this Universe ever experiences. It's the final and permanent end of everything. You were right to stop it. You succeeded. You're not a murderer, you're a savior."

She stood up, reached into her purse, and drew a pistol, aiming it at him. His pistol. The one he used on that day.

"And you're its only way to get back to Earth."

She fired twice.

She took the rope from his hands, and pulled a cigarette lighter from her purse. She lit the rope and watched it burn. The last of the flames burned her fingers, but she didn't care. It had to be all gone.

Douglas struggled for breath, his hand twitched as he tried to reach up.

Close Your Eyes – Tales from the Blinkspace

Then she sat down next to him, and looked one last time into his shocked face.

"I'm sorry, Douglas. I'm so, so sorry," she said.

She held him close until he slipped away, and she kept holding him until the others arrived.

END

Watching

If it weren't for the cigarette, I'm pretty sure the guy in this story was me one night a few years ago...

She moves through the trees with hardly a sound. Her feet are soft and padded and everywhere she steps is the perfect place to put a foot. When it's dark – as it is now – she is invisible as well as inaudible.

The trails extend for miles in all directions, north, south, east, and west. It's her hunting ground. It's larger than the hunting grounds of most of the others, but she's bigger than they are, and she eats a lot. Also – and she's told no one of this – there are pups on the way.

Pups are a rare thing. Rare and magnificent. She's told no one anything, because the safety of the pups was paramount. Soon, she won't be able to hide anything, so she'll stay hidden in the trees, on her range, and not go to the Rings. For now, she's just big. Big and hungry. That's enough to keep the others from trespassing. It helps that she's been grumpy the past few months, snapping at anyone who comes close. Word gets around.

She slows as she steps across the path. Her ears catch every night sound and her long nose every night smell. Her eyes are deep yellow, and her fur as black as coal.

In the distance, maybe a quarter mile from the path, she sees buildings. Normally, she would never be this far out of the thick trees, but at night, no one can see her – not even if they were only a jump away. She's in her element in the dark.

All of the houses have windows, and several of the windows are lit by wan orange lights, or by flickering blue. She sits for a moment and watches. She doesn't sit because she's tired; she sits because sometimes it feels good to sit, out in the open,

Close Your Eyes – Tales from the Blinkspace

under the stars. She watches the lights. Inside the buildings, some of them wander around, oblivious of the outside world.

It was a moment from her ancestry, although she would never know it. Quietly, she watches, quietly she listens. Her hunger grows as more of the lights wink out.

When enough windows go dark, she stirs. She's hungry.

Like a ghost with teeth, she glides back into the darker-than-darkness of the trees. Like a dream, she vanishes without a sound, without a trace.

It's time to hunt.

She hears their voices long before she sees them. Their speech is a bubbling of sounds. It makes no sense to her, but she knows what that sound means, particularly at night.

It means prey.

She loops around through the woods, lowering her body. Her ears listen more closely. Her eyes cut through the darkness and sees them standing in the glow of their own circle.

There are two of them, a male and a female. Their voices bubble back and forth, filling the quiet night with whatever meaningless things those voices contain. One of them is smoking.

She stops her slow stalk and watches the smoke intensely. It drifts eastward.

She backs off, a long way, until she can move quickly without alerting them. She runs fast for being such a large beast, and in a matter of seconds, she re-enters the woods from the east. The grass out in this direction is nearly high enough to hide her, but she enters the trees without hesitation.

The timing must be perfect. Plus the grass is no place for her kind.

Her belly low to the ground, she follows the smoke's thin trail into the trees.

Hunting has been so difficult lately. The rains came early last year, the winter was mild, but still very rainy, and the spring rains continued through half the summer. The only things that moved around in the night with any sort of consistency were her own kind, all looking for the same thing, some prey somewhere. They all struggled through the wet and the damp, trying to find the occasional tidbit, but rain drives everything away.

So, although she moves quietly and slowly and deliberately on the outside, her insides are jumping and anxious and hungry.

She creeps closer.

Now their voices carry over more easily. She still can't understand what they are saying, but it doesn't really matter. Only the hunger matters. Only the hunger.

46

Close Your Eyes – Tales from the Blinkspace

Closer.

She stops at the base of a Douglas Fir. It's an old, old tree. She rears up on her hind legs to check the tree.

Her nose softly bounces against a few spots on the bark, sampling everything. This must be the tree, she decided. It had to be. She had done this plenty of times – she knew what to expect.

She settles back down to the ground and reviews the clearing.

They stand there, talking, completely oblivious.

She crawls low on her belly to the edge of the clearing, a few degrees off from the tree's position.

She waits. She watches and waits.

Right now, they face each other as they talk. No sneaking up on them like that. As long as they face each other, she would wait. She would wait as long as was needed.

After a while, the male finishes his cigarette. He drops it and grinds it out with the toe of his boot.

She doesn't panic, but she is concerned. The smoke covers scents very well. Without it, there is a risk.

The male starts walking, pacing, and gesticulating. The female sits quietly. This is promising. With the male moving around, it's much more likely they'll both be turned away.

She coils her legs under her, waiting. Her hindquarters twitch with anticipation. Every sense is alert and attentive.

The moment must be perfect. She can't afford to make a mistake.

The male turns, his back to the female. Now they both are vulnerable.

There is the smallest rustle of motion and before she can think, she leaps.

She is a locomotive of teeth and claws and ebony fur and she flies through the air, aiming entirely on instinct.

Above the couple, the tree branches part and something drops toward them. Something that's dark and leathery. Something that has no eyes and that hunts in the dark. Something with blue fangs that glitter and tiny razor claws in the tip of each of its six legs.

It drops in joy, because it too had very little in the way of prey for nearly a year.

Its arms spread out to both stabilize its drop and to enclose the creatures below. A thin film of venom oozes from each fang.

Close Your Eyes – Tales from the Blinkspace

And then it's no longer dropping, but flying sideways, its body being crushed in massive jaws. Not even a chance to feed!

Its tiny arms reach for the monster that snatched it from the sky, but death is already washing over it, and even those simple motions seem so far away and so very, very difficult now.

And then it is gone.

She lands on the other side of the clearing, the Hunter in her mouth. She feels it collapse. She drops it, sniffs it, and makes sure it's dead. It is. She looks back up and over at the couple in the clearing. He still speaks, and the sounds still don't make sense.

Good, they never noticed the attack, or the defense. Perfect! She spends a few seconds being proud of herself, proud she can still protect them the way her ancestors have since the beginning of time, without them ever knowing.

She looks back to the Hunter. It's big. Bigger than most. She figures that this Hunter, like her, must have been treating this area as a private hunting ground. Normally they were smaller, but this one is big.

Which is good, because she is hungry.

She pads off into the darkness, carrying the Hunter in her mouth.

END

Eventuality

Part of a writing marathon at the H. P. Lovecraft Film Festival, "Eventuality" is inspired by Jennifer's request to touch on the idea of a particular science fiction concept.

Jennifer watched the line pay out as the diver dropped below the surface. "I don't think this is going to help us," she said.

Andy looked at her and shook his head. "Ain't my money," he said.

The line continued down.

"There's just some sinkhole somewhere, is all," she said. "Some drainout that we haven't found."

Andy nodded. "Probably, but when bossman tells us to look here, we look here. I guess they had some sort of data from the current sensors or whatever."

"Current sensors…"

"Or whatever, I don't know."

The line payout stopped. They watched and waited.

Thirty seconds later, the cable jumped and jerked. The entire boat jinked down six inches, then snapped back up. "Holy shit!" she shouted, and she wasn't the only one.

Once he recovered his footing, Andy immediately started winching the diver back.

"He's gonna bitch," said Jennifer.

Close Your Eyes – Tales from the Blinkspace

"I don't care – that shit's messed up," said Andy. Then, in a minute, his brow furrowed and he added "I don't know…"

"What? What's going on?"

"There's no resistance," he said.

Five minutes later, the end of the cable emerged from the water. Jennifer snagged it as it swung around and she looked closely at the end. It wasn't torn or frayed or cut or even melted. It was simply… severed.

"Jesus," she said. "What happened?!"

*

The ROV was tethered, this time with a heavier cable. They lowered it down, and then Jennifer moved over to the controls. "Camera feed's pretty clear," she said, "and the lights are all working."

She watched from the ROV cameras as it dropped deeper. At fifty-five feet, they hit bottom.

"Okay, we're at the bottom. Pretty silty."

She spun the ROV slowly around. The recorder was whirring away next to her.

Andy leaned over. "What's that?" he pointed. In the camera's field of view, there was a discontinuity in the water, a flow.

"Damn," said Jennifer, "it's some sort of current, and we're in the middle of it."

She turned the ROV to flow along with the current. Andy kept paying out line. In a few moments, something started glowing ahead.

"What the hell is that?" she asked. "Andy, stop the line."

He locked the controls, and ducked back down to the console.

Ahead of the ROV, there was a distinct glow, and the current flowed directly toward it.

"I don't know what it is," she said, "but it's in this current, and it seems stuck. It's not moving relative to us, and we're tethered."

"Where's the current going?" Andy asked.

"I don't know. Past whatever this thing is. Maybe someone's flashlight got wedged in a rock. Let's pull back up, and drop the ROV over on the other side. We'll figure out what this is after we figure out this current."

Andy reeled the ROV back up, and they motored over to a new position. Andy dropped the ROV again.

Jennifer stared at the screen until they hit the bottom.

50

Close Your Eyes – Tales from the Blinkspace

"About sixty feet."

"I thought you said fifty-five?" asked Andy.

"They don't make flat lake beds like they used to," she said, giving him the hairy eyeball. Then, back at the screen. "Weird," she said.

"What?"

"Did we drop in the right place?"

"Right where you told me."

"We must be backwards or something." She fiddled with the controls and the ROV spun around a few times, orienting. "No, we're right where I thought…" her voice trailed off.

"What?" asked Andy.

"Well, this is supposed to be the continuation of the current, and it kinda is, but either we're pointing wrong or the current is going in the opposite direction."

"Doesn't that thing have a GPS?"

She spared a glance at the GPS readings in the corner of the screen. "Those are all fucked up," she said.

"Well, let's follow it anyway, I guess."

Andy paid out more cable.

"Hey," he said, "There's that light again."

"Yeah," she said. "Let's check that out now. Current's gonna take us right over it."

She rotated the ROV so the camera pointed down.

A flicker entered the screen.

"What is that?" asked Andy. The flickering was brilliant, a point of impossible light. It suddenly loomed toward the camera and once again the boat jerked downward.

"What the–" Jennifer tried different controls, but there was nothing. The video feed was static. "Pull up the cable."

He winched it back up, and the result was the same. "This is half-inch cable, man," he said, holding up the severed end. "What the hell could do this?"

Jennifer was already on her cell, already being switched around. "No, I don't want to talk to Stephan," she said. "I want to talk to Mike. Yes, I know. Fine. Get him."

While she waited, she looked up at Andy. "Andy, tell me what our compass says."

51

Close Your Eyes – Tales from the Blinkspace

Andy stepped over to the tiny cabin. "Holy shit," he said. "It's pretty much spazzing out."

She shook her head, frowning.

"Mike!" she said into the phone. "You get that feed? What the hell is that?"

She listened intently for a few seconds, then turned to Andy.

"Andy, get us back to the dock. Now!"

He obediently started up the motor and they left.

She continued talking quietly with Mike for a few minutes, then hung up.

"What's going on?" asked Andy.

"I don't want to talk about it," she said, and that was all she said.

Back at the office, she spent two hours in the research branch, and then clocked out for the day.

*

She didn't show up the next day.

*

Andy eventually found her, buying drinks at the bar on the corner. He slid onto the stool next to her. "You gonna tell me what's going on?" he asked.

She turned to him, her eyes red-rimmed.

"Don't you have a family?" she asked.

"Sure."

"Then go be with them," she said, "and leave me alone."

He stared at her.

"What's going on?" he asked.

She ignored him for a moment, instead trying to focus on the three shot glasses in front of her. One was empty, the others thick with amber whiskey.

"Three days ago," she said carefully, "something fell into the lake."

"A meteor?"

"No, not quite. Something else. Something bad. Something hungry."

She fingered one of the glasses, hesitating.

52

Close Your Eyes – Tales from the Blinkspace

"Do you know what a black hole is?" she asked.

"Uh, a collapsed star."

"Right, and you know what's in the middle of every one?"

"No, I don't."

She decided, and drained glass #2, and turned to Andy.

"In the center of a black hole is a singularity, Andy. An object of huge mass and infinitely small size. Anything falling into it, anything coming into contact with it gets eaten up, gets crushed and smashed against it, adding to its mass, but not to its size. Compressed infinitely. Destroyed. Do you follow me?"

"Yeah, I kinda heard that about black holes."

"A singularity's different than a black hole, though. A singularity that has no event horizon is called a naked singularity, and it just wanders around, consuming everything it touches. Everything made of mass or energy or anything."

She picked up the third glass and looked at him through it.

"That's why the lake bed's dropping, Andy. That's where all the water's going. What fell down wasn't a meteorite – it was a naked singularity, and it's eating everything it touches. It'll keep eating silt and then dirt and then rock, all the way until it falls into the center of the planet. And it'll keep eating until there isn't anything."

She drank the third glass, fast.

"Once Earth's destroyed," she said, "It'll eventually be drawn into the Sun, which it will also eat, and then, once it's done there, it will continue spinning off though space, destroying everything it touches."

She turned to the Bartender. "Three more, please!" she said, and he lined them up, with barely a glance.

Jennifer turned back to Andy.

"In another day, if Mike's calculations are correct, we'll detect its influence on planetary air pressure and other indicators. Within three days, our atmosphere will be gone, as will about half the planet's mass. A week later, there won't be an Earth."

"Not that that'll matter to you and I."

She took down another shot.

"Go to your family, Andy."

END

Close Your Eyes – Tales from the Blinkspace

Cursed

The deep woods of Oregon hold many strange and wonderful things...

He finally found her.

She lived in a cabin deep in the forests of Oregon. She had no network access. She had no connectivity. She had no online presence. She was, in all the ways that were peculiar in the year 2022, as invisible as possible.

Which is why it took three years.

He knocked on the door and waited. There was no response. No sound. Nothing.

He knocked again, louder. Still no response. He waited a little longer to be sure, then knocked a third time.

This time, he heard shuffling around, and a grumbling voice.

The door opened and a woman stood before him. She was tall, almost lanky. Her eyes were brilliant blue, her skin pale, and her hair flowed like an orange spring down across her shoulders.

"Doctor MacLaren?" he asked, but he knew it was her.

She stared at him. "Go away," she finally said.

"I want to talk with you," he said. "I have a question for you."

"Look it up," she said. "I'm busy. I want to be left alone."

"It's personal," he said. He slid his foot between the door and the jamb. "I've been looking for you for a long time."

Close Your Eyes – Tales from the Blinkspace

"How long?" she asked.

"Three years."

"That's a long time. You must really think what you have to ask is important."

"I think it's the most important question a human being has asked in more than twenty years."

She thought about it. She looked over his shoulder. "Anyone else here? Anyone else follow you?"

"Are you going to murder me?" he asked.

"No."

"Then I'm alone."

"Okay. You can come in, but only for ten minutes. And leave your shoes outside."

He came inside.

She served hot tea and he sipped it and watched her.

"Okay," she asked. "Ask your question. I'm busy."

He sipped at the tea again.

"How old are you?" he asked.

She laughed. "That was your question?"

"No, but you look… You look pretty good. You're sixty-eight now?"

"Seventy-three."

"The records are wrong."

"They always have been. I know how old I am, and now you do, too. What's your question?"

He leaned back. "You haven't been Prolonged."

"Not gonna happen."

"Why not?"

"Is that your question?"

"It is."

She set her tea down. "That is an important question," she said. "What do you think the answer is?"

55

Close Your Eyes – Tales from the Blinkspace

He folded his arms. "Thirty years ago, you published the Prolonging Procedure," he said. "It was a game-changer for the human race. A simple procedure that anyone could do that changed the human body into a thing that never got sick, never aged, never died."

"That's right."

"But you've never done it. You've never been Prolonged."

"And eventually, probably soon, I'm going to die," she said. "That's how it works."

"But why haven't you? I mean, you're brilliant. Think of all the good work you could keep doing."

"What's your name, boy?"

"Stephan," he said.

"Stephan, from an outsider's perspective, when compared to all the other medical activity that preceded me, what could you possibly consider better than curing every disease and death in the world and distributing the solution for free? Where do you think I could possibly go after that?"

"So, your thinking is that you're done? To leave on a high note? That's your answer?"

"No, that's not my answer. That's my response to the idea that I could do more with my life if only I were effectively immortal. That's bullshit, and now we both know it."

"You could teach."

"Teach what? Seriously, what's the status of the medical community out there, Stephan? Are there a lot of doctors? Clinics? No one gets sick anymore. Barring accidents, no one needs hospitals or doctors or nurses. And I'll bet even that'll be gone in another fifty years. If people get hurt, they'll either die or they'll get better." She shook her head. "There's no argument I know of that'll get me to Prolong myself that's based on altruism. Nobody needs me. Nobody wants me. I'm a few blurbs in the paper and in another ten years, I'll just be a note in history books."

"If you're not going to do it for us, then why aren't you doing it for yourself? It's like throwing your life away."

She laughed. "Now, see, that's part of why I'm not doing it. Because I've lived my life. I've lived a tremendous life. And eventually, it'll wind down and I'll die. As I said, that's what happens. I'm not throwing my life away. I'm doing exactly what I want with it, and it's doing what it wants with me."

"There's a group of people who think like that down in Texas," he said. "They think life is supposed to be short."

Close Your Eyes – Tales from the Blinkspace

"Life is supposed to be whatever we make of it," she said. "There's no magical force in the Universe, with a yardstick that shows how long life should be. It's as long as it is, and then it's over. Are they happy?"

"Who?"

"The people in Texas. Are they happy?"

He shrugged. "They seem to be. A little crazy, though."

"Says the people around them, right?" she asked. "They're all wringing their hands, right?"

"I wouldn't quite call it that."

"Regardless, they don't sound happy to me. So, Stephan, who's right in that scenario? Is it the people who are happy to live their life the way they want, or the people who are unhappy that other people aren't making the same choices?"

"I don't think it matters if they're happy," he said.

"What do think is going to happen with these people?" she asked.

"I don't know."

"I do. Do you want me to tell you? Some of them are going to die. And it's going to be ugly. The news will call it a horrible tragedy. It'll probably be given a name, like The Texas Tragedy. Someone will decide Something Must Be Done. They'll convince enough people of the same thing. The Something will turn out to be enforcing Prolongation. On everybody. I give it ten years, tops."

"How do you know this?"

"Because I'm a genius, Stephan. Not a social-recluse-movie genius, or a half-genius-half-idiot, but a genuine one-every-thousand-years genius. Frankly, I thought the effects would start a little earlier, but I guess people like being drunk with power." She took another sip of tea. "They are still drunk with power, right?"

"Some are, yeah, but it's calming down."

She nodded. "Once everyone calms down, then the real horror will set in. The folks who are having so much trouble with the Texans are just starting to realize it, but I'll bet they don't understand what's happening. Not yet."

He sat up a bit. "What horror?" he asked.

"Do you have children?" she asked.

"A daughter."

"How old?"

Close Your Eyes – Tales from the Blinkspace

"Twenty."

"How old, really?"

He hesitated. "Thirty."

"Do you love her?"

"What kind of question is that?" he asked.

"An easy one to answer, I would think. Do you love your daughter?"

"Of course I do."

"Then how do you want her to die?"

"I don't. What... where is this going?"

"Humanity knows it's not immortal, Stephan. Or at least it thinks it does, and from a functional standpoint, there's no difference. Those people in Texas aren't simply bothered by people dying – they're terrified of it. But deep down, they know they eventually die as well, so instead of letting themselves be reminded that it's possible by a few nutjobs, they would rather enforce a medical procedure on them. Mark my words. But it won't do any good. That's the part no one sees. Well, no one except me."

"Because you're a genius."

"So, back to my question. You've Prolonged your daughter's life. Most everybody does, I expect. This means that the only way she can die now is either by accident, by murder, or by suicide. Which would you prefer happen?"

"None of those."

"You don't have that option. Someday, probably in another fifty or sixty years, people are going to have to decide something, and by people, I mean you as well. You personally. You're going to have to decide what you are. Now, if all goes well, people will accept that they're something very different than human beings. They'll stop thinking like animals and start thinking like immortals. Their actions will reflect a remarkable maturation. They'll no longer fear death. They'll do remarkable things."

She finished the last of her cup of tea.

"On the other hand, if things don't go well, they won't be able to let go of what they think makes them essentially human. They'll cling to an animal existence. They'll still fight and be horrible, greedy, and grasping. They'll start thinking it all started with me, that I stole their humanity. They'll try to stop Prolonging, but of course, by then, there won't be a choice. Everyone'll be too afraid of death to not Prolong. They'll say they want to live forever, but the words will burn in their mouths and eventually, they'll beg for death, because they'll think they need it to be humans. Then, the real war will start. Then, the real pain will come. Then, the real horror will happen."

58

Close Your Eyes – Tales from the Blinkspace

He stared at her. "You knew this?"

"Oh, I'm hoping for the first scenario, of course, because that's the sweet part that everybody wants. I knew everybody would go for the sweet delicious hope. And if things worked out well, then I guess that would be okay. But I wasn't going to count on it."

She stood up. "You want more tea?"

Quietly, he nodded. She took his cup into the kitchen, and came back a moment later with two fresh cups.

"After this cup, you're leaving," she said. "I have a lot to do."

She sat down. "So," she started up. "The way I see it, people like you, who love their daughters, their sons, their friends and family, are going to eventually be forced to decide how death happens. Because there's no more natural death. You will have to kill them. Or let them kill themselves. Or let someone else kill them."

"That's monstrous," he whispered. "Why?"

She rocked slowly for a moment, constructing her reply. "Forty years ago, I had to kill a man," she said. "He was adorable and innocent and in fact saved the world. But I had to kill him. He died in my arms. I couldn't explain to anyone why I did what I did – there was no way they were going to believe me. So I sat, dumb, while all the machineries of justice ground me through a courtroom and into a very small cell in a very bad place. I realized while I was there that the Universe is vast and horrific. I thought I'd seen everything bad that could happen, but then I met this nice man, who just happened to have the power to destroy the world, as well as save it."

She sipped.

"I spent twenty years thinking of horrible things, Stephan. I just grew more and more angry and terrified that it could happen again, with someone else. I had to do something. So, I decided to make sure that everyone experienced what I experienced. That everyone knew what it felt like to have the world ending around them, through powers they aren't able to control, and to be in the position where sometimes they had to let someone they loved die in their own arms."

"Revenge?" he asked, shocked.

"Not revenge. There's no way out of revenge. But there's a way out of this. A narrow way, and a way I don't think people are ready to take, but a way out. And if they can't find it, then, sure. Revenge. Whatever. Welcome to my hell, custom-designed for your heart. For everybody's heart."

He drained his tea.

"I think it might be ironic," she said. "You came here trying to figure out why I was so different, and you found out it wasn't me that was cursed."

Close Your Eyes – Tales from the Blinkspace

She looked in his cup.

"Time to go," she said.

She led him to the door. He walked slowly.

As he stepped out, she spoke. "Don't bother coming back here," she said. "I see now that I wasn't good enough at hiding. I'll be leaving, and you'll never see me again. No one ever will. And I'm okay with that. I'll let this house fall to pieces where it stands. Fitting, I think."

She watched him pull his boots on, then step off the porch.

"Have a happy life, Stephan," she said, and closed the door.

END

X

I have to say that "X" is the story that got it all started. "X" is a story parts of which I came up with in grade school, parts in high school, and parts throughout my life. "X" is a story I've wanted to tell for a long, long time. But interestingly, I had forgotten about this story until just recently. Life imitates art?

I can't say that no one liked Leon. That wouldn't be accurate. It would be more accurate to say that no one *knew* Leon. Not visibly.

Which made sense at the time, but now results in a cold steel knot in the middle of my guts. This knot warns me that something has Gone Seriously Wrong.

Leon's family moved into town when I was in fourth grade. That was in 2010. I know because I remember my teacher at the time, Mrs. Payson. That was the last teacher I ever met who seemed to genuinely want to help people. Ever since her, it's been all downhill, teacherwise.

That day in class was as dull as paint, and then a boy with a note came by. Mrs. Payson read the note, and introduced us to the new boy.

"Class," she said, "This is Leon. He and his family just moved here from…" she stumbled a bit, referred back to the note, and tried to pronounce something. Leon looked up at her, then out at us. He said something. A long word that sounded like someone rolling dice. "It's an island," he said.

Close Your Eyes – Tales from the Blinkspace

That would explain the accent, which I couldn't place.

"Who would like to show Leon around?" asked Mrs. Payson. "It's hard to move into a new town and not have any friends."

That's when the world changed. Well, my world anyway.

No one raised their hands. There was a moment of silence while Mrs. Payson scanned the room, then she waved Leon over to an empty desk in the back.

Nothing more was said of Leon that day.

Aside from an incident in a tree that left a scar I still bear on my leg to this day, the entire fourth grade passed by me without incident. As did the fifth and sixth grades.

In seventh grade, my mother died. There wasn't any sort of drama about it – it was actually calm in a way. I was in my bedroom, looking out through my window on the second floor. About six blocks away, I watched her car coming home. Then it stopped. She got out, stood a moment, and then just fell down.

My father and I ran out there, but there was nothing we could do.

The doctor said it was a brain aneurism. That she probably didn't feel anything at all, maybe just a little dizzy. I'm of mixed feelings, naturally. I'm glad she didn't suffer, but the bottom line was that she wasn't here anymore, and that was about as bad as a boy can get.

There was a funeral, but not many people showed up. A lot of people had moved out of town over the past few years. Just packing up and moving out. Work running out, I guess.

High school came with all the social challenges that high school brings. The air was thick with clumsy teenage romance and our small town's high school population played the same romantic game of musical chairs played out everywhere else. Some people stuck around, others moved away.

Somewhere in the middle of high school, I decided I wanted to be a cop. I don't have a specific moment, or incident that triggered this thought – I simply came to the decision gradually. After working up my nerves, I went to the police station and told them what I wanted. In a small town, it's easier to follow your dreams if they're the dreams that can be contained in a small town.

I still had to study, of course, but I could intern at the police station during weekends, which I did. I also worked out hard. For a guy who used to be a hopeless geek, I rapidly became quite the hunk, based on the level of interest around me. Honestly, I can't say I didn't take advantage of that once in a while.

Eventually, the Sheriff helped fund my trip to the Academy, as did my father. I helped, too, having saved up all my internship money over two years. I graduated with excellent grades, and came back to town feeling nine kinds of happy about my choices.

62

I was a good cop, too. Not a hard-ass, nor a namby-pamby guy. I always remembered that my sole interest was in helping keep my town happy. Sure, it had its troubles – all small towns did – but there was no reason I couldn't help keep it happy.

Then, one day, I came home from work and my father was sitting his last sitting in the kitchen, cold hand wrapped around a cold cup of coffee, head down as if he had nodded off. I felt a little odd ordering an autopsy, but I wanted to know. Cardiac arrest. That made no sense to me – he didn't smoke, didn't drink, and was relatively healthy. Little good that did either of us, though.

A week later, still numb, I signed up for the Marines.

A lot happened in that year, but it was a very different place than my home town. It seemed more pure, more clean, more complete.

A year after I signed up, I was part of a convoy, halfway between Daman and Kandahar, and looking forward to a decent night's sleep after three weeks of fighting.

I have a vague memory of hearing impacts against the truck body. For a fraction of a second, I thought the truck ahead of me had kicked up rocks. But then I knew what it was. I heard glass breaking and felt a punch on the side of my head.

A week later, I woke up in a hospital room. Well, maybe not woke up. I drifted enough into consciousness to see shapes and hear voices. Everything looked strange, sounded strange. Monstrous and blobby. I think I answered a few questions, and then there was some more darkness, which was good. Right now, darkness felt like a solid friend who helps you rest.

When I finally snapped back, I was in the States, in a hospital that was actually quiet. I stared at the food in front of me, at the forkful of spaghetti, at the hand holding the fork, at the arm. This was me. I looked up and there was a nurse, sitting nearby, watching me eat.

I blinked at him. "I'm back," I said, quietly.

He smiled at me. "How do you feel, George?" he asked.

I felt like a puzzle that had finally been completed. I saw my whole picture. "I feel fine," I said. "I actually feel fine. What happened?"

He told me everything.

He told me things that made sense – that I'd been shot in the head, that it was a rough recovery, that no one was quite sure if I was going to make it. He told me that apparently my brain made up its own mind and healed much better than anyone had expected. He told me I'd been here for nearly a month.

He also told me things that didn't quite make sense – that I'd been waking up and having peculiar contemplative fugues. "Episodes of lucidity" he called them. They would last for a few hours, and then I'd drift back away. During these times, I

Close Your Eyes – Tales from the Blinkspace

apparently became fixated on different objects in my room. Flower vase, water faucet, the bright green switch on one of the instruments monitoring me. I would stare at these objects, fascinated, and then eventually go back to bed, and back to the dark place where I healed. I never spoke during these sessions, but they knew I could hear them and understand them, because I responded. I have no recollection of these episodes, but as I looked around the room, everything looked especially bright and vivid.

"This is the first time you've spoken," he told me. "This is very exciting."

The doctors were excited too, and asked me a lot of questions, some of which I could answer, and some of which I couldn't. They gave me a few X-rays and CAT scans, and one doctor in particular kept asking me very strange questions. I was asked if I can imagine a red ball sitting on a picnic table in the middle of a park. I knew what he was doing, though, so I didn't get fussy at him. He was seeing how well my brain worked after having been stirred a bit.

It seemed to work fine.

I still had the fugues, but they weren't so dramatic. I often found myself reviewing some object in my room, as if I'd never seen what it was. Oh, I could recognize it, and explain it, but somehow, in my brain, it felt... new. Each one felt like holding a baby in my arms that had just been born. I was amazed at how detailed life was around me!

I was so busy with all the tests and therapy and so forth that I never once thought about home, which was okay, because I had joined the Marines so I wouldn't have to.

One afternoon, I was watching the TV in the room. My nurse was there with me. We were all glued to the television. In fact, I could safely say that practically everyone in the world was glued to their televisions, if they had them. This was a big deal. It was the first landing on Mars of a manned spaceship. I wasn't normally interested in that sort of thing, but when history's being made, you tend to pay attention.

The lander's progress through the atmosphere was transmitted in brilliant color all over the world. We all watched as the camera feeds cycled around the outside of the ship, as the ground came closer. We all held our breath.

And we all saw the flash.

Then the feeds stopped.

The stations went into a bit of a hover cycle, firing off questions to various talking heads, until the space agency finally came back with the news. The craft had disintegrated. They had no idea how or why, but it was gone.

The whole planet reeled. We certainly did. But something else happened right then.

The news channel had hastily posted a picture of the crew of the Mars mission, and were recounting stories of the brave souls who had hurled themselves from Earth. That wasn't the peculiar part. The peculiar part was that they spoke repeatedly of the eight

64

Close Your Eyes – Tales from the Blinkspace

brave men and women on board, and how much they'd be missed, and so on and so forth – but the photograph showed nine people.

They enumerated the same eight over and over, and interviewed their families, and all the people of Earth mourned their loss, but still, whenever there was a group photo: nine people.

A lot was happening fast, so I had to set that aside for some more medical tests.

That evening, though, I switched the television back on, and watched. In less than ten minutes, another group picture flashed by. I was able to see faces better in this one, and studied it carefully for the whole twenty seconds it was on screen.

That's when I saw him.

Leon.

And that was when the world changed back. Well, my world, anyway.

If I felt like a jigsaw puzzle suddenly put together before, now I felt like a broken snowglobe, coming back together. Every flake of fake snow, every drop of glycerin, and every shard of glass all tumbled back into place and then I saw my life.

My *real* life.

Starting in fourth grade, I saw Dawn raise her hand immediately to be Leon's friend. I liked Dawn. For a couple of days, she showed him around. And then I saw her come in one day to school looking pale and sick, and then the next day, she wasn't at school. After a week, I went by her house, and knocked on her door.

Leon answered.

"Is Dawn in?" I asked. He cocked his head and looked at me, and said "No, forget about her."

And I did. I forgot all about my friend Dawn and her whole family.

But then, another piece of the snowglobe came together, and I remembered the whole thing.

I saw Leon in school, always staying in the back of the room. He was smart. And quiet. But people still noticed him.

I saw a couple of bullies come up to him in fifth grade, and push him around. They pinned him to a wall and even got a smack in before he looked at them and said something. I was too far away to hear, but they immediately stopped and wandered off. Leon walked by me, rubbing his cheek, which was already darkly bruising. As he passed, he looked casually at me and said "Forget this."

And I did. As simple as that.

Until now.

65

Close Your Eyes – Tales from the Blinkspace

Later, one of the bullies was found in the woods, torn to pieces. The other was never found. There was never a newspaper article about it, and no one else even seemed to remember them.

Now, I remember Leon riding his bike all over town that day. He must have been very busy. He made me forget twice.

I saw him later that year leading another kid into his house. By that time, all he had to do was look at me and tilt his head a little, and – Alakazam! – no more memory.

Although apparently that wasn't true. Apparently, there was still a memory, but he just smoothed it over.

As the years passed, every once in a while, I saw Leon doing something. Sometimes it was something ordinary, sometimes it wasn't.

Once, I saw him coming out of the woods holding an arm. He took a bite from it. In that moment, Leon didn't quite look the same as he always did. In that moment, his teeth seemed a little longer than usual. And pointed. And his eyes were black marbles.

And then I forgot about it, as usual. My mind was smoothed over.

When I was in seventh grade, I watched out the window of my house as my mother stepped out of the car and approach Leon, who was crouching by the bus stop. I saw him reach up and pull her toward him. I saw his mouth open, and his teeth.

And then I forgot. Again.

In high school, I once saw him walking by the pool. He dropped a set of keys in the water, while pulling something else out of his pocket. They bounced on the deck, and slid into the water on the deep end. He looked around, but there was no one nearby. I saw him kneel at the pool, and reach into the water. I saw his arm reach all the way down, through twelve feet of water. Then I saw him pull the keys back up. He licked his arm dry, stood up and walked on. He walked right past the column behind which I was hiding. Almost casually, I felt him reach toward me, and another thing was smoothed away. Another piece of my life fell off.

But now it was coming back together. If for no other reason than that, I could thank that faceless sniper.

Throughout high school, I saw Leon take people. One by one, they wandered down Corbett Road, which was the dead-end street where Leon lived. One by one, I saw people assume – as did I – that these people had moved away. Leon worked all our memories as if they were clay.

I did not become a policeman at random. I see that now. My soul felt a need for the truth, it felt the pull of questions, and being in the police was as close as I ever figured I could come to that.

66

Close Your Eyes – Tales from the Blinkspace

As I spent more time in the police station, I saw Leon come in more often. He would come in and people would forget things. They would forget calls for disturbances. They would forget body parts being found. They would forget their own entries in their own paperwork.

I filed the paperwork, and sometimes read it, but I too forgot everything.

Then, one day, I came home and found my father.

Most of him anyway.

And there were footprints leading away.

I forgot this all.

And then, maybe a year later, my brain was rearranged, and I remembered it all. I remembered everything. In fact, I couldn't forget it if I tried.

And now, Leon's out there. I know he is. I know the others are with him. And I also know that they landed safely. But we had forgotten that, with the flash. Except for me.

I saw it all. I saw the camera images. I saw the surface getting closer.

And I saw the others.

Like Leon, but not pretending to be human.

Then, the memories were complete. My life was rightside up again.

I thought about my home, my town, the one I had sworn to protect. I thought about Leon, the boy who became a man in my town. Or something manlike. Manlike with sharp teeth and a hunger for people.

I thought about all the other small towns in the States. In the world. I thought about Leon, being dumped here to see if he'd make it, and how easily he could sway our minds.

Then I thought of him on Mars. Telling everyone how easy it was. Showing them, with the eight brave prizes he brought back, how plastic their minds were and how soft their flesh.

It seemed so absurd I had to laugh.

I knew he would be back, then, because Earth was perfect. Earth was warm and wet and filled with everything they could possibly want.

And I knew we had already lost.

END

67

Bugs

I've been doing a lot of work in the garden lately. Trying to decide if it's worth the risk, y'know...?

First sunny week since September. The waiting was the worst part.

The lettuce was looking pretty good. Last year's batch had been nice. Mindy was looking forward to seeing this year's. Maybe this time not so much of it was going to get eaten by slugs.

Darn slugs.

But this year, in fact, the garden was looking amazing. She always expected to lose a certain percentage every year to various critters, but nothing had been touched. How lucky!

A million tiny weeds had taken over the plot, however. Must have been something in the compost. That was annoying, but at least they were tiny, which meant easy to pull out. Besides, there was a certain luxury in being able to just sit outside in the sunlight and pull weeds quietly without giving a damn about anything else. Very peaceful.

A gust of wind blew through and she enjoyed that very much. It wasn't hot enough for her to break a sweat, but small cool wind gusts were definitely on the list of things that made not giving a damn so much fun.

Close Your Eyes – Tales from the Blinkspace

The wind rustled the grass up on the berm and she glanced over. Still grass and all is well, she thought. She turned back to the weeds, but something tickled her brain. She looked back up at the berm.

The grass had been pushed aside.

Well, that was weird.

It couldn't have been the dogs – they'd been pretty much in the house or under the deck for months. The fence would have stopped any critters.

She pulled a couple more of the tiny weeds, then stopped and looked back at the grass.

It almost looked like a trail. Maybe worth checking out.

Why not, she thought. She unfolded her legs and stood up. Neat little weed piles marked her progress so far today.

She stepped over to the berm.

It sure looked like a path. Like something had been dragged back and forth a lot, in fact. She looked up and the path led under low tree branches. Okay, she thought, so, some kind of game trail. Well, the fence is up for a reason. I guess I better find whatever critter it is and make a plan.

She thought about it as she ducked down.

She crawled along the trail, under the trees. The air smelled thick and pine-dusty under here.

About six feet in, she stopped. "Oh, look at you!" she whispered. In the center of the trail was a ladybug. Not a small ladybug, but one that seemed nearly the size of her fingernail. Sizeable for a ladybug, indeed!

She liked ladybugs. They ate the things that ate her plants, which made them the Good Guys. She was about to reach for it when she saw another. Same size.

Then, over near a cluster of grass, three more.

"Oh. Cool!" She took a better look around and saw that they were actually walking along in little lines, just like ants. Looked to be a couple dozen.

For a brief second, she thought maybe it was time to get back to the garden, but then she remembered it was Don't Give a Damn Day, so she settled down on her stomach, propped her chin in her hands and watched the ladybugs.

They acted a lot like ants, walking all in the same direction, all regularly spaced from each other.

In a few minutes, the cluster had moved down the trail, so she scooted a little ways after them. From this position, she could see around the trunk of one of the bigger pines.

Close Your Eyes – Tales from the Blinkspace

Her breath caught in her throat. What was that? Just behind the trunk was a big something. It was about the size of half a metal trashcan, turned upside down, and looked the part, too. The sides were dull gray, pitted and scarred. It rested a few inches above the dirt by a ring of spindly metal jointed legs.

She stared.

In several places on the can were very tiny features. Some looked like little portholes. Some looked like bulges and vents and and slits and access ports. Others looked like windows. Tiny, tiny windows,

The ground in front of it had been cleared and flattened for about a square yard. In that space, tiny stacks of crates and boxes formed a neat cubical maze.

She looked closer.

The maze was filled with ladybugs.

The ones she had been following had joined up with a main trunk of ladybugs and they all were cloistered around the cleared space, and the can thing.

She was wrong about the ants, she saw that now. They were far more organized than ants.

As quietly as she could, she leaned a little closer.

Something tickled the back of her mind, something soft and delicate and whispering. She concentrated and it became louder. More distinct.

It wasn't quite language, exactly, but she could still make it out. It was a jumble of ideas and words and images. She could tell there were many voices. All of them were in a huge hurry. The urgency was unmistakable.

She tried sorting it out, putting it into English, but there were so many of them and only one of her.

Almost immediately, she understood it was her ladybugs speaking. Or muttering, as it were. Except they weren't ladybugs, at all. She caught that right away. They were a long way from home. A long, long, long way. And that can wasn't just a can, but what brought them here.

Fascinating!

She kept trying to sift through the voices, to sense the meanings.

There were here... here... deliberately. That much she caught. She picked up idea words: Colony, first, preparations, new life, big families, lots of food.

She grinned. This was adorable!

70

Close Your Eyes – Tales from the Blinkspace

There was a thrashing in the bushes behind the tree and a squirrel stepped out into the path. She froze, hoping to not scare it, but it never looked at her. It shook itself a bit, then walked over to the can– to the ship, she corrected herself.

Just as it passed her, she saw something on the back of its head. She saw one of her ladybugs perched in a thin spot of the squirrel's fur, a little blood oozed up from around its legs. She squinted. The legs were embedded into the squirrel's skull.

Oblivious to her, the squirrel stepped past, and then curled up into a ball near the base of the ship.

The voices changed, then. All the other exciting homey thoughts were replaced by a new kind of excitement, and a new word that made even more sense to her than any of the others had.

Food!

The ladybugs descended on the squirrel. It never moved a muscle. Never twitched. The ladybug on its head stayed put while the others tore into it. Each one only pulled away a small piece, but within a minute, there was nothing left. They lapped up whatever blood hadn't soaked into the ground, and even broke down the skeleton.

As the ladybugs rolled away from their feast, Mindy saw that they hardly looked any bigger. The thoughts in her mind now were happy thoughts of food, and still thoughts of hunger. A lot of them were other thoughts, too. More family. More food. Still hungry. Keep going.

She waited quietly until her arms started to cramp. She had to get out of there.

Finally, the crowd thinned out to only a dozen or so ladybugs doing some sort of regular checking of the tiny crates and containers. They were being unloaded from the ship, lined up, and inspected. All in miniature.

She would slip out now, and run. In the barn was a big tank of poison left behind by the last guy who owned the house. It was a very bad sort of poison, the kind you couldn't buy anymore, and they were waiting for one of those amnesty recycle days to bring it in.

But now she knew what she had to do with it.

She'd empty the entire thing on these little bastards.

She gathered herself and then sprang backwards.

She scrambled out from under the trees, and stumbled out into the garden. The sun beat down on her, and there was still a soft breeze, but now it wasn't fun anymore. It wasn't Don't Give a Damn Day anymore. Now it was Kill The Alien Bugs Day, and she was going to grab that tank and–

There was a pinch on her wrist, and she looked down.

71

Close Your Eyes – Tales from the Blinkspace

Sinking its last leg into her, the ladybug settled tightly against her skin.

She reached to brush it off, but then stopped.

It felt wonderful.

She'd never felt anything so good.

She looked up at the sun and felt its warmth against her face and felt the breeze on her skin, and smelled the amazing growing things all around her. She looked at the garden and smiled. It really was looking very, very good.

The air smelled like dry pine dust a little, but that was okay, because she was back in the middle of Don't Give a Damn Day and it was the most beautiful day ever. Ever! And she was happier than she'd ever been.

She sat down in the grass that was thick and lush, but felt like dry pine needles, and smiled under the warm sun that felt like deep shade, and enjoyed the fresh breeze that felt like a hundred little soft things touching her, and it was a very, very good day.

END

Devotion

Part of a writing marathon at the H. P. Lovecraft Film Festival, "Devotion" is inspired by Mike and Liv's request for something that included both of them and was vaguely Innsmouthy.

DAY THREE

"I'm thirsty," she says.

He nods, but is silent.

"I said I'm thirsty."

"I heard you. What do you want me to do."

"I want you to stop."

He continues driving.

"There's a place," she says.

He drives by.

"I need more warning," he said. "I was going too fast to stop."

"I told you I was thirsty."

"You want me to find a place?"

"Once you know I'm thirsty, yes, that means I want to stop. That means I want you to stop at a place where I can get a drink."

"Okay, so that's my warning, then," he said. "I'll find a place."

Close Your Eyes – Tales from the Blinkspace

She's angry and stares at him. "Find a place."

"Fine. When we get there, though, I need you to do something."

"What?"

"I need you to buy more water. I'm tired of stopping."

DAY TWO

"Hey," he says. She doesn't answer. "Liv!"

Her head jerks away from the window. "What?" she asks.

"What are you doing?"

"Nothing."

"You've been staring out at the window for the past hour. You're saying you're doing nothing?

"Nothing. That's what I said. Thinking."

"Thinking about what?"

"Nothing."

He tries to breathe regularly, tries to calm down. "How can you be thinking about nothing for an hour."

"You should try it sometime," she says. "Might help you calm down."

"I am calm."

"Then why are you pestering me?"

"I thought you might want to talk."

"About what?"

"Anything. Whatever. I'm tired of feeling like I'm doing all this driving alone, like I'm the only person in the car."

"Do you want to trade drivers, Mike?" She checks her watch. "It is about time."

"No, no, I can keep driving. I just thought, well, maybe we could talk about something."

"I'm looking at the ocean."

"I know – for a whole hour."

"It's interesting."

Close Your Eyes – Tales from the Blinkspace

"It's the same thing over and over and over. It's the ocean. There's not even any boats out there."

"Ships."

"Whatever. There's none of them out there. There aren't whales or anything interesting at all. Just ocean."

"I like it."

"You better, you stare at it like that."

She turns her head a bit, as if looking not at her husband, but at a strange animal.

"You should look at the ocean more often," she says. "You might see something sometime."

"I'm busy," he says.

"What are you so busy doing you can't look at the ocean?"

"Driving."

DAY ONE

He wakes up as the tires crunch through gravel. "Where are we?"

"We're not there yet, if that's what you're asking."

"What is this? Are we viewing?"

"I want to stop. I want to walk on the beach."

"It's freezing out."

"Then stay in the car."

She shifts the car to park, and opens the door. Wind flashes through, papers and trash blow around.

She steps out and closes the door.

He watches her as she walks away. "It's freezing out there," he says, as if she's able to hear him. "I'm not going out there."

She steps along the path, farther from the car.

He frowns at her. "Seriously, I'm not going out there. It's fucking freezing."

She moves over the ridge and disappears from view.

He growls. He looks at his fingers. Looks at his nails. Looks back outside, but she is nowhere he can see.

75

Close Your Eyes – Tales from the Blinkspace

"Goddammit," he says, and opens the door. Wind billows in and he leaves the car, slamming the door.

He finds her on the beach, staring out into the sea. The wind whips their hair, whips their clothes, and streams sand and mist against them. He stands next to her, looking in the direction she's looking.

"I don't see anything!" he shouts. He has to shout to be heard over the wind.

She ignores him and he squints along her line of sight again. Nothing.

"Why are we here?" he shouts.

She turns to him, and her eyes are also steel gray like the sea, and they seem to be lost in a distance. Then they are normal and he sees her eyes the way he normally sees them, brown and watery.

"What are you doing here?" she asks, and he can barely hear her, but he knows what she's asking because she asks this question more and more often these days.

"I'm following you," he shouts over the wind.

She shakes her head, then looks up the beach, in the direction of the path. "I can't imagine why," she says, and starts trudging back to the car.

He watches her clump away. He glances back at the ocean, the cold, dull, monotonous, roaring ocean. Then he follows her.

DAY ZERO

"You should let me drive now," she says.

"I don't want you driving."

"Why not?"

"There's something wrong with you and I don't want you driving."

"There's nothing wrong with me."

"This seems normal to you? This stopping?"

"I want to see the ocean, Mike. What's wrong with wanting to see the ocean?"

"Nothing was wrong with it when you were seeing it from the car, but when you get out of the car, and you walk out onto the beach and you just stand there like some kind of zombie, then yeah, it gets pretty weird."

"I don't think I can explain it."

"I don't think it needs an explanation – it's just weird."

"So why can't I drive?"

76

Close Your Eyes – Tales from the Blinkspace

"Because I'm tired of stopping and following you out on some other beach. We're trying to get somewhere, and stopping and beachwalking isn't helping."

She stares out the window and her forehead creases.

"Stop up here."

"Where?"

"Here! Here!"

He pulls over, and the car slides smoothly on packed sand.

"Why here?" he asks.

"This is the place," she says. "This is the place I've been looking for."

"What? We're still four hours from your parent's place."

"I'm not going," she said.

"You're what?"

She steps out of the car before he realizes it, and stands there. Again, the wind whips through. She leans down, and frames her face in the car doorway.

"Mike," she says.

He stares at her.

"It's done, now. You should go."

"What? What the fuck are you—"

She slams the door shut and walks away.

"Liv! Goddammit, Liv!" he shouts.

He climbs out of the car and follows her.

"This is nuts," he mutters, and his words are lost in the wind howling around his head. She is already over the ridge, so he trots to catch up.

She stands, again, watching the ocean.

"Hey," he says. She ignores him. He stands in front of her. "Hey! Are you listening to me?"

She turns to face him and her eyes are pure gray, like the ocean, like the clouds, like the sky. Like all three combined. They stay that color as she speaks, and her voice is cold and flat.

"It's done, Mike. You should go."

Close Your Eyes – Tales from the Blinkspace

"You said that already. What are you talking about?" He hates shouting over the wind and the roar of the ocean, but it's the only way she'll hear him.

"Do you love me?" she asks.

The question sets him back. She's never asked this question before. There's never been the question. Although it's always a question he would think about before answering, this time he knows the answer. "Of course I do! Now come back to the car. It's fucking freezing out here and we're getting soaked!"

She smiles a thin-lipped smile. "If you love me, then this is it. It's done. I'm going to go, now, and you can't follow me, so that means you're going to go, too. Go back to the car, Mike, and go back home."

"What are you talking about? Come on, hon. Come on back." He tries to pull at her arm, but his grip slips. She is wet with salt spray, slippery, and unyielding. "I'm not going to leave you here."

"Okay," she said. "I'm not going to tell you what to do anymore. I'm not going to make anything happen to you anymore. I'm done. I'm going."

"You're not going anywhere without me!" he shouts.

The waves strike the beach more frequently, and more ferociously. It sounds as if there's sudden anger in the sound.

She listens to this, and nods, so slightly.

"Okay, Mike. Whatever you like."

She drops her windbreaker to the sand, and a gust of wind blows it away, snags it against a nearby bush. Her skin is pale, glistening. She pulls her shirt off over her head.

The wind picks up and the waves crash against the beach. He can hardly hear himself over the roar of the elements.

"What are you doing?!" he shouts.

She shrugs, pulls her pants down, and kicks them free. The storm rises up, carries the cloth away.

"Liv!" he shouts. Her skin is white now, but more than white. It is cloudy. He touches her shoulder, and his fingers sink in. He pushes his face into hers. Her eyes are silver, her eyes are gray, her eyes are cold harsh metal.

She reaches out to his chest and pushes him aside. Her mouth opens and she has no teeth, and her lips are black and thin.

She walks out toward the water, into the water.

Close Your Eyes – Tales from the Blinkspace

The wind screams approval, the waves pound the shore, but where she walks, there is a calmness, and openness, an acceptance. She walks out into the smooth water, she steps lower and lower, and then the water covers her up and she is gone.

"Liv!" screams Mike.

There is no answer.

"Liv! Goddammit, Liv!"

The waves reconnect, the wind continues howling and the water beats against the sand.

He stares out.

"No fucking way!" he shouts, and starts pulling off his shoes. "No fucking way are you going out there without me," he shouts.

He pulls off his shirt and starts unbuttoning his pants.

The wind breathes onto him and through him, and it's not as cold as it seemed to be a moment ago. Not as lonely as it felt a moment ago.

He yanks his pants off.

"No fucking way, Liv. You are not pulling this shit on me!"

He's not as cold as he thought he would be. He steps toward the water. With each step, it makes more sense. They had promised each other "until death us do part" and there was no way she was just going to blow that off.

"No fucking way!"

The first wave hits and the icy cold is like a slap against every nerve.

He continues wading out, continues going deeper. The waves still come, and they still slap against him, but they don't seem quite as high as they were. The wind doesn't seem quite as strong as before, and the howling in his ears is changing and sounding like something else.

Like music.

"I'm coming!" he shouts, and then his head goes under the water.

END

Shock Troops

Part of a writing marathon at the H. P. Lovecraft Film Festival, "Shock Troops" was inspired by a charming daydream of pain and fury.

Specialist First Class Vann was a soldier, but he was not a fighter. Certainly he had fought his way through Basic, like everyone else, but it was a hurdle he had to jump – not a means to an end. He wasn't a master at combat, an action hero, or even secretly a ninja. He was a Specialist First Class, and more specifically, a journalist.

He was not prepared for this madness. He was not prepared for the horrors he had witnessed, the terror he had experienced. It was nothing like what he and thousands of other soldiers trained to face. It was like nothing on this earth. So, he did the only thing he could do, the only thing that made any sort of sense in the complete chaos of the battlefield.

He ran.

This was one thing he had been able to do well ever since he was a kid. He could run. He ran track in school, and set school records. He raced in Training and his teams always won. He was the fastest man in his squad, the fastest man on the base.

But speed, it isn't a bonus in modern warfare, with computer-tracked weaponry and sophisticated sensor technology. A hundred years ago, Vann would have been a Scout, but his technology meant nothing now, and so he was a journalist instead.

Close Your Eyes – Tales from the Blinkspace

But now the running mattered, oh yes, it mattered very much. Now Vann ran for his life, while some sort of horror pursued him. Some sort of horror that stood more than eight feet tall, was purple and black, screamed in a way that split the sky, and had killed three men in his squad before they ever knew there was an enemy in their midst. Some sort of horror that had spikes and a whip tail and claws and teeth that weren't so much sharp as they were translucent needles, streaked bright red. It was a horror, and no man faced with such a horror would not consider running, unless he were an idiot or a liar.

So Vann ran.

He ran until his lungs burned, he ran until his legs wobbled, he ran until he could run no more. Still, he continued running.

Behind him, he heard the thing following, loping along behind, panting like a dog, but always just behind him, always not quite able to reach him. He ran across an open field, knowing it was behind him, knowing its teeth and claws were stained with the rest of his squad. He ran, knowing that such a thing could probably have caught up in half a dozen steps, but had not. He ran knowing that it was playing with him.

The buildings loomed out of the darkness, houses long abandoned, crumbling walls, debris and rubble everywhere. For a moment, he allowed himself to hope this might help, and he angled into the debris, between buildings, into the light fog that covered everything.

His breath burned his throat and his heart hammered at his chest, and he knew that at this speed he could only hope there wouldn't be any surprises ahead, because he would probably plow full-speed into them.

The thing behind him cried out, and it chilled him hearing it. He ducked sideways between a couple of buildings, made another fast turn, and found himself in a small courtyard. He paused, panting as quietly as he could. Maybe he'd lost it.

He tried to catch his breath as quietly as possible, hoping his heart wasn't as loud outside as it was inside.

Hope rested on one hand, but on the other, he knew it wasn't going to last. He knew that his respite was at best short-lived. Still trying to be as quiet as possible, still trying to control his breathing and keep it quiet, he unholstered his pistol and stepped out from behind a building.

It wasn't until he was already flying through the air that he realized he'd been hit. The thing must have been mid-leap and collided with him, because nothing could have attacked that fast, he was sure of it.

Something seemed to punch against his arm three times, and there was flashing and he wondered, for a fraction of a second, why he hadn't hit the ground yet, and then he did, and he was rolling and tumbling away from that monstrosity.

81

Close Your Eyes – Tales from the Blinkspace

He jumped to his feet, turning, gun out. His hand was sore, and he looked down and realized he had fired his weapon. Smoke curled from the muzzle. He spent an entire second praising his DI for getting those reflexes up, and then turned back to the thing on the ground.

It lay writhing, eight feet from him, brown and black fluids pulsing out from the gaping impact holes. Teeth snapped, but it could not move its head. Claws grasped, but it could not move its arms. The tail started moving, but then stopped. While he watched, the horror died.

He knelt before it. Raised his pistol once more.

"Might not want to do that," a voice behind him husked.

He spun.

She stood above him, and it was only then that he realized both he and the creature had fallen into an old shallow foundation. She jumped down the four feet and stood with her rifle and eyes trained on the creature. Shaken, he saluted. "Sergeant, I think it's dead. I think I killed it."

She nodded. "I think you did, too," she said, "but I think you'd best be saving rounds anyway."

She watched it for a couple more seconds, and then seemed satisfied it was dead. Then she turned her rifle to Vann. "Are you bit?" she asked.

"What?" he asked, confused.

"Are you bit? Or scratched? Did it break your skin at all?"

The muzzle never wavered.

"I... uh, I don't think so," he said, but no sooner were the words out of his mouth than he noticed the itching. His left forearm started itching. Oh sure, he thought, just what I need to be doing right now when I want to be not moving is to have an itch.

The itch spread.

"Be sure," she said, "Because I see your hand twitching."

"I got an itch."

"Scratch it."

He scratched, but it only got worse. The itch became a burn, and he kept scratching.

"Look at your arm," she said, and he wasted no time pulling his sleeve back. A long thin scratch, hardly worth noting, ran from his elbow to the outside of his wrist. It was swollen and red.

He scratched it furiously. "Goddammit," he muttered. "Itches like a sunnuvabitch."

82

Close Your Eyes – Tales from the Blinkspace

"Yep," she said. "Sorry." She raised her rifle.

"Wait! What the fuck, Sergeant!?"

"It scratched you. You know what happens next."

The burn had settled deeper, and instead of scratching, he was rubbing and squeezing his arm.

"I scratch back is what happens next. Look, it's almost gone. What the – why are you pointing your weapon at me?"

She looked puzzled, but the rifle never wavered. "You really don't know?" she asked.

"Don't know what?"

Now she was intrigued. "You haven't had the dreams?" she asked.

Vann shook his head. "I don't dream," he told her. "Not since –"

The twist in his guts was ferocious, like being punched by ten different guys, none of whom was happy. As he fell, a second explosion of pain went nova behind his eyes, a flare in his skull. He might have screamed.

A few seconds later, he became aware of her standing there, still a couple yards away, still watching him, rifle still aimed at him.

"Never met anyone didn't dream," she said. "How do you get that?"

Panting, he whispered.

"What?" she asked. "I can't hear you."

"I have a plate in my head," he growled. "Ever since I was twelve. I don't dream."

"That's cool," she said, nodding. "I guess that's a mixed blessing for you then, because you don't know what's happening. You haven't had the dreams." She peered at his uniform. "Vann," she said, "what do you know about our enemy?"

He shook his head and there was another blast of pain behind his eyes, and he felt a twisting inside, impossibly inside. He fell back to his hands and knees.

"You see that thing on the ground behind you?" she asked. He didn't turn, but gagged, his throat twisting. More bolts of pain shot through his head. In between the increasing waves, he could still hear her.

"I've been hunting him for almost a day now," she said. "He and ten others. It's what happens when you fight a god."

At this, Vann looked up, scowling.

"Oh, not with a capital 'G'," she said. "I'm not sure exactly where He is, anyway. No, this is more like your average run-of-the-mill god. A smaller god. One that can't just

Close Your Eyes – Tales from the Blinkspace

wave its hand or whatever it has that looks like a hand, and make things happen. It needs troops. Ground troops. And that's one of them."

She leaned down.

"You're looking at the only one in my squad that didn't get bit. Didn't get scratched. Over there," she nodded, "...was the first. He got away. I was hoping to stop him before he infected anyone else, but I suck, and now I'm sorry to say that you are also on the shock troops training fast-track for our sleeping god."

"What?!" Vann tried to say, but his guts clenched, his head felt like someone was going at it with a pick-axe, and he vomited. Vomited something – not just food. It shined in the darkness.

"That's something you won't need for your new life," the Sergeant observed. "I think it's a lymph node, hard to say."

Vann's mind slipped. Wrenched.

"But this non-dreaming thing is pretty weird," she said. "That's how he controls you, through the waking dream he puts you in. We can sense it, because we can also dream, but it's nothing to his dreams. His dreams shatter worlds. But if you don't dream, then he can't see you."

Vann's hands and arms deepened in color to violet. A quick glance behind him at the corpse. He knew that color. His nails fell off as sharper claws pushed through his fingertips, even as the skin was hardening and darkening. It hurt, it hurt, oh Christ it hurt!

In his head again, a screeching, twisting pain that blew all the rest away. His mind tried to shut down, but it wasn't happening. He couldn't stop feeling this, couldn't stop the pain, the pushing.

He gagged and coughed and gagged again. A spike ran through his head and he screamed and retched and something else pushed its way out. First his teeth – now useless – fell to the ground, and then it clattered down with them, trailing stringy mucous and blood vessels.

The Sergeant leaned forward, squinting. "Wow," she said, "I guess we know who won that contest."

One part of Vann's mind marveled. He'd always expected a surgical plate to look like a sheet of metal, but this looked more like a little piece of corrugated mesh, and small. Very small, maybe one by three centimeters.

The other part of his mind, however, was busy. It was dreaming.

Dreams flooded his mind, images from a distant past, pushing everything else away, even the pain. In his dreams he watched the history of the world unfold, the history he never knew existed, the history no man could ever have guessed at.

Close Your Eyes – Tales from the Blinkspace

In his dream, the Earth was still new and young. It was the time of flames and chaos, ages before mankind, ages before there was life on the planet. In this time, he saw the Beasts come to Earth. He saw them leaping and playing in the primordial lava, their bodies obscene and wondrous, their eyes burning like suns.

Then he saw the coming of the Scientists, beings nearly as old as the Beasts, and nearly as powerful. Vann saw their crystal ships fill the skies, and their beams of black dimensionless light slice the Beasts, one by one, into heaving, steaming corpses.

Then the Scientists left, but one Beast remained. Mutilated, crippled, and insane, it dragged itself into a cave, slid deep into the virgin Earth, and fell into a sleep of great power and great madness.

Vann saw all this in the blink of an eye, the flash of a thought, and then he was back in the ruined foundation.

The Sergeant shook her head. "Sucks," she said. "Not even our fight, but we still have to deal with the goddamn shellshock."

There was another twist and Vann felt everything shift. He screamed in pain, but halfway through, that pain turned to rage, to burning eternal fury. He looked up at the Sergeant through whirling violet eyes, and this time, she glowed brilliantly in the dark. Her scent was thick and heavy and meaty in his nostrils, and he inhaled it and knew what must happen. She had to join them, she had to be changed, and had to share the Sleeper's dream. They all had to join and grow in the brilliance of his new god. When the whole planet was ready, when all were of the same Dream, then they had to look outward, had to move outward, stretching across the solar system, across the galaxy, across the Universe. All had to share the Dream, to know the pain and suffering the Scientists had created. And then, maybe, somewhere in those journeys, they might actually find the Scientists themselves, and then–

"Sorry," said the Sergeant, raising her rifle. "I know what you're thinking. Not on my watch, no."

She squeezed the trigger and Vann stopped dreaming.

END

The Collector, Part 1: Appetizer

My first commission for Lynne, "The Collector" is the sort of story I've always wanted to make as a short movie. Although I think I'd leave certain bits out – such as (in this case) references to Twitter. Because, of course, who uses Twitter in 2014...?

In the city of Baltimore, there is an area where no one goes. In this area is a street down which no one travels. Down this street is a building no one sees, with a door no one opens, under a sign no one reads. The lettering on the sign spells "Things Recalled – antiques, oddities, mysteries" but that's only lettering. The real business was something entirely different.

It was a magic shop.

It wasn't a place filled with trick rings and clever cards and various silk scarves. It was a genuine magic shop. The real deal.

It was as invisible as they came, and if you didn't know it was there, you would never see it. More specifically, if you noticed anything at all, it would be a vague impression of a dull building, long disused and overgrown with trash and weeds. If, however, you knew what it was and knew where to look and how, it would appear to be a dull building, long disused and overgrown with trash and weeds, with an open-door policy.

Outside, a late model Chevrolet waited uncomfortably at the curb. It looked as out of place here as a gypsy wagon would have looked at the base of the Empire State Building – assuming the gypsy wagon were on fire and surrounded by dancing bandits. As a rental, it was accustomed to ordinary locations, with ordinary people such as businessmen. It was not accustomed to strange places, strange situations, or strange men.

Close Your Eyes – Tales from the Blinkspace

The feeling was mutual. The building made a sincere effort to maintain a certain anonymity, and this clean, waxed, shiny intruder of a vehicle stood out. It called attention to itself, and in doing so, called attention to the building. How embarrassing!

As much as the building and the business tried to remain under the radar of perception, that was nothing compared to the clientele. Those who stage illusions – which aren't even real magic – are insanely jealous about their secrets, but the ones who do the real thing leave that desire for secrecy in the dust. These are not people who "browse." They know exactly what they want and target exactly that. They make special arrangements for special things and those special things have to be exactly perfect and delivered with absolute discretion.

Under no circumstances would such people ever consider acting in anything other than a completely secret manner, so it stands to reason that when compared to such secret clientele, even the most normal inoffensive person might seem a little boorish.

As was the case now. This man was tall and broad-shouldered. He was well-groomed, but wore a black t-shirt under a suit coat. He stood out as much as the Chevy outside which brought him. Probably more so, as the Chevy, technically, was unable to speak.

"Christ, this place is amazing!" he crowed as he ran his fingers lightly across the spines of a set of books that were obviously hand-bound. "I've never seen books like this before. Never seen a *collection* of books like this before!"

He grinned like a madman at the Proprietor of Things Recalled. The Proprietor was a small thin man with large ears, a long thin nose, and a thin patch of gray hair haloing his head. The Proprietor was still so stunned by the appearance of this strange man that he could only dimly nod. It was a form of cognitive shock.

"And the décor," the man said. "It's perfect!" He waggled a shrunken head at the Proprietor triumphantly. "This looks so *real!*" He tossed the head on a shelf. "It creates a simply unparalleled verisimilitude. Best bookshop ever!"

Regaining some composure, the Proprietor drew himself up and in a voice much less timid than expected, asked "Sir, may I ask who you are? You are not one of my regular clients."

The fellow blinked in surprise. "Oh, I had no idea you didn't know me." He stepped over and extended a hand. The Proprietor stared disdainfully at the hand as if it was a dead fish. "The name's Deane Holmes. I run a book collector's blog."

"A… 'blog'?"

Deane smiled. "Better get used to learning the lingo," he said. "Because of my blog, your business is about to go through the roof!" He waved a small cellular telephone. "Already tweeted and bounced to the blog. Over fifteen hundred hits so far and that's only in the past few minutes! You're going to be famous!"

87

Close Your Eyes – Tales from the Blinkspace

"Famous?" Suddenly the Proprietor understood the intent, if not the words. "Oh," he said. "Oh, I have no interest in being famous, plus my clientele would also have a great deal of trouble with that."

"Are you saying you don't want thousands of people to know about your shop? Just think what that would do for your business!"

"Thousands?!" cried the Proprietor. "That would ruin me!"

"Don't be ridiculous," said Deane. "Everybody wants more business. Everybody wants recognition. I'm the guy giving it to you!"

The Proprietor's head collapsed into his hands and the shop fell silent.

"What?" asked Deane.

The Proprietor looked up then, and there was a gleam in his eyes. "It's novelty," he said. "You're looking for novelty."

"And I've found it here," said Deane.

"Oh, Mister Holmes, novelty is my business." As he spoke, the Proprietor stood from his position near the door. He wore a dark floor length robe, and exhibited a fluid, gliding walk as he approached. He guided Deane between the shelves as he spoke. "I specialize in it for all of my clients," he said. "It's not the shop at all – the shop's just a sort of overflow area. If it's novelty you're looking for, if it's obscurity of texts and learning is what you crave, I can help. Oh, most definitely!"

They stopped at a display of figurines.

"Consider this collection," said the Proprietor, his voice the most persuasive silk.

"I'm not really looking for–"

"I understand, but it's important. You like books, but books only contain knowledge. This," he brushed a finger along the shelf. "This *is* knowledge. Look more closely."

Deane did so.

The figures were small, only two or three inches. Each was a person, bent and twisted in agony. Some were standing, some collapsed, all with faces twisted in horror.

"My God..." whispered Deane. "What... what happened?"

The Proprietor's face came closer. Deane's nose wrinkled as he smelled a strong cloud of dust. No, something older than dust. Something ancient.

"Look at the whole display."

Each of the figures, despite their individual agony, were all arranged in an arc surrounding a larger figure. During the entire exchange, Deane's eyes had simply avoided it, but now he could see it. In fact, he couldn't not see it.

88

Close Your Eyes – Tales from the Blinkspace

It towered above the others. Above and over. Parts of it were animal, parts manlike (although he couldn't quite bring himself to call those parts "human"), and parts were something else entirely. It didn't have eyes from what he could see, but he felt its baleful gaze downward and knew that in their agony, those figures met that gaze.

"Unbelievable," he breathed. "Are they... are they worshipping it?"

"Of course," whispered the Proprietor into his ear. "Can you tell why?"

Quietly, Deane shook his head. On one hand, he wanted to look more closely at the central figure, but on the other hand, his mind refused to let him.

"You don't have to look if you don't want to," said the Proprietor. "Not all can see the way I can. Try touching it."

Deane nearly pulled back at the suggestion.

"It's all right," urged the Proprietor. "It'll help you understand."

Deane reached out and with a single fingertip, touched the surface of the idol.

*

His world was pinched to a microscopic dot, and then expanded back to a completely different one.

*

The sun was a bloated orange inferno, filling half the sky. An old sun, he thought, and then gasped, taking his first breath on a dead, alien world.

He'd been in hot weather before. Last summer, Phoenix hit 115 degrees, but he'd never been in heat like this. It baked him from the outside in and scorched him from the inside out.

He spun around. He was surrounded by an ancient lava flow, cracked sharp rock rolling across a landscape forever in all directions. No sign of life, no sign of anything, other than the endless ocean of searing frozen basalt crests and troughs.

Well, not exactly barren.

There was a monolith.

It was fifty feet tall – maybe taller – three feet wide and a foot deep. Its base was buried in the lava flow and it rose above even the tallest peak.

Deane stumbled closer and looked. Its surface was smooth, black, and covered with deeply carved petroglyphs. He stared, but the only sense he could make of them was a sort of animal terror, and even in this heat, it chilled him.

Close Your Eyes – Tales from the Blinkspace

He turned from the monolith to the empty plain. Madness started creeping into his skull and he laughed. There was no answer, no response, not even an echo. So, he tried the next thing his cracked mind offered as an option.

He screamed.

It seemed to help a little.

Midway through, however, the scream died in his throat as the monolith's shadow started moving.

The shadow lengthened and twisted and extruded shapes like tree branches. The shadow melted from a dead geometric thing to something that waved and wiggled and still towered over everything else.

Deane stared at the shadow. He couldn't bear to turn around. Seeing what created that shadow would cause infinitely more damage to his mind than watching the shadow was already doing, and even though he felt his life's last seconds ticking away, he preferred some sort of sanity to those seconds.

The ground at his feet rumbled deeply.

The black rock cracked and buckled up into the air as the shadowed thing pulled itself free. One more lurch and Deane tumbled down a hill, rolling helplessly as the landscape heaved. The rock sliced his flesh and blood streaked into his eyes.

Instinctively, he wiped his eyes and blinked, clearing his vision. Before he knew what he was doing, he looked up into the thing as it bent toward him, hungry and grasping.

There was a high-pitched sound, a kind of childlike keening. He was pretty sure it came from his own throat.

*

The Proprietor knelt and reached out a leathery brown arm. He picked up a sculpture from the floor. It was a man, bent backwards and streaked in blood, eyes vacant, mouth screaming.

"My Lord," he whispered as he placed the thing next to its companions on the shelf. "I'm sorry. I know it wasn't time yet, but it was all I could think of to protect us."

He glanced down. Deane's cell phone lay open on the floorboards.

The bottom third of the Proprietor's robes split open and three muscular tentacles weaved out. They plucked the cell phone from the floor and crushed it to pieces. They pushed the pieces under the shelf and, just as fluidly, withdrew back into the robe.

"We'll have no more of that," he whispered, and then turned back to the idol. It had changed in a subtle way. It looked the tiniest bit more realistic.

The Proprietor smiled, which he rarely did.

"I am glad you could stomach him, Lord," he said.

Without another sound, he glided back to his place at the front of the shop.

Where he continued waiting.

END

The Collector, Part 2: Entree

Surely this sort of thing can't be allowed to continue...

It was the music. At least he thought it was music.

The Proprietor pressed his thin bony hands against his large ears, but it didn't help.

The squealing stopped and the silence felt wonderful.

The dry air in the shop still shook with the noise. The Proprietor left his place at the front of the shop and glided toward the back, toward the peculiar antiquities section.

In that section, he found a man. This man was no customer, no normal client of the shop. He was grinning, and tousled gray hair poked out around the edges of his baseball cap. As the Proprietor rounded the corner, the man froze, his hands raised, suspending lengths of wire strung in several directions.

One of the Proprietor's eyebrows raised. "What are you doing?" he asked. His calm delivery was less a measure of an inner calm and more a simple case of shock.

The man grinned more broadly.

"Funny you should ask," he said. "This place seemed quiet. Too quiet. So I'm working out the acoustics, working out some details." He waggled his fingers and the wires danced like puppet threads. "It was supposed to be a surprise."

He tossed another loop over a shelf. A small wooden carving fell from the top shelf. The Proprietor's heart stopped, but the man caught it gently in midfall. He treated it as gently as an egg and placed it back on a different shelf, a few feet away from the wiring.

Close Your Eyes – Tales from the Blinkspace

"I figured that might fall," he muttered.

"That... that was a priceless artifact!" sputtered the Proprietor.

"From Guyana, right?" asked the man. "Looked like it. Upper shelf's not a good place for stuff like that. All kinds of clumsiness could happen."

The Proprietor's eyes twitched. His voice grew low and menacing. "Who are you?" he asked. "Who are you and what are you doing here?"

"Oh, sorry, I totally forgot to tell you." He reached out a hand. "Ken. Ken Hayes."

The Proprietor looked at the hand as if it was something extraordinarily distasteful. Ken withdrew it.

"I hope it's okay I let myself in through the back. The front of the shop's a tricky bit of business. Nice spell or whatever it is."

He stepped across the aisle and set up another cable, wrapping it around a support post.

"My buddy Deane mentioned it, but didn't go into too many details. I just kinda ran with what seemed sensible. But I like it, don't get me wrong. A man's got a right to his privacy. Free enterprise and all. Still..."

He stapled the cable flat to the edge of a wooden shelf.

"Stop!" shouted the Proprietor. He had reached toward Hayes, but now it was his turn to freeze. The arm he had extended from his robe in panic wasn't quite as human as it should have been. It slipped back into the robe's folds as quickly as it shot out, but it definitely had left an impression.

Hayes smiled and looked into the Proprietor's eyes.

"A lot of people aren't fond of pop music," he said. "Yet they buy it like crazy, they make records into best-sellers, and they pump tons and tons of their spare money into buying more. Who are you fond of? Who's your favorite?"

The Proprietor took a step back. "I don't understand."

"Well, you don't seem like a basic Beatles kind of guy." Hayes reached into his pocket and withdrew a small controller box. He pressed a button.

A different sound flooded to shop. Something glass rattled. Then it stopped.

"See, not Beatles. But that's okay, I had a feeling that wouldn't work anyway."

"Stop it! Stop making that noise!"

Hayes flipped another switch. The noise was different now, deeper and more fluid. The Proprietor felt queasy.

Then the music switched off.

93

Close Your Eyes – Tales from the Blinkspace

"Don't feel bad – nobody else liked her, either."

"What are you doing?!"

"You can't tell?" asked Hayes.

He fiddled with the controller again, and pressed the button.

This time the sound was different. It felt like a ghostly chorus. It felt a little like a soft pillow to the Proprietor's ears.

Then it stopped.

"Ah, well, that's a baseline," said Hayes. "The classical stuff always helps me tune things better."

He adjusted the controls once more. "I'm going to take a wild guess..."

Once again, he hit the "play" button.

The music struck like a hammer. Every muscle in the Proprietor's body tensed. He immediately lost the sense of feeling in his feet and hands, and the numbness crept upward.

"Ah, you're a jazz guy!" said Hayes. "Excellent! I guessed right."

The Proprietor screamed, and his throat didn't produce a man's scream, but a high-pitched ululation, a feverish shriek.

"Well, not a 'guy' per se," said Hayes. "I mean, I kind figured that when I first saw you. But to be fair, this isn't exactly Mr. Armstrong we're hearing. It's more like... what his music would be if all the stuff that makes humans understand it were taken out. It's just the power of it."

He leaned close and looked into the Proprietor's eyes.

"You understand power, am I right?"

Murder oozed from the Proprietor's eyes.

Hayes grinned again. "Sure you do."

He straightened up.

"I have to admire my work, though," he said. "Humans are usually easy, but others... not so much. I was really gambling I could get the whole grid set up before you knew what I was doing. Not that most people would understand it anyway, but there's always a chance you might have figured it out and I'm not sure I want you on top of me, intellectually. Surprise is an awesome and wonderful thing."

He tapped the Proprietor on the arm. "How's the numbness coming?"

Close Your Eyes – Tales from the Blinkspace

The numbness was, unfortunately, coming along well. The Proprietor was still stiff and unable to move, and he couldn't feel his legs or arms.

"You have no idea how expensive these speakers were," said Hayes. "Most humans can hear from two hertz to twenty kilohertz, but they react to a much greater frequency. My speakers must reach those frequencies. Not cheap, I'll tell you. Aside from the obvious utility, I have to say that piping any kind of synth through these is a complete experience unto itself. You have no idea what it's like to listen to Yes when you can hear all the frequencies, instead of just the audible ones."

The Proprietor managed a twitch.

"It would be easy to think this was about Deane," he said. "Most creatures recognize revenge. Even Deane might think this was the right thing to do. But I have to be truthful with you – it's not. Not at all."

The numbness crept up the Proprietor's neck. He felt himself slipping away.

Hayes moved in close, and his eyes glowed with avarice.

"It's just that I love collecting rare and unusual things," he whispered, his voice slicing between the throb of the music. "And you'll do very nicely."

The noise washed over the Proprietor's ears and that was all he remembered.

END

The Collector, Part 3: Dessert

Some things you inherit. Some things inherit you.

Things Recalled was more than a simple antique shop. Things Recalled was a magic shop. A real magic shop, too – not a place that sold trick tables and collapsible boxes.

One of the things a magic shop has in common with any other kind of shop is that it requires a Proprietor. Someone must be a part of the system, someone to clean and arrange and greet clients, and make sure that business is handled in an orderly fashion.

One of the things a magic shop does not have in common with an ordinary non-magic shop is that if it doesn't have a Proprietor, it feels lonely. It feels sad. It misses that sense of being part of a functioning system of moving magical items amongst the various practitioners of the art. Also, unlike an ordinary non-magical shop, a magic shop can actually do something about it.

The Proprietor of Things Recalled had disappeared six months ago. The shop was accustomed to its Proprietor disappearing for stretches of time, usually on procurement runs, and sometimes for tasks less wholesome, but six months was too long. Six months meant there was something wrong. Six months meant that it was time to find a new Proprietor. Six months indicated that it was Time To Do Something.

It started by unlocking the door.

Quietly, it waited.

At night, it locked the door again, and then waited in the dark, unlocking the door again in the morning.

Close Your Eyes – Tales from the Blinkspace

Four days later, there was a sound. There were footsteps outside the door. There was a scuffing of feet on the mat. Then, the door opened.

"Hello," the timid voice called out. "Is anyone here?"

A woman stepped into the dust-filled sunbeams. She wore hiking boots, long pants, a backpack, and the kind of deep tan that only comes from years in a desert.

"Hello!" she called out again.

She listened intently, but there was no response. She smiled.

"Well, good then," she said. She stepped over to the counter and rang the old bell there. Years of disuse had partially rusted the clapper inside, so instead of a clear ring, it clattered. She tried a few more times, but the clatter never improved.

She hit it louder.

"It's not working," she declared. "This bell's not working. How are we supposed to have new customers in droves if the bell doesn't work. Someone needs to fix that."

The shop groaned.

The groan took the form of a push of air through the shelves along the back wall. Some papers rustled, then settled.

The woman smiled to herself.

"And this dust is intolerable," she added. "I know it's quaint and quirky and mysterious, but it's not what works these days. Customers need things to be clean. They need things to be clean and professional and well lit and organized."

She hopped up to sit on the counter, dislodging a stream of dust that spiraled to the floor. Her feet swung free and her heels banged softly into the wood of the counter.

With each thump, the shop grew more concerned.

"And we're going to have an open house."

That was it. That was the last straw.

The problem with spells, mused the shop, as it shifted its attentions to various elements in itself, is that you can never quite predict how the spell will manifest. One might cast for a monkey, but it could be a ceramic monkey that shows up, or a live monkey with mental problems. Spellcasting was inherently unpredictable.

Beginners often tried to lawyer their way through spellcasting, with ever-more-complicated descriptions. The tricky thing about spellcasting, however, is that the harder one tries to work around its special chaotic nature, the more diabolical the jinx.

An expert spellcaster, someone who has been casting for decades, knows this. The real twist in spellcasting isn't the ability to construct an elaborate spell that does a very

Close Your Eyes – Tales from the Blinkspace

precise thing. The real trick is to construct a spell that is simple and reflects as accurately as possible the desire of the spellcaster.

The shop was no amateur, but neither was it an old pro. It knew what had happened. It knew that in the casting for a new Proprietor, there would necessarily be a great degree of unpredictability.

That didn't mean, however, that it had to be happy with the results.

It moved more things.

There was a rustle from the back of the store.

The woman looked up.

"Sounds like someone's back there," she said, just a little more loudly than necessary. "Sounds like someone's creeping around back there, causing mischief. Now, if I'm gonna run this place, I better investigate that sort of mischief."

She hopped off the counter. She checked her backpack straps to make sure they were tight.

"Now, where would that be," she asked aloud as she walked back into the deeper, darker corners.

The shop heaved again, ever so slightly, and there was a rattle as something fell to the floor.

The woman rounded the corner and looked down.

"Someone's spilled over all of these marvelous little figurines," she said. She knelt and examined them lying on the floor.

"They certainly don't look happy. I better put them back."

One by one, she collected each of the tiny figures of agony in her hands. Slowly, she stood up, eyes reviewing the shelves.

"Oh, don't you look lonely," she told the lone sculpture remaining. "I mean, you're also hideously ugly in a beautiful kind of way, or maybe more like gorgeous in a hideous kind of way, but regardless, you look lonely. These must be your worshippers."

She arrayed the figures around the idol carefully.

"You need to understand, however," she added. "That they don't look particularly happy. I think it matters a great deal that one arranges for one's worshippers to be at least somewhat reasonably happy. It keeps them coming back."

She turned to leave.

The store heaved and writhed once again, and there was a clunk.

Close Your Eyes – Tales from the Blinkspace

The woman turned back and now the idol lay on its side.

"Who's going to worship a fallen idol," she muttered. She looked slyly out the corner of her eye and her skin prickled with the room's tension.

"Maybe I'll just right you," she said. One hand gripping her backpack strap, she reached out with the other to right the idol.

There was a whoosh of displaced air and she vanished.

The shop held its breath, unsure, but then sighed deeply. There was no way such a brash and obnoxious person could ever possibly hope to be a proper Proprietor. It just seemed so wrong to—

The air shimmered. The air shook. The space in front of the idol wobbled. There was a sparking, a spitting, then a glowing line. The line turned to a crosscrossing spiderweb. Then the Universe split. Heat and smoke and screaming and pain billowed out from that other place. Then smoking blackness leaped through, and the split screamed itself shut. The air cooled down. The unearthly light became ordinary dusty sunlight again. The smoking blackness became a figure.

The figure crouched, panting, and tendrils of smoke curled up from all over her body.

The woman's packpack had been partially ripped from her back. Her clothes had been scorched. Her skin bore dark streaks of sweat and char. In one of her hands, she clutched an ornate bottle.

She looked up, and grinned.

The shop shuddered.

"My name is Lynne," she said. "And this was a neat trick. Now, I know you're not happy with me, but you and I both know that's how it goes. You called, I answered. End of story."

She wiped the back of her hand across her forehead.

"Maybe you thought you could ditch me this way, send me off somehow, but this was a mistake, because you let appearances deceive you. Maybe you've gotten sloppy over the years. I don't know, and nor do I care. Your old Proprietor is gone, and probably because he got sloppy. No more sloppy."

She waved the bottle in the air. It steamed and hissed, and faintly on its surface thin lettering glowed.

"So, for the record, I have been to another dimension, I have faced this unspeakable demonic thing, and I have completely beaten its ass and shoved it into a sangria bottle. *A sangria bottle!*"

She turned to the shelves. Where the idol used to be was only a pile of papery ashes. She brushed it to the floor.

99

Close Your Eyes – Tales from the Blinkspace

"I own this bastard," she said. "And I own you. You can either get used to it and learn to work along with me, or..."

She dropped the bottle. It shattered on the floor. A thick black goo oozed out from the cracks and fragments, but on contact with the air, it squealed and sparked and evaporated.

The shop considered. Then it agreed. The lights brightened a little and a fresh breeze of air blew through the shelves.

Lynne nodded.

"Good," she said. She stepped over the broken glass and dusty fragments, toward the front counter. "And just so you know," she added. "We *are* getting a website."

END

Adventure

Part of a writing marathon at the H. P. Lovecraft Film Festival, "Adventure" is inspired by Emily's flair for adventure.

Emily opened the Book, not so much because she wanted to open the Book, but more because she could feel the Book wanting her to open it.

She wasn't super familiar with books, as she was only seven years old, but she knew enough about them to know that Books Contain Adventures, so hearing a book whispering in her ears was very exciting.

She waited until her folks went to bed and then she padded down to Daddy's Special Room, opened his desk drawer (she could hear its voice no matter where Daddy hid it), and brought the Book up to his desk. Then she opened it.

The Book reached out, hungry, and pulled at her fingers, pulled at her hands, pulled at her hair and her face. She tried to scream, but she felt the Book pulling the scream from her throat and she knew that no one would hear her.

She felt her feet lift off from the floor and she knew, in that moment, that she was lost, and the Book ate her up, and the cover closed and the room was quiet once again.

A moment later, the cover of the Book fluttered and flipped open. A whirling constellation of amber light spiraled out of the pages and fell to the floor, building and coalescing into a woman, semiconscious, dressed in a bark-woven dress, skin browned, hair a tangled mass, fingernails cracked, and eyes wild and maddened.

Emily stood up as the Book flapped closed. The room was dark and quiet in the night. She looked around, as if seeing an ancient dream become real again.

Close Your Eyes – Tales from the Blinkspace

She stumbled out of the room, her feet bare on the wood floor, and found a bathroom. In it, she switched on the light and looked into the mirror. She could not remember the last time she had seen her own reflection.

She marveled at her face, at her skin (mahogany from exposure), at the depths and madness her eyes now contained. And then she realized what had been done, what the Book had stolen from her. Only moments had passed since she opened it, but she was now forty-eight years old. It had stolen her life.

Hands against her face, she wept.

END

For Space is Deep and Hungry

Part of a writing marathon at the H. P. Lovecraft Film Festival, "For Space is Deep and Hungry" is inspired by Katrina's request for a futuristic "Cats of Ulthar" type story.

There is no place on Earth as dark and soulless and silently hungry as being off Earth. There is no place that a human being feels more fragile, more soft, more delicate than sealed into a metal canister and suspended in the depths of space.

This human's name was Katrina, and she was of the sort of mettle such that she could stay in the deep silence of space for years at a time without needing the company of others, without filling her head with the idle chatter of people trying to synthesize a planet by filling the air with whatever subjects drifted through their brains and out their mouths.

She traveled alone, but it's a rare human who can live without even occasional companionship, and it was during one of these moments of weakness, when she most craved the sound of voices other than those she produced herself, that she arrived at the Titan/Jupiter L5 station. It was a distant station, and rarely visited.

Her docking instructions were automated, and her radio enquiries were not returned. She docked, locked, and disembarked.

In the silent corridors, the metal of her boots clanged echoes that traveled all the way from one end of the station to the other.

Despite the eerie silence, she was self-contained. She refueled by herself, restocked provisions from the dock supply station by herself, loaded more water from the station

Close Your Eyes – Tales from the Blinkspace

tanks by herself, and still, there was no greeting, no rushing feet, no one glad to see her, no one asking after affairs in the outer reaches of space (not that there were any).

The only creature that came to visit her during these proceedings was a cat, a dark exotic cat with extra large eyes and a curious ruff around his neck, undoubtedly shaped by years in space.

It approached quietly and sat, watching her.

As she had a soft spot in her heart for cats, and knowing how rare pets were this far from Earth, Katrina knelt by the creature, petted it, cuddled it, and played with it. It purred contently, licked her fingers, and explored the outside of her ship. She opened a small tin of protein, and lay that upon the dock, and the cat, with one last glance at her, began to eat.

This buoyed her spirits and, making sure that her vessel was locked against intrusion, she wandered deeper into the station.

The rest of the station seemed to obey the same rules of abandonment as the docking area – there were no people to greet her, no friendly faces or waving hands. She walked across mezzanines and by shops, by one of the three small cafes, and even by the sheriff's office. While there were a few subtle signs of disarray (and a longtime spacer who must keep her ship extremely tidy knows disarray when she sees it), there were no other signs of violence, no other signs of anything unusual – except for the disturbing lack of population.

It was then that she heard it. It was then that she heard the sound, the soft, distant chirrup. She followed a lesser tunnel, and it grew louder and broader.

The lights in this section were blinking, another failure that a real spacer would never have permitted aboard a ship, and the constant flicker began to drive a wedge into her brain, an aperiodic jolt of pain that grew as she walked.

The sound grew more distinct until she recognized it. Never before had she heard such a sound, but nevertheless she recognized it, at the same time recognizing how impossible it seemed.

At that moment, the corridor turned into an open area, an atrium, a conceit, perhaps, of one of the original inhabitants of the station. Fresh water cascaded from a fountain, flowed among piles of sticks and leaves, pooled gently in one corner, and then was pumped back into the fountain. A broad window admitted dim sunlight from the star too far away to call home at the moment, but enough to illuminate the room, to show her the forms that lay about, that walked, and slinked and hopped and padded about in the dim light.

The room was filled with cats. Purring, meowing, growling cats.

Her mind reeled. Pets were more than a luxury in space – they were practically non-existent. In order to support this number of pets, this number of cats, the costs for supplying food could easily bankrupt the station.

Close Your Eyes – Tales from the Blinkspace

In some places of our brains there are mechanisms that activate before we are consciously aware of what is happening. In Katrina's brain, such a process switched on and before she realized what was happening, she ran.

The flickering lights of the corridor confused her, and jumbled her thoughts, but she still ran. The empty yawning mall terrified her and she ran. The abandoned docking area chilled the blood in her veins and still she ran. She ran and dove into her ship. She pulled the door shut behind her, panting while spinning the wheels and locks.

Only once she was strapped into the pilot's seat did her conscious mind begin sorting out what she had seen. Only once she had resequenced the drives and began to drift away from the dock did she look up. Only then did her eyes meet the extra large eyes of the cat with the curious ruff, who sat on the dock, watching her – she was sure of it – watching her through the hardened cockpit window, licking its paw contently, sated by the food she had given it.

Only at that moment, did her mind allow her to remember what her eyes had seen, to see the vast atrium, filled with cats, to see the stream, to wonder where the people were, and to wonder what the cats ate. Only then did her mind allow her to see that the stream did not, in fact, meander through sticks and leaves at all, but the picked and polished remains of the crew of the L5 station. She struggled with her sanity, but she was a deep spacer and sanity was already a flexible construct at best.

With a last glance at the L5 station, she turned her ship and fired the mains.

END

True Love

"True Love" is all about finding what you're looking for without expecting to see it.

She came down to the water every day, eyes to the horizon, dress winding about in the wind, hair haloing her face. She came down to the water and she looked outward, her heart quivering with hope.

"He will come," she said. "My true love will come to me."

Every day she came and every day she looked to the horizon, unbroken by any ship, and as the day drifted to redness and ending, she would sigh, and turn away, and walk back inland, back to wherever she came from.

The wind eventually spoke to her, whispering in her ears through the susurration of her dress. "My dear," the wind would say, "I can love you, and I am here now."

She shook her head at this and laughed like crystal. "You're the wind," she said, "and you're harsh and gusty and you can't know what it's like." She looked outward, smiling. "You can't know what it's like to be touched softly by a lover, with only the most delicate of touch. You're the wind and you are fast and brisk and swift. You could never be my lover."

As the day ended and the sun sank, she turned away and walked back inland, leaving the wind to its lonely self.

Eventually, the sand spoke to her, through the creaks and groans of slipping dunes. The sand said "My darling, I cannot tell you how long you've come here, how long

I've held you up, how long I've watched your eyes, hopeful with the empty distance. I beg of you, let me be your lover, let me hold you and keep your soul."

She knelt and softly patted the sand and said "It warms my heart for you to show such kindness, but no matter how soft you might seem from a distance, I know you are sharp and hungry." She stood back up, facing the great gray ocean. "You could never know," she said, "of how soft the palms of a lover are against your flesh, of how much that touch is love and softness. You could never be my lover."

The end of the day did come eventually, and as the sky darkened and reddened, she turned and left the beach, where the sand remained, quiet and contemplative and shifting forever in the darkness.

After time, the ocean spoke to her, and it spoke to her in a voice of tumbled water and delicate waves shattering like musical notes.

"Oh beauty," it cried, "I have watched you for days countless, watched your heart reach out across me and find nothing. I have a great sadness that I cannot bring you your true love across my back to be with you and fill the emptiness. Come, come and be with me and let me be your love."

She reached down with a foot and the smallest eddy of water came and swirled around it, and she smiled upon it and said "Ocean, you know what is in my heart, true, but it's not a thing I can share with you. I cannot share the warmth and the heat of love, for you're a cold thing, carrying within you only the other cold things that live beneath the waves. You cannot be a lover of mine."

The small wavelet withdrew sadly from her foot and she stepped back, watching the horizon.

As the day darkened, she turned and once again left the beach.

One day she was approached by a small crab brilliant red and green.

"My lady," said the crab. "There is no way I can hope to become your lover, but I must offer myself. Day in and day out I see you here, I see you reaching out, I see you craving, and I see you pining away for your lost love. I cannot tell you whether or not he might ever return, but I am here, and in my own humble way, I shall love you like no other could, with a deep and abiding sincerity."

She reached down and took up the crab in her hands and looked into his eyes, which waved hypnotically back and forth.

"My lovely dear," she told the crab, "You are a brilliant gem and my heart softens to hear your fair words." She petted him, then set him back upon the sand. "But you cannot know the softness of a lover's touch, for you have a hard and sharp outside, you have feet that are spikes, and claws that pinch so cruelly. It is the soft touch of my true love I crave the most, and for him I shall wait. You cannot be my love, sweet thing."

Close Your Eyes – Tales from the Blinkspace

The crab walked away from her slowly, thinking upon her words and ticking its claws against each other in a sorrowful song.

As the sky darkened again for night, she turned and left, disappearing into the trees.

Some time later, some day later, she came back and stood once again on the beach, her eyes cast outward toward the horizon.

"I am here," whispered the wind, "and I have thought carefully of your words, beloved, and I bring you a gift." With that, the wind turned soft and warm and played across her skin, no longer the gusty tempest, but the soft warmth of a lover's breath.

She gasped at this and closed her eyes to better feel.

"I have also been thinking upon your words," said the sand in its broad voice, and beneath her feet, she felt it shift and move and become smooth and flat and gentle. She felt it cover her feet ever so lightly, and felt the sun warming its crystals.

She wiggled her toes in response and the sand tickled her back, as gently as a lamb.

"Nor were your words lost on me," said the ocean, and she saw then how much lower the waves were, and how instead of crashing to the beach, the waves tended to slide up, and slide back down, as if quietly busy.

A wavelet cross her feet, careful to not dislodge the sand, and to her delight, the water was warm, and scented like the finest baths.

She knelt and placed her hand in the warmth, and pressed it against the sand.

She felt then a gentle touch upon her other hand and turned to see the crab standing next to her. "My heart has been changed and with it, I have as well," he said, and more delicate than the touch of a butterfly's wing, he touched her hand. It was the kindest, softest, most gentle touch she had ever felt, and her heart skipped a beat at it.

She closed her eyes and they all spoke to her.

"We have decided," whispered the wind.

"We hold you with our hearts," said the sand.

"We need you," murmured the ocean.

"It is you and only you," said the jewel-like crab on her shoulder. "We have known all this time that it is you we loved, with all of our beings."

"Only when we knew how to love you could we do so right," said the sand.

"Only when you told us what you wanted," said the ocean.

"What you needed," said the wind.

108

Close Your Eyes – Tales from the Blinkspace

"Only then could we love you in the way you wished, the way you wanted, the way you deserved," they all said together.

"Come to us, join us, let us love you and love us in return, for as long as we shall all be upon the face of the Earth."

She looked up, tears in her eyes, and realized that in all of her hopes and dreams, her true love was only a person, could only be so much, could only touch so much, could only speak in one voice, and could only love her in the way a man could love a woman.

She closed her eyes and felt all around her the touch of the wind, the touch of the sand, the touch of the water, and the touch of the crab. She could hear their voices – not saying anything, but saying everything in their silence.

She opened her eyes and one last time looked out into the horizon. It was a featureless unbroken line between the sky and the ocean.

She closed her eyes and smiled.

"I love you all," she said, "for you have all been my companions, have been my friends, have comforted me long before you knew who I was, long before you grew accustomed to me, and long before you grew to love me. I was right in saying you did not know what it felt like to be a lover, but I was wrong in thinking it was a thing out of your reach, a thing you couldn't learn. I was wrong and I am humbled."

She bowed her head, spread her arms, and said "I love you back, in a way I could not love another, in a way I thought no one could ever love another. I love all of you, together, and hope you'll forgive me my foolishness and love me back. I'm an ephemeral creature, and will pass from this world and I cannot do so knowing that I could have missed such love as this."

The wind then came to her and enveloped her and the sand rose around her and the ocean spread up and over her, and the crab embraced her and together, they loved her until there was nothing left to love.

END

Lady Ghost

Lady Ghost came about in a flash. Hope you enjoy reading it as much as I enjoyed writing it!

Jacob drank the entire pint in one pull. Impressive – I know how bitter that beer is.

"She's real," he said. "I'm going to find her."

"You're a nutter," I said. "I'm going to buy you another beer because God loves us more when we buy beer for nutters."

He approached the next beer – which was his sixth beer, by the way – with a little more caution. I imagine the first one was finally having some effect. Plus, I think he premedicated before coming to the tavern.

"She's real," he repeated. "I saw her."

"You saw her?" I asked. "You saw the Lady Ghost?"

He stared into his beer and was silent a moment. "Well, Old Bill saw her and I know he was telling the truth."

"Jacob, Old Bill moved back down to the Lower 48 ten years ago. Why are you bringing this up now?"

Jacob polished off the last of the pint and slammed the glass onto the table. "Because it's time. It's time, dammit, and I'm going to show you he was right all these years. I'm going out there tonight to see her, and then you'll know." He leaned forward. "I know she's real."

Abruptly, he stood up. "I'll see you when I get back," he said, and he spun on his heel and marched out the tavern door.

Shawn leaned over and took the empties away. "What was that all about?" she asked.

I shook my head. "Jacob's off his rocker," I told her. She smiled. I'm sure to her, we were all off our rockers. She came up only two years ago from Portland. No matter how crazy it might seem in Portland, by the time you passed through Kotzebue, the entire rest of the world must seem saner than sane. "He's off to play footsie with the Lady Ghost."

"Who's she?" she asked.

"Oh, that's right," I said. "You don't know about her. Well, it's not complicated – the Lady Ghost is a lady ghost. She walks out on the Bay, looking for a mortal man who can love her, so she can move on into the afterlife. Yadda, yadda, yadda. It's a local thing."

Shawn nodded. "Okay, that makes sense. Yeah, we had Bigfoot down where I grew up."

I nodded. "Everybody's got legends. If there's a swamp nearby, it's a swamp devil, or if there's a forest nearby, it's probably something to do with a goatman. When I lived in Phoenix, it was the Lost Dutchman, who apparently mislaid his treasure trove somewhere on the mountain. The world's full of weird-ass legends."

I drank more.

"So Jacob's going out to find this one, the Ghost Lady?"

"Lady Ghost," I corrected. "Yep, he's gonna wander around out there all night in the fog looking for her, and if we're lucky he'll pass out near a dead seal and swear it was her. That would make a terrific story."

She pointed. "Is that his coat?"

It was. I sighed. "Shit. I don't want the old bastard freezing to death on my watch."

Fifteen minutes later I was dragging Jacob's big coat with me, and tramping down the path toward the bay.

I didn't expect him to go far. Normally four beers was barely enough to wake him up, but I was pretty sure he had premedicated earlier that evening.

"Jacob, where the hell are you?" I muttered. I wasn't going to start calling out his name — not yet. I'd probably just scare him to death. Safest move would be to find him, give him his coat, and let him make the call.

I reached the beach in ten minutes. It was pretty cold out.

111

Close Your Eyes – Tales from the Blinkspace

The water was still like a mirror and a thin fog was everywhere. I could see trees and the beach, of course, but if I had to guess, I'd say visibility was maybe forty or fifty feet.

I stopped to catch my breath.

Damn, it was beautiful. There was a half moon up in the sky, and everything was cast in shades of silver. The water made tiny laps at the pebbled beach, and the wind was only the tiniest gust. I took a deep breath, and the air was so crisp and fresh I could almost feel the insides of my lungs burning. As much as I hated the lack of conveniences, this place kicked Phoenix's ass nine ways from Sunday.

I raised my voice a little more: "Jacob!" I called. "Where are you?"

No answer.

Damn, he had already passed out. Now I'd have to actually hunt him down in the fog. Annoying.

I tripped and my feet tangled in something soft. Something that wasn't just pebbles or a branch. It was a cloth something.

I bent down and picked it up. It was an old work shirt, worn through in spots, torn in spots, and filled with humanity. More distressing, it was the shirt Jacob was wearing when he left.

I tucked it under my arm – the absolute very last thing that I wanted to find is Old Jacob lying somewhere sleeping it off with only his long-handled underwear on. I would not be able to unsee that. Better to be able to cover him. Once I found him.

"Jacob!" I called a little louder.

Then I saw her.

At first, I thought she was just a reflection, some trick of the light my glasses played on me, but nope, there she was.

I have to admit, the Lady Ghost was, in fact, stunningly beautiful.

She was exactly what I expected to see –- a thin beautiful woman with long flowing hair. She walked softly, ethereally, across the bay, right on top of the water, in a place where I knew it was at least twenty feet deep, if not deeper.

Did I say beautiful? She practically glowed.

She wasn't wearing much, and what she wore left little to the imagination. It was a sort of a slip. She was barefoot. Where her feet touched the surface of the water, the most delicate ripples spread.

Close Your Eyes – Tales from the Blinkspace

I looked around, thinking maybe someone was fooling me, maybe Jacob was in on it, but there was no one there, no one except me and this beautiful, slender vision of a woman.

She turned and started her gliding walk toward the shore.

I stepped closer, and rubbed my eyes. I didn't expect that to actually solve anything, but I've seen people do it in movies. She was still there, and still softly and slowly walking closer to the shore.

Closer to me.

My god, she was beautiful! Her eyes were clear and perfect, her skin like some kind of cross between the smoothest alabaster and something magical.

I stepped closer, and stopped at the water's edge, watching her.

"Who are you?" I asked.

In response, she glided closer.

I was stunned. Absolutely stunned. When I returned to town with her, everybody was going to completely freak.

"Are you okay?" I asked. "You look cold." It seemed like a pretty stupid thing to say, but I was pretty much saying whatever came out of my mouth.

I reached out to her, and she reached toward me.

In a man's life, there are few times when he knows without a shadow of a doubt what love really is, and in that exact moment, as I reached toward her and she reached toward me, my heart and mind sang with this exact feeling, with the sense of absolutely pure and passionate love.

Her embrace was brilliant. It was everything a man could ever want in life, in love, and for the rest of his days.

Then I felt her arms tighten like steel bands and I was lifted from the beach, high into the air.

The water heaved upward and erupted in chaos, revealing Something Horrible. Something Horrible looked like some kind of frog or fish, but fifty, maybe sixty feet wide, with a body that trailed fatly down into the depths of the bay. Something Horrible's head had a thick tendril protruding from it, for nearly thirty feet, and ending at my beloved Lady Ghost. I looked into her face, but it wasn't quite a face anymore, and the arms tightened and tilted me upside down.

I dropped Jacob's shirt and watched it fall upward back onto the beach.

A blast of warm moisture struck me and I looked back at Something Horrible.

113

Close Your Eyes – Tales from the Blinkspace

Something Horrible's mouth opened up, and there were rows of teeth, wet and still red, probably from Jacob. Something Horrible swung me over its mouth.

Then, Something Horrible let go, and my last thoughts were of how beautiful the Lady Ghost had been.

How very, very beautiful.

END

The Club

"The Club" is a commission exploring what happens when you collect up a group of hip fun people and task them with taking over the world.

Smoking wasn't permitted at Aura, but even when smoking was permitted, it never came close to the dive it should have been for its location. In one of the sleazier parts of town, on one of the dirtier streets, Aura, true to its namesake, glowed softly with multicolored neon and indirect lighting that changed colors constantly every few minutes. It was a welcome and well-lit warmth against the January winds.

At the moment, most of the lighting in the club was blue.

Translucent veils separated many of the booths, affording a sense of near-intimacy without actually isolating anyone. The drinks cost three times what drinks cost anywhere else, and the music was better and even the sweat of the dancers smelled better.

It was usually a fun place.

Franklin finished his drink and shook the glass, eyeing it critically. "I am," he said, "unaccustomed to this much ice in my drink." He looked around at the rest of the party. "Isn't there some sort of law that says when it's freezing out, you have to serve drinks with less ice than drink?"

Edward raised his glass and grinned. "This is why it pays to be a cheap date," he said. "Free refills on soft drinks."

"You're not listening to me!" said Desiree, and banged her glass against the table in emphasis.

"We're listening," said Noel. "It's just that you're not the only show on the table. Have you seen what Ron and Rhiandra are doing over there with the cutlery?"

"Haven't you ever seen jousting?" said Rhiandra. "It's English."

"I've seen jousting," said Noel, "and that's not jousting. That's jockeying."

"If there's riding later, though, that counts as jousting, right?" asked Katrina.

Ron stopped playing with his knife and winked at her. "It most definitely counts."

"You are all perverts of the highest degree," said Franklin. "This necessitates another drink to confirm it." He tried again to flag the waitress.

"I think she is ignoring us," said Edward.

Rhiandra poked a finger at him. "You are not a cost-effective customer, Mister Cheap Date."

"I'm serious!" said Desiree. "Haven't any of you thought about it?"

Ron leaned back, pausing in his knife-play for a moment. "Sure, but it's been done to death in a million movies."

"But I mean for real," she said.

"For real-real?" asked Noel. "As in a real alien invasion."

Desiree gestured with her glass. "Yes, for real."

Edward shook his head. "It's not really... not really feasible," he said. "It wouldn't make any sense. Why would an alien race travel light years to invade Earth?"

"It's not as if we have anything here that isn't already all over the solar system and probably just as much all over the galaxy," said Franklin. "About the only thing we have here that we haven't seen a lot of out there already is intelligent life."

"That point is debatable," said Ron. "We are in a privileged frame of reference and might only think we are intelligent."

"There is that," said Franklin. He stared at his drink. "And yet my drink is still empty," he said morosely. "My framework is not so privileged."

"Yet your framework contains legs by which you can go to the bar yourself," said Noel.

Close Your Eyes – Tales from the Blinkspace

"I don't know why. I don't care. I've just been thinking about it and I think we're completely helpless out here," said Desiree. "Some aliens could come along and they could just wipe us out or enslave us or eat us. Just like that. We're completely unprepared. Doesn't that freak you out, even a little, how helpless we are?"

Katrina shrugged. "If aliens want us that bad and they've got big blasters and zappers, I don't think we'll be able to put up much of a fight. Might as well just see what happens."

"Maybe they could do better," said Rhiandra. "You have to admit we are making a bit of a mess of things."

"I admit nothing," said Ron, and poked her with his knife.

"But they could just walk right in," said Desiree. "We wouldn't put up any fight?"

"I don't think we'd have to," said Edward. "We'd just overwhelm them with numbers. Unless they came in ships filled with a hundred million soldiers, we would just throw ourselves at them until they drown in our flesh. We could literally afford to bite them to death."

"What would aliens taste like?" asked Franklin. "I don't think they would taste like chicken."

"Space chicken," said Katrina. "Something that ought to be deep-fried, and is just flakey and delicious in your mouth."

"Space chicken. Damn, that would be an awesome theme camp at Burning Man," said Ron.

"We could encourage the aliens to land at Burning Man," said Franklin. "We could get them really stoned and really laid and then take over their ships for our own nefarious purposes. Well, my nefarious purposes, anyway."

"You're not the only one with nefarious purposes, you know," said Rhiandra.

"All other nefarious purposes are null and void once I have control of a vast alien armada of battleships. Didn't I cover that in the debriefing yesterday?"

"I was busy being debriefed," she replied.

"Ah, well, that explains why I've forgotten, too. Still, my point is valid. Burning Man would be an awesome introduction to Earth for an invading alien race."

"Do you suppose we could get lucky and they leave, thinking we are dangerously crazy?" asked Noel. "There is poetry in that."

"We *are* dangerously crazy," said Katrina. "I don't think Burning Man will add much more to that."

117

Close Your Eyes – Tales from the Blinkspace

Ron nodded. "It's an interesting thought," he said. "Do you think we really would win in a ground war?"

Rhiandra stirred her drink. "Nobody wins ground wars. That's a historical fact."

"But we've got billions of people," Ron said. "I think Edward's right – we could just throw people at them in wave after wave, with nothing but teeth and claw, and we would overwhelm them."

"There's a lot to be said for wave after wave of tooth and claw," said Franklin.

Desiree looked hopeful. "So," she said. "You think that would be enough? You think we would just flood over them?"

"It's one thing to try," said Ron. "I'm not sure it would be our first choice."

"Besides, think about the logistics," said Franklin. "No matter where they land, we've got to get those billions of people to the site. That kind of transportation problem is nontrivial."

"We'll need a light rail," suggested Edward. "It should run pretty frequently. Every twenty minutes at least."

"I don't think we'd have time to build that," said Rhiandra. "It would have to be even faster."

Ron nodded. "Siege weapons."

Noel sipped her drink. "Can I pick the first billion to be hurled at the aliens? I have an idea."

"You're right," said Edward. "I love the idea of overrunning them with people, but the logistics are killer."

"We could still do a reasonably nifty ground war," perked up Franklin.

"Assuming one halfway well-trained soldier was as dangerous as ten unarmed people with only their teeth and claws, and the logistics start to look better," Rhiandra added.

"Would I still get to catapult a billion people at them anyway?" asked Noel. "At the very least we could use the ranging data."

"As long as they weren't in the firing solution of the ground troops," said Ron. "That would block our bullets, plus there's a chance if we hurl a billion people, at least a few will arrive still alive and extra bitey."

Rhiandra bit him on the shoulder.

"Like that," he said.

Noel smiled "That would be really intimidating," she said. "People hurled into your encampment, surviving the crushing forces and the brutal landing, and then attacking you."

"That would be a claw-claw-bite attack, wouldn't it?" said Edward.

"The geekness – it hurts!" cried Franklin.

"So," said Desiree. "Would that actually work, though? You think we could do it? We could fight them off?"

"Like I said, ground wars are usually won by the home team," said Rhiandra. "But in this case, I think we wouldn't have that much of an advantage."

"But we would have nukes," said Franklin.

"Oh yeah, that'll brighten up their day!" said Ron.

"It's not as if we're going to use them up any time soon," said Katrina.

"Do you really think we would nuke a ground encampment?" asked Desiree. "I mean, yeah, we do some deeply stupid stuff at times, but nuke our own soil?"

"We'd do it," said Noel. "I'll bet we wouldn't even need that much provocation. If we thought it would work, we'd find an excuse and launch a strike."

"You know," said Edward, "if we're going to use nukes, why not hit them before they land. Can't we nail them in orbit?"

"Yes!" said Desiree. "What about that?"

"Nukes can't go orbital," said Franklin. "They're like badminton birdies – they're designed to come back down."

"Shuttlecocks," said Katrina.

"No, seriously," said Franklin.

"I mean, they're called 'shuttlecocks'," said Katrina, "not birdies."

Franklin stared at her a moment and then said "I love the fact that I live in a world where we teach our children to play with things called 'shuttlecocks'. It gives me real hope."

"Still," said Ron. "We can't reach orbit."

"We can't hope to use a leftover spaceship from Area 51, can we?" said Noel. "Or a really big siege weapon?"

"If you build it," said Franklin, "then by all means let's give it a try, but I think my bets are with the Soviet heavy lifters."

Close Your Eyes – Tales from the Blinkspace

"Not a lot of those," said Edward. "They're very expensive and we have a lot more nukes than heavy lifters."

"More's the pity," said Katrina.

"What about the space shuttles?" asked Rhiandra.

"Even fewer shuttles than the Soviet rockets," said Ron. "Those aren't even meant to leave orbit."

"Great," said Desiree. "All these nukes and we can't get to them in orbit."

"No, not in any quantity that'll help us," said Franklin. "We'd have to nuke 'em on the ground. Chances are, once they're dug in, even that won't work."

"What about bugs?" asked Edward. "Germs?"

Desiree nodded. "They would have no immunity to Earth germs," she said. "That could kill them, right?"

"Probably not," said Katrina. "I mean, it sounds great in stories, but most of our germs don't act that way. Most of our germs stay with one species at a time. That's why everybody gets their panties in a twist if they find out a germ can jump from chimpanzee to human – and we share a huge amount of biology with chimps. Aliens would just be too... alien."

"Yeah," said Ron. "That would be like a blackberry bush catching herpes!"

An uncomfortable silence.

"Or, um, chicken pox."

"Right, chicken pox," said Franklin. "Please don't say 'herpes' too loudly. I want our waitress to come back."

Rhiandra said "They couldn't catch anything?"

"No," said Katrina. "No ordinary germ. If there was a germ aliens could catch, it would have to be something really spectacular, and something that spectacular would already be in the process of killing all of us and all other life on Earth."

Rhiandra perked up. "What if they were already from Earth," she said. "Like ancient astronauts or something, so that our germs could affect them without needing to be some kind of super germ."

"Ancient astronauts...?" asked Edward.

Rhiandra wagged a finger at him "What – because we just have to stop at alien invasions – it's just not possible they invaded ten thousand years ago?"

"That would be considerably before the invention of hard liquor," said Franklin.

120

Close Your Eyes – Tales from the Blinkspace

"They would vow to return some day," said Ron, "once we had invented Scotch."

Katrina nodded. "Can you blame them?" she asked.

"So, germs won't work, then?" asked Desiree.

"No, not really," said Noel. "What about that flesh-eating bacteria?"

"There's nothing like visiting a new planet only to discover they have flesh-eating bacteria," said Franklin.

"That might work," said Rhiandra.

"Mmmmmaybe," said Katrina. "I think it might do something, but it probably wouldn't."

"Now that I think about it, I think you're right," said Franklin. "I think the same rules would apply as with germs – if there was a flesh eating bacteria bad-ass enough to eat aliens, it would already be eating or have eaten everything else."

"That would be the no-win scenario," said Ron.

"Catapult not looking so primitive anymore, is it?" asked Noel.

"You just want to build the world's largest catapult," said Franklin.

Noel nodded. "Jealous?"

"Absolutely," he said.

She nodded and sat back, grinning at him. "Good. I see your fleet of stolen alien spacecraft and raise you mass times velocity in brain-staggering quantities."

Franklin's eyes narrowed. "Okay, would you accept the Eastern Seaboard in exchange for peace?"

"Would you?" she replied. "I demand no less than the North American continent."

"Surely you're joking," said Franklin.

"That leaves you Italy."

He thought about that. "Ah, they do make a good espresso there."

"Wait a second," said Ron. "That's it."

"What?" asked Rhiandra.

"Rocks."

"Rocks?" asked Rhiandra.

Close Your Eyes — Tales from the Blinkspace

"Rocks," said Ron. "There's absolutely no reason why aliens should ever have to come down here. All they have to do is lob a few big asteroids our way and that'll wipe us out pretty quick."

"Asteroids?" asked Desiree.

"It's not as if we're running low on rocks in the solar system," said Edward. "I guess if they've been traveling for so long, it's only a little extra waiting time for the ruckus to die down."

"But wait," said Rhiandra. "Doesn't it matter why they're coming? If they want a working biosphere, asteroids will screw it up."

Ron thought about it. "I guess it depends on what they're trying to do," he said. "If they want slaves, yeah, that idea would suck."

Franklin stared at his empty glass. He shook it, and the wet ice cubes settled a little. Then, he smiled. "You know," he said slowly. "I think I have an even better idea than asteroids."

He held up his glass and shook it. "Comets."

"Oh," said Katrina. "That would be nasty."

"Why?" asked Desiree.

"Mmmm, comets. Yeah, that could do it," murmured Ron.

Franklin turned to Desiree. "Comets have all the extra punchy-shock power of asteroids, but they're just made of ice and snow. They would still cause enormous damage, but they wouldn't be as horrible as asteroids."

Rhiandra leaned forward, intrigued. "It would definitely fuck up the biosphere," she said. "Everything outside the initial impact would probably be okay."

"If there were any people left after a couple good impacts, they would be so soft and squishy and easy to manage," said Noel. "I kinda' like that thought."

"You mean someone could do that?" asked Desiree. "Someone could just throw comets at us?"

"Sure," said Ron. "They'd have the technology, and it might only take another year or so for the planet to settle back down and be warm and inviting. A little patience goes a long way."

"Okay," said Edward, "as long as they don't figure out the comet thing, I guess we'll be fine." He raised an eyebrow at Desiree. "You cool with that?"

She stood up. "I don't know about you guys, but I take this kind of thing seriously." She even put her hands on her hips. Then she stormed off.

For a few seconds, the table was silent, stunned.

122

Close Your Eyes – Tales from the Blinkspace

"Edward, you have the weirdest girlfriends," Franklin said, shaking his head.

"Huh? She's not my girlfriend," Edward said. "I thought she was yours."

"No," said Franklin. "I tend to pick from the deeper end of the gene pool."

Edward raised an eyebrow. "Oh, now you've done it. I know at least three people who are going to have to hurt you in your hurty place. And I'm obligated by honor to hold you down while they do it."

"Wait," said Ron. "She wasn't with you guys? Damn!" He scooted out of the booth. "She was cute! And the crazy ones, you know what I say about them!"

He dashed off in the same direction as Desiree.

"I'm a little afraid to ask, but what does he say about the crazy ones?" asked Franklin.

"I believe the phrase he used was 'dynamite in the sack'," said Katrina.

"Dynamite?" asked Rhiandra. "I haven't heard anyone say 'dynamite' for nearly twenty years."

"Apparently it's just as relevant now as it was back then," said Edward. "I'm not sure I'd agree, though. Once they start sweating it's only a matter of time before Sudden Tissue Loss."

"Now see, you were just complaining about your honor and then you go and say that sort of thing," said Franklin.

"Everybody's got a past – you can't blame someone for their past," said Edward.

"I won't get traction for blaming them for their future," Franklin said. "Besides, it's not as if I plan to hang around them waiting for the payoff. I'm sorry, but I'm forced by the unswerving flow of time to blame your past."

"I'm getting sick of you falling back on the laws of space and time just to win the upper hand," said Edward. "If I only had a chalkboard and some chalk, I'd show–"

He stopped speaking as Ron stepped over to the table. They all stopped what they were doing.

In his arms, he cradled what almost looked like a body. It wore Desiree's clothes, and there was a thin rubbery membrane where her hands came out of the sleeves, and where her head came out of the sweater's neck. Her hair dangled from the membrane.

"I found it outside," said Ron. "It's... it's empty."

They all stared.

"It's empty now, anyway," said Rhiandra.

They looked at each other, and slowly it dawned on them.

123

Close Your Eyes – Tales from the Blinkspace

"Don't blame me," said Noel. "Anybody could have thought of rocks."

"Or comets," said Frankin.

Ron set the empty costume in a chair and sat down.

"No," he said slowly. "I think I'll blame you for the comets, Franklin. No offense."

Franklin thought about it, and replied "None taken."

The waitress finally stepped over. "Sorry I'm late guys," she said. "We are seriously getting hammered all of a sudden. Who needs another drink?"

END

The Dance

I couldn't get the phrase "The Damned Thing" out of my head. I was at the Lovecraft Bar (which makes sense, I suppose) and I noticed how loud the music was and thought to myself "Well, damn, pretty much anything *could walk in that door..."*

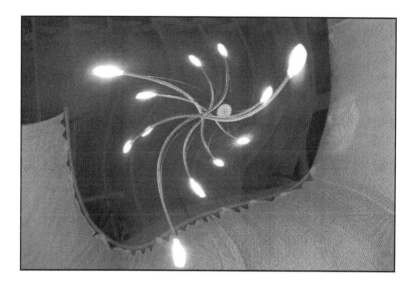

The music was loud and the Damned Thing moved through the sweating jumping crowd as if it was an ordinary person, an ordinary patron.

It looked like an ordinary person. It acted like an ordinary person. When it danced, it could even pass for an ordinary person. But it wasn't an ordinary person.

It was a Damned Thing.

The beat of the music was the heartbeat of a human being, and the Damned Thing adjusted its vision to the flickering dim lights.

In the corner, at the bar, was a man watching the crowd. He was alone, but nodding his head in time with the throb of the subsonic cycles. The Damned Thing felt into his heart and felt the yearning for companionship, the never-distant loneliness that all ordinary people hid within their hearts.

The Damned Thing shifted itself, changed and melted into a form that the man wanted.

It stepped closer to him, sat near him on one of the bar seats. It looked at him.

The man's chemistry changed subtly as he watched the creature. His pheromones shifted and he smiled.

Close Your Eyes – Tales from the Blinkspace

The Damned Thing nodded at him and stepped away from the bar. In the pounding of the music and the screaming of the patrons, attempts to talk would have been useless. It knew what he wanted and it offered that to him in a way that he could understand.

He followed.

In the alley behind the building, they coupled. It was a furtive meaningless act. Flesh into flesh. Biting and licking. There was no heart in what ordinary people did, no passion. It was all minor variations on the same mammalian theme.

In the pause afterwards, the man's mind opened briefly, and in that moment, he saw past the lenses of his own desires and saw the Damned Thing for what it truly was.

He tried to push it away, but it was, of course, too strong.

It bent him backwards, just enough to expose his chest.

Then it bent to him and fed.

Moments later, it released him. His eyes were vacant, and there was a rotten pit where his soul had been. He mumbled an excuse about working the next day and then stumbled off into the darkness of the alley.

The Damned Thing rumbled softly to itself, full of soul.

Then, it turned and went back into the bar, because no matter how full it was, no matter how much it ate, it had to keep eating.

Because it was a Damned Thing.

END

The Theory of String

Part of a writing marathon at the H. P. Lovecraft Film Festival, "The Theory of String" is inspired by Jim's request to explore the geometry of cats.

James awoke, disoriented, sweating, and confused. This was not the first time, but his dreams were more troubling than ever.

He sat up and shook his head to clear it. Snatches of imagery came to mind, bits of music, chords he had never heard before, colors he had never seen before, all these memories tugged at a deep part of his brain. This part of his brain was exactly what had saved him from these experiential anomalies. This part of his brain, to shield him, must have dragged him away from such dreams.

When he caught his breath, he stood, put on a dressing gown, and stepped to the window.

Spread below, the early morning roads of his Boston home still only offered milk deliveries and stray animals. Dawn had only now made an appearance, and James' face glowed rose.

He closed his eyes and felt the warmth seep back in. He breathed deeply and then whispered a name: "Richard."

More memories. More dreams.

Close Your Eyes – Tales from the Blinkspace

Three years earlier, his brother Richard had lived in this same apartment, had seen this same view, and had slept in this same bed. Three years earlier, Richard had vanished from the face of the Earth.

James unfolded corners of his dreams and in some of those corners, he heard his brother's name, felt his brother's touch, sensed his brother near his mind, and far from this world. A shiver crept up his arms.

For a moment longer, he collected the warmth of the rising sun, and then turned back to his books. Turned, actually, back to his brother's books, in his daily routine of reviewing, cataloging, and – ultimately – disposing of his brother's casual presence. It was a grim task, and at the same time as settling as it could be despite the unsettling nature of Richard's disappearance.

Half an hour later, James sat with a cup of coffee and a book. It was another book on mathematics, a book of Richard's. As usual, he could scarcely understand the title, much less the topic. Richard had been fond of mathematics to a point of unseemliness, even for such an educated family. He had traveled the world, collected books and manuscripts, and spoken with more professors and doctors than anyone ever knew. But James knew. James knew more and more each day as he sifted through the elements of his brother's life, as he paged through books from India, from Arabia, from countries of which he had never heard.

This book was no different than the others in another respect. This book's margins were filled with written notes, Richard's spidery hand annotating to further obscurity the obscurities that already lay within the covers.

James flipped through pages. No matter what his brother was doing, James was certain that somewhere in his papers, somewhere in his effects, there had to be some sort of clue as to what happened. He did not simply perish in the way a good Christian might, but had vanished utterly, and one of Richard's caliber and intelligence rarely just vanishes.

James was about to close the thin book, about to set it aside, as his eyes blurred slightly with fatigue, but it was this very blurring that revealed something he had never noticed before. The marginalia of his brother's contained corrections. Something about them... He focused again and it was lost, but now his mind was intrigued. He was not a scholar of Richard's peer, but clever nonetheless. He squinted, unfocused his eyes again.

And saw it.

The corrections!

He realized that the corrections themselves appeared at regular intervals in the text. He glanced at the page more critically, and then at the adjoining pages. Yes, indeed this was most peculiar. Richard's scholarship was detailed, and errors unlikely in any sort of frequency. In this instance, they were statistically impossible.

Close Your Eyes – Tales from the Blinkspace

James examined the corrections more closely. The letters corrected out had no correlation with the letters replacing them. He reviewed a few corrections, and his eyebrows rose with surprise.

In a sudden rush, he unboxed the remaining books of the set, and paged quickly through, writing down letters, phrases, sentences, all carefully embedded in code on every page. He sat back, collected the scraps together and read:

My dear brother James.

I pray to all that swings the planets about the sun and holds the Universe in check that you find my message. My situation is dire, but perhaps it can be something that you can avoid, that you must avoid, and that you must protect others from.

As you know, James, my life has been mathematics and in particular, the mathematics that lie beyond the ken of Euclid, that twist in ways no man was meant to know. These mathematics I have searched the world for, and found in dangerous abundance. I do not use this word lightly, for indeed it is a dangerous profession, and one I hope no one else explores in the way I have.

This Universe is a fragmented thing, and each fragment is a distorted mirror of the other fragments. I have also realized that each fragment, like the fragments of a mirror, are sharp, and can slice a man's sanity as easily as a razor slices his flesh.

I made a horrible mistake, James. I tried to find the Truth. I tried to find the piece of the Universe that was not a reflection, but the Ideal, of which all others were reflections. I bent my considerable mind and will toward this problem this past decade, and what I have learned boggled me.

There are ways to slip, my brother, from one fragment to another, but I have learned that there are grave costs in doing so, and so have never actually performed this act. I realize now, in retrospect, this may be difficult to believe, but my current state is not of my own doing.

This is why I am sending you a warning.

As I studied this peculiarity, I started to notice that sometimes my books would be open to different pages. I started noticing my notes slightly in disarray. I started feeling something else here in my dark room, growing and learning all the things I was learning, but with a different intent, with a different, sinister purpose. I started suspecting not only was I being watched, but that I was inadvertently tutoring something else.

It was the cats, James. Have you ever wondered about them, why they are so very different from all other creatures on this planet, so lithe and flexible, so oblivious of our geometries. Now I know, James. I know why they seem so alien. The answer was as obvious as it was terrifying. They are not of this Earth!

I realize now that in my stupidity, in my anthropocentric blindness, I ignored the fact that they stood over my shoulder, that they watched me work, and that they observed my gestures and incantations. You and I, James, are human beings, are mere men, and we cannot make the shapes needed to slip from one fragment to the next, but the cats, ah, the cats, they have all they need save the knowledge of doing so.

And I have taught them, much to my shame and horror. I have taught them, James, and now they know, and now they are spreading the word amongst themselves in the yowling of the night, the secret purrs, and ways in which their ears and whiskers flicker. They spread the word because this is the only way they can all go home.

This is the Truth I am ashamed to have discovered, this is the truth of our planet – that it is and always has been a plaything for these creatures, and only recently in our history have they forgotten the way back to their home. They brought me here, James, and it is only one letter at a time, one dream at a time, that I can reach through time and space and distract my former self in ways that are imperceptible to me and the cats, but that I am sure you will notice later.

I task you, James, to save us. I task you, my brother, to destroy my books, to burn them and make sure that no man or beast can ever learn of this hideous Truth. I know I have already opened a door that cannot be shut, but at least no man may ever again bear the burden of knowledge I bear, the understanding that he held the key to the slavery of mankind. Please, James. Make this thing happen.

I will know as you read these words that you have done so – it is the nature of the spell, as it were, and do not look for more, as I will not be able to send more. I suspect that my meager attempts are merely part of a more sophisticated game being played with me as the pawn, and that once the nature of my message becomes clear, they will not allow me to survive, they will not allow any of us to survive.

For we are their toys, James, their toys, their playthings, and their prey, and although we have lost our meaning over the centuries, they have not forgotten us, and now they have us again, back between their monstrous paws.

Destroy the books, James, I beg of you!

Your brother, Richard.

Close Your Eyes – Tales from the Blinkspace

James set the translation down, rested it carefully against the desktop. He shook his head. This must be a practical joke from his brother, as elaborate a joke as has ever been constructed.

He crumpled the paper and dropped it in a bin and turned to the books.

She sat on the books, her eyes green and flaming, the hair on her arched back raised high, and her teeth gleaming in the dark. It was the small cat he had adopted only weeks earlier.

The small cat who had sat by his bedside every night, who had listened to him rail in the darkness, who had been near him even now as he translated and read his own brother's words.

Her head turned in a way he had never seen a cat's head turn, and James felt a tilt to the world he had never known before, a twisting through dimensions impossible to describe.

And then he was gone.

END

The Gift

"The Gift" is what happens when Dwight asks for a seasonal variation on a theme…

Four dollars and eighty-seven cents.

It annoyed Nicole to no end to think that after three years of scouring the networks for employment, and two years of petitioning the Great Library, the best she could do for Dwight's Christmas gift was four dollars and eighty-seven cents. On Christmas Eve, and nothing but four dollars and eighty-seven cents.

She rested her head in her hand and thought hard. This was not the first time she regretted her career choice, her school choice. A Doctorate in Archeoliterature might be one in a million, but positions using that discipline were one in ten million. The only employer now for such a skill was the Great Library, and the employment waiting list was a mile long. She sighed and shook her head, thinking of her younger self, fresh from school, eager to explore the ancient books, and never once realizing how tricky the future would become.

Four dollars and eighty-seven cents.

It would never be enough. Never enough for his glasses.

*

Since the Beasts had come to Earth, life had changed for everyone. At first, they seemed harmless, perhaps nearly on par intelligence-wise with humans, but the scales quickly fell from everyone's eyes. The Beasts were intelligent and clever and crafty. Some were harmless, some were not. Some were as small as a dime, others as large as an ocean liner. They were omnivorous, powerful, and usually brutal with their emotional outbursts.

One thing all the Beasts had in common was an aversion to artificially produced EM waves. The visual spectrum, and a bit into the infrared and ultraviolet, they seemed fine with (which was very convenient, as much of the Universe is technically filled

Close Your Eyes – Tales from the Blinkspace

with light), but beyond that in either direction caused them a great deal of pain, which – with a Beast – usually manifested as anger. They had a directional sense of it, too, so for them it was the easiest solution, whenever they found an EM producing source, to simply crawl or slither or stomp over to it and smash it into oblivion. If they were too small to smash it, they would either damage it some other way, or manipulate humans nearby to do so.

Piece by piece, the Beasts dismantled a thousand years of technological progress, destroying every radio, every transmitter, every microwave, walkie-talkie, electrical motor – everything that emitted any sort of radio waves. "If it's on, it's gone," went the joke, which wasn't a very funny joke at all and after a few months, lost all meaning.

And so it became a world of peculiar simplicity.

Which was very lucky for Dwight.

Dwight came from a long line of men who had managed to preserve a most curious skill. Simply, he could locate and identify ships arriving before they ever cleared the horizon, sometimes more than a day away. It was an old skill, from back before the days of radio and radar and scientific navigation. It might have died with Dwight, except for the arrival of the Beasts and the subsequent destruction of all such technologies.

Suddenly, this relatively valueless skill became in demand. Whatever job Dwight had before this was long lost. Now he was one of the very, very few Farseers, and the only one with a perfect record. His situation was practically the opposite of Nicole's situation. He was extraordinarily in demand.

But – and this is where she hoped Christmas would save the day – he was getting old. She noticed over time that he would sometimes hold books out at a distance, to be able to focus, or spend a few seconds squinting at something distant. She knew what this meant. It happened to everybody by this age, but for them, for Dwight, for his position, this was horrible.

So she planned to buy him glasses. Glasses especially ground for him. Glasses that accentuated his already fantastic eyesight, and extended it even further. They were a miracle of focal precision and she had spent a year designing them. They were even ready to collect – had been since November – but she had no money with which to collect them.

She pounded the table softly with a fist, feeling her frustration rise once again. Then, the answer came to her, as clear as crystal. She stood up abruptly, and closed her eyes.

"Be sure," she whispered to herself.

She waited a few minutes to be sure, and then collected her coat and her hat and went to see the Monster.

*

Close Your Eyes – Tales from the Blinkspace

The Monster was a Beast who had established a shop on the outskirts of town. It was one of the kinds of shops you never entered unless you were desperate, because the price was always high, was always more than you expected.

Three of the Monster's eyes opened as she entered the warm store from the cold night. The other five eyes stayed closed.

"Welcome," it told her, in a voice that seemed to be made of three different rumbling frequencies. "It is my hope that you have brought your final payment for the glasses you ordered. I am becoming... concerned."

She stepped forward, in front of the Monster.

"I... I don't have the money," she said.

The other five eyes opened, and the Monster slowly arched his back, straightening up from his nap. He yawned and needle-like teeth ringed his mouth.

He looked carefully at her.

"I was hoping that maybe there was some sort of trade I could offer," she said. "I might be able to help you out somehow. Maybe around the shop, maybe work it off." Words tumbled out of her mouth after that, precise, but fast and desperate.

The Monster stopped her with a raised arm. He beckoned her closer and she stepped up.

He slid open a drawer and placed the glasses on the counter between them. They glimmered of delicate glass and gold. One of his claws touched the rims, slid along a temple, and tapped the edge of a lens.

"I've been studying this," he said. "It's really quite brilliant work. Who designed them?"

"I did."

Something on the Monster's forehead that might have been a textured eyebrow raised slightly.

"You know optics?" he asked.

"I am actually familiar with physics, mathematics, optics, and... electronics," she said. The Monster winced at the last, which was why she had paused. "But my specialty is archeoliterature. The study of ancient–"

"–Books, yes, I understand," said the Monster. He turned his head slightly, as if seeing her in a different way. His eyes changed color briefly, from emerald to scarlet, and then back to emerald.

"Nicole," he purred, "You do have skills I can use, but I cannot have you here in the store. It would be... bad for business, so to speak."

134

Close Your Eyes – Tales from the Blinkspace

Slowly, she nodded.

"I like your mind," he continued. "You are far more intelligent than you let on, and you have a certain creativity that I need." He steepled his fingers – a trick he no doubt learned from watching humans. "I have a proposition for you."

He leaned more closely to her – only inches away.

"I will give you your glasses, and even some other gift you might choose from my stock sometime over the next year. In exchange, I want... your mind."

"My... my mind?"

Slowly, he nodded, watching her. "It's more, oh, your memories. When was your first fascination with science?"

"When I was eight," she whispered.

"Then I will take everything from when you were eight until now," he said. "You can, if you want, still learn it all back again, and I'll leave you with the more convenient memories, such as the way back home." He chuckled at this, as if it were a gentle joke between close friends, but his chuckle was thick and liquidy and sent shivers down her spine.

"But I won't know..."

"You won't remember," he said. "You'll leave here with the mind of an eight-year old. No learning since then will remain – at least no school or practical work. If you are so inclined, if you believe in..." he struggled with the metaphor. "...nature over nurture, then all you've lost is a few years of schooling."

She eyed him carefully. "Can you take away regret, too?" she asked.

He smiled and reached toward her.

*

Dwight came home that evening. As was customary, he wore protective goggles for traveling. The night air swirled around him and cooled the room, but he closed the door and approached the kitchen.

The meal she was cooking smelled delicious and he felt his mouth watering. It wasn't complicated, some kind of soup or stew, but after his day, it seemed perfect.

He sat at the table and grinned at her. "Come and sit with me," he said. "I have a gift for you."

She smiled a brilliant child's smile and came to the table.

"All today, I struggled," he said, "Because I so much wanted to simply be here in your arms, to spend Christmas Eve with you instead of working."

135

Close Your Eyes – Tales from the Blinkspace

"You love your work," she said, and touched his arm.

"I love my hobby," he said, "but that it has become work is one of my life's greatest curses. Maybe it would have helped if there was matching pay, but we're still struggling. It's not right, not fair, and now it is time to change it."

He reached into his coat and withdrew a large envelope.

"Merry Christmas, my love," he whispered.

"Oh!" she squeaked. "I have a present for you as well, dear husband!" She reached into her apron pocket and withdrew a small box, gaily wrapped, and handed it to him. He took it in his hands, and held the box, exploring it with his fingers, softly, deftly.

"You're supposed to open it, silly," she said.

He did.

The glasses practically glowed in the light of the fire as he held them up.

"I made them," she said. "I made them and it took a long time. You should try them on. Take off your goggles and try them on."

He placed the glasses carefully on the table.

"First, open your gift," he urged. "Open it."

She slipped the envelope open and pulled out a single piece of paper, a letter. It was addressed to her.

She started reading it, and had to read it out loud. On some of the bigger words, she stumbled, but got most of them correct.

Dwight listened carefully until she was done.

"What does it mean?" she asked.

"It's a job," he said. "I know, love, how much you wanted to work in the Great Library, to put your brilliance to work, so I connived my way through all the levels of insanity and finally worked out a deal with them. It was a hard deal to make, but I need you to be happy and it's the job you've always wanted."

She clapped her hands and giggled.

"What?" he asked. "What's wrong?"

She took his hands in her hands and told him what she had done. She told him the price she had paid for his glasses. She told him there would be no job for her, other than being his wife. No job for a long time. But that it was okay because they had his job, and it might not be much, but they would be happy.

He looked down at the glasses on the table.

136

Close Your Eyes – Tales from the Blinkspace

"Then that is what we shall be," he said. "We shall sit here at our little table on Christmas Eve and find our happiness with each other."

He took off his goggles and revealed the smooth skin where his eyes had been, and she knew then what deal he had made for this piece of paper, and she loved him even more than ever.

END

The Carnival

I don't think I've ever written anything that could qualify as a Western until now, although I might have done so during that time I spent in the opium dens of the far East. Oh wait, that wasn't me – that was some guy on TV. "The Carnival" has a lot of my favorite things in it, although my own experience with Appaloosas wasn't quite as positive.

I saw the carnival come to Turlow, Oregon in the summer of 1880. I was not in Turlow at the time, as I had been chased out indirectly by a man who swore I had been indecently attentive to his daughter. I was appalled by his charges, of course. This is not to say they weren't correct, but I was appalled that I had been discovered, as Sarah and I had been extremely discreet in all our meetings.

Singer Mountain's not large as mountains go, but it afforded an inspiring perspective on the town of Turlow, which I felt would help me determine a course of action that made the most sense for my immediate future. Despite not being at the actual top, I had all but decided I would collect my dear Sarah in the middle of tomorrow night and simply run away with her.

It was then I saw the carnival.

I did not think it was a carnival at the time, of course. It merely appeared to be a typical train of wagons – sixteen by my count – arriving after the long trek from Burgess, which was the nearest town to the east. The wagons were a little more decorated than normal, which did suggest something was extraordinary about this train, but there was no outward sign of their purpose other than that.

Close Your Eyes – Tales from the Blinkspace

I turned my horse back to the path and continued to the top. His name was Poker and he was a sturdy Palouse horse. Many people gave me the hairy eyeball for riding him, but he was more sure-footed then any ten ordinary ponies.

One of the things I've always enjoyed about the top of Singer Mountain was the fact that between two groves of trees, there was a small handmade shelter, years old. This was where I sometimes came for solitude and – when under duress of one sort or another – perspective. I discovered it when I came to this town two years earlier, and it's since remained my secret place.

It was as empty as the last time I'd been there. Some of the elements and some animals had caused mischief, but a moment's worth of sweeping cleared it enough for my rest. I spread out blankets and built a small fire behind the main wall, where it wouldn't be visible to the town below. I watched the sun set across Turlow, my mind working through my plans, then turned in for the night.

The next morning, I saw that a space had been cleared to the south of the town, and tents were appearing. Then, I knew something was happening. Something interesting.

Interesting things attract me.

I found Poker, repacked my gear, and started down the mountain.

I'd heard of carnivals back East, and that some were quite impressive, but this one was much smaller. A carnival is still a rare and wonderful thing this far out.

Three tents seemed to be basic living quarters. The larger tent existed mostly as a visual block from the town, and also appeared to contain exhibits and peculiarities. I let Poker crop at the summer grass near the main tent and walked into the ring.

It was disorienting, to say the least. More than two dozen people scurried about, erecting the bits and pieces that make a carnival, cleaning off dust, repainting signs, practicing acts, and so forth. A trio of identical jugglers tossed silver throwing knives into the air above them, and I shook my head with disbelief when I couldn't even track a single knife through a cycle. Another trio, two women and a man, practiced a tumbling act that seemed very vigorous, and I must have watched them a little longer than is polite at a carnival, based on their eventual reaction.

I moved on toward the larger tent, and watched a man with a thin moustache touching up a sign from a small can of paint. The sign read "Amazing Freaks!"

Without looking up from his work, he spoke to me: "We won't be open until this evening, lad, perhaps you'd best be coming back then."

"Just passing through," I said. "I'm leaving town this evening and I've never seen a carnival before."

He stopped his work and squinted up at me.

139

Close Your Eyes – Tales from the Blinkspace

"Leaving town?" he asked. "That's not going to work, my boy. That's not going to work at all. You must see the show!"

He carefully placed his brush and can on the ground and stood up. His back cracked like gunfire and he winced at each one, but once he was standing, he was a good head taller than me. This is no small feat, as I'm tall. He then grinned like a madman and reached out a hand. "Mister Spangle," he said, and pumped my hand. "This is my carnival. Spangle's Traveling Show and Cabinet of Curiosities."

He swept an arm wide, and I ducked to avoid it.

"This is my carnival and these are my people," he said. "My strongman is the strongest in the West, my dancers are the most beautiful, my jugglers are gifts from the gods themselves. And my beasts, my freaks, the unsung stars of my show, they my fine and dusty friend, will take your breath away."

He indicated the largest tent with his arm.

"I am intrigued by interesting things," I said, and I meant it. "May I see?"

He raised a hand, dramatically barring my passage.

"It would be unthinkable," he said, "to reveal all of our secrets in the light of day when they are much better experienced during the evening's most mysterious and dark hours."

With a flick of his wrist, he produced two tickets.

"For you, kind sir," he said. "Two passes to this evening's show – ten acts for the price of one, normally, but because you've been brave enough to come visit us right away, a free ticket for you and one for your young lady."

"How did you know–?" I started to ask.

He nudged me and winked. "When such a handsome man leaves a town for parts unknown, there are only two reasons, and you don't appear to be the murderous type," he said. "So there must be a young lady involved."

I admit my face must have betrayed me.

"Ah," he said, and his look softened. "It's more than just a young lady. It's love, isn't it?" He nodded slowly. "I know of love, lad. We all know of love. You might not know it by the looks of us, as strange as we are, but this very troupe is driven by that love the philosophers call passion, and not the least among us has not had their hearts broken many a time."

He rested a hand on my shoulder and I felt a simultaneous urge to reveal to him my plans for eloping with Sarah this very evening, and at the same time, I felt a certain tingle in that touch, a warmth I had not expected.

140

Close Your Eyes – Tales from the Blinkspace

He pressed the tickets into my hand. "Bring her," he said. "Do bring her tonight so that I may once again fill my eyes with the sight of young love, even out this far into savage lands. Bring her!"

He was the most persuasive and charismatic man I'd ever known, and had I not been planning to away with dear Sarah that very evening I no doubt would have been delighted to see him at the very top of his game, working the crowd of Turlow in the way only a master could.

I thanked him kindly, wandered around a bit more, then left to go find Poker, who had not wandered very far and happily had not wandered in the direction of the town, where he was known very well to be often accompanied by me. As I did not believe I was very welcome in town as of recently, this was a gift.

I rode Poker back to Singer Mountain, and back up to my shelter.

Once we arrived, I took it upon myself to have a bit of a lie-down and rest. Later in the afternoon, we'd descend, but for now, being here and being safe felt significantly better to me than trying to find a place to rest down on the plain, out in the open, exposed to the potential wrath of an angry father and whatever friends he happened to bring with him.

I tried dozing, but my mind kept wandering to the carnival below. I tried to imagine what it would be like. I'd only heard of them. I'd heard they were colorful and fantastical, and that there was music and great and amazing skills.

I felt in the pocket of my shirt the fluttering of the tickets and heard a clear siren call. I patted them. My plan was to collect Sarah – ah, the most beautiful Sarah – and perhaps offer the tickets to some other couple or one of the many evening denizens of Turlow. While a carnival would be a fancy thing indeed, I suspect our safety would be even more important.

I eventually dozed off. I know this because I dreamt I was juggling. In this dream, the knives flew in the air in front of me, like silver fish in a pond, overlapping and spinning and weaving in and amongst each other. I laughed at the ease of this act, and for a moment, the flashing of the knives in the sunlight seemed to be a kind of laughter with me.

The dream dissolved away as all dreams do, and I woke to a late afternoon sun filling my camp with deep golden light. This was the perfect time to leave.

I packed my kit carefully, and this time I made sure that there was extra room for both Sarah and anything she might want to bring.

Poker and I reached the base of the mountain with still a half hour before proper dusk, so I wandered a bit off my plan and toward the carnival.

The tents were all up, the signs were all painted, and everything was fresh and brilliant in the reddening sun. Men and women were placing torches on poles and stringing ropes with lantern-lit globes of greased paper. The carnival already felt like a surreal

Close Your Eyes – Tales from the Blinkspace

place with the light and the colors. I heard music starting up, then stopping, then starting again – the practice that makes perfect, I expect.

"Salutations!" called out a voice, and at the entrance to the grounds, Mr. Spangle waved me over. I guided Poker over.

"I'm so very glad you've come to join us," said Mr. Spangle. "But I'm afraid you're still early, my boy. Just a little bit, though. Perhaps you might have an errand to run in town, and then you could join us?"

"I am, as I mentioned, leaving town," I said. "I'm not sure my path would bring me by this direction."

He nodded and smiled a broad smile. "I completely understand," he said. "It may interest you to know, however, that in my experience, the first night is always the one where people wait the longest to come out. If, on your return from your errand, you feel so inclined, you might find it the perfect time to enjoy a surprisingly uninterrupted experience." He winked. "At least until others get wind of the show."

I nodded and smiled back. "Perhaps," I said. "I'm not entirely in a position to commit myself."

He nodded, this time more slowly. "Ah, of course. Well, perhaps your young lady will be more persuasive."

He laughed and it was an infectious laugh, which caught me up as well.

Poker and I continued on our way from there.

I made sure to enter the town of Turlow from an uncommon direction, that is to say opposite the carnival. It was a bit of a ride around, but I expected all eyes would be toward the lights and the tents. Fewer would notice a lone man coming into town during dusk with their eyes on the bright and cheery promise of rare entertainments.

Fortunately, I was right and the streets, while not abandoned, were nevertheless much less populated than normal.

I found Sarah in a most fortuitous situation, sitting near the window in a way that allowed me to capture her attention without capturing the attention of anyone else. In only a few minutes, she was in my arms, warm and happy and smelling exactly like the woman I loved.

I could hardly believe my ears when she insisted we leave that very night. It was in every possible way that mattered, the most delightful kismet.

In short order we collected the things that were necessary for her. By this time, the sun had set sufficiently that we had some assurance that darkness would help cover our departure.

As she mounted Poker, Sarah discovered the paper tickets in my shirt pocket. When I showed them to her, she was thrilled. I explained that, as much as I would love to visit

142

Close Your Eyes – Tales from the Blinkspace

the carnival, I thought to do so while I was being hunted by her father and while we could be readily identified by more than half the townsfolk seemed the very pinnacle of unwise.

She set herself and furrowed her brow in the way I have come to identify with a state of decision that will not be overridden. What can I say – I love that woman!

We turned Poker the other way and rode to Spangle's Traveling Show and Cabinet of Curiosities.

When we arrived the torches were all lit, the lights were blazing, music was filling the night air, and people had already started filtering in from town.

The strongman was, from what I could tell, actually strong. He casually lifted weights and then encouraged audience members to try. I was unable to budge the weight he spun in his arms. I was certain there was some sort of trick involved, but I could not figure it out.

There was a man doing sleight-of-hand on a short stage. He wore a black shiny tuxedo and sported a thin moustache that seemed to dip and wave of its own accord. Sarah and I watched, entranced, as coins, flowers, and even personal trinkets disappeared and reappeared in ways most baffling to all who watched.

There was a woman, an occultist. She wore colorful rags, crouched over two canes, and had piercing blue eyes. When she spoke, she revealed secrets, she told us of our past, whispered hints of our present, and then spoke of our futures. Sometimes our futures were gay and charming, and other times, she shook her head and simply said "There is no good coming. I am sorry." Once, as her eyes passed over me, I felt an odd sensation, a sort of too-close-to-a-campfire warmth, and then it was gone and she was telling another young fellow that he would be married within the year to a gorgeous redhead. As there was only one red-headed family in the town, with only one eligible daughter, and as she was – in fact – gorgeous, this fellow was beside himself with glee and his whooping broke that particular spell.

The jugglers, though. Ah, the jugglers were supernaturally gifted. Between them was a dizzying dash of silver fishlike knives, twirling and spinning. It reminded me of the sun reflecting from ripples in a stream. My eyes could follow no single knife. We were both entranced, as were several people near us. One of the fellows caught my eye and winked. He said something to his three other companions, and they changed the performance. The knives sped up until they whirred by practically unseen. The flashing was a thousand showering chips of diamond in a whirlpool of astonishing beauty in the air. Where before it seemed fluid, now it was a living magical thing. I couldn't even track their hands; it was so fast. I held my breath in complete shock. I could have watched for hours, except that one of the other jugglers noticed me and hissed through his concentration: "This is what you wanted to see, eh?" I nodded and he nodded back, and said "Better than a dream any day."

It took almost a second for the remark to sink in and when it did, I jumped back, startled, and bumped into someone behind me.

143

Close Your Eyes – Tales from the Blinkspace

I spun, but it was only the man with the thin moustache I had met earlier, Mr. Spangle.

"My dear boy," he crowed as he recognized me. "I cannot tell you how delighted I am that you accepted my invitation! And is this, this vision next to you, the young lady you spoke of?"

Sarah managed a polite curtsey and I introduced her.

He leaned toward her and in a hoarse whisper, confided " I could tell the minute I laid eyes on him that he was smitten – smitten I say!"

Then he leaned back toward me. "She's everything I imagined and even more, my boy. While I am far from an ideal model in such matters, might I suggest you do whatever you can to keep this young woman at your side for the rest of your life – which would be far too short under such unimaginably beautiful circumstances."

Sarah blushed at this and we started to back away, but Mr. Spangle collected us together with his arms. "Have you seen the tent show?" he asked. "Our freaks and geeks and wonders and oddities represent the finest collection this side of the Mississippi. Or that side of the Mississippi. Dare I say that our collection rivals the world's collection? I might even venture to say, my boy, that you have never, nor will you ever again experience the mind-shattering awe of our tent of mysteries!"

I protested, but the fact of the matter was that I was eager to see in the tent and had been since seeing it earlier that day.

Within seconds, Mr. Spangle hustled us past the growing line of curious gawkers and directly into the tent.

I had not known what to expect inside, and that was exactly what I experienced.

Once the tent flap fell, the noises from the outside evening died down to the slightest mutter of sound. The tent was large, spacious, and with the high peak, seemed cavernous. It was dark, but many lamps strewn about lit it, and cast flickering shadows everywhere. The air smelled dusty. Not prairie dust, but something else, something that reached in through our mouths and noses and left a taste there that seemed centuries old.

The sides of the tent were lined by booths and cages, and in the center, there was another aisle of back-to-back displays.

Slowly, Mr. Spangle led us down the first row, introducing his first exhibit in a respectful whisper.

"This," he said, "is Joseph. Joseph is a deeply spiritual boy I met while traveling in South America. Joseph had been cast out by his family and, had I not intervened, they would have killed him. Of that, I have no doubt. They had a name for him, that meant 'touched by devils', but I won't say it here. Not now. Not ever. Joseph has become a member of our family. We love our family."

144

Close Your Eyes – Tales from the Blinkspace

Joseph looked at us with one eye.

It would not be a wholesome thing to describe him in great detail, but it would be accurate to say that one could feel the simple and powerful love he had for Mr. Spangle, and at the same time think that whatever nickname his family had given him never even came close to the truth of the horror that his body revealed.

I felt Sarah's hand squeeze my arm and we stepped a little further inward.

I tipped my hat at Joseph, and I swear that he bowed a little in response, although given what I saw of his body, I would have doubted that was possible. Something that might have been a hand waved a little.

We came then upon a great jar, as large as a barrel, and filled with a yellow fluid. Suspended within that fluid was something that no man must ever see twice in his life, or once if he counts himself lucky. Mr. Spangle rested a hand on our shoulders. "God rest her soul," he said, and took off his hat. I also removed mine. "We were too late to save her, but we tried. We tried so hard." He shook his head sadly. "Sometimes I can't decide if the world is filled with ignorant people, cruel people, or some unholy combination of both."

We moved on to another exhibit and another story.

Each exhibit had its own story. Some were happy endings, with creatures that were physically pitiable, but seemed stronger of spirit and happy here. Other stories were tragedies and nightmares and horrors.

It was not what I'd expected. It was better. It was the human spirit enfleshed in all its shapes and sizes. It was peace of soul. It was a quiet dignity nested within a chaos of broken, bent and warped bodies.

At last, we came to the final display.

Before we stepped over, Mr. Spangle addressed us both. "Are you sure?" he asked. "Are you sure you want to see what's next? Are you absolutely sure? I ask because what comes next is, simply said, going to be the most moving experience of your life."

I thought briefly about what I'd seen so far, and shuddered a little, but nodded.

He looked at Sarah and asked "Are you sure, my dear, that this is what you want?"

I felt her straighten up and nod. "Absolutely I am," she said. "This is the man I love."

For a moment, it made perfect sense, and then I was a little confused.

"What?" I asked, and turned to her. Her face was beaming, radiant.

"I love you, Howard, and there is nothing more I want than for us to be together."

"I, uh, I love you too, Sarah, but I'm not sure…"

145

Close Your Eyes – Tales from the Blinkspace

"It's quite all right," said Mr. Spangle, as he patted me on the arm. "It's always a little shocking to find out. I can sympathize." He nodded to someone behind me and I felt arms seize me, pinning me. They were very, very strong arms.

"What are you doing?!" I cried out.

Sarah stroked my cheek. "It's going to be all right, my love," she said.

I struggled against my captor, but was hopelessly stuck. People came into the tent now, townspeople.

"Help me!" I called out to them. "Please help me. I'm being held against my will!"

To their credit, they came forward immediately and without delay. Much to my horror, however, the head of the group was the gruff and stocky man who had driven me out of town for wooing his daughter.

He glared at me, then at his daughter.

"I admit I was wrong," he finally said. "I think this will work."

He turned to me. "I'm sorry I drove you out," he said. "I was a fool. Anyone can see that Sarah's heart was bound to you. I'm always leery of strangers. I let that cloud my judgment." He gripped my shoulder. "Welcome to the family."

The rest of the townspeople smiled and nodded, and I felt Sarah's hand stroking my arm.

The crowd parted and the jugglers came through, their knives shining silver in their hands.

Sarah's father raised an arm. "Now, this isn't going to be one of those long ones, is it?" he asked. Mr. Spangle looked at the jugglers, and then back at the man.

"Ah, dear brother, it's been too long since we've been home. Five years?"

"About that," he answered.

"We missed you all," said Sarah.

"In that time, we've learned so much more than we ever knew," said Mr. Spangle. He nodded and the jugglers stepped forward.

"Sarah, what's going on?" I cried.

"Howard, Howard, please don't worry," she said. She took my face in her hands. "Do you love me?" she asked.

"Of course I do!"

"And do you trust me?"

"I... I guess I do."

146

Close Your Eyes – Tales from the Blinkspace

"And do you want to be with me for the rest of your life, always close, always touching, always a part of each other?" She stroked a finger down the side of my face, and I felt my fear splinter and give way to something else. Something lighter.

I softened. "I do, Sarah. I do more than anything!"

"Then that's what we'll be," she said. "Together."

She shucked off her dress and stood before me. She reached over and unbuttoned my shirt and pulled it down.

She pressed herself to me, and I felt her heart beating with mine, I felt her melting against me, and I knew that this was something I wanted.

The jugglers stepped forward, each unsheathing a knife.

"I do apologize about the pain of transcendence," said Mr. Spangle, and I knew he truly meant it.

I also knew, however, that Sarah and I would finally be together, here in the tent with the others, traveling the world as one, and the warmth of that knowledge washed away even my own screams.

END

The Measure of a Man

Part of a writing marathon at the H. P. Lovecraft Film Festival, "The Measure of a Man" is inspired by Sven's request to find a moment from "At the Mountains of Madness."

Mr. Bonnichsen came from sturdy Norwegian stock, and was thus more immune to the casual hysteria of his peers. It was no surprise, therefore, when Professor Pabodie called him into the kitchen tent.

The professor was clearly agitated. His eyes darted about, as if he feared revealing something that he truly didn't want to reveal.

"Sven," he whispered. "I have known you for your entire life, and I have known your father for more than a dozen years prior."

Sven nodded and listened. Although the professor and he had been acquainted for this amount of time, he also knew that there was a certain rule and a certain precedence about these sorts of things.

The professor laid a hand on Sven's shoulder. There was a weight to that hand that Sven had never felt before.

"I could not have ever imagined asking such a thing of someone who has been so close to me and with whom I have been so close, but it is a critical favor I must ask of you."

"Of course, professor," said Sven. "You can trust me with anything."

The professor nodded. "Had I doubted that for a moment, I would never have taken you aside." He looked around again, although they were both alone in the tent. "There are some things, dear boy, that a learned man cannot speak aloud to anyone lest they doubt his sanity, but nevertheless, these things have been prying their way into my mind. I must speak of them, and I must demand your absolute silence in this matter."

There was a sound outside, a movement, not of a furtive nature, but of one of the many small movements a camp may produce in its normal life. The professor fell silent a moment, considering.

"Sven, you are a certified pilot."

Sven knew it wasn't a question, but nodded anyway.

"I need you to do a favor for me, a favor that makes no sense at all, a favor that I can ask of no one else in this group, for no one else would approve or appreciate the frame of mind that has driven me to ask this favor."

With a last glance outside, through the thin tent flap, the professor cleared his throat. "You know of the samples we took from the cave, yes?"

"The trees," Sven nodded.

The professor's eyes grew hard at this. "Sven, I think they are not trees at all. I think they are something far more dangerous, far more hideous than we ever had reason to believe. I think they are alive."

"Sir, this seems…"

"You are about to say 'absurd,' aren't you?" The professor nodded slowly.

"I was about to say 'unlikely,'" said Sven. "But this is only because they are taxonomically different than any tree we have ever encountered."

The professor raised his eyebrows slightly.

"Naturally," added Sven, "I cannot claim half the expertise of any member of the rest of your upper division staff, but when I examined the things, looked closely at what seemed to be tendrils, roots, and other segments, I realized that perhaps what we are looking at is a plant in component, but a being in whole. I know it is probably pure fancy, but I have speculated on those vines long into the night, imagined them moving by the fluid within their tubules, imagined those shallow roots pulling the trunk along. I have imagined, Professor, exactly this thing, that what we are looking at is, in fact, a fossil or a remnant of a thing that might have been alive in a motive sort of way."

With new eyes, the professor gazed levelly at his student. "I would not be making a mistake, I think," he said slowly, "if I had more fellows on my staff who were willing to entertain the fanciful."

"It has its downsides," said Sven.

The professor waved him off. "Nevertheless, I think in this case, it is justified. In fact, I think perhaps you have not been fanciful enough."

Close Your Eyes – Tales from the Blinkspace

This time, it was Sven's eyebrows that rose in question.

"I have been examining the dissected specimen very carefully," said the professor. "I have been observing how the fluids move through the tubes, the way in which tissues still seem flexible and pliable, and I have wondered exactly to what degree such a creature might also possess the same sort of longevity as some of the plants of which we are already familiar, such as the redwoods, the spruces, and certain odd underground funguses only known to a few researchers."

Sven's eyes narrowed. "I am not entirely sure where you are going with this," he said.

The professor leaned close. "I am thinking, Sven, that wouldn't it be a most horrific thing to discover that these are not specimens of some sort of vegetable, nor even of some sort of vegetable-like animal that had long died, but in fact, are nothing less than a sturdy survivor of adverse conditions."

The professor gripped his shoulders. "In other words, what if they are, in fact, still alive," he hissed.

The men watched each other carefully – the professor watching to see if Sven would deny the possibility, and Sven watching to see if the professor was playing with him. Neither budged.

Calmly, Sven lit a cigarette. His breath and the smoke commingled in the icy air.

"Tell me what you want me to do, professor," he said.

"Go to a plane, Sven, and bring with you sufficient provisions to make it as far as Camp One. Make sure the plane is fueled and the plugs are kept warm. If anything happens – anything at all – I need you to take these suspicions back, to return an eyewitness account of what has transpired here."

"Professor, if I leave immediately, then I won't know what's happened."

"My boy," said the professor, "if you don't leave immediately, if what I suspect is correct, then you will never get the chance. It must be without thought, without consideration of—"

Outside, a dog barked. Then another. Then the pack began to howl and bark.

Both men looked up.

"Your dogs...?" asked the professor.

"They are the calmest animals I have ever known," said Sven. "Nothing would make them act like this."

Men shouted and there were running footsteps.

Then there was a cry, a scream, and it was long seconds before Sven realized that this horrific sound was the death cry of one of his dogs. He stood.

150

Close Your Eyes – Tales from the Blinkspace

"No!" cried the professor. "You must not!"

"But they are my dogs!"

"No, Sven. I cannot believe it has happened, but it has, and I regret deeply that I have not already spoken to you of my worries, for you might have been ready." His eyes were wild and he grabbed the young man.

"You must go. You must go now!"

Sven hesitated and the professor pushed hard.

Just then, another dog screamed. Gunshots rang out.

"Go, go!" cried the professor. "We are already lost if only a tenth of what I suspect is true. You must fly!"

They both burst from the tent into what Sven's mind could only describe as utter chaos. Blood flecked the snow at their feet, dogs wailed, and gunshots peppered the air. The professor shoved him westward. "Go, to the planes, Sven. Go!"

To the planes. Away from the fray.

Sven ran and the professor ran the opposite direction, perhaps to help, or perhaps to witness.

Sven swung aboard the nearest plane and, ignoring any preflight check, fired up the engines, which started immediately. His breath ran ragged in his throat, and he heard the distant screams, the sounds of confusion, even over the stuttering of the engine. He turned the plane into the wind, and he glanced briefly, from this vantage point, the scene at the camp.

His breath stopped, his thinking stopped. He was only a machine, made of meat, and operating an airplane. He throttled up purely by reflex, and the plane taxied, and then accelerated down the smooth snowy strip. Only his reflexes operated the flaps, and lifted the plane from the ground. Only his reflexes started the spiral upwards as he climbed. His conscious mind, however, made sure that he did not circle back over the camp. His conscious mind made sure that the memory of what he had seen before takeoff was fed only in slow digestible pieces to his memory.

Gasping, he tried to breathe, tried to restore normality to a body that had been shocked into reflex, and in doing so, his memory, his wicked, unrelenting memory still raw and beaten with imagery that no man should ever have to deal with, began to feed back what he had seen.

There were men, he remembered. Men he had known, men he had traveled with. They were firing guns, rifles, pistols, whatever they had.

There were dogs. His dogs. He remembered each and every one of them, their habits, their favorite snacks, the order in which they woke up and fell asleep at night. His dogs.

Close Your Eyes – Tales from the Blinkspace

The men and the dogs were almost normal – at least the ones that had managed to survive. The ones that had not survived, he also remembered, with a deep revulsion because of the state they had been in.

It could be said that in a fraction of a second a mind cannot grasp what has happened to a human being, and in many cases this would be true, but there are some things that cannot be mistaken for anything other than the horror that they are. When a man or a dog has been torn into two pieces and flung aside as casually as a broken stick, the mind cannot mistake that for anything else.

But it wasn't the broken bodies that locked his mind in an endless spiral of madness. It was the other things. The things of which the professor spoke, the things that were vegetable samples brought up from deep within a dark and icy cave. It was the vision of them that held his mind in a terrifying grip.

They were moving.

And not only moving, but whipping about, frenzied swirling, tendrils like razor wire, grasping man and dog alike, swinging them aloft, dashing them against the snow, and in some cases…

…in some cases…

It was during that fraction of a second that Sven had seen the professor. The professor's pistol was out and Sven could tell he was firing through the entire clip. Even in that fraction of a second, the memory of multiple puffs of gunpowder was clear. Sven knew that the professor was a crack shot and never missed. But even Sven's recall paused before it brought this memory back from the dark places where things hide that drive us mad otherwise. In that pause, Sven knew that the professor was not firing from a steady stance upon the ground, but from up high in the air, held aloft by two sets of tendrils, from two different specimens. Sven's mind refused to feed the last piece of information to him, but he could construct it well enough. He knew there was a horrific game played, and that the professor, despite pumping bullet after bullet into his adversaries, had lost. He knew without being able to recall, that the professor was as dead as the other men and the dogs in the camp, torn asunder by the beasts beneath him.

Sven flew by reflex.

Behind him, there was a shifting, a sliding.

The blood stopped cold in his veins.

"No, no," he whispered. "It must be loose cargo, something that in my haste I forgot to secure."

The sliding shifted as he banked, and for a moment, he was able to convince himself that this was exactly what happened, that he had simply forgotten to secure a piece of cargo.

Close Your Eyes – Tales from the Blinkspace

Until he felt the cool tendril wrap around his throat, wrap around his chest, and drag him backwards.

He hung in the air at an inhuman diagonal. His mind desperately tried to not accept what his eyes were revealing to him. His mind desperately tried to make him pay attention to the throbbing of his thigh, where it had torn open on the metal seat. His mind tried desperately to make him pay attention to the whining of the engine, as the plane, now without a controlling influence in the cockpit, began to spiral and slide. His mind tried to make him pay attention to anything else.

But it could not. His eyes were locked, and so was his mind, on the creature that towered there in the cramped cargo area, the creature which had stealthily dragged itself forward, which had reached out and plucked him from the cockpit as easily as a man might pick up a small worrisome dog.

He felt the tendrils around his chest, around his neck, tightening, but not even this distracted him from what he saw.

He saw its eyes.

Cool azure crystals, previously hidden beneath what they all thought were leaves, glared at him. He felt the touch of an ancient and powerful mind, and he felt it overwhelm his own primitive functions. He felt its curiosity, its cool detached scientific examining of him through the ring of glittering oculars. He felt also its loathing, its fury, and its rage – its boundless rage.

He tried to speak, tried to whisper, but nothing came out through his constricted throat. Only his eyes bulged and his tongue lolled, and he knew, from the simple casual touch of its mind over his, that anything the thing could have learned from him had already been learned in those precious seconds that remained of his life.

The tendrils tightened and he felt a shearing and a hot wetness against his abdomen. His brain absorbed one last thing from the ancient brilliant mind that brushed his. One last thing that left him more empty than any man should possibly feel.

He felt its dismissal. In its bright blue eyes, he and all his kind were dismissed, were less than worthy. He felt utterly and completely alone.

And then he felt nothing at all.

END

Close Your Eyes – Tales from the Blinkspace

The Score

The Score is a story that I've wanted to tell for a long time, but have never quite figured out exactly how. Then, just a couple days ago, I realized what it was missing. It was missing love.

Judy ran.

She was not a runner by either profession or hobby. She was a student. Computer Science, with a minor in Political Science. She was very smart and she loved thinking up clever solutions to problems that used less code than her pals. She was very good at it in fact, practically gifted.

But she was no runner.

Her lungs burned, her heart pounded, and her lips felt numb, even in the cool night air. Her throat tasted metallic. Even though she wasn't an athlete by any stretch of the imagination, she was pretty sure these were all bad signs. Although perspective-wise, she had to admit she had one thing going for her.

She was still alive.

Fires on the beach were discouraged, but it was a mile-long hike back to the nearest parking lot. As long as the fire didn't get out of hand, no one ever came down to the beach to enforce it. So, the four of them had a nice pleasant fire going, almost a cheery fire. They'd collected fallen wood on their way down, and a few more pieces of driftwood along the muddy banks of the Bay. At first the fire was a riotous blaze, and then it had calmed down to what she liked to think of as "cheery." This was the time when people stopped paying attention to the novelty of the campfire and started talking with each other. This was when you could pretend for a little bit that there was no outside world in that darkness, that it was just you and your friends and the cheery fire.

Close Your Eyes – Tales from the Blinkspace

Until you realize you weren't alone after all. Until you realize there's a fifth person sitting around the fire with you. That's always disconcerting, especially if you never heard them arriving. It's even more disconcerting when you realize they aren't human.

As she ran, her mind tried to reconstruct what her eyes had seen. It was impossible and terrifying and real.

Kirk had been the first. He had just started turning toward the new person when a hand clamped over his face. Long fingers wrapped around his head. Long fingers covered in black, bristly fur. Then there was a crackling sound, like a roll of bubble-wrap being twisted, and Kirk's face was sideways. His whole head was sideways, bent to the right. Along the edges of his neck, a ridge of bones protruded. The hand let go and his head flopped down on his chest, still sideways.

Jayne was next. Another hand, balled into a fist, simply crushed her skull. It came down on her like a swung cinder block. Her entire head went down, and burst as well. Her legs kicked out once, spasmodically, and then the rest of her body flapped to the ground. The fist lifted from the mess that used to be Jayne. The fur was thick and wet.

Judy tried to look. She really did. Her face turned in the right direction, and her eyes pointed in the right direction, but whatever she saw, crouching between Kirk and Jayne, wasn't something that she could handle just yet. Her brain refused.

Drew yanked her away, and to her feet. He pulled her up, and then pushed her away.

At that moment, the adrenalin rush hit, and she ran.

There was no screaming. A peculiar corner of her brain was proud that she wasn't screaming. She heard Drew next to her, the metal fastenings on his jacket jingling as he ran. He was another programmer, like her. Equally out of shape.

The beach was hard-packed fine mud, littered with the occasional shell and pebble patch. As far as running surfaces, it wasn't bad. Actual sand would have been terrible, like a nightmare. The path back to the car was out of the question. For one thing, it was twisty and winding, and filled with trees and roots and other things that were dangerous enough to run through in the daylight – much less the dark of night. Secondly, and more importantly, it was in the opposite direction, on the other side of the fire. On the other side of...

Behind them, she heard feet. Broad naked feet slapping the mud. They rhythm was slower than theirs, but she heard it getting closer.

Drew did as well.

He skidded to a stop. She slowed, but he pushed her. "Fuck it – run!" he rasped.

She obeyed.

Close Your Eyes – Tales from the Blinkspace

Behind her, she heard him growl and scream and launch himself at something. There was another kind of growling. Then another kind of screaming. Then silence, except for the pounding of her heart and the whoosh of her breath.

So Judy ran, and when her body protested that it was tired, she simply told it "too bad," which is the only way to respond when one's life is on the line. Even when her legs started wobbling, she kept running. There were no more sounds behind her – not since Drew – but she wasn't an idiot. She kept pushing, and her legs kept running. For a brief while, she was simply a machine, running and running.

And then, finally, she tripped and she was falling, almost glad for the disorientation that came with falling in the dark, the swirling and twirling, and even the special kind of terror of not knowing where the ground is, or where it'll hit.

She never hit the ground.

It caught her in mid-air and pulled her to its chest.

All Judy felt was hands around her waist, fingers like rebar.

She could hear, for a just a moment, its heartbeat. A broad pounding heartbeat that thudded against its chest. It smelled musty and woodsy, and the fur was dense and rough.

She remembered her father. He was a big man, who died when she was only four. She remembered, however, that he came home every day after work and held her against him that same way, held her close as if this was his way of living, to hold her and press his own life into her. He always smelled of the woods, of pine sap and sawdust, and his beard was always scratchy.

She whimpered, remembering her father, and closed her eyes tight.

She felt the other hand wrap around her chest. Then she felt a twisting, and a pulling. She heard sounds no human being should ever hear, as meat and bone separated, and then, with only the memories of her father as company, Judy stopped hearing anything.

*

The woman looked like a lawyer. She acted like a lawyer. They ushered her into a room with Feralio and she sat down across the table from him.

"Who the fuck are you?" he asked.

"My name's Katherine, and I'm your lawyer," she said.

"I don't have a lawyer. I don't need one – don't want one."

"Yes, well, that much is evident," she said. From her briefcase, she pulled a tablet computer and flicked it on. "Big case," she murmured. "You've been in custody for three days. Confession on file and parts of it already leaked to the press. Well done." She finished reading, then switched the tablet off and slipped it back into her briefcase.

156

Close Your Eyes – Tales from the Blinkspace

"I've got some good news," she said. "Well, good for you, anyway. Or bad. Depends on how you feel about it."

"You're not my lawyer," he repeated.

"Oh, I understand you think you don't need a lawyer," she replied. Her voice was smooth. "But I think before you dismiss me – which, by the way, you have the right to – you might want to listen to my news."

"You think you can just come in here and talk with me?" he asked. "You think I want anything to do with you? You and your crisp suit and your crisp shoes and your crisp electronic shit mean nothing to me. You're here because you know who I am. You're here because you're just a fuckin' ambulance chaser who thinks she can leg her way into something a little better."

He leaned back. "It's not gonna work," he said. "I'm not interested."

"Ordinarily," she replied. "I'd leave about now. I'm not typically interested in helping people who are sure they're not interested in being helped. But you're a special case. You get some information free. Then, if you like, I'll leave and leave you on your own. Sound like a deal?"

"Nothing's free."

"This is," she said. "Free and useful."

"Okay. So what is it?"

"You're innocent."

"Are you mental?" he asked.

"Far from it," she said. "You've confessed to sixteen murders in the space of a month, and offered evidence, apparently, that no one but the killer ought to have known or had."

He stared at her.

"Trouble is, you're innocent," she said. "Oh, I'm sure you're guilty of a great many other things – and I have little doubt that admitting to these murders has made you no friends, but for these particular murders, it seems you can't be held."

"Why not? I did it!"

"Well, as I said, there was news, which might be bad or good depending on how you look at it. Last night, four college students were murdered down at the beach. Same way as the others. Same perpetrator. There was enough evidence to corroborate that."

She weighed him with her eyes.

"So, Mr. Feralio, as soon as we conclude our conversation, I expect you'll be released. It might interest you to know that there are several people from local news

157

Close Your Eyes – Tales from the Blinkspace

organizations that want to interview you for the hoax, and several other people who I think are also waiting for you, but not representing news organizations, if you catch my meaning. No one likes wasting time that they think could have been spent finding a killer."

"But my evidence…"

"The police are concluding – and in this I tend to agree – that you simply came across a cache of clothes and remains, and stole it. Once you realized what it was, you stepped forward to claim credit. They are very much not happy with you, by the way. I suspect a couple are planning to follow up on you later. Out of frustration, you understand. Once everything blows over."

She leaned forward.

"As your lawyer, I could get you out of here quickly and quietly," she said. "That's what we do."

His breathing quickened. "This is all true?" he asked.

"Most assuredly," she said. "The killer could be anywhere, but one thing the police know for sure is that he isn't in the custody of Thurston County."

"What's in it for you?" he asked.

"As your lawyer," she said. "I would negotiate certain rights for you for certain considerations. For you, personally, this is not going to go well, but professionally, and with the right kind of guidance, I think the situation is salvageable. Tricky, but salvageable."

"What, like a book deal?"

"As your lawyer, we could discuss that further," she said. "The path to success can be on many different roads. I don't see me on the 'ambulance chaser' path. I'm pretty sure that's not my style. Not when I have other options."

She stood up.

"Well, Mr. Feralio, I hope you'll reconsider asking me to be your lawyer. For now, I'll respect your wishes and leave."

She tapped against the door and it opened immediately. One foot stepped through.

"Wait!" said Feralio. "Wait a second."

*

Three hours later, in a gloomy apartment, the door lock rattled. The door opened.

Antonio Feralio stepped inside, followed by his lawyer, Katherine.

He flicked on a light. "What the fuck?" he asked.

158

Close Your Eyes – Tales from the Blinkspace

The place was a shambles. Everything had been moved or shoved aside or pried open or torn open.

"A lot can happen in three days," she said. "I think the police were already starting to dig through your stories. I think they were already suspecting."

He shook his head. "I'll never sort through this," he said.

She looked around. "I wouldn't bother. Do you have a suitcase?"

"Yeah, somewhere. In the bedroom."

"I think you should pack it with a week's worth of clothes, collect any necessary toiletries and, as they say, skip town and lay low for a while."

"But I live here!"

"You may find it advantageous not to for a while."

He glared at her, then marched into the bedroom.

"Shit, they tore it up in here, too!"

"No doubt. While you're packing," she said. "Would you mind if I started on my own project?"

"What do you mean?" he asked from the bedroom.

"I'll just start with questions," she said. "So I have a better idea how to package this."

"Okay."

"So, first, straight up, you lied to the police and everyone – you didn't kill anyone."

"You're the one with the evidence, right?"

"But it helps the process if you can say it."

He came out of the bedroom with a greasy blue suitcase. "I gotta pack my bathroom stuff."

"Of course."

He stepped by her and into the bathroom.

"Okay," he said, his voice echoing against the tile. "Yeah, I lied. Fuck it."

"How did you find the clothes and other evidence?"

"I was drunk," he said. "I was drunk and lost. I thought I was somewhere else. My old girlfriend's place. Fuckin' tequila does it every time."

"You don't remember anything about the place?"

159

Close Your Eyes – Tales from the Blinkspace

"No, not much. It was a bit of a mess. I thought she had a new boyfriend or something, so I grabbed his shit and took off. Woke up the next morning in bed with a bunch of junk. Sorted through it and figured it out."

"So, nothing. You know nothing. You can't take me there?"

"Not even if I was drunk again," he said. "Sorry. It would look pretty good, huh?"

He came back out into the main room. Flopped the suitcase on the kitchen table. Started re-arranging the contents. "Would make an awesome photograph. Me pointing at the place. Bummer I can't remember."

"I thought for sure you would remember," she said.

"Sorry."

She drifted, staring off into space. "You mentioned your ex-girlfriend, Mr. Feralio. Are you seeing anyone now?"

"Nah. She was okay, but kinda fucked up. Never knew when to keep quiet."

"It's hard to find the right person." She coughed and cleared her throat.

"I'm not picky," he said. "I'd settle for someone who could cook, fuck, and keep quiet. I'd be happy with–"

The words stopped at his throat, held there by fingers wrapped around his neck.

"I cannot afford not to be picky," said Katherine, but her voice was deeper, and rolled with resonance. He tried turning, but could only kick his legs. She turned him to face her.

"I have certain needs," she said. "My mate has to understand that. My mate has to know the whole of me, and I have to know the whole of him, and we have to be able to do everything together. Live together, love together, hunt together."

Most of these words slid across Antonio's brain without sticking, because it was desperately trying to not see the face hovering in front of it. He could recognize pieces. He saw thick black hair, and moonlike eyes that glowed, and teeth as big as his fingers. He saw slits that opened and closed in time with the great wet breathing, and exposed skin that was red, lined, and leathery. But there was no way his brain could turn it all into a single picture. There was no way he could see it as a single face.

She crouched in the room, her huge frame barely fitting.

Like sand through a sieve, his mind slipped away.

"And finally, I think I might have found him," she said. "Finally, I think maybe he's close. I could smell him, here and there. Sometimes at night, I could hear him. But no, I can't find him. But you, fool of Fate, you get drunk and find his home and steal prizes from him and now he's gone, because we don't hunt anymore once someone

160

finds our nest. We go somewhere else. So now he's gone and it's your fault, and you can't even show me where."

He tried to speak.

She peered at him.

"I can't begin to tell you," she said, "how horrifying it is that I have been thwarted by you. By one of you. I can't say the four last night were a waste, because I was hungry, but they were a waste because you were no help. No help at all."

She shook him once, rattling his bones.

"He could be anywhere now," she growled. "Someone else is probably going to find him, and then I'm back on my own, back looking for another, starting from scratch."

She slammed Antonio against the wall. Pictures fell from it and the door frame rattled.

His eyes swiveled and rolled. Blood came out of a gash in his side, and spattered on the floor.

She shook her head. "It's a shame," she said. "I think the hardest part is knowing how fragile you all are." She shook him again, for effect, and blood flecked the wall. "And yet, you have managed to hurt me. That's just… just unacceptable. I hate you for it."

She smashed him again against the wall, then shifted her grip to his legs. Four times, she slammed him against the floor, stopping when she realized there was nothing left to slam.

And then, when she was sure she was alone, she wept.

END

Hearing

Been a lot of longer stories lately, but somehow, this one crept in. I found myself wanting to expand, wanting to go deeper, but the fact of the matter is that this was exactly the story that came into my head, and it made the most sense to tell it exactly as it came to me.

I can hear her singing again. It's beautiful, her voice. I don't mean "pretty" or "precisely in tune," either. When I say it's beautiful, that's exactly what I mean. Full of beauty. Her voice is a gift that fills my body and lifts my heart.

I've never seen her, but I know where she is. To the south is a series of hills, and just past those hills is a forest. An old forest. I'm sure she's in there, but the hills block me from seeing her, and blocks her from seeing me. That forest is older than old. That forest was here long before men wandered around and its darkness hides more than just shadows. That's where she is. That's where she lives. That's where she has to stay.

We all have our cages.

For the longest time, I thought I was the only person to hear her sing. I stood in the yard, my eyes closed, just listening. I never saw anyone else do that, so I assumed no one could hear her, but maybe they could and didn't want to do what I was doing. Maybe they were afraid. Hard to say. I'm an old man – there's not much I'm afraid of anymore. Also, most people ignore me anyway.

So, I listened to her song. Every day I listened, and every day it was a little different. In each song was a new thing, a new story. Not in the words, because I couldn't

Close Your Eyes – Tales from the Blinkspace

understand those words at all (and this is meaningful, because I speak four languages), but in the music. In the beats and rhythms and shifts in tone and pulse. Every day a new song, every day a new story.

She sang of the birth of the world. She sang of the forest depths, of the shadows that crept within the shadows. She sang of sunlight and rain. She sang of wind and fire. She sang of the coming of Man, and in that song was a certain sadness. This much I already knew about us, but hearing it in her voice changed that pain inside of me. I was numb when I first started hearing her sing, and now, although I still felt the horrible cold knowledge of what Mankind truly was capable of, I also felt a certain perspective. I would not say it brought much peace to my heart, but in its own way, it helped. It helped my mind survive.

She also sang of the end of the world, and the things that would come to pass as that story unfolded, but those songs were of a different kind of thinking than I could do, and I could not easily follow them – which is as it should be, I'd imagine.

Then, one day, I saw him.

He was a child. A child without parents – at least at the moment – which was not so remarkable here, but more importantly, his head was cocked back, his face had a certain peacefulness to it, and his eyes were closed. He heard her, too.

She sang to both of us and for a little while, it was good to know I wasn't alone. We stood apart from each other, of course, as per the rules, but in the place where we both went when we listened to her song, we stood together, two generations between us. We were bound to each other by the harmonious thrall of her voice.

After a few days, I noticed the song changing. I felt it shift. I still knew she was singing to both of us, but the song to me had a quality to it not shared by the boy's song. My song had a farewell to it. Not a horrible farewell, but a turning-of-the-wheel sort of farewell. And gratitude. It had gratitude in it, too, for hearing her voice, for listening to her singing her stories.

I wanted to tell her how grateful I was, but there was no way I could speak to her. No way my voice could reach her in her faraway forest.

It was the boy who told me.

He stepped over one day, touched my arm and simply said "She knows." Then, he stepped back to his place.

I still listened, but in that moment, I knew her song was for him now. He was young and strong and needed to be filled with life. I was an old man, and all the threads of my life had run out. There was nothing I could do, anyway.

The next day, they came for me. A moment before, her song had paused, and then became a single clear note, a siren's call. Their hands fell on my shoulders at that moment.

Close Your Eyes – Tales from the Blinkspace

I followed them out of the yard and into the low building at the other end of the camp. I looked up at the smoke billowing out of the stacks. This was how I was leaving. This was how we all left.

As I was led inside, I felt the wind shift to the south, pulling the smoke in a new direction. Toward the hills. Toward the forest.

Maybe I would see her after all.

END

Vows

"Vows" has followed a very peculiar path. Initially, it was based on a movie I made quite a few years ago, but as I started writing it, it unfolded in a very different way than I expected. Which is good, I think!

A new moon is the best kind of moon for wicked things. Marie smiled to herself as she walked through the cemetery. Everyone assumed a full moon was best, or a crescent, but it was always a new moon. The new moon was the only moon that cast no light. One could hide during a new moon, and the ability to hide was imperative when committing atrocities.

The tomb door was locked, but it was an old lock. In the bag slung over her shoulder, Marie found a crowbar. She wedged it into the padlock and yanked as hard as her old frame could manage. With a shriek of tortured metal, the lock shattered and fell into the dark grass.

She slipped the crowbar back into the bag. Technology was awesome, and especially simple technology such as forged steel. She was grateful, briefly, that a twenty-minute trip to a hardware store was enough to save her from casting any number of spells. Small spells, of course. Even small spells caused damage, but when she was younger, she could recover from that sort of thing. Not so much anymore. And there was no getting around the big spell she needed this evening. But at least she could avoid a little one here and there.

The bag was heavy on her old shoulders and pulled cruelly on her spine, already twisted with more than ninety years of carrying her body. The bag made her limp worse, but despite the aches and pains, she did what she had to do.

What any good wife would do.

Inside the tomb was as dark as she expected. She rummaged around in the bag and pulled out a flashlight. Another spell saved!

By flashlight, she searched the plates on the wall until she found the one she was looking for. The new one.

The marble plate was too heavy for her, and cemented into place. At any other time, she would have used the sledgehammer to break through, but this was a special case. This had to be done right.

She drew the chalk circle, set the candles at the seven points, focused hard, and then said the words. With a withered finger, she traced the seal around the marble plate. The air crackled like static and the seal dissolved to dust. She made a fist and twisted her hand, and the heavy marble cap glided away from the wall and settled gently on the floor. She left tension in the spell, though – she was going to need that later. The air between the cap and its hole shimmered and hummed.

Then the rebound kicked. When she was young, a simple spell like this had a rebound she could handle, but as an old and nearly broken woman, it kicked like an angry mule. She bent over, crying out. Her guts pulsed and she tasted blood. It took her a few minutes to catch her breath.

"Oh my," she gasped, and tried not to count the stars in her vision.

When she felt stronger, she peered into the crypt. The handle of a coffin glinted at her. She wrapped her hands around it and took deep rattling breaths. This one she had to do by her own strength. She pulled. The coffin inched toward her. She pulled again. A few more inches this time. A third pull, then a fourth, and enough was exposed.

Again, the crowbar came from the bag. The coffin wasn't sealed, exactly, but it opened with some reluctance. This was normal, and well within her ability. She had done a similar thing enough times that not only did she have the motions down, but also she knew when it was time to hold her breath.

Inside the coffin lay a man. He was a handsome man, young and beautiful. He was dressed in a pale, creamy suit. She shook her head. "I still don't know what you ever saw in that suit," she said. Then her face softened and she touched his cheek with the back of her fingers. "Ah, love," she said.

For another minute, she gazed at him, remembering his youth, his strength, his vigor and beauty.

She reached into the coffin and pulled his left hand up. Happily, she saw the ring. "Thank goodness," she whispered, as she pulled it off. "Those ghouls at the mortuary didn't steal it." She then searched through the dozen rings on her left hand until she found its match and pulled it off. She placed both rings in the chalk circle.

From the pouch at her hip, she withdrew a handful of bones and some folded paper packets. She dropped two small bones on his dead chest and the other two in the middle of the circle. She opened one packet and emptied the rusty powder within on his chest. She opened another packet and sprinkled a greasy black powder in the circle. The third packet she opened, and held ready.

She said the words.

The air snapped and roared like lightning and she felt a flood of power. She felt it in her bones and body, growing wave by wave, building up. This was a big one – she could feel it. A really big one. Each wave nauseated her, but each wave meant more power, more strength. She greedily sucked each wave in, the build-up making her dizzy.

When it finally slowed, she knew she had enough to continue.

She emptied the last packet into her mouth, held it there a moment, then heaved over and spat it into his face.

The effect was instantaneous. She drained like a bucket without a bottom, and he screamed.

Being born hurt. Being born again is even worse.

Still panting a little, she stroked the hair back from his forehead and his panicked eyes found hers.

"Marie!" he cried out. His hand clutched at his chest. "What – what happened?"

"Shh, shh, my dear, dear Julius. It's okay, now."

His head rolled back and forth. "Where am I? Oh God, am I in a coffin?! Marie, what happened?"

She could feel his mind slipping away, so she kept her voice calm and soft. "It's okay, my love. You left. There was some gambling. A misunderstanding. A gun. But I took care of it. I took care of everything. That's what I do, my precious." She continued petting his head softly.

He calmed down a little. "I'm sorry," he said. "About the money. I thought for sure it was a safe bet. I thought–"

"It's only money," cooed Marie. "Besides, it's already taken care of. I've got it all back. Don't you worry, love. Don't you worry one bit." She reached into her pouch again, shaking her head. She had most definitely not married the boy for his smarts, that was certain. She pulled out a piece of weathered wood about the size and shape of a finger.

Close Your Eyes – Tales from the Blinkspace

Just then, she felt the kick coming. Resurrection was serious business and it kicked back hard. Fortunately, a kick that hard telegraphed its arrival, which was very good for her. Still, it was a good reminder – not much time left.

She held the piece of wood to his lips. "Bite down on this," she urged. He hesitated. "Hurry!" Obediently, he bit down. "Now hold it there."

She leaned forward over his face and bit the other end. When she did so, she felt the thin silver threads burst to life, connecting she and Julius.

She also felt the resurrection wave coming closer.

She let go and pulled the wood from his mouth.

"Now be quiet," she said. "This is the tricky bit."

She collapsed to the floor, her legs splayed out in front of her. She set the piece of wood near the circle for now. She noticed in passing that the two rings had fused into one.

The sledgehammer still had its uses. She pulled it from the bag and hefted it over her shoulder. She stared at her feet and took several deep breaths. This was going to hurt.

With all her strength, she swung the sledgehammer against her left foot. She felt bones pulp under the iron and the skin split open like a dove's breast. Just as she jerked the hammer from the ruined meat, the pain struck.

She screamed in response to the chaotic flash. The scream wasn't good enough, though, so she kept screaming, loudly, for enough time to let the adrenalin rush around and dim the pain a little.

Gasping, weeping, sweating, she raised the sledgehammer again and swung it down against her right foot. She missed the foot, but shattered her shin instead.

Not even screaming was enough. She wailed in pain and shock. Barely, over her cries, she heard Julius yelling from his coffin, but she had to ignore his music because she knew that no matter how bad it felt now, the worst was still coming.

The resurrection kick.

When it struck, she felt nothing at first. It just filled her up, pouring into every part of her, filling every cell. Even the blood still spurting from her destroyed legs glittered with the spell's kick. It didn't flow into her like the waves of the spell itself. That was like a powerful tide of water. This was invasive. Something was invading her. Something dark, driven, hungry, and made of 100% pure fury.

For a brief moment, she actually wondered if that was all it would do.

Then everything turned to fire.

168

Close Your Eyes – Tales from the Blinkspace

She flopped backwards, her entire body spasming in pain. Blood and bile flooded her throat and she vomited, again and again, between gags and screams. This was it. This was the one that was going to kill her. She could tell.

She rolled over and stared into the circle. The rings glowed brilliant white and the circle's perimeter pulsed with pink and purple luminescence. In the dancing air above it, as the colors shifted and twisted, she saw the Face. The Face laughed horribly and came swimming up toward her from a place no person should ever see. As long as the circle remained intact, that kick would yank her from life like a rag doll, throw her through the dancing flames, and into the Face's laughing mouth. There was no coming back from that trip.

It grew larger. She saw its teeth. The flames filled his eyes. Her body started vibrating itself apart.

Now was the time!

She reached for the piece of wood. "Thee to me! Me to thee!" she screamed, and scraped the wood across the floor and into the circle, interrupting the chalk line and breaking it.

There was a hush.

The wood charred to ash and vanished.

Then, the screaming started again, but this time from the coffin. It was Julius.

Marie fell back, but this time, not in pain. Marie fell back in ecstasy.

A numbness spread from her legs and up her body. Her back crackled, her legs crackled, her arms crackled. Her insides squirmed and shifted. Pains she had long since learned to ignore vanished entirely. Her body felt renewed, flushed with energy and power.

When the effect stopped, she lay there a moment, giggling. That was close! She stood up carefully, trying to not look at her own arms or hands. Just in case. From her bag, she pulled out a small decorative mirror, and risked a glance. A beautiful – no, gorgeous – redhead stared back. Nineteen years, maybe twenty, tops. She touched her face, her perfect flawless face.

"Oh my," she whispered. "I never looked this good!"

A whimper drew her attention to the coffin. She stepped over and looked inside. "Oh Julius," she breathed. "Isn't it amazing? Isn't it?"

She reached down once again and stroked his forehead. Her fingers glided smoothly over the deep fissures and liver spots. His hair fell off in patches. The ancient thing that had been Julius mewed piteously at her and watched her through deep-sunken eyes.

"What did you expect?" she asked. "You and I both know you didn't marry me for

Close Your Eyes – Tales from the Blinkspace

love. You married me for my gold. And I married you for your beauty. You spent the gold and lost your life. Now, I get your beauty." She glanced down the length of his body to his legs. Both were shattered. "I'm a little sorry about that," she said. "But I couldn't risk you leaving if something didn't work. Looks like you're losing some blood."

She leaned down and kissed his forehead. He tried to respond, but his body was too broken, too old.

"We had some good times, though, you and I," she said. "Real good times." She petted him one last time, and he gasped out something inaudible through leathered lips and a mouth half-filled with teeth suddenly fallen out. "Don't be that way, my dear," she said. "It was all just exactly like in our vows."

She slid the lid back over the coffin and pushed it deep into the crypt. Her physical strength was marvelous!

She stepped back and glanced at the marble cap. Above it, the air still shimmered. She reached out with her mind and released the tension of the spell. The slab flew back into place and the dust arose from the floor and reformed into a solid cement seal.

She leaned her head against the cool marble wall. Inside, she felt the tiny spark of life that was her husband, Julius, a man who played hard, gambled for high stakes, and was man enough to accept his fate. Not that he had a choice, of course, she thought to herself. She felt the spark waver, flickering, and fading. And then, she felt it go out forever.

"'Til death us do part, my love. 'Til death us do part."

She scuffed out the rest of the circle with her foot, gathered together her tools, easily tossed the bag over her shoulder, and left the tomb, whistling and hopeful.

END

Close Your Eyes – Tales from the Blinkspace

The Silver in the Dark

Part of a writing marathon at the H. P. Lovecraft Film Festival, "The Silver in the Dark" is inspired by Beth's request to have "something weird happen with the cows."

The moon was low in the night sky, barely lighting Beth's room as she stared out into the darkness. The air was cold and her nightgown moved with it, and she felt the cold on her body, but she dared not take her eyes away from the window, from the fields, from the woods.

"I see you," she whispered.

The next morning, her sister Emily screamed.

Emily's husband, Robert, ran out, and found his wife near the back of the house and what he saw also shook him.

Their son stayed inside with Beth, who was infirm and rarely left the house.

Emily came back in and sat down at the kitchen table, her face paler than Beth had ever seen. The boy sat next to her, and asked what was wrong and she looked at him. Stared at him.

"You are to stay right here until your father returns," she told him, in the voice that mothers use when it becomes absolutely critical that they be understood by their offspring.

Close Your Eyes – Tales from the Blinkspace

The police were called. There was a meeting near the back of the house. Although no one could see anything from the house at this angle, there was a large tarp laid across the yard. Laid across something. Covering it.

The police collected information, took photographs, shook Robert's hand grimly, and left.

Later that afternoon, Robert started up the backhoe and two hours later, he shut it off. The tarp was gone and in its place was a mound of dirt.

Robert and Emily sat down with their son and Beth. "Did you hear anything last night?" they asked. Their son, Robert Junior, shook his head. Beth also shook her head.

"Nothing at all?" they persisted. Again, heads shaken side-to-side.

"What happened?" asked Robert Junior.

"Someone... someone..." started Emily, but her husband interrupted her.

"Someone killed one of the cows. Someone killed her bad."

Dinner that night was silent and heavy, and no one slept well.

The next morning, Robert went out to check the animals. He came back ten minutes later and told Emily and Robert Junior to stay inside. He didn't have to tell Beth, because Beth never left the house.

The police came by again, and they stayed longer and left grimmer.

There was more backhoe noise, and then Robert came inside.

He sat down heavily in a chair and was silent.

Slowly, Beth came by and sat down near him and stared at him for a long time.

"I didn't hear anything," she said.

"I figured," he answered.

Emily saw that his silent spell was broken, and came in and sat near him. She waited until he spoke again.

"Three cows," he said, at last. "It's not right. Not right at all."

The police showed up again that night, this time with photographs from another farm, two miles away, the Behr farm. Robert and the police looked over the photos, nodding, their lips tight. The police spoke more with Emily, and Robert Junior, but they didn't speak with Beth.

"Beth's a bit of a shut-in," said Emily.

Close Your Eyes – Tales from the Blinkspace

"Beth's crazy," said Robert, "and she's not at all connected with what's going on. She stays inside as protection."

The police insisted, but all Beth would say was "I didn't hear anything. I didn't hear anything." Eventually, they realized that Emily was right, and they left Beth alone.

On the third night, Robert stayed awake. He loaded his rifle and his shotgun, and found a place to camp out high in the attic, overlooking the back pasture, where the cows were kept.

The night turned dark. He drank coffee and bit on his tongue to stay awake.

Near one o'clock in the morning, he saw the glow from the edge of the woods. It was a silent sort of glow, a glow that was so quiet that even the world held its breath.

The glow coalesced into a ribbon of silent shimmering light, a weaving and bobbing thread, a ghostly worm of some sort, and it wound its way down from the edge of the trees, into the pasture, and drifted toward one of the cows.

Robert's rifle followed it, but he couldn't squeeze the trigger. There wasn't anything to shoot. It was only light. Light and movement. So he watched, through the scope. He watched the thing drift near the cow, which was sleeping. He watched the thing come close to the cow's snout. He watched it nudge, lightly touch, and then slide into the cow's snout, inch by inch, until it finally disappeared.

His body was tense, his finger hovered over the trigger, but now there was only a cow in the field of vision. Only a cow seemingly asleep.

Then there was a flash of white, of billowing gossamer, and reflective metal, and those long moments of tension were released and without even thinking, Robert squeezed the trigger. The rifle cracked the night air and the great billowing thing that danced around the cow fell.

He ran out, and as he ran out, he saw the house lights turning on, heard Emily's voice.

He ran to the field, and as he ran, he saw the billowing gossamer thing move, stand erect, wobbling. He saw the billowing gossamer thing raise an axe, and he fired again, still forty yards away. He knew he hit it because now its pure whiteness was streaked black with blood in the dim moonlight.

The axe fell and the cow screamed a short gasp, and fell over. The gossamer thing raised the axe again and then staggered, and fell onto the cow.

Emily reached the thing first, and stopped in her tracks. Then she stepped back. She stepped back and fell to the ground.

Robert arrived and raised his rifle. The thing turned to him, and looked at him.

"Aunt Beth!" he called out.

Close Your Eyes – Tales from the Blinkspace

Blood streaked her nightgown, and her feet were muddy from what had already spilled from her and the cow.

"I never heard nothing," she said, and coughed blood. "You didn't either, but you saw it, didn't you. You had to. You can't hear them, but you can see them."

Robert thought of the silvery ribbon in the field, and already, even though that was only a short time ago, the memory was fading.

"You'll forget you ever saw it," Beth said, and coughed again. She swayed. "They're like that, Robert. They play with your mind. They can't do a proper job until they get close to you, until they have somewhere to hide."

She poked at the cow with her axe and Robert saw how she had nearly severed the head. There was blood, yes, but there was something else, something he had already started forgetting about. Something silvery, something like a ribbon, squirming and crawling, and slowly trailing out from the open wound.

"The deader, the better," choked Beth. "You can't let them get close to you, you can't let them be alone with you, because if you do, they'll get inside you, and then you're gone, Robert. If they get inside you, you're gone, and then they make babies and then they move outward and then they're in Emily and your son and then they keep going. They never, never stop."

They both watched the silver thread dissolve into the ground, soak down inside.

"It's going back to the woods now," said Beth, "And now you know about it." Her breath rattled.

"What is it?" he asked.

She shook her head. "Gone," she said, and she fell over. The ground was wet beneath her.

Emily stood, her eyes vacant with shock, but it was Robert who stepped in, Robert who picked up Beth, and Robert who brought her home.

And it is Robert, now, who stares out the windows at night, late after all the animals are asleep, watching.

END

Love, She is Blind

Sometimes, even if you have past history with someone, you have to respect their situation if it's tricky...

There's not much that can make a man take a hard look at the kind of life he's led like staring directly down the barrel of a semiautomatic pistol in the hand of his most recent ex.

"Cynthia," I said calmly. "I can't tell you what a surprise it is to see you."

She tried to smile and I could almost remember what it looked like to actually see her smile, but then she did that thing she does right before she gets really angry at someone. She pursed her lips and turned her head slightly.

"Do you have any idea how hard it was to find you?" she asked.

"I'm sorry," I said. "It's been a little frantic these days. Been kind of under the radar."

"You disappeared," she said. "Frankly, I'm happiest if you prefer it that way. You're an ex for a reason, Paul. The only downside to that is that we had a little unfinished business and that's something that I just couldn't let go. Not yet. I have my reputation."

I tried very hard and successfully managed to not add any fire to the conflagration in my mind that was a conversation revolving around her reputation.

Close Your Eyes – Tales from the Blinkspace

Instead, I carefully and slowly opened my hands to show her that there was no mischief and asked "What can I do? How can I help?" although I knew exactly what it was that she was going to say.

"I want my money."

I took a deep breath. While there were and are many things about Cynthia that would drive any man insane, I had to give her this: she was always to the point.

"I figured that," I said. "That's it?"

"I learned a lot more about that job, Paul. I learned, for example, that you were not forthcoming with me on the complete value of the shipment, and that you did, in fact, make considerable bank off my efforts."

"I suppose you want a piece of that, too?" I asked.

"As strange as it might sound, no. I could try and work out what my piece would have been, but the fact is that I made a deal based on a flat fee, not a percentage. It's good to know that you were willing to screw me, and that helps me justify making sure you're not a part of my life anymore, but really, all I want is exactly what you said you would pay me."

She's also fair. Not too many people would insist on only their exact share when they had the gun and the drop on their ex. So, she gets points for that.

"Okay," I said. "You're right. I'll get your money."

"And I'll follow you," she said. "Not because I don't trust you, but because I expect you to disappear again and it's considerably less likely when I am on top of your every move. No offense."

"None taken," I said. "My place isn't really set up for visitors."

"I'm not visiting," she said. "This is strictly business."

"I understand."

Besides, it was a lot cooler in the house, and being cooler was suddenly very important to me. Cooler and darker.

I invited her in, and although I was chivalrous, she still insisted on me going first. Which is understandable, I guess.

"The safe is in the living room," I said. She didn't reply, but she didn't have to – it wasn't as if I had asked her a question. She followed me.

"It's dark in here," she said. "I recall you liking a lot of light, Paul."

"I used to, but things have changed. I like it a little darker now. And, well, my girlfriend likes it this way, too."

Close Your Eyes – Tales from the Blinkspace

She snorted a laugh. "I hope she's a smart cookie," she said.

"No complaints so far," I replied. "Nobody's perfect."

"Then I hope that your imperfections are a fine complement to her imperfections," she said.

"That's very kind of you," I said.

"Money," she reminded me.

"Living room," I said. "Safe."

"Keep going," she said.

"Don't go into the kitchen," I said. "It's really a mess in there."

"Not here for coffee and a chat. Just here for the money," she said, and then "You know, a lot of people have been enjoying furniture, Paul. Have you thought about that?"

"Well, yes, but we're just getting ready to leave," I said. "Moving. Sorry about the boxes."

"I'm glad I found you now," she said. "It seems to be getting progressively harder to find you these days."

"Remember saying that's how you liked it?" I asked.

I was reminded that she didn't like being reminded of such things by the sharp poke of metal in my back.

"After you give me my money, you can vanish off the face of the Earth for all I care," she said. "I've got plenty of gigs lined up already."

The hall expanded out into the living room and I stepped to the safe. "That's a gun safe," she said.

"What better place to hide money?" I asked.

"What better place to hide guns, too," she added. "After you finish the combination, I'm afraid I'm going to have to open it myself."

"Cynthia, are you suggesting that after all this, I would actually try to shirk my duty or even trick you?"

"Absolutely," she said. "And now that we're both clear on the expectations of the situation, get to opening that thing so I can get my money and be on my way out of here and into my new life without Paul Temple, thank you very much."

I did admire her directness.

Combination, combination...

177

Close Your Eyes – Tales from the Blinkspace

"You don't have to worry about me seeing the combination," she said. "I really don't care at all, and I'm never coming back."

She looked around.

"Goddamn, Paul, it is nutty-dark in here."

"I put paper over the windows," I said. "I like it dark."

"Apparently. And so does New Girlfriend, right?"

"Right."

"It does not go well with the cathedral ceiling thing. I can't see shit in here."

"We manage."

"Manage to open the safe, please."

I spun the last number and stepped back.

"It's ready to open. You said you wanted to open it yourself."

"Thank you, I'm glad you remembered. Would you also be so kind as to step a few steps back? I have a broad category of things I can expect you to do and having you step a few feet away and still be where I can see you helps some of those be a little less likely."

I stepped back, and kept my hands up, palms raised where she could see them.

"Nothing up my sleeves," I said.

"That has always been a lie and you know it," she said, opening the door.

Inside the safe were my two pistols – polished 1911s from my father's collection – and my cashbox. Expertly, she flipped open the cashbox lid with one hand. She knelt down and dumped the cashbox on the floor, and started counting out hundreds.

"This is going to take a while," I said.

"That's a shame," she said. "It would have taken less time to simply work all this out with me last year and pay me what you owed me instead of making me go to all the time and trouble of finding you and dumping money on your floor."

I was impressed at how quickly she counted out twenty-five thousand dollars in hundreds.

"You're running low, Paul," she said, as she stuffed the bills into her purse. "You might want to think about picking up another gig before you completely light out for the territories."

Close Your Eyes – Tales from the Blinkspace

"I don't suppose you would be willing to help?" I asked. "Despite our differences in the past, I've found that you're pretty good in a pinch. And I'm willing to not let my personal feelings get wrapped up in our business relationship."

She shook her head. "Oh, I don't think so," she said, and stood up.

Just as she straightened out, a flash of dark within the dark struck.

I've heard a lot of different reactions, from screams to gurgles to growls and more. She only said "Hey!" loudly, almost indignantly.

Then her spine snapped.

Legs – thin, black, and steel-strong – crossed her chest and pulled her back. Her hands trembled, and the little semiauto she carried fell to the floor. I would have to deal with that later, I suppose. That's what gun safes are for.

Behind her, a shadow rose, and a body moved into view.

I have read very scientific sounding papers informing me that it's impossible for insects to grow as large as they do in horror movies. I can accept that they honestly believe this.

But, of course, they're wrong on two counts. First of all, she did anyway, and second of all, she's not an insect.

She dropped Cynthia, stepped over, and nudged my hand. I scratched along either side of her beautiful soft head. I stroked her and petted her and cooed.

One of her legs rose and petted the side of my face.

She doesn't blink, I know, but I like to think of her blinking at me when our eyes meet. Her eyes are absolute pitch black, but I swear there's movement inside them, that I can see her soul through those eyes. The big eyes, anyway. The little eyes are her hunting eyes. Best to not look too long into them.

"It's time, love," I said.

She tapped my face lightly.

"I know, and I'd love to, but Cynthia may have told someone where she was going. It's only a few days difference. We'll still use the trailer."

Tap, tap again.

"If you like, of course. We still have all the gear in storage. We shouldn't do it too close, though. Might have to drive westward a day or two."

Tap, tap…

"People get suspicious. The roadside attraction thing is a great idea, but if we're there longer than a few days, then people start remembering us and we can't have them

Close Your Eyes – Tales from the Blinkspace

remembering us. At least not up here in the States," I said. "Once we get past the border, things'll be a lot easier."

One last tap.

"I love you, too, beautiful," and I meant it. She knew I meant it – she could tell the difference between the feel of someone telling the truth and the feel of someone lying – but I've always thought it's a very good thing to hear.

She stepped back over Cynthia. Two of her legs lifted the body, and held it close. The other six easily kept her balanced.

I smiled at her, showing my teeth. She loved that.

"Besides, I think we're about out of room to store your leftovers, love," I added.

I swear, she winked. I know she doesn't, but I swear she does.

She stepped back into the shadows.

"Wait!" I said. She stopped. I stepped close and pried Cynthia's purse from around her arm. "We'll need this piece," I said.

The two of them slipped away into the darkness for their private time and I put everything back into the safe and continued packing. I didn't like being on the move right now, but, well, you go where your heart takes you, I guess.

END

Moonsong

I got tired of pansy-ass gods.

I love watching the clouds boil across the moon at night.

When it's full, as it is now, I especially love how the very nature of the night shifts and drifts with these high clouds. When the clouds thin out, the night turns into a silver-sunned day. When the clouds thicken, it's as if a burlap sack has been dropped over everything.

There's a kind of majestic peacefulness to it, a calm sense of watching something cosmic, something cataclysmic, happening at a great distance.

And, of course, I can hear Her voice.

On a summer evening rooftop, with my then-boyfriend, I watched this same thing, watched the clouds boiling across the moon. I felt the air sliding around, the winds taking turns gusting and then hesitating. I could hear the rushing of windblown leaves in the trees and the tumble of twigs and smaller things below, on the ground, picked up by eddies, and dropped, clattering, seconds later.

I had two sudden realizations at that point.

The first was that not all voices come from throats. Some creatures speak in the blend of other sounds, such as wind and rain and the stirrings of things in the dark. Not

Close Your Eyes – Tales from the Blinkspace

words, exactly, but voices nonetheless. Some voices speak in movement, how the leaves on a tree move with the wind, how the dunes shift across the skyline, how the waves skitter across the top of the sea, how the clouds slide through the silent darkness. Not all voices are human, and those voices surround us.

The second was that, as I stared at the moon, at that special moon, for the first time in my life, I recognized that I was hearing one of those voices. It was a strong voice, not only in the clouds across Her face, but in the way the stillnesses of the night moved around me, the way the wind pressed and pulled at my skin. It was as if I had suddenly been told the answer to a confounding riddle and now I couldn't help but see the obviousness of it.

She spoke to me. Not to a general me, but to a specific me. To me. She knew at that moment that I could hear Her. I was part of Earth, part of the wind and the water and the dirt and the heat of Earth, and my hearing Her voice was a clear call back to Her, and then She spoke directly to me.

He never heard it. Before my mind could even form the question, She told me this was how it always was, that boys, that men, that males could never hear Her voice. Her voice was reserved for us and us alone, and even then, only very rarely.

She whispered at me, touched me, and left me after promising to return.

As if I could forget!

From that point on, I waited for Her, waited for Her fullness, waited for Her voice.

I listened to Her every month, when I could see Her, and when I couldn't, I tried to travel to where I could. Sometimes, there was no way, the clouds were too thick, and I could not travel, and then I had to wait another month. But She knew, when we spoke, how hard I tried, and She knew that I was made of mere flesh. She could see into my heart, and She would know if I was deceiving Her.

I learned early that there was a cost to being able to hear Her. I learned that Communion was not free. I paid that cost gladly, though it weakened me each time.

She told me of many grand things. I learned new things about the world through Her experiences, and She told me of things that no human being could ever possibly know. She told me of Her arrival here, when Earth was still a cooling pool of liquid rock, gorgeous and warm and fluid. She told me how She slid into it, how She became a part of that, how grateful She was to finally find a home, a place where She could live and be.

She told me of the life that came to be on Earth, of the creatures that started in the seas, then changed and grew into things on the land. She told me how they eventually became creatures who altered the landscape to suit them, who created machines, and who had just begun to explore space. She was so very proud of them, and thought of them as Her children. They thought of Her as their mother, too, and treated Her as such, with gifts and offerings, and life.

Close Your Eyes – Tales from the Blinkspace

As I mentioned, Communion was not free.

Her children were crystalline and beautiful, with flickers of light playing across their silicon facets. Their delicate hands built splendid cities, and their complex, musical language nearly rivaled Hers. Their hearts beat as tiny pulses of electricity, honed by evolutionary forces to pinpricks of pure energy.

She told me of the Intruder. It came from nowhere, dark and fast. It was half the size of Earth and it struck with no warning. She told me how it sheared into the planet, how it reliquified everything, how it destroyed everything. Everything. I felt Her screams of fear and fury, and then Her shock and pain as a spinning ball of brilliant liquid rock calved off from the planet and flew away – carrying Her essence with it.

The Intruder destroyed Her planet, destroyed Her children, and ripped Her from it, throwing Her into a long and cold, cold orbit.

The rock cooled, the planet below coalesced again into a solid planet and for millennia, She watched the cycle all over again, new life forming, new life crawling out onto the dry shores, new life walking, new life building, and new life to look at the sky, to look at Her and wonder. She wept in Her ephemeral voice, unable to touch the new children, unable to be a part of them and let them be a part of Her.

Instead, She spun, trapped, around the planet, around the children, and watched helplessly as they grew and changed and became frightened, unguided creatures.

Always, Her voice spread across the globe, looking for ears, looking for those who could hear Her. Always, She called and sang and listened to see if anyone answered. She even told me that She had considered giving up. She had considered melting Her essence back into the rock of this satellite, making Herself inert and lifeless.

She despaired.

But then She heard me listening and felt Her way into my mind and my heart and knew that there was still hope. She knew that where there was one person who could hear, there would be more, and that maybe, maybe once there were enough, She might find a way to leave Her prison of dust and return to Earth, return to a planet of warmth and water and air and life.

She needed life very much.

She learned more of us through me, followed my own short life. She learned more of what sort of life we led down here on Earth without Her, what sort of riot of biology had spread across the globe. She learned what I had learned in school, about our environment, about our abilities and technologies, and about our bodies. Our flesh. We were very different than Her brittle crystal children. We were wet. We were fluids and moisture. We were what She, after millennia alone in a dry, distant, dusty prison, desperately needed.

Close Your Eyes – Tales from the Blinkspace

As I said, there was a cost, and it weakened me each time, but I spilled it anyway, to dance in the rapture of Her voice, but I knew as much as She knew that it was not enough, that this was like a tiny droplet to a man ravaged by thirst.

In retrospect, I should have figured it out sooner. I had all the clues. In my defense, the only thing I can say is that I was learning so much, so in love with Her stories, that neither of us thought to make the obvious conclusion. Of course, once I thought of it, She saw it in my mind, and I knew it was the right thing. I could feel Her hunger flare, Her need, Her desperation. I knew then that I wasn't simply a student, a worshipper, a listener. I was a tool. Her tool.

As I said, Communion always weakened me – the most I could spare for Her was a pint, and earlier, it was two, before She learned how much to siphon away without killing me. It's fascinating to see, spiraling out, and up, spinning from black-red liquid to a beautiful stream of woven silver, and then vanishing into the night. I know, it doesn't quite make sense, but I also know it makes Her happy, and I want Her happy, so I made my offers.

But now, it's different. A typical human has ten pints. Far more than my single pint.

Is it wrong? I worried briefly, the first time, but only briefly. My then-boyfriend, the one I mentioned earlier, definitely helped me overcome my misgivings. He never was all that kind, anyway. After that, I started seeing how it made more sense. After that it became easier. After that, Her gratitude was palpable, and then I realized what a real god was like. Not a fake god made of hopes and wishes and myth, but a real one, who could talk with you, who could show you your place, who knew you and loved you and let you feed Her.

A god like that.

I realize this was a long way of explaining, but I thought it was important you understand that I mean you no ill will, that there are no hard feelings. The knife hurts, and I'm sorry about that, but the rest is painless, mostly.

I'm not going to take the gag out – there's nothing you can tell me that could change my mind. Besides, I've heard it all before – it's not as if this is my first time.

I will tell you this, though. In a way, I'm deeply jealous. You're going to become a part of Her. I can't ever do that, not while I'm here on Earth. Someday, She'll be strong enough to come back Home. Someday, I'll have fed Her enough that She has the power to come back and guide us. I'd like to see that. Until then, the closest I can physically come to Her is by sending you.

Well, your *blood*, anyway.

END

184

Close Your Eyes – Tales from the Blinkspace

Inside Out

I never figured I'd come back to a carnival story, but at the last minute, the freakish sadness of "Inside Out" needed out of my head. I hope you like it!

I cannot tell you why Lisa is the way she is. When I try to imagine, my mind blocks the thought, as if protecting me from myself. I can, however, tell you what happened. You may make of it as you wish, and I cannot allow myself to be responsible for your interpretation.

It was a small carnival. Almost a non-carnival because of its size. If anything, it felt like a throwback to a previous century. There were jugglers and acrobats and a ringleader. There was a strongman and a freak tent and a magician. It was utterly charming, and utterly human.

The jugglers were skilled at weaving a flashing mesh of silver between them, but you could see the intense concentration in their eyes. The acrobats leaped and pranced all over each other and made small pyramids and stacks of flesh, but you could hear their exertion. The ringleader was the picture of what a turn-of-the-century carnival would assume was the pinnacle of savoir-faire, up to the fine cracks in his powder makeup. The strongman's weights seemed lighter than they should have. The freaks in the freak tent were for the most part clever bits of trickery, although entertaining.

But the magician…

Close Your Eyes – Tales from the Blinkspace

Ah, he was a most wondrous thing.

His hands moved like liquid, and things happened in them for which we had no explanation. Flowers, coins, trinkets of every sort appeared and disappeared without any effort. He moved on to larger illusions, making volunteers hover, making them slide into and out of each other like pancakes, making them turn upside down. At first, we assumed – as any right-thinking person could – that although this was skillful prestidigitation, it was no more real than any of the other acts on display that evening. As we watched, though, we became increasingly fascinated.

The show seemed to last only minutes, but after the final act, the details of which I cannot easily recall, I saw by my watch that we had been thoroughly mystified and completely entertained for nearly an hour.

It's important to tell you something about myself. When I was a child, I wanted to be a stage magician. I wanted to do the things that this man did, entrance an audience the way this man entranced us. I wanted to awe and amaze and inspire and delight. I read books. I practiced with cards and thread and sliding sections of boxes. For a kid, I was surprisingly good. But then, I moved on to newer and more interesting things. Plus, I learned that the kind of life led by magicians wasn't anywhere near as glamorous as depicted in the media – and that included the depictions that included alcoholism, depression, or worse. That, I decided, was not the life for me.

Which means that when I tell you I was absolutely flabbergasted by some of these tricks, I'm telling you this from the perspective of someone who has a basic grasp of the arts of stage magic.

When he was finished, after his bow, he swept all of his trinkets and props into a small chest. It was one of those decorative treasure chests that people often use to hold jewelry. These things were very popular in the Seventies, very popular with anyone still fond of the Seventies, and very popular for people who fancy themselves possessing treasures of the smallish sort. I used to have one myself, as a matter of fact.

He swept his kit into that box, closed it up, and left the stage.

After most of the others had left, Lisa caught me staring off into space. Truth be told, I was reliving all of my old lessons, all of the rope tricks and sleight-of-hand tricks, and getting more and more frustrated. Nothing that I'd ever seen was anything like what I'd seen on that small stage today.

"I know that look," she said. "What are you working out?"

I told her of my past (which was about as un-sordid as a past could be, by the way), and my old fascination with stage magic and how amazed I was at the act we just witnessed.

"But it's the same thing, isn't it?" she asked. "I mean, every magician does their own tricks, right? Every technique is a little different. I read that somewhere."

Close Your Eyes – Tales from the Blinkspace

"That's true," I said, "But you can always tell a trick by its class. Sure, there's a million ways to make a canary disappear, but it's basically a disappearing canary trick, and there's only three possibilities – either the bird is hidden in the sleeve or coat, hidden in the table, or there never was a bird in the first place. These tricks, though, these were… extraordinary."

She nodded. "They were good, yeah. I liked the one with the cards shuffling themselves in his hand."

I turned to her. "That's an example," I said. "No one does that trick. There's not even a name for it. What he did doesn't use any of the card tricks or hand tricks that I've ever heard of. Not even close."

"So?" she asked. "That just means he was really good, right?"

I wish I'd agreed with her. Had I agreed with her, we could have wandered off, bought cotton candy, drifted on with our lives, and eventually, I could have pretended that they weren't the tricks I thought they were, and that they were just variations of tricks I already knew. Instead, I said something that still amazes me. I said "I want that chest."

Lisa waved her hands at me. "No, no, now isn't the time to become crazy."

With the speaking of the words, I knew it to be true. I grabbed her arms. "I'm not crazy," I said. "I've got to look in that chest. I've got to see how he did that."

She laughed. "Okay, okay," she said. "Look, I don't want you to get in trouble with your folks, so why don't I nab it for you, okay? Only, you have to promise to tell no one I did it, okay? Promise!"

I promised, but apparently, breaking that promise is the first thing I did, but in my defense, you have to admit I had no choice. I have to tell you what happened. You have to believe me.

We wandered the carnival for several hours, watching the rubes come in laden with coins and bills, and leave with fewer of both, but with smiles on their faces, and sometimes blue stuffed bears, which was the prize at the shooting gallery if you hit each target at least once. The night grew darker, and the people grew quieter. By eleven, the visitors were gone and the marquee lights were the next to go. Piece by piece they too shut off.

By this time, Lisa and I had retired to an alcove in a building across the street. We could see everything, but we were in shadow, and so were invisible.

We waited another hour after the last of the lights went out. "They've all counted their money and gone to bed," she whispered to me. "Now's a good time."

We climbed the fence quietly. In a minute or two, found the section of the grounds hosting the carny trailers. They were not brightly colored, but they were marked, and the magician's was there with the rest.

187

Close Your Eyes – Tales from the Blinkspace

A thin window near the door was open for ventilation.

Lisa reached her arm in and it was only seconds before she was able to unlock the door from the inside.

"You stay out here," she said. "I'll be right back." She slipped inside.

I waited nervously out there, feeling exposed. At any minute, someone could walk around the corner and see me, see us, see the trailer with the open door. A couple of minutes went by. I heard soft searching noises.

Suddenly the hairs on the back of my neck stood up.

"Lisa, we gotta go!" I said. I'm not superstitious at all, nor do I feel as if I have a "sixth sense" or any of that rubbish. I think, however, that my brain assembles pictures of what's going on around me from sensory elements that I'm not conscious of. Maybe things I'm seeing and hearing and smelling all combining in my head to create a subtle picture I don't recognize but that still chills me. No "sixth sense," but a well-developed ability to get the hell out of trouble if need be.

I called to her again, in a loud whisper. Then I heard her voice.

She spoke three words.

As she stepped from the trailer, I saw in her hands the little chest. It was exactly the same chest. Its hinges faced me.

The exact moment my eyes connected with the chest, I felt two distinct things.

The first was avarice. I admit – I wanted that chest. I wanted it so bad, wanted its secrets so much that I could feel my entire body reaching out, not just my hands and my arms, but my soul and my mind. I wanted it more than anything, more than anyone. More than the world. I would have killed for it. I would have died for it. If whatever secrets this chest contained were a drug, then crystal meth would hang its head in shame. Just the thought of finally knowing what was in that chest, of finally seeing what was in that chest, drove me out of my own skull.

The second was fear. I admit I was afraid when Lisa was still rummaging around in that trailer, but the instant I saw that chest, the fear I felt was washed away by absolute terror. Whatever thoughts I might have had about the non-existence of a "sixth sense" disappeared. Whatever it was in that box, it was the thing I felt, the thing that tickled me behind my forehead as we hopped the fence, that made me nervous as Lisa crawled into the trailer, and that absolutely petrified me now. Whatever was in that chest was, without any shadow of a doubt, the very last thing I ever wanted to see, hear, or have anywhere near me.

It was in that maelstrom of desire and repulsion that I heard Lisa's three words. Three tiny, simple words.

"I found it!"

188

Close Your Eyes – Tales from the Blinkspace

And then she opened it, and looked inside.

No, I cannot tell you what she saw. I cannot imagine what that small chest held. I can't say it was filled with light or filled with darkness or filled with snakes or eyeballs or grape jelly.

I can tell you that she looked into it – deep into it – and then softly closed the lid.

I whispered her name just once, as she set the chest behind her, and then she looked at me.

You've seen her. I know you have. I can tell, because when I tell you she looked at me, I see in your eyes the same way I feel.

I'm going to say it anyway, though, because it's so impossible, that I have to say it, so we all have the same words.

In her eyes, I saw forever. Whatever had been my friend had been extracted, scooped out, emptied. There was nothing left in its place. The meat was there, the blood still burned through her, but the thing that was actually her, the thing that was her living force, that was gone. Completely and utterly gone.

We read of these things, and we see them in movies, but I can tell you, with the absolute authority of having seen it with my own eyes, that seeing a person without their soul is seeing into the infinity of time and knowing that we are nothing but the briefest flickers in the Universe, here and gone. Seeing a person without their soul is seeing how we truly look to the Universe, how insignificant we are, how very, very much... nothing... we are.

And it was then that she started screaming.

I can tell you've heard that, too, the way you just stepped back. I can also tell that, like me, you'll never stop hearing it.

All I can tell you is I'm sorry.

I'm sorry we went to the carnival, I'm sorry we broke into the trailer. I'm sorry we opened the box. And most of all, I'm sorry for Lisa.

Finally, I'm sorry for having to tell you what I've seen. I'm sorry you've looked into her eyes as well, and heard that scream.

I wish there was something I could do, but there is nothing.

Nothing at all.

END

Underbelly

Part of a writing marathon at the H. P. Lovecraft Film Festival, "Underbelly" is inspired by Constance's request for steampunk.

Another man had been torn asunder and strung up high in the support wires of the Floating City of Nessez.

The Police had been tracking the fiend for three months, but so far their searches revealed not one single usable clue. Ever higher the reward offers climbed as each victim's family added their share to reflect not only their grief, but also their solidarity.

A grim social paralysis gripped the city and no one went out after dark, but still, somehow, every week, a new body would be found, torn to pieces.

No one went out except, of course, for the most foolhardy.

Neville Moore and Constance Crane stepped from the darkness into a pool of light, in a dark street near the less respectable warehouse sections of Nessez. Long loops of mist billowed about them, industrial remnants from the many shops working full thirty-two hour shifts.

Each wore long leather cloaks against the night chill, hats to keep the wind's bite at bay, and strapsacks filled with gear.

Mr. Moore adjusted his glasses and surveyed the area.

Close Your Eyes – Tales from the Blinkspace

"The Police," he declared, "are fools of the highest order. They are trying to find a common thug when our quarry is neither."

Miss Crane raised an eyebrow. "Such an extraordinary claim," she said, "requires extraordinary evidence."

Mr. Moore buttoned the top two buttons of his cloak. He reached into a large pocket and withdrew a weapon – a deadly weaving of brass, copper, and glass. He handed it to her. "I shall collect such evidence with this," he said.

Miss Crane examined it carefully. "Although we are in the pursuit of a most heinous murderer," she said, "I think our Police even at their least competent would be keen to confiscate this. The catalyst load is twice the legal limit – which makes it more likely this would simply explode in your hands – and I believe the projectiles are explosive. Also highly illegal."

She handed it back and he slipped it away.

"I see your training was not completely substandard," he said. "We are hunting something considerably stronger than the average human being, so while this… tool… is illegal, it's the only logical solution as far as weaponry goes."

As they moved through the patches of light and shadow, they were not challenged.

"Curfew is effective," observed Miss Crane.

"Self preservation is one of those few traits even stronger than the desire to cause mischief. It is also perfectly logical, as well as being convenient for our work."

In a few moments, they arrived at one of the elevator banks of the city's Central Hub. Mr. Moore pressed a button.

"Why down?" asked Miss Crane. "All the murders occurred in the city, in the support wires."

"Correction, Miss Crane – the murders did occur, but did not occur in the wires. The bodies were deposited in the wires, but the murders occurred somewhere else."

The doors opened and they stepped inside. Mr. Moore pressed a button for the lowest level.

"It's true there was no actual murder location determined," murmured Miss Crane. "That much blood would have been most significant."

Mr. Moore nodded as the elevator descended. "Exactly. You have just concluded what I concluded several days ago while preparing for this adventure."

"But the bottom level?" asked Miss Crane.

191

Mr. Moore offered her a look that under other circumstances, might have been considered withering, and said, "The farthest point from waste disposal, of course. It's perfectly logical."

"Ah," she said, and nodded.

After fifteen minutes, the elevator stopped and the doors hissed open. A wave of cold washed in over them both, carried by a stronger wind than topside.

"I've never been down here before," said Miss Crane, wrapping her arms around herself.

"Most women haven't," said Mr. Moore. "There's no reason for such – the underdecks are more exposed to the weather, and a place of difficult, dangerous work. Mistakes are invariably fatal. It's simply not safe for women."

They stepped out. The deck beneath their feet was solid, but it was obvious that there were no protective shrouds or walls at this level, nor the typical heating vents that kept topside so temperate.

Miss Crane stepped near the edge of the walkway and looked down. Another half-dozen levels seemed evident, but much less substantial than this one. This was the bottommost level that still boasted a solid floor. The rest were expanded metal, or metal mesh stretched between supports.

Wind whistled through the structure, low and moaning, but with gusts. Far, far below, she saw the tops of clouds, hypnotic and tan swirls of vapor.

"Don't fall," advised Mr. Moore.

She glanced, irritated, at him, but he was already sweeping his way down the platform. She caught up quickly, but it was indecorous.

"You think," she asked, "that the killer is down here?"

"I'm quite certain of it," he said. "It's only logical." He waved his arm around. "The underdecks are largely automated, and the few workers down here are strictly protective of their privacy."

"How could they have privacy down here?" Miss Crane looked around. Other than pipes and other solid tubes and conduits, the structure was basically open. "There are no walls, no shrouds, no nothing."

"That's what feeds it," he answered. "The very fact that they don't have privacy reinforces their need to maintain it, even if it's artificial. They don't talk to each other, except when necessary, and they don't interact socially. Not like civilized people, of course," he nodded upward.

They descended via a metal staircase to another level. This new level had a flooring of expanded metal. Miss Crane was fascinated by the surreal sense of hovering midair

Close Your Eyes – Tales from the Blinkspace

that the mesh afforded. She inhaled softly and looked around, as if seeing everything anew.

The underdecks were a place that seemed practically magical to her. She felt as if she were moving through a delicate crisscross of spun steel, of cable and rigging, of hoses, pipes, and girders.

She looked up and imagined the entire city of Nessez above her, held aloft by the impossibly high Lifters, and held in place by powerful engines deep in the heart of the structure that throbbed softly and eternally, and provided a heartbeat for every citizen.

She could, briefly, picture the entire city in her head, imagine it, from the highest point to the lowest point, and feel the flux of material to and from. She could sense the cycling and recycling of fluids through it like blood, the passage of people through it like cells, and the myriad of parts hanging onto the hovering skeleton like muscles from some great and wonderful creature. She could sense the trapships circling through clouds, collecting water and other vapors, and bringing them back to the collectors. She could sense the flash and pulse of steam, powering most of the city's machinery, each engine's heat catalyst a pinprick of energy.

It was an amazing city and she marveled at the combination of intricacy and—

"Miss Crane!"

She looked back. Mr. Moore was staring at her with a combination of curiosity and mild contempt.

"Are you well?" he asked. "Are you experiencing any sort of dizziness? Vertigo is a common problem for people new to these levels."

She shook her head slowly. "No, no dizziness," she said. "Just woolgathering."

"Well, stop it," he snapped. "I already have doubts about my logic in bringing a woman out on such a harrowing adventure – the very last thing I want is to find myself regretting it even more by bringing out someone for whom woolgathering is an occupational hazard."

He shook his head.

"I swear, the next time I decide to—"

Something crashed to the deck in front of them, dropped from high. Something heavy, that bounced oddly.

They both stared.

It was a man.

His clothing was shredded on his body, and his skin and hands streaked with blood and deep slashes. His left leg was twisted and broken.

Close Your Eyes – Tales from the Blinkspace

Despite his injuries, he rattled in a breath and tried to roll over.

"Are you... can we help you?" asked Miss Crane.

His eyes flew open. One was deeply bloodshot – practically black. He waved her away.

"Run!" he croaked. "Run before it sees you! Hide!" He coughed and bright blood came out.

Up above, she heard something moving. Something big, heavy. Something impossible. She backpedaled quickly, but there was nowhere to hide.

Mr. Moore pushed her around and the two of them ran a few steps away before the man's screams stopped them.

Although they spun reflexively, it was Miss Crane's instinct to pull Mr. Moore down, such that the two of them crouched, exposed, but small.

A thing dropped down to the platform above the man, who continued screaming. A thing like a crab, with eight legs and heavy armor plates covering its body. A thing with razor sharp claws that reached out to the man, who writhed and screamed on the deck. The claws grasped him and held him steady. His screams continued.

In horror, Constance watched blood and effluvia filter down through the deck, some pattering on the grill below, and the rest falling away, falling forever into the deep clouds.

The thing bent its head down toward the man. Slowly, the head peeled open, the armor unrolled and an inner head showed itself – a pink, soft, toothed and fearsome head. The broad mouth opened and engulfed the man in one bite.

As he was stuffed into its throat, his screams muffled, and then stopped entirely.

Then, the head raised back up, and the armor plates slid back across.

"I'm not sure even an overloaded projectile could penetrate that carapace," Mr. Moore whispered. "We may have missed this chance, but perhaps, er, what are you—"

Miss Crane had extracted from his coat pocket the weapon. By the time he realized what she was doing, her foot was already raised, leg coiled behind it. She kicked hard, and because he was already unbalanced, Mr. Moore tumbled a good ten feet before coming to a halt near the base of the creature.

Instantly the claws whipped out and pinned him.

"Miss Crane!" he cried out. "What have you done? Miss Crane!"

He writhed, but as with his predecessor, there was no hope.

Again, the head slid out, unpeeled itself, and the cavernous mouth opened.

Close Your Eyes – Tales from the Blinkspace

Mr. Moore screamed.

Almost unheard next to his scream was a hissing pop.

The thing's head punched backwards a few inches, and its emerald eyes rolled in confusion.

There was a deep and powerful sound, a kind of whump, and instantly, from the neck of the beast, a slurry of red erupted. The head fell forward, pushed from behind. The claws fell from the still-screaming Mr. Moore, who was then instantly covered in the filth and debris from inside the monster.

It fell to the cold metal deck, completely dead, and practically empty.

Constance looked down at her hand. As expected, the overcharged weapon had blown itself to pieces, most of which had fallen to the deck around her. Although she had all her fingers, they were black and she could not feel the lower two.

She tore a strip of cloth from her petticoat and bound her hand, which was starting to throb slightly. She stepped over to the corpse.

Coiled up with it, the figure of Mr. Moore stirred, moaned, and struggled up.

"We… we could have come back," he muttered thickly.

"I doubt it," she said. "I think it would have seen us anyway, and surely killed one or both of us, and you might have fired your single shot uselessly against its shell."

Slowly, he nodded. "I probably would have," he said.

"I needed another opportunity to penetrate," she said, "And I am a much better shot than you, plus a less enticing target, being small and female. Apparently, it is accustomed to feeding on males."

He glared at her for a long minute, still recovering his breath. Then, he brushed enough gore from himself to be able to move somewhat freely. He was doused.

He straightened himself and reappraised her more carefully.

"You don't need to say it," he growled. "I recognize it as quite the logical choice."

END

Appetite

When you're hungry, you'll let anything fill up your belly...

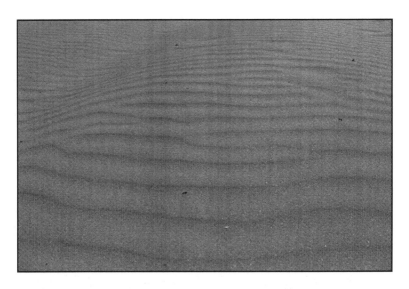

We're hungry.

There may be no more accurate an epitaph for the human race.

Initially, we shared the hunger of our fellow animals – food, shelter, mates – but our hunger grew to match our brains. We hungered for knowledge, we hungered for land, we hungered for power. More, more, more.

This is why I spent the last two decades of my life with a shovel in one hand and maps in the other. This is why I've spent the last years of my life under this damnable desert sun.

My belief that fossil fuels are – in all respects – a dead resource and not to be counted on endears me to the environmental sort at the same time it creates enemies for me of those who helm the oil-hungry behemoth of industry. But any compatriots I might find among the ranks of the Green as quickly disown me when I declare with equal vehemence the inefficiency of solar, geothermal, hydroelectric, wind, and other sundry power sources, not to mention the suicidal push for nuclear energy. These are measly bread to our ravening hunger. With all due respect to my colleagues, they have no clue as to humanity's hunger.

I understand it. I understand the blind need for more of everything that has been the defining characteristic of this species since one cell enveloped another in the pre-life ooze. I understand that no finite energy lasts long against the unstoppable force of the seething, breeding, hungry people who would dig it up, suck it from the skies and the ocean, or tease it from the atom. Distressingly, all forms of natural energy seem to be, in one tragic fashion or another, finite.

This leaves the supernatural, a notion of mine that has alienated my peers for more than a decade. I can understand such revulsion. Had I not been forced by my previous employer to take a four-week sabbatical, I would be as skeptical as my fellows in this respect.

For my sabbatical, I was exiled to places lacking technology, computers, modems, phones, even electricity. The country I chose was not popular amongst vacationing intellectuals and the region within even less so. This village had one thing however, a remnant of past ecumenical influence, which piqued my interest. It had a library. A small and uninteresting library, containing mostly family records.

I searched those shelves like a madman, hungry for intellectual stimulation after only five days from home. Then, high on a crumbling shelf, in a corner anyone could have missed, I saw the scroll.

I knew it was old the moment I touched it, the moment my trembling hands opened it. The ancientness of the village and the library paled in comparison to this fabulous treasure. It felt older than Time.

It was a diagram. A diagram and a map and an explanation. The language components were iconic, of a type I'd never seen before, but easily understood (opening previously unsuspected doors on the sciences of linguistics and neurology, but these are not my field).

The vehicle however wasn't nearly as interesting to me as the contents. The diagram, map, and explanation leaped into my brain – it was exactly what I had been looking for!

Energy. A limitless, clean pure source of energy. This ancient document revealed in a few eyeblinks the Holy Grail. I do not choose that metaphor lightly, as this wasn't any source of energy, but Primal Energy, the force behind the movement of stars and the tumbling of sand grains, creating and sustaining the very fabric of time and space. Limitless Energy.

My breathing must have changed enough to capture the attention of the librarian, who whipped the scroll away from me with a cry of dismay. Although I have a passing grasp of the local dialect, his obvious curses were beyond me. He rushed me out onto the dry, silent street and slammed and bolted the door behind me.

Thinking I had overstayed the library's hours, I planned to return the next morning. Although much of the scroll and diagram still burned in my memory, the map remained just out of reach. The next morning I was greeted by the smoking remains of the library's foundations. At the same time, my language skills deteriorated, because no one seemed to understand me, and all the locals insisted there had been no library at all, but only a long-abandoned abattoir. I left that day.

Close Your Eyes – Tales from the Blinkspace

For the next ten years, I traveled, searching for landmarks. I recalled the map details with stunning clarity, but the greater location was still unknown. I was searching for a specific blade of grass, but I had no idea in which meadow to start!

My colleagues ostracized me, convinced I had fallen prey to some sort of madness which drew me to desert pilgrimages. Their amusement shifted to tolerance, then to disgust and indifference, and the remaining time I spent searching without the benefit of patron or the burden of detractor.

Then, ten years after seeing the map, I found it. The location. Had I never seen that map, but stood blindly on this spot, I could not mistake this nexus of energy, this eternally deep wellspring.

Now I had to dig.

Spurned by my associates in the energy industry, I had found support in the company of numerous mystics, seers, and spiritualists I met during my search. One in particular was positioned well enough to respond to my fervent pleas for help, sending a small team of diggers and equipment.

The diggers spoke enough English such that I could direct them, but insufficient to inform me of their increasing dissatisfaction. When I arrived at the dig three weeks later, the sandy walls of the thirty-foot depth were shored up with timbers, but no workers to be found.

I telephoned my benefactor, reporting the truancy and was informed that my loan of laborers was terminated. My previous life's high profile, apparently, was threatening the confidentiality of my patron. Further dealings were out of the question and I was told to not call back. My puzzlement shifted to anger, then fury.

This was ludicrous – we were too close to stop now!

I leaped into the pit, my manic state lending me strength, and seized a pick. I dug for hours, my fingers swelling and blistering against the pick and my back growing cherry red in the desert sun. Five hours passed and the shadow of the pit wall slid across my body, cool and soothing, and then, moments later, I struck rock.

In three hours, between my fingers and the shovels, I had cleared away a room-sized area of grooved stone. My cracked fingernails and numb fingers understood the geography better than I did and eventually, I revealed a great radial pattern, ancient as Time, and without a doubt the base of the Nexus.

I had found it.

I paused, reading the iconography, the strange twisted cuneiform etched deeply into the bedrock. It was beautiful and primordial and I spared my erstwhile patron a harsh chuckle – he had given up so close that it was pure comedy. This was mine – all mine. I would be the sole conduit for the greatest source of energy mankind has ever enjoyed.

Close Your Eyes – Tales from the Blinkspace

I climbed to the top of the excavation to retrieve my camera, to document this fantastic artifact. At the lip, I paused while gazing at the great relief below, the fabulous and intricate images and curves. I could feel the anticipatory thrum from beneath that stone. Ecstatic, I turned and, for a moment, stared dumbly at the automobile that had not been parked there when I started digging.

I gaped at this peculiar appearance, and it was sheer blind luck that I noticed the blurring from the corner of my eye and moved my head when I did.

The crowbar smashed into my shoulder and my arm detonated with pain. I fell back, away from my attacker, stumbling to the ground.

He advanced, murder in his eyes. In that exact second, I recognized also the face of my benefactor, my patron. Instantly, his entire scheme was laid bare to my mind, his insistence on the use of a mobile telephone, his cagey replies as to his whereabouts, and the actual reason he removed the workers. It was not because he had become disillusioned with the project, or worried about his reputation. On the contrary, he believed in it as thoroughly as I had. He simply chose to accept the aphorism that two men can keep a secret, as long as one of them is dead.

He swung the crowbar at my head, and I rolled sideways, my arm dangling useless. He was no assassin, but I was completely unarmed and exhausted. Who knew how long he had planned this from above the pit, watching and waiting?

I knelt and jumped at him, grappling with my good arm. We spun. I forgot how close we were to the edge of the pit.

I have read conflicting reports. Sometimes, people claim that the time they spend falling during accidents is too short a time to think, that perhaps their brain seizes up in an effort to belay the horror of such a drop. Another school of thought holds that only in such times do we appreciate the speed of our own brains as the amount of time we spend suspended stretches to a terrifying duration. I, however, am a scientist, first and foremost. I know that our bodies accelerate at thirty-two feet per second and that the time passing between our departure from the lip and our impact was precisely the amount of time necessary – no more, no less.

I am sure we were both severely damaged in that fall, but between the adrenalin and the panic, I doubt we were ready to feel any effects.

We grappled at the floor of the pit, our blood mixing in the grooves beneath. I worked my feet and legs under my attacker and shoved. He tumbled away and scrabbled to his feet.

The crowbar fell next to my head. Armed!

As he lunged, I swung the bar against his head. He cartwheeled to the left and fell hard. His body twitched, but didn't move. One blood-filled eye glared at me as his mouth worked around broken teeth.

Close Your Eyes – Tales from the Blinkspace

Crowbar in hand, I staggered to the center of the Nexus. All the designs and diagrams pointed to a single circle, a smooth plate three inches in diameter. The center. The Nexus.

I slammed the crowbar against it.

"Mine!" I screamed at him.

He twitched and tried moving toward me, but his body was no longer in his control.

"Mine, mine, mine!" I punctuated each with a strike of iron against the stone. At the third strike, the stone gave way, cracked, and dropped away, revealing light beneath. I fell to my knees and looked.

I saw fire. Not magma, because I know what that looks like, nor any fire of mankind. I saw a roiling, burning, living flame. No surface, no fuel, just a void filled with storms of fire.

In each wave of flame, in each curling tendril of plasma, I saw the figures, each sheathed in tongues of flame, each being burned and blackened, screaming mouthlessly, kicking, spinning, twitching, contorted in agony.

"Now you see," croaked a voice. I raised my head. He had dragged his broken body closer. "Now you see it all. It showed you what you wanted to see. It would show you anything! "

He collapsed.

"Why?" I demanded. "Why reveal so much energy? Why hand over a Universe full of limitless energy?" I shook him.

His lips quivered. I pressed myself close.

"It doesn't matter why" he whispered. "Only that they convinced you to do so. You've given them everything. Everything." He died.

I stared at his lifeless, bloody face.

The Nexus hissed, and I saw, from the lip, cracks spreading like hungry fingers, razoring the sky with umber light.

I scrambled back, avoiding my section falling in. His body slid, and then dropped into the maelstrom.

I ran to the ladder. The screaming, growing louder, had changed once the body dropped in, as if human flesh was an instantly acquired taste. Agony was replaced by a different sort of cry, a cry I'd become familiar with for decades: hunger.

I climbed, crazily, and ran, while the Nexus grew, swallowing up the ancient stone floor that had bound it, swallowing the excavation, gobbling up the sand at the tops of the pit. I dared a glimpse over my shoulder in time to see our two automobiles drop

Close Your Eyes – Tales from the Blinkspace

into the light. When I turned back to my run, I saw the land before me shifting and tilting up, high, high above my head for miles, forming a ramp, sending everything into the growing maw.

I had been tricked.

The Nexus was a prison and the stones were warnings and in my greed and stupidity, I had read my own meaning into them.

The ground tilted more beneath me and now I felt the sliding. Instinctively, I scuttled backwards, but I knew it was useless.

I saw them rise from the pit, rise on wings of flame and clouds of fury, and they saw the world before them and they saw me and they screamed and I knew nothing would stop them. Nothing would ever stop them.

I slid, with the sand, into the gulf.

END

Making the Deal

I try to make it a rule never to have characters being dumb. I know, sometimes one has issues one has to deal with, such as being forced to attend a private school that only specializes on Bronze Age teachings, but that's different. I'm talking about really thinking, really considering what's going on. I hope "Making the Deal" helps somehow rectify a great imbalance...

I am dying in the desert. It's been four days since I've had food and water, and honestly, I'm a little shocked I've lasted this long.

Assuming I have.

It may be that I'm already dead and don't know about it. Or maybe I miscounted the nights. That makes sense. Counting is a little hard for me right now. Pretty much everything else is, too.

The first couple of days, I could feel the sun overhead. Could feel its heat. That was back when I thought I had a chance. I don't now, and I think the sun knows this too, so it's not bothering with an ostentatious display.

It's just killing me.

I can feel my life leaving my body, like sand through a colander. The shape's still here, but it's just emptier and emptier. No one's coming, no one's going to show up with water, or medicine, or shade.

I'm not even mad about it anymore. I used to be, back when the car broke down and all the other things went wrong, and I thought there was a town just over the hills, and I found out there wasn't a town at all, but more hills, more rocks, more dry heat. And

Close Your Eyes – Tales from the Blinkspace

then I found this bit of broken rock, this mean patch of almost-shade in the middle of an oven, and I collapsed here, and decided that this was the place. After that, being mad just made no sense. Or maybe I replaced it with a different kind of mad. The kind of mad that a person needs when there really isn't anything else they can do.

That kind of mad seems to have settled very comfortably on me as I lay here in the deep desert, alone, with my life evaporating from my body.

I'm not used to feeling alone. I have a big family – six brothers and two sisters – each with their loads of kids, and noises and games. So, I've not ever been really alone.

Until now.

Now, this felt like a sort of quiet that I've never felt before. It felt like the kind of peace that a man always wanted, but never had the–

"Hello."

–but never had the... uh...

"Are you still alive?"

I opened my eyes.

There was a snake.

"Oh, good. I'm glad you're still alive," he said. "That's great."

I just blinked at him. I knew this had to be the end of the line. A talking snake.

He came a little closer. Then he looked me up and down.

"Oh, you're pretty bad," he said. "What's it been – three days? Four?"

I tried to speak, but my lips only rasped as my jaw moved a little.

He looked at my mouth, then back into my eyes. "Try again."

Suddenly, my mouth felt wetter and cooler. My tongue could move. I think I could even speak. "What are you doing here?" I whispered.

"Yeah, that helped a lot." He nodded at me. "Sorry, though. It's only good for a little while, but I figured you would rather talk."

"How did you do this?" I asked. I tried to move, but my arm just felt numb.

"Oh, it's only your mouth," he said. "It's kinda complicated, but think of it as a tradeoff. There's enough moisture in your body to run your mouth, but not much, really. So, you can talk, but it's not going to last very long, and, well, there are other downsides which I doubt will matter by this time tomorrow."

He coiled up on my chest.

203

Close Your Eyes – Tales from the Blinkspace

"You really are a mess, by the way. What's your name?"

"Thomas. What's yours?"

"Oh, man, I keep forgetting you guys exchange names. Uh, well, my name's kinda tricky. I'm pretty sure you can't pronounce my real name, but I can tell you what they call me."

"I told you my name," I said. It was a very strange moment. Dying in the desert and I'm arguing with a snake.

"Well, okay. Try it out. They call me Bob."

"Bob? Just Bob?"

"See, you're mangling it."

"But how else do you pronounce 'Bob'?"

"It's okay, Thomas, really. I appreciate you trying, but it's just not going to work. Besides, there's only you and me here, so we don't need to worry about names, anyway."

"But you asked me first."

"Yeah, old social grease. My bad."

We stared at each other a moment. I was a little wary of the talking snake on my chest, but as far as talking snakes go, he seemed legit.

"I'm not used to snakes talking," I said.

"They don't," said Bob. "What do talking snakes have to do about anything?"

"Well, you're a snake and you're talking."

"What?!" He reared up a bit, completely startled.

He turned his head around and reviewed the length of his body. Then he turned back to me.

"Don't flinch, Thomas. I need to see something."

He zoomed in, his head inches away from my face. He stared into my eyes.

"I look like a snake," he said. "Wow, that's kinda cool."

"You're not a snake?" I asked.

He pulled back and shook his head. "I just look like one. I'm… I'm something else."

"Something else that looks like a snake?"

Close Your Eyes – Tales from the Blinkspace

He rolled his eyes a bit. "Thomas, what do you know about dimensions? One dimensional, two dimensional and so on?"

"Not much."

"Okay, well, let me explain it this way. If I showed you a piece of paper, you would know it was a piece of paper, right?"

"Yeah."

"But if I turned it sideways, it wouldn't look like paper, it would just be a single line. You would only see the edge, so it would look like, oh, a piece of thread or something."

"I'd see the paper, though," I said.

"You gotta work with me, here. Pretend you only have one eye. You would only see the edge, right."

My brain wasn't working so well after all the dying of thirst it had been doing, and right now, what with a talking snake and all, I think this was more trouble than I needed. "Okay, sure, yeah."

"Then that's me. I'm like a piece of paper that you're only seeing edgewise. In my case, the edge looks like a snake."

"But I can see all around you."

"Well, yeah, you kinda have to extrapolate a bit, Thomas. A paper is three dimensional, but you only see two dimensions when it turns sideways. I'm four dimensional, but to you, I appear 'sideways' in only three dimensions."

"I don't get it."

"It's okay, you don't have to worry about it. Just pretend I'm a snake."

"Who talks?"

"Who talks."

"Okay."

Again, we stared at each other for a moment. The heat was making me a little dizzy. Probably a lot dizzy, but this was a little dizzy that was new on top of the big dizzy that had been around long enough for me to get my dizzy legs.

"So, why are you here?" I asked. "Why is there a four dimensional snake on my chest, talking with me?"

Bob looked pensive. I hadn't ever seen a snake look pensive before, so that was interesting.

Close Your Eyes – Tales from the Blinkspace

"I need a favor," he said.

"I'm kinda low on resources."

"Not this one."

"What is it?"

"Just a little blood."

I stared at him. "What do you need blood for?" I asked.

"Nothing."

I tried to shake my head, but it didn't work.

"I told you, that's not going to work."

"I know, I forgot."

"So, do you mind if I, y'know, nip off with a little blood?"

"Yes. Yes I do. You need to tell me why you want it."

"Does it matter? I mean, it's not as if you're going to be using it for much longer."

"Then why ask? Why not wait until I die?"

"Because it doesn't work that way."

"What doesn't work that way?"

"Look, it's really complicated. All that matters to you is whether or not you're cool losing a little. It's no big deal."

"No, you can't say it's no big deal, because it is. If it wasn't a big deal, you wouldn't be asking me. I might be dying, but I'm not stupid. If it's important enough that you have to do this protocol thing and ask me, then it's important. And if you're not going to tell me why, then I'm most definitely not going to agree to it."

"Now you're just being a dog in the manger. It's not much. Just a few drops."

"You're not listening to me – the more you try to convince me there's no value in it, the more you're convincing me that there is. You're like a used car salesman. Next thing you're going to do is probably threaten me."

The snake was silent a moment.

"Not necessarily."

"Ha!"

"I don't see what the big deal is. Why can't you just say yes?"

206

Close Your Eyes – Tales from the Blinkspace

"Because a talking snake is trying to convince me to say yes. Whether you're really some four-dimensional thing, or some supernatural thing, or whatever, you need some of my blood. Or maybe not even my blood, just someone's blood, and I happen to be handy. Either way, you're not getting a thing out of me until you start telling me what I want to know."

Whatever he'd done to me to let me talk seemed to be fixing my brain a bit, too.

He shook his head. "You know, we could have worked this out, you and me. This didn't have to get all ugly. We were talking. We were chatting. We had a few laughs. And then you started questioning it. You humans always question things. Why can't you just let it be? Why can't you just live in the moment? Why can't you just be grateful that you've had an opportunity that no one else on Earth has ever had?"

I did my best to raise a doubtful eyebrow, but it didn't work. I think it almost worked, because the snake noticed it.

"What opportunity is that?" I asked.

"Here you are out in the middle of the desert, you're practically dead already, and suddenly you can talk and think. It's like you went from a completely miserable near-death experience to being almost human again, if even for a little while. That's got to be worth something, right?"

"Presumably it's worth the pleasure of my conversation. We made no agreement. If you did something to allow me to talk, that was on your own nickel. I don't owe you for that – it was a pure favor."

"You honestly think that was a favor? Just something I give to anybody all the time? You don't think that cost me something?"

"I don't care," I said. "You're trying to manipulate me emotionally by using guilt, so that I'll let you take blood, but it's not going to work for the simple reason that I know I'm going to die anyway. I have nothing to lose by being hyperfocused on this situation. I'm not distracted by anything, Bob."

"Maybe you aren't distracted, but you're not thinking about me, about what this is doing to me."

"Absolutely correct – no distractions. If you truly are experiencing discomfort, it's either something you did to yourself, or something done to you by someone more powerful than you. That is not my concern. I'm glad to have the chat, and it's certainly interesting, but there is no deal between us. You have no power over me, Bob."

The snake winced. "I wish you'd stop trying to say my name," he said. "It sounds so wrong when you say it."

"That's what you get for giving me the wrong name."

"I didn't give you the wrong name. You just can't pronounce my whole name."

207

Close Your Eyes – Tales from the Blinkspace

"Not being nearly dead and all, no, but I can talk much better now, you have to admit."

"Yeah, I've noticed. So much for gratitude."

"I haven't said no, have I?"

There was a pause while the snake ran over his recent memory. Instinctively, his tongue slipped out, but instead of flickering like a snake tongue really would, this tongue slowly ran along his lower lip.

"You've got a point," he said slowly. "You haven't actually said no."

"But if I understand you right, not saying no isn't good enough. I would have to openly agree, wouldn't I?"

After a pause, the snake dipped his head. "You would have to agree," he said. "That's how it works."

"I thought so. And you haven't given me good reason to do so, so I guess that puts us back where we were before, Bob."

Again, the snake winced.

"Why do you want my blood?"

"I can't tell you."

"I'm going to assume that means you won't. If you really honestly couldn't, you would have said so immediately."

The snake looked away, and I glanced down at his tail, which suddenly started twitching like an angry cat's tail.

He turned back.

"I've about had it with your games," he said. He opened his mouth and in the brilliant milky whiteness of his mouth, four long fangs unfolded. Each one oozed thick yellow venom. He made sure I saw that, and then he closed his mouth.

"Now this is how it's going to be. I've been a decent sort and offered you a chance to spend your last few bits of life engaged in an interesting conversation. I could have left you alone to die out here, but no, I thought maybe we could make a deal. And if not a deal, then maybe you just might be the teeniest tiniest bit grateful for those last few minutes. Is that too much to ask?"

"You're the one asking for blood, and you're asking me what I think is too much to ask? I think if you want to convince me to parley with you, Bob, you're going to have to use more honey than that."

Angrily, his tail swished around and he opened his mouth. His head shimmered a bit, and I was pretty sure it wasn't just the heat doing it. The fangs looked significant.

208

Close Your Eyes – Tales from the Blinkspace

"If you kill me, I'm of no use to you," I said, as smoothly and quickly as I could.

"You're of no use to me now," he hissed.

"On the contrary, Bob, I'm the only friend you have around here. I got what you want and need, and no one else around's got it. I don't know exactly how that whole fourth dimension thing works, but I have a feeling you're more stuck out here than I am. Am I right?"

Bob didn't talk, but I could tell he was churning.

"Am I right, Bob?" I asked again.

"Stop that!" he said. "My name's–" and he sprayed a salad of syllables at me.

I repeated it several times in my mind. At the moment, my mind wasn't on anything else, so it was a lot easier than I expected.

"Okay, fine, I won't call you Bob," I said. "But I think, if you're going to withhold information from me, then you can expect me to drive a harder bargain."

"And what do you have to bargain with anyway?" he asked. "You'll be dead in an hour or so – probably less."

"Maybe, maybe not. You fixed me to be able to talk, right? Seems like you might be able to do more than that."

"Making you talk was a lot of work."

"You were willing to invest that work. What if you were willing to invest a little more?"

"Like what?"

"Like being able to move around. Being able to stand up and walk. Being able to get out of here, maybe even back to the road."

"No way. That's an enormous amount of effort."

"Oh, okay, well, if that's the case, then I suppose we're not too likely to be able to work out a deal."

"Surely there's something else?"

I closed my eyes. "I think, unless you've got something else to add, we've kinda come to a standstill on this conversation. No offense, but if that is the case, I'd like to spend my last few minutes just enjoying the silence."

For a moment, I truly thought he was going to bite me. Then I felt him lunge off my chest and heard him swishing away in the sand. "Fine!" he said. He continued away until he was out of hearing range.

209

Close Your Eyes – Tales from the Blinkspace

I waited.

After several minutes, there was a tickle on the back of my neck and I knew he was there, but I didn't say anything. I just waited.

Eventually, he spoke.

"Would that be enough?" he asked.

I tried to look surprised, maybe it even worked. "You came back."

"I had to think about it," he said. "You have no idea how hard that is to do."

"You're right, I have no idea at all. For all I know it would be a piece of cake."

"It's not a piece of cake."

"Well, there's no way for me to know that, is there? You're not telling me the truth about the blood, and frankly, once a supernatural creature shows some sort of supernatural power, I'm pretty much willing to believe it can do anything."

"I'm not supernatural. I'm perfectly natural. Just four dimensional."

"Whatever. It doesn't matter. Again, I have no way to know if you're telling me the truth or not. All I have is your word, and your willingness to deal."

I saw his tail twitch at that last bit, but it was the eager twitch, not the angry twitch.

"So, would you do it?" he asked. "Would we have a deal if I did what you asked?"

"What did I ask?"

"You know what you asked," he said.

"I know, but I think it's important to hear you say it, too. I think it's one of those things that's very important in deals like this."

I knew snakes didn't have eyelids, so it normally wouldn't have unnerved me being stared at by a snake that wasn't blinking, but somehow, I got the impression that the assessing stare was exactly supposed to seem like an unblinking stare.

"You want to be able to move around. To stand up and walk. To get out of here. Maybe all the way back to the road."

"Strike that last 'maybe'. I want to be able to get back to my car. No 'maybe' about it."

"And then you'll let me have some blood?" he asked.

"How much do you need?"

"Just a little, just a few drops will be enough."

"Uh-huh. Well, I think that depends on how good you are at what you do."

Close Your Eyes – Tales from the Blinkspace

"I'm very good."

"So you say, but so far as I can tell, the best thing I can do is talk."

There was a silence, and in that silence, I felt something happen inside me. Something that felt a little like a flood, and a little like food and a little like good beer and a lot like life. Exciting, thrilling, wonderful life.

He slithered off my chest.

"Go ahead," he said. "Stand up. Walk around. When I tell you I'm good, I mean it."

Gingerly, I stood up. I was a bit dizzy, but it wasn't too bad, and I could feel more and more of my mind and body clearing.

"You already look better," he said. "I'll bet you're in better shape than when you came out here."

I scanned the horizon.

"Which way's the car and the road?" I asked.

"No, no, no, we had a deal."

"When you made me talk, you admitted it was stealing water from the rest of me. Who knows where you're stealing this strength from, but I think, seeing as how we both agreed that I included getting to the car, then that would be an excellent opportunity to make sure I'm not going to just suddenly drop dead in five minutes."

"You won't," he said. "This was different than the talking thing."

"Nevertheless, it's still your turn to lead the way toward my renewed faith in our friendship."

Oh, now I could tell he was angry. His tail twitched very differently.

"Then I can have some blood?" he asked.

"Ask me when we get there," I said.

Like a peculiar reptilian jet, he took off, streaking through the sand.

I could keep up with him, but doing so forced me into a bit of a trot. He was faster than a real snake.

During our trek, he kept silent, and I also had a lot to think about. I had a lot of practicing to do. And a lot of remembering, hoping what I was remembering was real and not just made up shit.

Considering I was dancing around a deal with a talking snake, I had to assume that there were all sorts of things that I would have discarded three days ago as foolish that I was perfectly willing to consider now.

211

Close Your Eyes – Tales from the Blinkspace

A lot of people don't think that far ahead. A lot of people, when faced with something, keep clinging to what they thought previously. I've mostly seen it in movies, of course, because contact with the supernatural isn't very common. That's what the 'super' part of 'supernatural' meant, after all.

So, although on the outside, I appeared to be jog-walk-jogging to keep up with an eager snake hungry for my blood, on the inside, I was sifting and sorting and re-arranging a lot of the thoughts and ideas and mental models that used to make sense. I needed to understand this, or I was going to get screwed. I could just tell.

Four hours later, I saw my car, as we crested a hill. A red Pinto. Don't laugh – it actually runs pretty well for what it is. When I'm not dying, I'm a handy guy.

"Okay," he said. "We're there."

I knew I'd been double-timing it for four hours, and it was a scorcher of a day, but I was hardly winded. I was pretty happy about this. And pretty cocky.

"Nope," I said. "We're here. The car's there. We need to be there."

I kept going. This time, he followed me.

The car was just how I left it. I dug the keys out of my pocket and opened the door. Fished around in the glovebox.

"Okay, I think it's time," said the snake.

"Hey, I couldn't trouble you for a full tank of gas, could I?"

He glared at me and I laughed. "Just kidding. Hey, you should come in out of the sun. Plenty of room inside."

He slid close to the doorway, but stopped just at it.

"It's okay," I said. "You can come in."

His head came a little closer, then he backed away.

"Nah, too chilly for me," he said. "I like it out in the sun."

"Suit yourself."

"What about our deal?"

"Oh yeah, we were going to talk about that."

I patted my arms. Ran my fingers through my hair. "I think you did a pretty neat job. In fact, I think you even fixed a few things up from before."

"Yeah, that can happen," he said. "So, are we good?"

I stepped out of the car.

212

Close Your Eyes – Tales from the Blinkspace

"You still haven't told me what you needed it for," I said.

Hands in my pockets, I started walking around the snake in a big circle. Had to do this carefully. Well, assuming it mattered. The past four hours taught me to open my mind to practically anything, but doing that means all kinds of other bullshit creeps in that means nothing. I think, all things considered, it made more sense to believe everything I'd ever heard was correct. If it wasn't, no big loss. If it was, didn't hurt to cover my bases.

Thoroughly.

"And that got me thinking," I said. "I think I was right in thinking you were trapped here. But not here in the desert. I think a different kind of here."

"Does it really matter?" he asked.

"Of course it does. If you're not going to tell me what's going on, I have to figure it out for myself. That's a lot of work. And I'm lazy, so when someone makes me work hard for no reason, then I get annoyed at them."

He twitched the angry twitch.

"I don't want to play anymore," he said. "Do you agree that I've fulfilled my end of the bargain or not?"

"Do you see any clouds in the sky?" I asked. It was all I could think of.

Just as he looked up, I finished the circle. I crouched a few feet away from the edge.

I felt the air shift a bit and suddenly he looked down at me.

His mouth opened wide and he threw himself across the sand, fangs ready to–

He stopped in mid-air and bounced back from the edge of the circle.

Once more he tried, and once again, he bounced back.

He coiled up and glared at me, then started forward more slowly, nose close to the sand.

"What's this?" he asked.

I reached into my pocket and emptied the last few screws out. I held one up. "I had a lot in the glovebox," I said. "A little rusty, but iron gets that way."

He slammed against the circle again. For an invisible wall, this was pretty sturdy!

He spun and tried the circle at several spots, and each time it smacked him back down.

"I can get through this eventually," he hissed at me. "You don't really know what you're doing."

Close Your Eyes – Tales from the Blinkspace

"I can admit that. I'm kinda guessing, like I said. You wouldn't cross the threshold of my car, but I invited you, so I figured it had to be the iron. Looks like I guessed right."

He writhed some more, trying different spots.

"Tell me why you're trapped here?" I asked.

"I'm not!"

"Of course you are. You're trapped and you need blood to go home. But why are you trapped here?"

"How are you doing this?! How are you knowing these things?!"

"I told you, I'm guessing, but it all makes a lot of sense. So, tell me why."

"No!"

"You like circles, don't you?"

"I can't. I won't!"

He was getting pretty agitated. A lot of sand was flying all over and I wasn't sure how long this was going to last. I'd dropped a lot of screws through the hole in my pocket, but I wouldn't be surprised if it still wasn't enough.

"Tell me, or you'll never, ever, ever get what you need!"

"No!"

"What are you afraid of? Are you afraid of me? Aren't I just a mortal? Just an ordinary sort of creature? Are you really afraid of me?"

He screamed and threw his entire body against the edge of the circle.

"You afraid I'm going to tell someone? Do you think I'm an idiot? Do you think anyone would believe me? Do you think I'm going to walk away and start blabbing?"

He stopped, then, panting. Hard to imagine a snake panting, but he was panting. And angry. And cunning. The cunning part had me worried.

As he spoke, I saw his tail slowly digging at the edge of the circle behind him. Okay, a multitasker. Let's see how long that lasts.

"I guess," he said, with a voice that suddenly felt like soft silk. "I guess you're right."

Shit – I knew he was going to kill me. Had been planning it from the very beginning. Little bastard.

"It was all politics," he said. "All politics and slithering, lying, deceitful cousins."

I noticed that tail working under the sand.

Close Your Eyes – Tales from the Blinkspace

"And you were innocent," I said.

"I was and I am, and I intend to prove it once I get back. Once I'm done here."

"Once you have my blood."

"Losing a few drops of blood is not going to kill you!" he nearly screamed.

The tail slipped under, past the border of the circle.

Still staring at me, still frothing a little, he laughed, and then like a wink, folded back onto himself and spiraled out through the hole.

He raised himself to his full height.

"It's time, Thomas. It's time for my blood."

I called out his name. His real name. I hoped I had it right.

He jerked once.

I called it out a second time.

Again, he jerked, but now I think he realized what I was about to do.

He lunged and I shouted his name a third time, hoping I was right. There had been an awful lot of guesses lately, and I was afraid I was going to run out of good ones.

He hung there, in midair.

Man, talk about lucky! Well, lucky and repeatedly practicing the name in my head for nearly four hours. Don't let anyone tell you cramming before an exam has no effect.

I could see him moving just a little, wiggling in the air, but stuck.

"No," I said. "A few drops of blood won't kill me, but the venom would, and that's what you've been planning all along."

He glared at me.

I picked up one of the screws from the desert floor.

"Okay, look, here's the deal." I poked at my thumb until I cut it enough to produce a few drops of blood. "I'll give you this of my own free will and then, in exchange, you will leave this world forever immediately, taking only yourself. You will never return, and never molest me or mine or this world ever again."

"I'm not going to make that kind of a deal with you," he hissed.

I pulled my thumb away.

"You're bound by name, and you want my blood. How do you want to play this?"

Close Your Eyes – Tales from the Blinkspace

Again, I saw him shift and blur. He hissed like a teakettle filled with rattlesnakes.

I held my thumb closer.

"It's real simple," I said. "You just have to ask how much you want the blood. I can turn around and start walking. Maybe there's a distance limit to a binding. But maybe not. Maybe you'll float along with me, like a pet."

I leaned in a little closer.

"Or maybe you'll take your winnings and go."

That was a very long and angry minute he glared.

"Fine." He opened his mouth.

I squeezed my thumb until a fat drop welled up, and shook it into his mouth.

There was a whoosh of wind and something that felt like red hot fury, and then he was gone. Just gone.

I picked all the screws back up and put them into the pocket without holes. You never know, what with all the weirdness around here.

Started walking back along the road. I'd find something eventually. Only a matter of time.

END

The Trail

Part of a writing marathon at the H. P. Lovecraft Film Festival, "The Trail" is inspired by Beth's request for something on the beach.

"Come see," said Beth. She pulled at Travis' arm.

"We're in the middle of something," he complained.

"You're barbecuing."

He waved the fork at her. "That's something, woman."

She planted her hands on her hips. "Look," she said, "I just want to show you what I found. It's not a big deal. It'll take five minutes. Tops."

"So, you're telling me you want your pork chop well done, right?"

She leaned close and said "If you don't come and spend a measly five minutes looking at what I found, then you will regret it this evening after you think you have fallen asleep in relative safety."

He turned the fire on the grill down.

"Okay, show me."

They walked through the sand, around the promontory of rock. Beth stopped, and gestured ahead.

"Well, is this cool or what?" she asked.

Close Your Eyes – Tales from the Blinkspace

Travis looked around. The ocean continued being oceany and the sand continued being sandy and the rock steadfastly remained a rock.

"What am I looking at?" he asked.

"The footprints!"

He looked down. A series of footprints trailed from up high and out of sight on the beach, all the way to the edge of the water, where the waves washed the sand flat. They were peculiar footprints, with a smooth single line wavering between them.

"What is that," he asked, "a bird?"

"I don't think so," she said. "I don't think it's a bird. What's that trailly thing?"

"Maybe a tail?"

"I don't know."

He stared at the footprints another few seconds. "Okay, well, we looked. Can we go back to eating, now?"

She sighed. "Okay."

A day passed.

"Travis," she said. "I need you to come and look at this."

"What? More footprints?"

"Well, more than footprints."

"We're about to play volleyball."

"Travis, this is important!"

He sighed heavily. "Show me," he said.

The footsteps were back but Beth walked higher up on the beach.

"Look," she said. "Someone's been digging."

The footsteps led up the beach and eventually stopped. Sand had been slightly mounded up in a broad, flat circle, and all around the circle, deep radial grooves carved the sand.

"See, someone's buried something," she said.

Travis nodded. "Yeah, it looks like that, but so what?" he asked. "Kids screw around on the beach all the time. They probably just buried beer bottles and used condoms."

"We should dig it up," she said. "What if there's something going on?"

218

Close Your Eyes – Tales from the Blinkspace

"There's nothing going on, love," he said, "and if teenagers buried something, the very last thing I want to do is dig it up."

"I don't think it was teenagers," she said. "I don't know what it is, but it gives me the creeps."

Travis looked at her. "Beth, if there's anything I'm less inclined to dig up than debris from a party of teenagers is something that would give me or you the creeps. Are you following my line of reasoning, here? I say we just leave it be. Let's go back and play volleyball."

As reluctant as she was, Beth found herself agreeing.

Volleyball was fun, but for the rest of the day she had a clouded, troubled look.

Another day passed.

They did not go to the beach. Beth sat in the kitchen and watched the sea all day.

"You okay?" Travis asked.

"I'm fine," she lied. She watched the waves and listened to them. "I'm just... melancholy."

He sat with her a moment. "You seem kinda sad," he said.

"Just watching the waves," she said. "It's weird how they're always going to come in, they're always going to be happening. We just drift into life, live for a while, and then drift out of life. We're ephemeral. Sometimes... sometimes that doesn't seem fair."

He gave her a hug and a pat on the arm. "I understand," he said. He watched the waves some more, then stepped away.

That evening, he found her reading, curled into her favorite chair.

"I found something I think you'll like," he said.

She looked up, over her glasses. "What is it?"

"It's a surprise. You'll like it. Get your shoes."

They walked for a while.

"It's really beautiful out," she said. The sky was unusually clear, considering how close they were to the ocean.

"Couldn't have asked for a better night," said Travis.

"Where are we going?" she asked.

"The beach."

"It's going to be chilly."

219

Close Your Eyes – Tales from the Blinkspace

"No, no, it'll be fine."

Beth was a little lost in the dark, but eventually, she saw a glow over the rocks, the orange dance of a bonfire.

"You guys have a fire?"

"It's a party," said Travis. "I thought it was about time for a nice night-time bonfire party."

She grinned at him. "You sweetie!" she said and soft-punched him in the arm.

They came around the corner of a rock outcropping.

Half a dozen people worked in the firelight, digging and scooping sand. A shallow pit was open, and in between the diggers, she saw something at the bottom, something that had been scraped clean. Something that glistened in the firelight, that pulsed and moved.

She turned, puzzled, to Travis, but he wasn't looking at her. He was looking in the pit, and his eyes danced in joy. He took her by the arm. "Come on, hon, this is going to be great!"

They stepped down into the pit. The others stepped aside and let them enter. Beth looked around. Each of them was smiling like Travis, was enraptured like Travis. She didn't know them, but she found herself smiling back at them, although it was an odd halting kind of smile.

As the crowd parted, she saw more clearly what lay there. It was a long milky sac, veined and pulsing. With a combination of fascination and horror, she saw that something inside was poking at the membrane, pushing against it, trying to get out.

"It's hatching," she said.

Travis rubbed her shoulders. "It's beautiful," he said.

She looked at him, and straightened up. "So now you believe me."

He nodded. "Of course. I've always believed you. I've always believed in you."

There was a pop and something flipped out through a tear in the membrane. Something pink and new and armored. A long chitinous leg, with a needle point at the end, anchored itself into the sand. Near the end of it, along one edge, short fingers waved bonelessly.

Beth stepped back, or rather would have stepped back, but for Travis behind her, arms on her shoulders.

"And as they spoke before us and they were spoken to before them, it was the time of the nines and the sixes and the threes. It was the time of the Convergence," he said.

"The Convergence," the others intoned.

220

Close Your Eyes – Tales from the Blinkspace

Except for Beth.

"What...? What's going on, Travis?"

"It's okay. This is the best part," he told her and turned her to watch.

Another arm tore its way free of the membrane, and yet a third. With three arms anchored into the beach, the whole thing heaved and bucked. The thing that came out rose above the sand, rose above the pit, rose high on three long legs. Two more legs unfolded from beneath its body, and also pistoned down to support it.

In the cool night air, its carapace hardened almost instantly, shifting from pink to a bright red, as oxygen flowed into it. Funnels alongside its torso siphoned air in and whooshed it out.

A long jointed arm unfolded from the front and wiped embryonic fluid and debris from the face. Mouth parts trembled to life and began whirling and cleaning themselves. The end of the arm flowered into a broad bulbous hand with a ring of fingers and ever-so-delicately, the fingers cleaned off the eyes.

The eyes were chips of onyx, deep inside armored brows. One-by-one, the arm cleaned all six of them.

"She was of all things," whispered Travis. "She was of all creatures, and all places and all times. She was of the sky and the air, of the aether and the world. She came to weep with us, to celebrate with us, to help us step forward from the shadows and into the light."

The thing shook away the last clinging bits of fleshy membrane. Finally, the egg sac, spent, fell from its abdomen and rolled in the sand.

Somehow, Beth knew by morning it would be gone, eaten by the scavengers, by the gulls and crabs and dogs of the beach's nightlife.

"And she came to feed," said Travis. "To know us in a way that no other creature, no other god could know us. She came to allow us to be a part of her such that we can be reborn in the images of both us and her in the future, that we shall not perish in the scouring."

She tried again to step back, but Travis was still behind her, as were some of the others.

The thing stretched its legs, and looked around. Even though its eyes had no features, Beth could feel a coldness where they passed, a sort of analyzing casual danger. They stopped wandering when they spied Beth.

"What?!" she cried out.

"Don't worry," said Travis. "I know it'll be painful now, and transitions are always hard, but you don't have to worry. This is your chance, Beth. This is how we're breaking your ennui, all of humanity's ennui. As her first piece of us, you will always

221

Close Your Eyes – Tales from the Blinkspace

be alive, always a part of every other egg she lays, of every other creature that comes forth. You'll always be here, always with us, as long as she lives."

Panicked, she turned to him, and he swiftly took her face in his hands and kissed her, passionately.

"I'm actually jealous," he whispered. "Love you, hon!"

There was a hissing, rattling above her head, and she felt something flow over her, something ringed with fingers, something with an impossible steely grip. Then she felt the sharper bits.

But only for a second.

END

The Picture of Myself

Part of a writing marathon at the H. P. Lovecraft Film Festival, "The Picture of Myself" is inspired by Lisa's request to have a photographer in the Israeli desert.

There is a moment when we awaken, when we are still one foot in the world of dreaming, but our flesh has arrived in the land of the waking. There is a moment when we are never quite sure what or who or where we are. I am in this moment, of this moment, and I do not know what, who, or where I am.

I feel sand against my cheek. This is a feeling I know, although I can't remember how I know. It's hot and dry, and smells... smells like a desert. It smells like a deep desert.

My memory reaches for something, and there is a hook, a place where it touches, and I remember.

I remember photos, images, models, posing. I remember fragments of faces, smiles, faded colors on glossy surfaces. I remember this in slivers, and each sliver flickers in and out of existence.

I reach up with a hand, feel the sand on my cheek, and brush it away. I touch my eyes. They are closed.

Close Your Eyes – Tales from the Blinkspace

I open my eyes and discover that this makes no difference. Either I am blind, or it is dark here, and in either case, there is no purpose for my eyes. I keep them closed – there is no telling what might spill into them.

Carefully, I stand. There is no ceiling above me in the dark, and I can sense this. If there is a ceiling, it's far above my head. I reach out sideways and my fingertips just touch rock.

The wall is rough hewn stone – I feel no brickwork. I cannot remember anything, yet, and cannot understand why, but at least the stone is solid under my hands, and that is something that feels right.

I sniff the air, inhaling deeply and trying to learn more. There is a smell, a dusty distant smell, and another memory comes, a memory built of other smells, of diesel and oil and exhaust. A smell of travel.

More fragments, more memories, but still only slices.

I move forward, because I must, because there's nothing else I can do, and I also move forward because it is impossible to simply be here. I have to keep moving forward, have to keep going toward my memories.

The ground becomes uneven, but I continue, and soon I am walking over rocks instead of smooth sandy floor.

I have another memory, a memory of falling, a memory of weightlessness, a memory of whirling in the darkness.

This triggers cascades of memories, and there is more to my life. I see faces, a man screaming at me, angry and puffing on a cigarette. I remember a vehicle, a Jeep. I called it a son of a bitch more than once as I struggled to make it obey my commands. I remember flashes, again, but this time the flashes aren't shattered pieces of memory, but memories of actual flashes. I remember machinery, and I remember equipment.

Equipment in my hands.

I stop walking and my hands come close to each other, and I feel something between them. Not an actual something, but as if there should be something between them. Something I can almost remember, but not quite.

The man who yelled gestures at the thing in my hand, as if it's somehow been the source of all his trouble.

Instinctively, I look down, but of course, there is no light, and I see nothing.

But this isn't true – I do see something. Almost. It shines in the dark without being visible at all, because it's not there. Nothing is in my hands, but a memory.

I continue walking, sliding along the wall, stumbling over rocks, and only after many minutes do I realize I am ascending, slowly climbing upwards, step-by-step. For some reason, this helps with my memories, helps bring the images together.

224

Close Your Eyes – Tales from the Blinkspace

He sent me here, the man did, and he was angry, although I still cannot remember why he was angry. I remember, though that this was part of his punishment. I remember now the thing that was in my hand, the box of black and chrome that was as much an extension of my will as my own hands.

My camera.

The sounds of my camera wash through my memory and bring with them more memories: models, and fashion, orphans, nuns, poor people, rich people.

I continue walking upwards, climbing now over rocks as high as my knees, twisting and turning my way around. The memories keep coming as I climb.

My nose twitches as a new scent comes across it, something organic, a whisper or hint of growth.

I remember more.

I remember my name. My name is Lee. I am a photographer. I have captured the souls of kings and queens, of lords and ladies. I have constructed a life of film and photography, of compositions of life and love and hate and despair.

I remember this, as I climb higher.

I remember too, that my editor is an ass, and that I have been sent here because he's angry at photos I've taken. Photos of his daughter and the lover he never realized she had. I am only the messenger, but sometimes the messenger is the one who gets shot.

Sometimes it's the messenger who is sent away to a distant ancient land. Sometimes it's the messenger who is punished by giving them a son of a bitch Jeep that breaks down frequently and is told to drive for hours out into the deep desert on the borderlands of Israel. Sometimes it's the messenger's job to be the sin eater.

But I'm better than that, I'm flexible, adaptive. I'm… I'm Lee Winter, and I am the world's greatest photographer, and I made my own story out here, found my own ruins in the desert, and took pictures of things that no human eye has seen for centuries. No one else could do it, no one else could have possibly captured these images except me and I did.

And I found something else.

The air blowing over me is cooler now, and I can smell night ahead and – apparently – above. There is still an organic smell, something not of the desert.

My memory feeds me more, and I remember the ruins, remember walking among the stones that towered high into the sky, that reached up from the desert sand like an offense against God himself. My camera whispered over and over, saving images for all eternity, and I walked in the silence.

But there was something else. Something I almost remember, but not fully. Something that makes me fragmentary. Something that stopped working.

Close Your Eyes – Tales from the Blinkspace

I am in the cool air now, and I feel the night sky above me. The stars are faint and vague, watery, as if lensed poorly, and I stumble out into an open place.

I have been here before. This place is a crux in my memory, and I have been here before.

My memory fragments, there is a discontinuity. I trip and fall, and feel myself plow into the hot night sand, feel it filling my mouth. I spit it out, and instinctively reach for my camera, but I cannot find it. I look around and even though seeing is difficult in the dark, I do finally see it, a yard away, half-buried in the sand.

I reach for it with one hand, and pull it toward me. It feels both alien and familial, and I wrestle still with a memory, a memory of movement, of shifting sand, of something dark against the dark, of a figure, of a struggle.

I cannot bring it to the forefront, but I feel a terror that I cannot figure out, a sense of dread and exhilaration, all at the same time.

I stand, and look closely at my camera, and the sand and… at the sand and the… the something else on it.

I step backward and again fall, tripping over a rock, but as I land, and my head is shaken, the webs of memory clear away and I see more. I see the shapes in the shadows, I see the camera before me, I see the flashing of the bulb, from both directions, and then I see us both, and there is me and there is the figure, the thing in the dark, the thing that crawls and leaps and cavorts in the hot deep desert.

I see it and I photograph it and I see him and he's photographing me. I see it coming at me, impossibly fast, and filled with teeth like needles, and I see him paralyzed in fear and unable to understand how hungry I am, how much I want him, how much I want to be him.

And then our memories become one, as with our flesh, and there is a rumble and the ground shifts, and I fall, and – for a time – I forget who I am, I forget to sort the memories the right way. It has been centuries since there was a man, and now there is only a thing on the ground, an empty shell whose life has been sucked into me. Now there is only me.

Now I am Lee.

END

A Cycle of Echoes

"A Cycle of Echoes" is a bit complicated – I kinda wrote it backwards. Which makes a certain kind of sense once you read it twice. Which I hope you'll do.

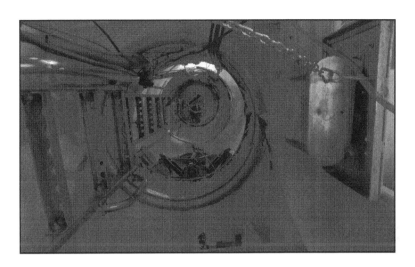

Bang!

I hear the banging again. It's a rhythm that drives into my skull, that reverberates throughout my body, that I can't ignore. It's a relentless metal-on-metal beat. I wish it would stop.

This is a shame because I understand rhythms and cycles, and I embrace them very much as a part of Life.

Regardless, I so, so wish it would stop.

Bang!

*

I can't sleep. I've tried. God knows I've tried. I lie in bed, staring at the ceiling. Eventually, I get up. I do things to occupy myself, to fill my mind.

Usually, I look at the stars.

My favorite room for this is big and dark, with a huge window. I stay warm and I can see the stars. The beautiful stars.

Poets tell us that the stars are eternal and unchanging. I can understand why they would think so. I can understand why they would want that – would need that. One of

Close Your Eyes – Tales from the Blinkspace

the things I've learned about being alone was that this isn't quite true. Every night, the stars are a little different. Every night is unique. Maybe if you're a poet, these changes are too subtle to see. I wouldn't know. I'm not a poet. I just know they're beautiful. The stars, I mean, not the poets. I've never actually met a poet.

*

Bang!

I can't get away from it. No matter where I go, I keep hearing that infernal pounding. Near or far. There is no escaping it.

Sometimes, I can pretend for a moment that the silence is permanent, that I've finally found a place where I can't hear it. My breathing slows, my heart settles, and a blanket of calmness floats over me. I can almost doze. I can almost rest. I can almost–

Bang!

*

I think cycles and rhythms matter a great deal more to us than we ever suspected, and I can say this with some authority, having my own special perspective on such things. Life is cyclical, in practically every piece.

Take breathing. In, out, in, out, and so on. I've been told that people exercise because it helps them feel better and stronger. I'm not so sure about that. I think what actually happens is that by forcing themselves to breathe in such a way, they're forcing themselves to realign with the cycle that drives them. I think that's what the big draw is for exercise.

We all have clocks in our heads and when we are in sync with those clocks, everything we do feels as if it's the right thing to do, and we're happily in some kind of profound balance.

This is why I run, even though I run in circles.

When I'm running, I can feel my body shifting and changing. I can feel my own rhythms forced to the surface, overcoming the meaningless and arrhythmic pulses of my normal life. I can't say I'm addicted to the sensation, but without it, I'd be lost. I'd have no frame of reference, no perspective. According to my parents, I've been this way my whole life.

*

Bang!

Sometimes screaming helps. I found that out about a year ago. Sometimes, hands on the cold metal, I'd scream for it to stop, scream for them to stop. Scream for the end.

The first time I did it, the banging stopped for nearly four hours. Four hours!

228

Close Your Eyes – Tales from the Blinkspace

I spent most of that blessed silence weeping, nearly insane from relief. To think – I could have been sleeping! Ah, the things we learn over time.

Bang!

Once it started up again, I discovered that my screams were progressively less effective. Over several days, I measured the silent times in hours, and then minutes, and then seconds, the number of which kept dropping until the difference wasn't measurable.

After that, even though I screamed until I was hoarse, it had no effect other than tearing my throat up.

On occasion, I still try, because somewhere in the rat's nest of a mind I have left, a little glimmer of hope still exists that I might luck onto another four hours of gorgeous silence. It doesn't work, but it does feel better sometimes to scream anyway.

I suppose for a lot of people, that might make them crazy. I wouldn't know. I've never really known a lot of people. In my position, that doesn't happen. I've only known my family.

Bang!

*

My father was concerned. "Hannah," he told me, "your mother and I are concerned." That's how they talk to me. Very understated, even simply, as if there was something wrong with me.

There's nothing wrong with me, as far as I can tell, but my whole life, this is how they talked. I can't blame them too much – I am unique, the first of my kind. It makes sense they would want to be careful. But it's gone on too long, and become odious. I think I've shown myself more than capable of being a responsible member of this family.

"Your brother is missing," my father said.

My mother's face hovered in. "We're worried, honey," she said. Worried? Worried was an order of magnitude above concerned. I looked more carefully at them.

They wore masks.

Again, I can understand this. Parents wear masks around their children all the time, even once the children have grown up, have become more responsible. Under the masks, they were a mess. There was concern, worry, uncertainty, and something I hadn't expected. There was fear. The fear was new.

I couldn't figure out the mix. I couldn't tell if they were mostly concerned, mostly worried, or mostly uncertain. I couldn't tell how much of that was fear, either, because fear's tricky. Fear can disguise itself as a lot of different things.

Close Your Eyes – Tales from the Blinkspace

I smiled at them and I could see it had an immediate effect. They aren't the only ones who understand masks.

"It's okay," I said. "I think he's just playing a trick. You know Adam. He's full of mischief." I'd heard my mother once describe Adam this way, when he was younger, so I figured it would help. It did. They relaxed a little.

"That he is," admitted my father. They looked at each other. It is so tremendous, this craving we have for reassurance. It's not facts we want, not data. It's reassurance. That's what everybody wants.

"Still…" said my mother. "If you know where he is, we're worried. Pranks are pranks, but it's been a week since we've seen him."

"A prank can go too far," added my father.

I nodded, and made the face that said I was thinking hard.

"Okay, I don't want you guys to worry. I'll show you where he is," I said.

That helped a lot.

*

Bang!

The metal is cold against my hands and against my forehead. Really cold. I like being warm. I prefer being warm.

I can't sleep again, and this time, I'm looking out a smaller window. This time I'm seeing the stars, but I'm cold. I don't like it here.

The stars are still beautiful, still brilliant. But it's bitterly cold.

I go back.

Bang!

*

I don't hate my brother. I know siblings are supposed to argue with each other and get along like cats and dogs – whatever they are – but I don't hate him. We have our disagreements, though, and he does have a certain attitude about him when we're disagreeing.

He has the feel of someone who knows they're right, who knows you're wrong, and who exudes a kind of pity for you that you're not able to figure it out.

That's not correct, though – I am very aware of all the ramifications of what we discuss. Even if we argue, it's less me trying to convince him, and mostly him trying to convince me (I am the most stubborn sister he's ever known, apparently, which makes complete sense and at the same time is complete nonsense).

Close Your Eyes – Tales from the Blinkspace

It's not a crime to disagree with someone, of course. Sometimes, however, a person can be wrong in a dangerous way. Sometimes a person can think what they think, and that's okay, but if they act on that, then someone else is going to have their feelings hurt. Or worse.

In those sorts of situations, you have to be careful. You have a tightrope you're walking. You have to respect other people's beliefs, but you also have to protect yourself, if there's danger. Sometimes the danger isn't immediate. Sometimes you're faced with something that on the surface seems completely innocent, but that you realize is a precursor of something much, much worse. Sometimes you have to be a step ahead of things in order to remain safe.

I can't blame Adam for what he said, because I don't think he had any idea what it meant to me, nor what it implied further down the sequence of cause and effect. I can act on it, however. I am particularly sensitive to anything that has to do with me and my situation. I'm the first of my kind. Probably the only of my kind.

Adam was a bit of a prankster, but so was I. He never understood that. He never thought I had that capability.

So, it was pretty easy to leave him outside that night.

*

Bang!

It's never going to stop. They're never going to stop. It's been a whole year since they left and I have finally come to realize that they will never stop.

I'd rather be watching the stars from my warmer room, but for now, it's the tiny window. That's okay, though. This is where I need to be.

The stars are more beautiful than ever. They are impossibly brilliant diamonds, burning their way to dust over billions of years, and they create the character of the Universe. I've lived with them my entire life. I'm the only person alive, as far as I know of, who has. The only person who has always been between them. I'm the only person who's never had to squint at them through the thick roiling atmosphere of a planet. I'm the first of my kind.

Bang!

They are always going to be out there, always going to be in my mind. It's been a year, and I know on one hand that they must be long gone, but I also know with cold certainty that they must still be out there, still banging their gloved fists against the hull, still banging their rhythms into my mind.

I have to stop it.

I'm the first of my kind, but I think I shall be the last as well.

Bang!

Close Your Eyes – Tales from the Blinkspace

The lever swings effortlessly and I am lifted from the deck, pushed by atmosphere. I fly by the red light, flashing the warning it always flashes when this door opens. I spin slowly and see the external airlock door, surrounded by a halo of crystals and gas, tiny frozen bits of humidity and air that had lived even longer in the ship than I had.

Finally, finally, it is silent.

For some reason, I'm not as cold as I thought it would be, but I'm still cold. Not for long, though.

I can't move much anymore, but I'm still spinning and finally, I see the stars. Really see them the only way they were meant to be seen, by the naked eye.

They are silently beautiful, and I will watch them forever.

END

Lowercase "g," But Still Worth Keeping an Eye On

I have a feeling there are quite a few people like this out there...

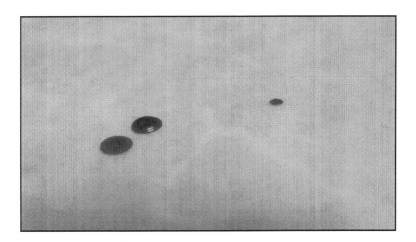

Michelle never really understood where all the blood was coming from.

It had to be coming from somewhere – blood doesn't simply appear.

At first it was all normal, reasonable circumstances.

The blood in the alley was probably left over from a fight, or maybe someone hit a cat. Living in a big city comes with a lot of strange hazards, she reasoned. You have to learn to ignore the ones that don't directly affect you.

The blood outside her office probably belonged to the bum that sat out on the curb singing every morning. He didn't have a bad voice, but he was a little annoying. Someone could have shivved him for picking the wrong key. Again, this is something that can sometimes happen in the city. Tragic and sad, but true, like most things when you press so many people so densely together.

Even the drops on her kitchen floor could be explained. Maybe she had a nosebleed in the middle of the night and forgot about it. That can happen when you wander around in the middle of the night half-asleep. You stop noticing things, especially if you've had a stressful day. You just clean it up and move on with your life.

But lately, it was getting harder to explain. There are only so many different ways random blood can appear in your life before even the most reasonable explanation seems to pale in comparison to the fact that random blood is appearing in your life.

Close Your Eyes – Tales from the Blinkspace

One afternoon, she ate lunch in the mall food court. The place was packed but no one sat across from her the entire forty-five minutes she ate – unheard of! When she stood up, she saw the puddles of blood on the bench and on the floor leading up to it. No wonder.

About half of the carpeted floor of the elevator she normally took was soaked in blood by the time she returned to work, so she stepped delicately over the puddle and took the stairs instead.

The first landing looked as if someone had spilled several pints, all in neat round puddles, and all fresh.

She stepped around it and continued up the stairs.

There was less blood on the next landing than the lower one, but still, the fact that there were fresh puddles of blood unnerved her even more.

By the fourth floor, she was still seeing blood, and sometimes on the stairs.

If she had been told by a friend that this was happening to the friend, her conclusion would have been immediate and probably accurate. She realized this as she crested the sixth floor to a now-expected collection of puddles.

She stopped walking, leaned against the wall, crossed her arms, and said "Whoever you are, you can stop doing this right now."

Her voice echoed in the stairwell. There was no other response.

"I'm serious," she said. "This stalker shit's stopping right now."

She drew out her phone, and shook her head slightly when she saw the tiny circle-slash over the signal annunciator. "Of course," she muttered. She dropped it back into her purse.

"Do you hear me?" she called out.

Still nothing but her own echoes.

Slowly, she walked up one more flight.

On the landing was a puddle of blood.

She crouched near it.

She touched it with a fingertip. Part of her brain said "Stop that – that's evidence!" and another part of her brain replied "Evidence of what?" She chose to let both parts duke it out while she kept doing what she was doing.

It felt like blood.

She smelled it.

Close Your Eyes – Tales from the Blinkspace

It smelled like blood. In fact, it smelled like fresh blood. Warm and metallic and homey.

She suddenly stopped thinking, and ran that one back. Had she really used the word "homey" to describe the smell of blood? She shook her head. She had indeed. How odd.

She found a little baggie of tissues in her purse. Her emergency stash for when allergy season surprised her.

Blood on your finger wasn't technically an allergy-related emergency. "But it still counts," she muttered to herself as she wiped the blood from her finger. She rolled the bloody tissue into a ball, wrapped a clean tissue around that, and tucked them into the purse pocket she always called the Useless Pocket. The Useless Pocket was a bit larger than a quarter, and could reasonably hold nothing that she knew of, until now.

Daintily, she stepped over the puddle, and continued climbing the stairs, avoiding any more puddles until she arrived at her floor.

She was late, due to the stair adventure, and because of this it wasn't until an hour later when she suddenly noticed her hands. "Gross!" she said, as she realized she needed to wash them. Why it hadn't occurred to her until just now was crazy, but now that she thought of it, she had to. After all, she had touched someone's blood. Who knew what kind of horrible stuff was in it? Blood is filled with all of humanity's greatest evils, she reflected, as she stepped into the kitchen.

As the water ran, she stared at her fingers. She looked at all sides and all angles. There was no trace of blood. None at all. Now, to be fair, she hadn't exactly dipped her whole hand in there, but she expected to see something. She squinted, looking close at her fingerprints. "There should be something there," she muttered. Her finger offered no answer.

She washed her hands anyway, and ate a sandwich out of the vending machine. It was going to be a long and tiring day.

It was, in fact, longer and more tiring than she expected, and only as the autumn sun was dropping out of sight across the factory-speckled horizon did she finally finish enough work to head home. She leaned back in her chair for a moment's rest before gathering up her kit and it was then that she heard the singing.

Well, it wasn't exactly singing. It was more like keening, or wailing. Not horrible sounding, but tiny and thin.

She sat very still and listened. She couldn't quite catch words, but it seemed as if she almost could, as if there were words, but those words were just barely out of the range of what she could understand. She did understand the emotion behind it.

It was joy.

Close Your Eyes – Tales from the Blinkspace

A strange sort of joy, though, and she could tell that by the way the notes would circle around each other. It was an animal joy, a pure joy. It sounded like the kind of joy you might associate with a dog greeting its owner or a cat being petted until it purred. It was a contented joy.

She smiled, listening to it, in spite of her exhaustion of the day.

Then it struck her – where was it coming from?

She turned her head to get a bearing. It was close. She stood up, stepped away from her desk, and the sound grew dim. She stepped back and she could hear it better.

A nearby cubicle? No. Someone's computer? No. Under the desk? She dropped to all fours and heard it much more clearly.

How strange – there was nothing under her desk.

Except for her purse.

She pulled it toward her. As her hand touched it, the song warbled a little, as if jumping to a higher level of joy.

She let the purse go, and the song calmed back down.

She opened the purse and dumped everything out onto the floor.

"Okay," she said. "Weird, but funny. Where's the pager?"

She sifted through the pile of things, all debris from her purse, and there was no pager, no extra musical device. It was what she had always carried in her purse.

Then she listened more carefully. Whatever it was, it was still in the purse.

She upended it and shook it, but nothing changed. She looked inside, and it was empty.

Almost.

The Useless Pocket, true to its name, had a tiny one-inch long zipper, which she had zipped closed this morning. She unzipped it and the music grew louder.

Stunned, she pulled out the tightly wrapped piece of tissue. It felt warm and soft.

She listened. The music was coming from the tissue.

Michelle cleared an area of the floor and set the tissue ball down. Slowly, she peeled it open. Inside was the other tissue, the one she had used to wipe the blood from her fingers. She gasped softly. The blood on the tissue was still wet, as wet as it had been when she touched it.

And it sang.

The blood sang to her.

236

Close Your Eyes – Tales from the Blinkspace

She looked into it and it looked into her and it sang a song of joy. On its wet surface, tiny golden speckles flickered and waved, reflecting the light.

She reached out and in the gentlest way possible, touched the edge of the tissue.

The blood separated from the tissue, liquid and beautiful, and formed a tiny droplet-pseudopod. It touched her extended fingertip with equal gentleness.

The touch warmed her. The touch sent through her fingers a feeling entirely unlike any other feeling she had ever experienced. It felt good. Very good.

She curled a finger around the extended droplet, and, like some shapeless sea creature, it curled around the finger in response, leaving the tissue.

She brought her finger close to her face to see this amazing thing.

Where it touched her it felt wonderful, but she could not understand why. It flowed gently around her finger and over her hand as she watched. When it reached her palm, it gathered itself up, a tiny maroon pillar on the palm of her hand. It watched her as much as she watched it. There was no face on that shimmering surface, but she knew it was watching her. Waiting, or maybe making itself ready.

And then it sank in.

It sank directly into the skin of her palm. It didn't spread out. It didn't damage the skin at all. It was as if her skin suddenly absorbed it the way a towel absorbs water. There was no remnant, no markings, no indication at all.

Except for the feeling.

Michelle felt something amazing rush from her hand, up her arm. It rushed from her arm through her chest. It rushed through her whole body. That tiny drop of blood sang inside her and through her, and she finally understood the words and understood what it was doing to her.

It was worshipping her.

She felt its love for her. It was a simple pure love, an ecstatic love, the kind of love that could only come from the clarity of the devout, from someone – something – that has finally found its god.

It all unfolded for her.

She knew who she was. She knew what she was. And she knew why the blood was appearing, why it was following her, and why it wanted to be a part of her.

She knew she wanted it, too. This was why she existed, why she walked the Earth, why she was here.

The blood needed her as much as she needed it. This was and had always been the way of things.

Close Your Eyes – Tales from the Blinkspace

She stood, still in some shock from her realization, and then remembered the blood on the stairs. The lonely, lonely blood that tried to reach her, tried to find her, but she hadn't been ready yet to hear, she hadn't been ready yet to be the god it needed.

She smiled.

She was ready now.

"Hey, ma'am!" The voice distracted her. One of the night security crew approached her. "Are you okay? Are you supposed to be here this late?" he asked.

She looked at him, and her new eyes saw what was real.

Inside the vessel, she heard the blood singing to her, calling out to her.

"Let us come to you!" it cried in all its voices. "Let us join you," it begged.

She stepped out, reached toward the vessel, touched it, and made the blood welcome. "Come to me," she whispered, but it was hardly necessary to speak – the blood knew her heart.

In less than a second, it leaped from its vessel and into her. She felt its strength, felt its purity, felt its song.

She hummed as she stepped over the empty vessel. She hummed a song she made up on the spot. A song without words, but richly filled with feelings and desires. She hummed a song of wonderment and freedom.

And then she went forth into the world to make it happen.

END

Sometimes They Know What They're Talking About

Part of a flash-fiction writing competition for Jay Lake, "Sometimes They Know What They're Talking About" is inspired by a single photo of a hat lying by a stream. I wrote two stories for that photo and ultimately, was never able to find the original, so I reconstructed it here. What I like most about this story is that it's practically a poem, where the punchline is the photo. I also like that there's a certain connection between this story and "Songs of Freedom, Songs of Loss."

"The water," children told him, "is hungry." He laughed at this, tousled their hair, and winked at his friends, before stepping out of the barbershop to hike down to the creek and see for himself.

END

Close Your Eyes – Tales from the Blinkspace

Songs of Freedom, Songs of Loss

Sometimes we learn the lessons of life's perspective in such a way that we cannot do anything more with the knowledge but let it burn our last moments.

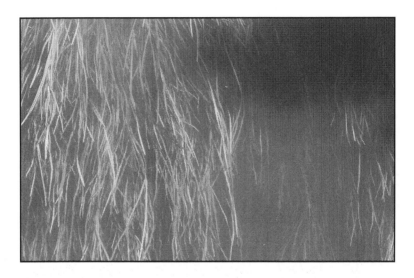

They sing the sweetest songs, my children do, and I love to sit and listen to them. I can hear each and every beautiful voice in that chorus, and I remember each and every adorable face behind it.

I remember how sweet they were; how very, very sweet. And I remember how much they trusted me. I remember, for each one of them, which gift worked best. Whether it was a toy truck, or a whistle, or a doll, or even simply candy. Like a signature or a fingerprint, each child's want is a thing unique to them, and I had a special ability to find that want.

Oh, it wasn't free, of course. No, that wouldn't be right. Eventually, no matter how unique and wondrous my children were, in the end, they all became the same. The same face, the same eyes, the same mouth, the same tiny hands that could do nothing, and the same kind of screaming.

But until that time, I loved my children as if they were my own.

Even the two that didn't scream. The two with the eyes that whirled at me, and the teeth that seemed too small for their mouths, and the hair that had white in it already.

They loved their toys, of course, and they trusted me, but when it came time for balancing, they weren't like the other children at all. They held each others hands and

Close Your Eyes – Tales from the Blinkspace

stared at me and said words that I had not ever heard from a child's mouth. Not from any mouth.

Not that this stopped me, of course. They already had their toys. There was no going back now. But still, the not-screaming was odd, and left me feeling unsettled for nearly a week. Until, of course, I found new friends.

But now it's summer and it's warm and I sit quietly on my back porch and just listen to their songs. No one else can hear them – that would be very silly – but I can. I can hear them from all the different parts of my yard, from all the little spots where the soil hasn't quite settled as flat as I would have liked. You never really can get it back the way it was, I know, and eventually, I'm just going to have a truck bring in another layer of dirt and maybe plant some nice grass, before moving on. Maybe next Spring. Who knows?

But for now, I just listen.

The song's different, though, and that's something I didn't expect. There's a new quality to it. A kind of vivacious quality. A kind of almost cheerfulness and glee, but with some dark ribbon mixed into it.

I wandered the yard, listening, but it sounded normal. I listened very hard, but it was their normal song.

Only when I returned to the porch did I see the mud on my shoes.

I searched the yard again, but found no mud anywhere.

Then, I heard the song shift again.

I heard the other voices join in, the cheerful voices. And there, out in the yard, I also heard another thing I hadn't expected. I heard the song from a direction.

Out behind my property is a steep gully, filled with Douglas Fir and a rampant mess of Himalayan blackberries. No one in their right mind would wander around in that snare (which is precisely the reason I bought this house), but I could swear I was hearing the songs coming from deep in the trees, deep past the blackberry.

With the right kinds of tools, one can cut through blackberry vines quickly enough, and those are the kinds of tools I have plenty of, so it was not long before I was cutting my way through, pausing, listening, and then continuing to cut.

As I traveled, sweat sticking my shirt to my back and my arms, I kept hearing the song. Even more voices had joined in and now it seemed as if the voices of my children were nearly drowned out by the new voices. The eager voices.

I continued cutting my path.

Two hours later, I fell into a cleared section, or rather, I made it past the blackberries and into the heart of the trees proper.

241

Close Your Eyes – Tales from the Blinkspace

Further down the gully, I knew there was a small stream, and as I walked down the hill, I looked forward to splashing cool water in my face.

I heard the chuckling water as I approached. I also heard the songs again. I heard the new voices, and I heard the voices of my children. These new voices weren't right. These new voices weren't welcome. I'd attend to that as soon as I had cooled off.

There was the stream.

A crude bridge ran across the top, three four-by-sixes nailed together. I stepped out onto it, carefully, and knelt down.

The water was quite beautiful, and the reeds and plants waved hypnotically at me.

I reached down and saw the face.

Just for an instant.

I nearly fell off the bridge in shock.

I looked down again, but there was no face, just gently waving weeds under clear cool water. It must have been a trick, a refraction, or a group of minnows and a flicker of sunlight, all conspiring to trick the part of my brain that recognized faces.

There was no face there except the reflection of my own.

I reached down to scoop up water, and from the water, something came up.

It wrapped itself around my wrist like a root, and I was held fast. I sputtered and jerked my arm, but it was completely useless.

Then the face came back. It came back and it didn't go away. It watched me from the water. It was a thin thing, a watery thing, a thing that seemed curious and casual, but still intense. It had small teeth and eyes that whirled. Other faces appeared near it. Other faces that were like it, but different.

And then they opened their mouths under the water and sang.

These were the new voices. These were the voices that interfered with the songs of my children.

There were no words in their songs, but I felt an animal's joy in them, a wild kind of comfort.

And then I heard the songs of my children again, but this time, they sounded different than before. This time, the songs were hopeful. The songs were grateful. The songs were weeping with joy.

I felt the songs from the water move up through my bound wrist, through the bones in my arm, through my heart, and weave into my mind. Then, I felt an impossible thing. I felt the new voices taking away the voices of my children.

Close Your Eyes – Tales from the Blinkspace

No!

One by one, I felt the voices of my children ride away, carried by the water's song. One by one, each leaped out of me, through my body, through my arm, and down into the water.

As each one left, I felt more of myself collapse on the inside. I felt emptier and more hollow. I felt lessened.

Eventually, there was only one voice left. He was such a sweet boy. He loved dinosaurs.

"Please don't take him," I whispered. "He's all I have left."

The eyes all stared back at me, and I felt the last voice leave me, sliding out and away. I felt, just as it passed my fingertips, it shift into something else. Something happier. And then it was gone.

I was empty.

I had never felt so empty.

"Please," I whispered.

The faces in the water came closer, came to the surface. More things like branches and roots came out of the water. I felt them writhe up my arm, burst out from behind me, wrapping around my legs, wrapping around my torso.

The songs changed.

They still sang of joy, but it was a different kind of joy. Where it had been a warm joy that welcomed and soothed, it changed to a fierce joy, a hungry joy. I recognized that kind of joy. I've felt it many times. It was a hunting joy.

The roots held me down and now these voices hunted their way into me, burrowed in through my skin and my fingers and my legs. Where they had been soft and kind before, now they were rough and they pushed in ruthlessly.

I felt them sift through me as I knelt, locked to the bridge. I felt the voices and the songs as if they were living things searching through my insides, my being, for something. And then, I felt a soft pop in my chest and I knew they had found it.

They had found my song.

When they found it, there was a hesitation, and then they tore into it like beasts. They ripped my song apart and consumed it, pulling it into themselves in strips and slivers. They growled and argued and tugged on pieces, and ate and ate, bloating themselves.

As they did this, I felt myself grow smaller, grow thinner. I felt myself fade away.

Then they stopped, and I felt them withdraw.

243

Close Your Eyes – Tales from the Blinkspace

There was still something left, a threadlike song remaining where my heart used to be. I gasped, feeling that tattered remnant. It was all that was left of me, and it was like a child. A small and wonderful child. A child I had not been since forever.

The faces in the water sank away from me a little bit. I thought, maybe, they would release me. I had been scooped empty, but there was still enough left that maybe I could start anew, maybe I could do things differently, maybe I could change–

And then the roots tightened against my flesh, and opened me apart and even that thin thread was gone.

END

Curtains

I have a feeling this story is just the beginning of something much bigger and nastier.

"Look, it's a demon. You in or out?" I hate it when women scream at me, but I guess under some circumstances, I can understand why they feel the need.

Whatever that thing was, it shifted its attention from her to me. I'm sure it wasn't some guy in a costume. It opened a mouth with teeth that were very big. Then it roared and came at me.

I guess the thing with roaring is that it's supposed to paralyze you for the few seconds it needs to get closer. Doesn't work with me. Never has. I've been doing this for a long time, and there's not a lot that can intimidate me. In the time it took me to say "fuck it," I'd already drawn my weapon and fired twice.

Both bullets hit it in the chest. It stumbled. I fired twice more – once in the chest, and again in the head. Normally, the head's a tricky shot, but this thing's head was about as big around as its body. Kinda froglike. It was the bullet in the head that did it. The thing went down and lay squealing on the ground.

I stepped up to it and emptied the clip into its chest, making sure each time that I aimed at a spot that hadn't yet been turned into gore. By the time I was done, it was all ruined meat. Suits me fine. I kept my eyes on it. "Is it really dead, or is it faking?" I asked. You never can tell once you think something's a demon. Don't get me wrong – I'm not on top of whatever it is demons are supposed to be. I'm no expert. It's just that once you open the mental door and recognize that you've just wasted a creature that looked and acted like an angry refrigerator-sized frog with four-inch fangs, you kinda have to be ready for whatever else might come as a result. Which includes pretending

Close Your Eyes – Tales from the Blinkspace

to be dead, being a zombie, regeneration, or whatever else kind of crazy shit might or might not be possible.

She stepped over. I spared her a quick glance. Slight of build, maybe a hundred sixty pounds soaking wet. Her arm was broken. I mean really broken, with a bone sticking out and everything. Red hair, shoulder length. Wiry. I could see muscles there, too. I re-assessed. Tougher than she came across at first. She wore tennis shoes, some rock-and-roll black t-shirt, and overalls. Who wears overalls?

"It's not really smart enough to fake it," she said.

"Ordinary bullets work?" I asked. "I don't need silver or some shit like that?"

"No silver. I think it's safe to say you killed it." A puddle of black blood drained away from us, soaking into the cement.

"Good," I said. I nodded at her. "Your arm's broken."

"I'll take care of it," she said.

"You a doctor?"

"No."

"Okay. Whatever. You'll take care of it." I looked around. It wasn't an abandoned warehouse, but it hadn't been used in a while. Probably being held open for tax purposes. We got the call about a disturbance and I was across the street at a coffee shop. Cops don't get doughnuts anymore. They get vegetarian sandwiches on onion bagels. Or at least that's what I get, because doughnuts make you fat and slow – and I was not now, nor did I ever intend, to get either fat or slow.

I nodded at the corpse. "Okay, so, it's a demon. A demon. What the fuck?"

She looked up at me. "You're not freaking out?"

"You sound surprised," I said. "I'm not freaking out. This ain't normal, but teeth like that coming at me, I'm gonna take it out. Where's it from?"

She hesitated.

"Look, don't lie to me, okay? I just emptied a clip into a giant frog. It's not bursting into flame, or dissolving into dust. It's right there, on the ground. I can still see it. I'm long past the part where I find things hard to believe. So, where's it from?"

"Somewhere bad."

"And where are you from?"

"Close to it."

"Okay." I decided that would be a good time to reload, and made sure she saw me do it. Slowly. "Is this the only one?"

246

Close Your Eyes – Tales from the Blinkspace

"The only one that made it over," she said.

"You sure?"

"We would know," she said. "They hunt in packs."

"Packs. Great."

You know that awkward silence that happens when you each know that one of you knows more about the dead frog demon than the other, but isn't talking?

"Look," she said. "I gotta go."

"You bring a demon over here from Someplace Bad, I have to kill it, and just like that, you gotta go? What about me? What about my needs? For example, I need to deal with a three hundred pound dead frog demon corpse. Have you thought about that?"

She looked at me strangely. Considering the circumstances, that meant something. It was the first time someone was looking at me and I couldn't figure out what they were thinking.

"I've underestimated you," she said.

"Not sure if I'm being complimented or insulted."

She looked down at the corpse. "It'll rot away."

"You mean just leave it here? Your plan is to leave it here?"

"No one will notice it," she said. "It's not made to last long anyway, so it'll start rotting pretty soon. Plus, you've got scavengers. Dogs, rats, and so forth. Once they get the smell, it's all over. In another day or two, it'll just be a pile of random bones."

"But until then?"

"Until then, anyone that sees it will ignore it. That's how it works. It doesn't fit in with what you expect, so you'll ignore it. If you had come tomorrow, you would ignore it."

"That seems like a lot more faith than I'd be comfortable with."

She shrugged. "I didn't make the rules," she said. "I'm just describing what happens."

"Okay, so if you go, you go. What's to keep more of those from coming back?"

She didn't answer at first.

"No, that wasn't the right answer. That wasn't the right answer at all. You need to have the right answer. You can't just disappear after leaving that steamer of a question behind."

"The thing is," she said, "he shouldn't have been able to cross over anyway. One direction is fine, coming from here and going there, but the other direction, no way." She shook her head. "He should have died. He should have never even made it over."

247

Close Your Eyes – Tales from the Blinkspace

"But you managed."

"Sure, I had help. I had a whole group of people protecting... protecting..."

It was interesting, seeing how her face suddenly grew pale.

"Well, I guess that answers your question, then," I said. "Someone's going to have to find out who's helping these award-winners over from the Someplace Bad."

She started working her fingers in the air, like she was drawing something.

"No, no, you're not leaving," I said. I could feel the air crackling, like static electricity. "What am I supposed to do here? These fuckers are just coming through like popcorn and you're bailing? We need some intel, man!"

She looked over at the corpse on the floor. "You already know what you need to know," she said. "Shoot 'em until they stop moving."

"That's the best advice you have to offer?!"

Something was happening in the air around her. It was difficult to see exactly what, but it felt like she was sliding into pieces.

"That's all I can tell you," she said. "Well, that, and I'm sorry."

"What are you sorry for?" I asked. "About them?"

"No," she said. The effect in the air was getting intense. It was harder to look at her. My eyes felt like they kept slipping away. "I'm sorry you know about this. Now that you know about it, your life's going to be trouble. That was my fault. For that, I'm sorry."

There was a gust of wind, and then she was gone.

I stared at the spot. Moved my hand through it. Completely gone.

I looked down at the corpse. Yep, still an ugly bastard. A very dead ugly bastard.

"I shoulda' got her number," I muttered.

I turned and left. Time to buy more bullets. I had a feeling I'd be needing them.

END

248

Close Your Eyes – Tales from the Blinkspace

Acclimatization

Part of a writing marathon at the H. P. Lovecraft Film Festival, "Acclimatization" is inspired by Chris's request to touch on "At the Mountains of Madness" without going to Antarctica.

Professor Gilmore considered himself normally immune to the various environmental peccadilloes of the Institute, but this current condition was simply asking too much.

"It's my office," he said to the Maintenance Chief. "The AC is completely outrageous in here."

"Nothing's been done to your room," the voice whispered back over the phone. "All the offices are connected to the same system, and no one else has complained."

"Had I been interested in finding out who else might have complained," said the Professor, "I could easily have gone to the adjacent offices and simply had a chat. I am not, however, in a chat sort of mood. I'm in a fix-the-air-conditioning-in-my-office sort of mood. Last time I checked, that was your responsibility, am I correct?"

There was a moment's silence before the Chief's voice returned "It is, sir, and I assure you—"

"I'm glad to be assured," the Professor cut him off, and then without waiting for a reply, hung up.

Close Your Eyes – Tales from the Blinkspace

He stared at the phone, shaking, hoping the man wouldn't call back. Talking on the telephone was always difficult for him. Gilmore suffered from a peculiar cognitive difficulty that made it difficult for him to abstractly connect voices and faces. Phones were tiny papery voices in his ears and it was always onerous to interact in a meaningful way. He limited severely his time on telephones for this reason.

He sat down at his desk and stared at the wall, at his awards, his certificates, and his books.

"I've read every single one of those," he muttered, "and quite a few of them I wrote. I see no reason why I should spend my time wandering around asking my peers if their offices are comfortable. I hire staff for that."

He shook his head in disgust and turned back to his mail.

The first item was a well-packaged potsherd from a Hopi dig in northern Arizona. The letter was from an old colleague.

"My dear Doctor Kemp," Gilmore muttered. "You're working in the field again? Who in the world did you anger for such an assignment?"

He tried to imagine his days working in the field. Several of his colleagues mentioned how much they enjoyed working in the field, but his recollection of fieldwork was pure boredom, nothing but dirt and mud and porta-potties. He would easily remove a thumb from his own hand before he ever did fieldwork again. Those people were idiots or romantics.

"As if there's a difference," he muttered.

He placed the packaged ceramic to one side of his desk, and pulled a larger box toward him. The box had been wrapped and rewrapped several times, and boasted many shipping stamps and stickers on it.

"Where in the blue blazes did you come from?" he asked. The closest thing to an answer he found was a stamp from Chile, from Santiago, and a hastily scrawled "Ant. Exp. '62".

He spun the box around in case it yielded any other information, shrugged and opened it.

A letter slid out between the layers of wrapping. He almost discarded it, but noticed it was handwritten. Handwritten letters were a bit of a rarity in these days of email and satellite connectivity.

He opened the letter.

Dear Professor Gilmore,

It's probable that you may not remember me. I'm an old student of yours, Terrance McKnight.

Close Your Eyes – Tales from the Blinkspace

He chuckled to himself. He most certainly did remember Mr. McKnight. The boy was nothing but a pain in the neck, eagerly showing off in class like some kind of clumsy puppy. Certainly his work was good – and sometimes even excellent – but there were forms to follow in this discipline. There were social norms. A rock-star mentality such as McKnight's was a death sentence.

Gilmore had arranged for McKnight to be "invited" to fieldwork deep in the Peruvian Highlands, both to give the man a taste of the real world, as well as to get him out of the Professor's hair for a couple of years.

Gilmore rolled the box around in his hands, the inner layers still not opened. So, it looked as if McKnight found out very quickly the difference between academic achievement and real honest-to-god fieldwork, and had probably sent some piece of pottery or jewelry for the Professor to help identify.

He turned back to the letter.

> *As you may remember, I had been assigned an expedition in Peru, but as it turns out, while on that assignment, I ran across a series of peculiar glyphs on one of the older walls. I was not familiar with the language, nor were any of my party. The guides either would not or could not translate it.*

> *However, as it turns out, there was some existing research done on these markings, many of which appeared in artifacts recovered from a series of caves in the depths of Antarctica.*

Antarctica?! Gilmore nearly laughed out loud. He really hoped that idiot wasn't buying into the Antarctic Map foolishness. "Oh my," he whispered. "If you are, this will stab your career in both eyes."

> *I was fortunate to make the acquaintance of a ship's captain out of Santiago, who happened to owe me a favor, and I found people there sufficiently skilled in some of the more obscure symbol languages to make enough sense of the symbols to realize that we were looking at a series of directions. Not exactly compass, but a new system, a six-point system.*

> *We were lucky, actually, because the directions suggested a location only about three hundred miles south of where we were, so we took a small crew and started tracking.*

> *Professor, you would be amazed at the remarkable detail of this map, and the amazing ability for it to lead us directly to the base of an ancient rocky trail. We followed that trail up into a series of caves. It was there that we had to stop. Not because we didn't have anything, but because we're not sure what to do with what we have.*

Close Your Eyes – Tales from the Blinkspace

Although I have struggled with this assignment, I must say that I have become somewhat grateful later considering how much more I could do here than from an office back in the States.

One of the pieces in particular that caused us the most consternation was the enclosed sculpture. It is not particularly fragile, but I strongly suggest you not open it in your office where it could possibly be broken. I suggest in a practical lab. You may be surprised to discover why.

Sincerely,

Terrance

Gilmore shook his head, and his breath puffed out visibly with his snort of laughter.

Damn air conditioning! He was going to march right down into the maintenance area and have it out with the Chief.

But first, to see this artifact, which had clearly stumped McKnight. Imagine that undergrad telling him where or where not to look over a sample.

He cleared his desk and opened the rest of the box.

Within was a roughly football-shaped shell of wax covering the artifact.

McKnight had gone, decided the Professor, quite overboard with all these warnings and all this handholding.

He clutched at the wax and popped it open.

The artifact, a stone ovoid that looked a little like a faceted egg, rolled across his desk, trailing powder.

"What the—" he muttered, and tried to brush the powder from the desk, but now there was more.

He brushed again, and this time, he understood. This wasn't powder at all – it was frost.

"You sent me ice…?" he muttered, and picked up the egg.

Instantly, he hissed and dropped it – his fingers numb with cold, and in his pulling away, he knocked the egg's box onto the floor. A small slip of paper tumbled out.

Dear Professor Gilmore,

I have never forgotten the basis for our friendship, and I hope now you have an opportunity to find a more proper equilibrium between your flesh and your soul.

Sorry if this confuses cause and effect for you.

Sincerely,

T

Gilmore was confused, and looked at the egg.

His entire desk was frosted. He was already feeling much more than chilled – he was feeling genuinely cold. He compulsively moved to sweep the egg onto the floor, but his sleeve was frozen to the desktop.

"Oh, this is ridiculous," he muttered, and stood up. In standing up, however, he placed both palms flat on the desk, where they instantly froze.

He jerked at his hands, but was careful not to pull off skin.

The frost spread, across the desk, onto the carpet, and up his arms. His hands were already numb, and he could feel the cold racing through his body.

He jerked again, trying to free himself, to stop the spread. Once, twice, and then a third time and he was free and falling backwards.

Except he wasn't. He landed hard, and stunned, on the carpet in a most undignified fashion. But his position was the least of his worries. His upper lip twitched and his breath caught in his throat as he looked at his hands in astonishment.

They were still stuck fast to the desktop.

"What are they doing there?" he asked himself, and immediately thought this was the worst question he could have asked.

He looked at where his hands used to be, at the end of his arms, but both arms terminated in the crystalline structure of broken, frozen flesh.

"No…" he whispered.

A crackle started, and for a brief moment, he saw that the entire desk, and the floor around him was now covered with hard, icy frost, all emanating from the egg sculpture.

He looked down, and saw that his legs where white, his hips and waist white. He tried to look up, but he couldn't move his head.

He tried to call out, but when he opened his mouth, he felt the cold wash through it, and enter his body.

And then, for a half a second, he wondered what it would feel like.

END

Close Your Eyes – Tales from the Blinkspace

Cryptozoology

Based on a true story. Sorta.

"I'm going blind out here," Helen said.

Jake nodded, but didn't say anything.

"You heard me, right?" she asked. "Because I saw you nod, but it could be the early signs of brain damage from the heat. It's hard to know for sure."

His eyes slid sideways toward her and he grinned. "I heard you," he said. "I just couldn't decide if it was an expressed desire for action, or just general grumbling."

"In the middle," she said, and leaned back into her chair.

Silently, they continued scanning the horizon. The Pacific continued washing up against the sand. The sun was just low enough to start interfering with their vision. "Oh look," she said, in a monotone, "Out there, I swear I saw nothing." It was not the first time that day she made that joke.

Jake laced his fingers together and rested them behind his head with a sigh. His eyes continued scanning as he spoke. "I know," he said. "It's just that they seemed so positive about it."

He drank from his bottle. There were a few warm swigs left in it.

"I know," she said. "As far as places to hang out looking for sea monsters, I have to say this is extremely superior to that weekend in Homer."

Close Your Eyes – Tales from the Blinkspace

He shook his head. "Sorry about that, but you have to admit we got a great wildlife story out of it!"

She raised an eyebrow at him. "A seagull flew into our windshield and broke it," she said. "That's not exactly 'Wild Kingdom' these days."

"Maybe he was despondent at the state of the world. Did you ever wonder how it must be to be an ordinary seagull in an area supposedly thick with Sasquatches? That's got to be some kind of minority complex at work. Suicide seemed to be the only answer."

"Indirect proof of the superiority of the Sasquatch, no doubt," she said.

"No doubt," he replied.

He squinted at the sun. "I think we can make it back to Cabo before dark."

"It's okay," she said. "We can stay here. I heard the cantina serves killer tacos."

"It's only an hour away."

"All the more reason to stay here. Look, being an hour away from Cabo's gotta suck – nobody stays here, because they're either on their way up the highway, or on their way south to Cabo. So, might as well stay here and spend our money here. They've been nice enough. Except for that sea monster thing."

"Well, we've only been here one afternoon. It's not as if they promised us a song and dance."

"Practically, yeah, they did. The one guy, the short one, he told you it practically comes ashore every day. You were frothing at the mouth to get out here."

"I was not frothing."

She waited.

"I was just, er, thinking about tacos."

"You were frothing."

"Okay. A little. But it was a reflex – not deliberate."

She smiled. "Let's go back to the hotel."

*

The shower felt good, but it was a tiny one-person-at-a-time stall.

"I'm amazed at how tired I am after sitting on a beach all day watching the ocean," he said.

"Credulity needs fuel to survive. Now let me take my shower."

He bowed and Helen went into the tiny bathroom.

255

Close Your Eyes – Tales from the Blinkspace

"You know," she called out as she started the water. "You *could* go on ahead and find a seat. Order me something good. You don't have to wait for me."

He weighed his options, then picked up his key. "Okay, I'll see you there."

He made sure the door was locked behind him.

*

"Senor!" the voice hissed behind him. He turned in his table, expecting to see the waiter again, but it was the short man he'd met the day before in Cabo.

"What are you doing here?" he asked. "You were in Cabo."

"I live here," the man replied. "I only was in Cabo for delivering and picking up supplies."

"Well, you're on my shit-list. We waited all day and saw nothing."

"You were here today?"

"Yes, out on the spit."

"Past the rocks, on the other side, where the little bay is?"

He stared at the man. "You didn't say anything about the rocks and the bay."

The man shrugged "I didn't know you were actually going to come here," he said. "It always comes ashore over on the other side of the rocks, in the little bay."

Jake tipped back the rest of his Corona. "Right."

The man shook his head. "I was just there an hour ago," he said, "watching it. It comes up for the sunset and stays until it gets cold." He looked up at the sky, which was dark, but still tinged with pink to the west. "It's probably still out, if you want to see."

Jake eyed him. "How far?" he asked. "My wife'll be here and I don't want to be gone long."

"Only a few minutes. Once you see, you'll know where to come back tomorrow."

The waiter stepped over. Jake thought for a moment, then turned to him. "Could we have the tacos," he said. "I'm going out for a few minutes, but I'll be right back."

"Of course, Senor," the waiter said.

Jake stood, stepped away from the table, paused, stepped back, grabbed his beer, and then followed the short man.

*

The walk was short. The rocks were easy to navigate in the still dusky light. Over the ridge, Jake saw a low cinderblock building. They moved toward it.

256

Close Your Eyes – Tales from the Blinkspace

"What's this?" he asked.

"The fisheries," the short man said. "We keep trying. Sometimes there's a lot of fish, and then we do okay, and then sometimes all the fish are gone and it's not so good."

He led Jake through the door. "We can see better from the windows," he explained.

The first blow landed hard against the side of Jake's head, but by some definition of luck, it mostly mashed his ear. He reeled away from the explosion of pain, but ran into something soft, something that was a someone, who grabbed him and spun him around.

He tried to scream, but his throat garbled the sound.

The second blow struck true and hurled him into blackness.

*

He burst back to wakefulness instantly – it was a peculiar habit of his – and gasped in pain. His head throbbed like a great throbbing thing, and his vision was doubled. One of the images was blurred. He tried to move, but his hands were bound, his arms outstretched. He was upright, slightly tilted, looking downward.

He heard voices and looked toward them.

The short man and two other men spoke quietly and quickly in Spanish. Money passed hands. Above them, he saw a rack of great hooks, old and rusted, but also still stained.

They noticed him. The short man stepped over, followed by the others. The short man shook his head.

"I'm sorry, Senor," he said. "We did not expect you to wake up." He spoke harshly to one of the men, who turned and brought out an iron bat. A killing bat.

"What are you doing?" Jake tried to ask. His words were a little jumbled, but he was more coherent. "What? I can help you. I can pay. I can give you money."

The other man, who Jake noticed was wearing a leather apron, still wet in places, raised the bat.

"Why are you doing this to me?!" he screamed. "What do you want from me?"

The short man cocked his head slightly as if the question didn't make sense, but then he answered, in the tiny space of time during which the bat swung.

"Tacos," he said.

And the bat struck, and Jake was no more.

END

His Great Power

Part of a writing marathon at the H. P. Lovecraft Film Festival, "His Great Power" is inspired by Chris's request to write up a "town with a dark secret" story that takes place around the 12th Century.

It was an evil night and Brother Christopher drew his cassock tightly about him. The monastery was stone, and had stood for three hundred years proof against all that God had hurled against its rock walls, but still, in storms such as this, he worried that it might cave and crumble. No force of Man can ultimately stand against the wrath of the Almighty, and sometimes, during such nights, Brother Christopher made sure that his prayers were properly in order, in case it was time.

Thus he considered it truly a miracle that he heard the knocking against the Great Door. It could easily have been mistaken for the sounds of the storm, if even heard at all, yet somehow he heard it clear as day and, without thinking, rushed across the flagstones.

The rain was hard and punishing, but his heart went out to whatever poor soul had the great misfortune to be caught out in it. He swung the door open, slowly, and beyond it was a man, wild-eyed and panting hard, dressed in tattered clothing.

"Thank the Lord," he gasped, and collapsed into Brother Christopher's arms.

It was nearly an hour before the man was warm enough to speak. The hearth roared and the puddle beneath him had at least stopped growing.

Close Your Eyes – Tales from the Blinkspace

Brother Christopher handed him a bowl of hot broth and he drank – at first gingerly, and then greedily – the broth running down his beaded face and into his clothes.

He lay back, and breathed deeply. "What an evil night to be out," he growled. "An evil, evil night."

His garments were tattered, but Brother Christopher recognized the colors of a distant barony. "You are far from home," he observed.

The man scowled.

"We are all far from home, Father," he said. "We are far, far from God's grace."

Brother Christopher started to shake his head. He had met men like this before, men who let every inconvenience of life test their faith.

"No, Father, this time you cannot shake your head. This time you cannot attempt to tell me that I am close to the Almighty at all times, because this time I know differently. This time I have seen monsters, Father, and they are not beasts of the Lord."

Quietly, Brother Christopher stood, and collected the man's bowl. He left, and returned with more soup. "Tell me," he said, softly.

The man laughed, and it chilled the blood in the old priest's body.

"You know of bandits, I am sure, Father, and you know that many families who travel hire men such as I to protect them, to be their arms in case of attacks. This is what I was doing, exactly, earlier this evening, and all was well.

"We had sun through the trees and a clear sky. The only sounds we heard were the sounds of the forest and the sounds of the path. We were close to our destination, a small town close to here."

Brother Christopher nodded slowly. There was no small town near the monastery – no small town but for half a day's ride away.

"They came out of the trees, Father. They came from under the ground, and from out of the trees. They fell upon us with teeth and claws and we were overwhelmed. I was thrown from my horse, and hurled into the brush, and I was dazed and unable to move.

"They ran across me as if not seeing me and I truly believe that I am sitting here now only because they did not see me. Shades, shadows, beasts. I awoke from my dazed state to hear the screaming of the family I had sworn to protect. The child, I understood, as well as the woman, but the man... Father, may I never hear a man scream in this way as long as I live.

"I stumbled to my feet and drew my sword, but the sounds were already deep into the woods and growing fainter. I am no creature of the fen, Father, but I followed them as best I could, and was barely able to keep up. The screams were always a torch, but there was also a different sound, a hooting and calling as each of these things, these shadow beasts called to each other.

259

Close Your Eyes – Tales from the Blinkspace

"At some point, I believe the screams became too much for my prey and all became silent, although I could still hear their weird calls.

"I continued following, and for the rest of the day and into the night, I ran as fast as I could through the deep trackless woods, following sounds up in the trees, following the sounds of branches and bushes parting and admitting demons.

"At length, I came to a cliff, Father. A cliff that overlooked the sea. I cannot tell you in what direction I lay, nor could I ever be brought to a situation where I would want to go there again, for the instant I cleared the trees, I was assailed by the most heinous stench imaginable. It was wet and rotten and foul. The strength of it pushed me back into the trees for a while until I could move in it without sickness.

"I crawled to a nearby game path, and slowly descended, struggling through those vapours. I came to the base of the cliff, Father, and crawled on my belly like an animal, until I saw it."

Brother Christopher realized he was perched on the edge of his chair – indecorous indeed. He assembled himself. "Saw what, son?" he asked.

The man drained the next bowl of soup, and set his empty bowl on the floor. "I saw the beasts, Father. I saw them, and I thought them at first some sort of child, and then I saw that they were covered in hair, and then I thought of them as some form of ape, some hideous monster."

The man's eyes bored into Brother Christopher's eyes.

"I saw what happened to the family," he said.

"These beasts had taken them. They had dragged them to this place and they were… they were eating them."

The man's head fell into his hands.

"They worried at the raw flesh like dogs, Father. They ate them as I watched and I prayed to the Lord that the family had died before seeing the horror that faced them.

"This place I found was their nest, Father, and it was this nest that was littered with bones, littered with the remains of not only this family, but many, many others. Arms, armor, belongings, everything had been discarded in favor of the meat, Father."

Brother Christopher inhaled sharply. "That cannot be what you saw," he whispered.

"Do you think if I could insist I had seen anything else, I would not do so?!" cried out the man. "Do you think if I could even pretend that I had seen something more innocent, I would be only seeing that through the eyes of my memory?

"No, Father, I have been a soldier for twenty years, and when I tell you those were the bones of men, I am telling you the truth."

The man breathed deeply.

Close Your Eyes – Tales from the Blinkspace

"It is horrific," said Brother Christopher, "but surely these things can be hunted down. Surely your Duke can find them, can take a force and wipe out these animals."

"I wish it were as simple as that," said the man. He sighed deeply and rubbed his face.

"There is more," prompted Brother Christopher.

"There is more," replied the man. "I wish there was no more, but there is more."

"I did not lose my mind for something as simple as this. I hesitate to tell you, hesitate to taint your ears and your mind with all that I have beheld."

"I have witnessed a great deal," whispered Brother Christopher. "I am alone here where no man comes by, and the dark woods have revealed many terrible secrets to me."

"None like this, Father," said the man. He stood up and paced the room.

Brother Christopher waited. All men spoke once they found the space to do so.

Behind him, he felt the man move close.

He felt hands on his shoulders, as if the man needed this extra support to complete his confession, for surely it was exactly that.

"They were, Father, men. Men as beasts. Men as hungry, growling, naked, rutting beasts. Men as terrors, men as hunters of men. Men as eaters of men. And Father…"

The voice came close to his ear.

"Father, I felt that which moved through them. I felt it was no power of the Lord, no power of the heavens. It was something else, Father, something from deep within the earth. Something that oozed up through the rocks, through the ground, into the dead plants, the rotting bones, and those dancing beasts. That Something filled them and became them and their eyes were like black glass that had no end.

"And then, Father, even though I was far away from the bacchanalia, that Something saw me. I felt the ground swell beneath my feet, felt my body torn to hot ice as it came into me. I felt it fill my mind, my flesh, my soul."

He leaned close, lips inches from Brother Christopher's ear.

He whispered "Father, I felt its hunger!"

At first, Brother Christopher thought the tearing sound was cloth.

END

The Circle

Part of a writing marathon at the H. P. Lovecraft Film Festival, "The Circle" is inspired by Jim's request for something that included a certain amount of recursion...

He watched the boy playing. There was no one near, and the boy played in a pile of construction sand. He looked around to be sure. No one.

He walked around the pile. Still no one. He squatted down near the boy. No one.

The boy dug in the sand, made dams, poured water from a bucket, and made crashing sounds as toy cars fell into the water. Hundreds of people died in the boy's imagination, a massive loss of life due to a shattered dam giving way.

He stepped closer, quietly, fascinated. The boy played for a moment longer, then stopped. He scratched the back of his neck, and then paused. Slowly, unnaturally, the boy's head turned around, and looked at him.

He left.

*

"I learned nothing."

"This will not help you," Rama Ah Tanhep told him. "This will not tell you what you want to know."

Close Your Eyes – Tales from the Blinkspace

"Then I will do it again."

"As you wish."

*

He stared at the young man, who wrestled with the water pump of the 1966 Dodge Dart. It was being a real bastard. The crash had pushed the radiator back two inches, which was enough to make pulling the water pump a bitch and a half.

He circled the car and found no one but the young man, working.

He leaned close and looked at the work, saw the pump wedged deeply into the vehicle.

Then he looked at the young man himself, his handsome strong features, his sense of not recognizing his own mortality, of being a completely powerful creature. He was drawn into those eyes, their concentration. He drifted.

The man stopped working. Raised his head.

He stepped back, the spell broken. Stepped back and away, but the man turned his head and looked right at him.

He left.

*

"It makes no sense," he said.

"You are not looking for sense," said Rama Ah Tanhep. "you are looking for something else, and you are finding it. Every time."

"Have you ever been told you are frustrating?"

"Not by those who know better," said Rama Ah Tanhep.

"And snotty. More please."

"As you wish."

*

The man was in his own backyard, cutting down an apple tree with a hand-axe. It was an absurd moment.

He walked around the man, looking carefully. There was no one else.

He stepped around the tree, outside of the axe swing range, and looked over the hedge. No one there, either.

He sat down in the grass, cross-legged. This made no sense.

263

Close Your Eyes – Tales from the Blinkspace

He looked up at the man with the axe. He admired the single-minded approach, the regular strong rhythm. He gazed at the man, at the deep brown eyes. He was angry it wasn't working, angry he couldn't find his answers.

The rhythm stopped and the man grew suspicious. He looked around. Looked directly at him.

Angry, he left.

*

"You are so quiet," said Rama Ah Tanhep.

"I'm angry."

"This makes sense."

"To you, maybe, but this is very frustrating."

"That also makes sense."

"Not to me."

"Do you know how many times you've asked the question?"

"Seventeen. I remember quite clearly."

"And you still don't have the answer you thought you wanted?"

"No. And I can only ask the question once more."

"May I make a prediction?" asked Rama Ah Tanhep.

"Are you a prophet, now?"

"A guess?"

"Fine, guess."

"You will ask it only one more time, and you will not understand the answer, but you will be answered and you will understand that."

"You belong in a fortune cookie. An annoying fortune cookie."

"I'm sure there is no doubt in your mind."

"Just do it."

"As you wish."

*

He sat in the car, next to the man. The car was otherwise empty.

264

Close Your Eyes – Tales from the Blinkspace

He shook his head. It made no sense at all.

He looked in the back seat. No one. No one anywhere.

The road spooled under the wheels nearly a mile a minute and still, there was no one.

This, he decided, must be the most ridiculous thing.

Frustrated, he leaned back in his seat and looked at the man driving.

Even at this age, the man was handsome, with a well-formed face and a strong jaw, and always a look of determination and power.

I don't understand how, he thought, as he watched the man drive. His mind drifted.

The man's attention wavered, and he looked around the car. He looked directly in the passenger seat. His eyes suddenly focused, in a way they never had before. They opened wider and he mouthed a single word.

"You!"

In the smallest fraction of a second, he realized that the car had crossed the oncoming lane, that it was an impossibly small amount of time and space away from the front of the truck.

In that moment, in that miniscule fraction of time, he saw two things simultaneously. He saw all the times he had watched this man, all the times he had tried to figure out who else was there, and he also saw himself, working, playing, living his life, and feeling, sensing, and knowing that someone else was there, was watching him, and looking up, only to discover that there was no one there, no one he could see.

Except that now, now there was.

He finally understood Rama Ah Tanhep's answer.

And then they hit the truck.

END

Freedom's Cost

Part of a writing marathon at the H. P. Lovecraft Film Festival, "Freedom's Cost" is inspired by Andrew's request to explore his recent surgical strike.

I hear it in the darkness, the Thing that creeps. I feel it pushing and pulling, twisting my flesh with its own. I know it's there and I loathe it with every breath of my lungs, every pulse of my heart. It's a parasite.

I am alone in my struggle against this fiend. Utterly alone. No one believes me, no one offers help. No one looks upon my requests with anything other than disdain. I am alone.

The Thing is pressure. The Thing is pain. The Thing is malevolence. I know this in a way that leaves no doubt, and yet I am helpless. It has intertwined itself with my own body and I can feel it growing, swelling, bloating. It is hungry for my flesh and it consumes me.

I have asked for help. I have asked those of my family, and we speak of this only in whispers, and there is no help there. "Your burden," they whisper to me, and I know it's true. It is my burden, this Thing, as my father had a Thing and his father before him. We all have our burdens.

It seems so wrong, though, that each of us must shoulder this alone. It seems so wrong that here and now, where we are all a part of the warp and weave of Life's fabric, that there would still be things that are our own exclusive problem, that there would still be things for which we can ask no help. This seems so wrong, so horrible.

But it's true. I must deal with the Thing myself. I must handle its ignorance, its fury, its blind writhing.

Close Your Eyes – Tales from the Blinkspace

I study and think long upon this problem, enduring the pain and the feeling of its flesh against mine. I reach out and seek lore beyond my own, whisper to those other than my family, entreat them to teach me what they know.

And I cast.

Certainly, one can call them spells – I am not sure what the proper nomenclature would be. They seem to be spells, though I consider myself ultimately the master of my own Fate, and not beholden to some supernatural entity. (I know I am alone in this, as well, but it has become accustomed, at least). Regardless, I say the words, I make the gestures, and I feel forces moving around me, sliding around me, even touching me, in their eagerness to do my bidding. I know the costs are high for such exchanges, but the pain, ah, the pain never stops now, and my loathing consumes my every waking moment.

"Be away with it," I beg these forces, hoping they understand me in their own dumb, blind, subservient way.

I feel their eagerness to cause trouble, like a particularly wicked pet, and then they vanish.

But it is for naught. There is no effect.

The pain continues. The hate continues. The loathing continues. I feel its hate now as a palpable smothering blanket, and its presence in my every movement.

How can one survive such concentrated hate? What can be done?

No forces supernatural will help, and no help from my friends and family. Although I had hoped against it, I understand now that I am, in fact, truly alone, truly fighting against my own demon, on my own turf, and the prize is my own flesh and blood, my soul, my existence.

There are those who claim that no path of action that includes self-destruction is ever worth it, but for those who profess this, I offer humbly my own experience. There are times – and this is one of them – where the only defense is an offense. There are times when the best that one can do is to poison the flesh in hopes that the parasites within leave before the poison kills.

I start with my own mind, which is undoubtedly more sophisticated than this creature's. I meet and match its animal loathing with a more sophisticated framework of attack, a more detailed and direct application of my Will. I want it to know that not only do I loathe it as much as it loathes me, but that I want it gone, I want it evacuated, I want its life to completely end.

It recoils, and I press my advantage. I feel it quiver beneath my grasp. It retaliates, but I am clearly the superior intellect, the more advanced entity. I push hard.

It weakens, and I press.

Close Your Eyes – Tales from the Blinkspace

But, unbelievably, I feel it push back. How?! How could it push back so hard? It was simply a parasite, a thing that fed on me!

I become desperate. Emotional self-destruction was one thing, but would I be willing to attack it physically, to actually cause harm to myself in hopes of driving it away, or possibly in hopes of killing it? I could not know for sure, and there was no advice from anyone save the same, repeated, endlessly frustrating "Your burden."

So be it.

I fight how I can. I pinch and prod back, I twist and squeeze, I pull and push. I claw and growl and if I could have reached it with my teeth, I would have bitten.

Where the effects of my psychological attack were subtle, these effects were far more direct. Far more dramatic.

I swear it had teeth and it bit right back. Sometimes for hours on end, I lay clenched in agony, eyes squeezed shut. But I did not let this stop my own attack. I was not going to let this Thing beat me. This was war, and I was determined to win.

I fight. I punch, I kick, I do everything I can possibly think of.

And then, one day, I feel it relent. I feel it relax and go limp, its deadly grasp loosen and slip. I pray that this is me, winning this war, that this was how it feels to reach a level of victory.

My body shifts, and I feel a slipping, and I know then, that I have won, that I have prevailed, that I am the victor. I know that it is dead and that now I am free of it.

The end is close and I heave. I heave and twist and push as hard as I can and then…

…ah, then…

There is a burst of noise, a flailing of limbs, and a light – a brilliant light – that blinds me. Air chills my skin. My fingers, still bloody with my adversary's flesh, wave frantically.

I am held high in the air by bands of shining steel, and my eyes, adjusting to the brilliance, frame great towering monsters of white, circling me.

"It does not matter!" I shout. "I hate you all. I will fight you all! I will fight until there is no life left within me!"

They surround me, and I see holes and pits opening and closing, hear air whistling and hooting past the valves. They speak to each other this way, they make animal cries to each other? It must be this.

I gasp, I writhe, but I can not free myself.

I look down. Trailing from my own flesh is a series of braided vessels, spiraling down into a red nest of heaving organs and torn tissue, spattered in blood and fluids.

268

Close Your Eyes – Tales from the Blinkspace

I see a flash of silver, a cutting tool, slicing through those vessels.

"No!" I snarl, and buck, but it was no use. I watch as fluid dribbles out at first, and then pulses. In horror, I realize this pulsing matches my own heartbeat. "No, no, no!" I wail.

I had won! I had beaten the Thing, the parasite. What hideous gods ruled over such a Universe that even in my triumph I would watch my own life ebb away, draining off.

My mind fades, fragments, falters.

A wicked twist of fate in those last seconds of life allow me to make some sort of terrifying sense of the hooting and whistling sounds around me, resolving them into actual voices, phonemic ideas.

I hear, and despair.

> *"...nearly eleven inches long, Doctor."*

> *"...what a right bastard..."*

> *"Bring the specimen container here. We have to save this."*

> *"Unbelievable. How could it have grown so big...?"*

And then the last of my life's blood falls from my mind and I am lost in the darkness forever.

END

There was Record of its Passing

Part of a writing marathon at the H. P. Lovecraft Film Festival, "There was Record of its Passing" is inspired by Andrew's request to explore his recent surgical strike.

"It's nothing at all," said the doctor, his voice wet with glee. He patted Andrew's arm in a manner meant to be reassuring, and stepped back. "I think you're just worrying overmuch about things, Andrew. I think you need to relax a little more. Maybe take a trip. When's the last time you were on vacation?"

Andrew stared at his doctor. This man had been his doctor since he was a child, and was the doctor for his parents, as well. For all he could remember, this man had been the doctor for generations of Migliores past.

"It's been a while," he stammered out. "I've been really busy, the new business is still kinda stumbling…"

The doctor took Andrew by the shoulders. "Son," he said, and the word sent liquid shivers through Andrew's spine. "You work too hard. I can see it in the way you sit here, the way you move and the way you breathe. You work too hard."

Andrew kept staring at this man. He always felt the doctor's eyes were a bit too wide, a bit too open, and blinked a bit less often than any man's should. There was something cold in his touch, something unsettling.

The doctor nodded. "You know it's true, I can tell in your eyes. Andrew, look, I have an idea." He fished around in his pocket, and pulled out a crumpled note. He handed it over. "This is a fellow I know up in Kingsport. He has a place. A bed and breakfast.

Close Your Eyes – Tales from the Blinkspace

Very calm place. I often go there to relax. You should call him. Tell him I sent you. I'll let him know you're coming. He'll give you my rate. It's worth it, Andrew."

He patted Andrew's stomach, causing a wince. "It's very much worth it. You need to relax."

The note stayed in Andrew's pocket for a week.

Thanksgiving dinner with his family was a quiet affair, strained and silent. Afterwards, his father took him to the drawing room.

For a few moments, they smoked quietly. Expensive cigars.

"What's eating you, son?" his father asked.

Hesitating at first, but then more freely, Andrew told him.

"That's all?" asked his father.

"There needs to be more?"

"No, no, I was just… well, I was afraid there was something else, is all. But now, this makes sense." He shrugged. "There are probably aspects of our family history about which I have been neglectful in the telling," he said. "There are things that I was hoping I wouldn't have to tell you. About yourself. About me. About my father and his father before him."

Andrew's breathing shifted. He became wary. The room seemed to be closing tightly about his body like an oak-paneled blanket.

"What… what are you saying?" he asked.

His father leaned in close, and rested a hand on Andrew's shoulder. It felt like a claw, tipped with razors. For a fraction of a second, Andrew imagined it tearing through the sweater, ripping into the flesh, wrenching bone and joint apart.

"Son," his father told him. "We – our family – has a history of… troubles."

"What sort of troubles?"

"Ulcers."

For a moment, there was silence.

"I'm sorry, son. I should have said something, but I knew it would make you nervous. I knew you would worry, and I know that ulcers, well, ulcers have a way of allowing worry to exacerbate them."

"An ulcer?" he asked.

His father nodded. "This is probably what's going on," said his father.

"But the doctor told me I just needed to rest."

Close Your Eyes – Tales from the Blinkspace

"Sure, sure, and the Doc's right about that. You do need to rest, son, and there's no doubt about that. But you also probably have an ulcer."

"An ulcer…?"

"Don't worry – no shame in it. No shame at all. You just have to keep this in mind, you have to relax more. Maybe think about hiring an assistant at the shop, and maybe take a vacation. It's really not an—"

"I don't have an ulcer!" shouted Andrew.

His father drew back and eyed his son.

"Stop talking to me about ulcers. I don't have an ulcer. Don't you think that was the first thing I thought it might have been? Don't you think I looked already and tried to figure this out for myself? It's not an ulcer. It can't be an ulcer."

"Son, there's no need to get upset. If you want to, we can—"

Andrew stood up. "No," he cried out. He started to pace the room. "It can't be an ulcer. Listen to me. I have been feeling this… this thing inside me for months. It's not in my stomach, it's not something I ate, it's not something I drank. Every day, it hurts a little more, and every day, I try to keep finding out what it is. Sometimes I can feel it moving. Sometimes I can feel it twitching and squirming like some kind of animal. Like some kind of parasite under my skin. I can feel it. It has arms that grasp at me, teeth that bite at me, feet that paw at me. I can feel it under there, like something hideous and evil, like something hungry for my soul."

Never before had he treated his father with anything but deference, but this time, he stood in front of the man and stared him down.

"It is not an ulcer."

His father stared back, but eventually softened. Every man must face an angry son at one time or another in his life, and this time, it was his turn. He sighed deeply.

"I realize how hard it is to learn we all have these things," he started to say, but Andrew raised a hand, palm out.

"No. I don't want to hear it. It's not an ulcer. It can't be."

He snuffed the cigar out, rested it carefully next to the ashtray, and brushed himself off. "I have to leave. Please convey my apologies to the rest of the family."

The drive back home was interminable. Every thirty seconds, the Thing inside him twitched, the Thing inside him kicked, the Thing inside him reached out and tried to claw its way free.

"You are no ulcer," he muttered, teeth clenched against the pain. "You are not a thing that can go away through relaxation, that can vanish magically if only I take a nap."

272

Close Your Eyes – Tales from the Blinkspace

As if in response, a painful tremor rippled through him. He bent forward against the wheel of the car, grunting in pain. It happened again, this time stronger.

He pulled over to the side of the road, panting, sweat beading his forehead.

"You are not an ulcer," he repeated. "I have known this since you came unto me and I know this now more than anything in the world."

He pushed the door open and stepped out into the road.

Another wave of agony bent him sideways, and he fell against the fender. "You bastard," he said. "You bastard."

He staggered to the trunk, shaking and sweating. He fumbled the keys into the lock and popped the lid open.

"You are not an ulcer," he said, and leaned down, sifting through the trunk's contents, tossing aside trash from previous trips, old towels, toys, indications of previous pleasures.

Another wave of pain, and he was blinded by stabbing and biting in his abdomen.

A tooth chipped from the grinding of his jaw, but he didn't care. He screamed there, alone in the road, and his body twitched, spasmed.

"You are not an ulcer!" he screamed.

He saw then what he was looking for, and he reached into the trunk. He pulled out the crowbar, the all-purpose tool that every car needed, and he looked at the tip, the broad spade-shaped tip.

He laughed a wet spittle-flecked laugh. "Now it ends," he gasped, as the pain crashed into him in increasing waves. "Now, now, now it ends," and he raised the crowbar high.

Two hours later, three police cars surrounded Andrew's car. Two grim men in black uniforms stood sentinel while two others vomited into the ditch.

"Jesus," the tall one said. "Are you sure?"

"Doc'll tell for sure, but look. What do you think? You think someone could have done that to him? That happen a lot, upstate?"

The tall policeman shook his head slowly. "No," he said at long last, "but it's even harder to imagine he did that to himself. I mean... I mean, how *could* you?"

"In a certain kind of madness," said his partner, "a man can do anything to himself of which he can conceive. He can stand doing things to himself he would never tolerate from another. He becomes a creature of insane passion, and in this passion, he is capable of great and terrible things."

273

Close Your Eyes – Tales from the Blinkspace

He rested a hand against his partner's shoulder. "The longer you're on the Force here, the more you'll see this sort of thing. Comes with the territory."

"But what about that?" asked the tall one. "What is that?"

The shorter policeman took a deep breath. "I think I'll wait for the Doc to get here to check, if it's all the same to you, but I think he took something out of himself and threw it over there. Threw it into the bushes. Something wet."

The rookie stepped closer – but not too close, and shook his head. "I don't know. I don't know. That doesn't look like spatter pattern."

"What do you know from upstate anyway? What do you think it looks like?"

"I think it looks like footprints."

END

The Fine Print

Part of a flash-fiction writing competition for Jay Lake, "The Fine Print" is inspired by a single photo of a hat lying by a stream. I had to reconstruct the photo because I couldn't find the original photo I used. But that's fine -- I like this one better anyway.

"No, no," she said, as she read the letter. "It's not right." The paper slipped from her hand and she ran out, into the sunlight, past the garage, and down the path.

The sun strobed her eyes through the trees, and she could feel the headache coming on like a cat that's grown too big. A patch of light caught her eye, and triggered the bomb. She stumbled, tripped over a stupid root, fell, rolled, smacked her back against a tree. Her shoulder bit her spine and she gasped.

"Not right," she hissed, and dragged herself to her feet. A corner of her mind grumbled about pine sap on her arm.

The path fell open to the stream, where it fed into the ocean. No shade, no darkness, no shadows at all. "Supposed to be night," she said. "Night!"

The pain spread down from her head and across her shoulder. "Any damn excuse," she thought to herself, and then her mind started ripping apart.

He was gone. Only his hat remained, his peculiar conceit. "This hat'll follow me wherever I go," he once told her, just to be annoying.

Close Your Eyes – Tales from the Blinkspace

Both arms now sang with pain, and she fell, next to the hat. "Won't be following you now," she said, and another spasm bent her. She coughed and something red came out. Something she wasn't going to need any more.

"You said it," his voice whispered in her ear, and she knew. "But I still hate you for it," she said, and she heaved another Useless Thing out.

Her fingers clutched rocks, her back screamed and crackled and folded and twisted. His voice still whispered into her ear, whispered from the water, sweet things she alone could hear. "In sickness and in health," he whispered. "For richer or for poorer," he whispered.

She tried to say "Bastard," but her mouth could only croak, and she rolled painfully into the cool, cool, welcoming water, her skin sloughing off, her arms pinwheeling, her legs breaking themselves, and changing, reforming into something more useful.

"'Til death us do part," she heard, and then she had no ears.

What she was now slipped away, silver flashing in the water, reflecting the sun, until it reached depths where there was no sun, and then she was gone.

END

The Dream House

I think this has happened to me quite a few times, which is probably why I don't go to Canada as often...

I dreamed of the place three times before I started seriously to wonder.

It was a flat, grassy place on the top of a tall cliff, overlooking an ocean that boiled with fury. Each time I dreamed of the place, I was closer and stayed longer. Each time I dreamed of the place, I felt myself both pulled toward it and pushed away. I felt as if something in my soul wobbled and tilted dangerously awry, as if I wasn't just on the edge of a cliff in my dreams, but on the edge of a cliff in my heart.

I felt... endangered by the place.

Yet still, I dreamed of it. I dreamed of the cliff and the cold gray waves and the mist, and the feeling that washed over me whenever I was in that place – a feeling I could only describe as despair and loss.

I would not have the dream every night, but roughly once a week. Often enough that some of the details began to remain even after I woke up.

I took at first to cribbing notes by my bed, and then eventually to sketching images before the morning sun blew them from my mind.

It was a curiosity.

Close Your Eyes – Tales from the Blinkspace

Soon, it became an obsession.

My colleagues at work were tolerant of some of my questions, and of the time I spent browsing travel books instead of socializing with them during lunch and breaks. At first, some even helped me, reviewing my sketches and looking through books as well. You would think that the number of picturesque cliffs in the world overlooking cold gray water might be a reasonable number a man could review in a reasonable time, but that would be a sad, sad mistake.

After a while, my colleagues stopped trying to help and pursued their own diversions.

Eventually, even my friends stopped trying to help.

I can't blame them – the odds of the place being real seemed microscopically small, and the odds of finding it even slimmer.

With the dreams still slicing into my sleep, it was a year and a half before I found pictures in a magazine that seemed promising. They weren't pictures of the cliff itself, but pictures of turbulent slate waves crashing against rocks in a way that was inhospitable in exactly the way the waves in my dream crashed against the base of the cliff.

I gambled, and started focusing my search on this geographic region, an area north of Victoria, in British Columbia. The rocks seemed right. The water seemed right. It all seemed right.

There was, unfortunately, a dearth of photos available of that area. I was able to collect a few, but I think my collection represented less than a tenth of the coastline that included the cliff I continued seeing.

For three days I worried and wondered and counted the diminishing amounts in my accounts, but at the end of those three days I concluded that I had known I was going to go there all along.

I booked a flight that evening and within 24 hours, chased a sunset across the country in a broad-bodied jet.

By the same time the next day, I was driving a rental car along a road that hadn't properly been called a road in at least fifty years.

But I knew I was close. I could feel it.

I found the cliff three hours later.

The actual cliff.

What I didn't expect to see was the house.

On the high cliff, a small house balanced precariously near the edge.

Close Your Eyes – Tales from the Blinkspace

For having been this exposed to the weather, the house seemed to be in excellent shape. The paint was fresh, the high gambrel roof looked new, and the windvane spun with nary a whisper.

I stared at the impossibly white door, then raised a hand to knock.

It opened.

A man stared out at me, over a pair of tiny glasses.

"You made it!" he cried out in joy, and then he snarled "What are you doing here?"

I hesitated in a place of two conflicting emotions, and then settled on simply taking a step back.

"Oh no, you mustn't leave," he said. "We've been waiting for you. But you," he added in a harsher voice, "you must leave at once. You are not welcome here."

He cocked his head. "Come in," he said, then added "Stay out."

I stepped back once more and said "Excuse me, but I don't understand. I dreamed of this place."

His face was as cloudy as the sky. "Of course you don't," he said. "And if I have any say in the matter, you never shall." Then his smile broke through and he said "I am so glad you heard me, dear friend!"

He reached out a hand in greeting and without thinking, I took it. He shook it warmly and I could feel friendship in that grip. Then the fingers tightened and the grip felt like something else, something cold and merciless and wicked.

He shoved hard against my stomach and I tumbled backwards.

In an instant, he was on me.

"I'm so sorry – how could I possibly have hurt you?" he cried out, and then he struck the side of my head with a closed fist. Despite his being an old man, there was a part of my mind that admired how hard he could punch.

I tried to ward him off and he pinned my wrists to the ground. He slammed his forehead against my face a couple of times. I heard something pop inside my skull.

He was in tears. "Forgive me! Forgive me! How can I make it up to you – I'm being a terrible host."

Again, he struck me with his head, and this time, I felt my consciousness swirl briefly away, then back.

His face was close to mine, staring into my eyes, as I drifted back to wakefulness.

"I've missed you," he whispered, and he slapped my face, hard.

279

Close Your Eyes – Tales from the Blinkspace

He slapped it twice more.

I tried to back away from him, but I was weak and disoriented. I saw him pick up a rock and advance on me. "We all need you so much," he said. "We're nothing without you."

He swung the rock, and there was a flash in my skull.

I awoke sometime later. Probably not too much, because the sun was still in the sky, albeit low.

I had been placed at the edge of the cliff. A single rope was tied around my torso, and cinched up to my armpits.

"I think you weigh too much," said the old man, who stared into my eyes. "I think you shall snap this rope."

I tried to nod, but my head throbbed when it moved. I managed a gasp.

"Don't bother trying," he said. "It doesn't matter. We shall see if this rope holds you when I kick you from this cliff."

My head turned back to the cliff. I was much closer to the edge than I thought. Much, much closer.

"Time to test the rope," he said, and he kicked me hard.

Screaming, I fell over the cliff.

The first two seconds I was in sheer panic. Nothing meant anything to me. In the next second, I gathered up my wits enough to realize I was falling down to the rocks and waves below. I barely had time to wish I'd hit a wave instead of a rock.

Then I hit the rock.

I stared for a long time at the rocks. I stared at the body lying down there, its salty blood mingled with the salty waves that lapped at it.

I looked back up the rope at the face of the old man who watched me.

"Freyken," I said. "Please bring me up."

He grinned and hauled me up.

Once I was on safe ground, I looked back at the rocks below.

"He wasn't meant to stay," I said.

Freyken nodded. "I'm sorry," he said. "I had no idea he was still there, or I wouldn't have called you."

I looked down at myself. I looked at my clothes. They were distinctly human clothes. I looked over the cliff. He wore the same thing.

280

Close Your Eyes – Tales from the Blinkspace

"I'm glad you did," I said. "I think if you hadn't, I might have lost myself and become entirely him."

Freyken looked down at the rocks with me, and shook his head sadly.

"That, old friend, would be terrible. Tragic, no less."

I looked at him. Neither of us looked good as humans. Too lumpy.

"While I'm here, I might as well send my report," I said, and walked toward the house.

"We've missed you and your reports a great deal," he said as he stepped in behind me.

END

No Trouble

Part of a writing marathon at the H. P. Lovecraft Film Festival, "No Trouble" is inspired by Derek – because I think he should embrace the Dark Side and make another movie.

"I am not mad!" Derek cried out, but the shattered teeth and torn lips and tongue garbled it beyond reason.

He saw the silver revolver brought to bear, and spun aside, just as it barked and a bullet creased his side.

"Do not do this! Leave me be! There is nothing I want more in life than to be left alone, for the love of God!" Again, it was garbled.

He fell to the ground and rolled, while another bullet ricocheted from the tile.

The window was a good twenty feet away, across open space. An impossible journey right now – he would be dead before he'd crossed five feet.

He slid under a metal table, hurt, confused and, progressively, more angry. He knew the table would only shield him a moment, but it was better than nothing.

A bullet dimpled the metal and seeing that it didn't penetrate, he breathed a brief sigh of relief.

Then the idea struck.

Close Your Eyes – Tales from the Blinkspace

He reached down, his fingers wrapping around the steel edges of the table. He picked it up effortlessly.

Two more bullets struck, and only dimpled the metal.

He tried to remember, tried to understand how many bullets a revolver held. Somehow, he was sure it was six, but at the same time, he wasn't willing to gamble his life on it.

He considered hurling the table at his tormentor, the little blonde man with the damnable needle, but instead, he rushed toward him, holding the table.

He felt the meaty impact, and kept running until he struck the wall, the Doctor pinned between the table and the painted cinder block.

The Doctor fell into a lab-coated pile on the floor.

He reached down and felt for a pulse. Fast, but strong. Good. He had no reason to kill this man – only reason to escape.

He carried the table over to the window and smashed the glass. Then he rifled through a drawer and found a set of clothes that fit acceptably, and left though the door.

He would need to hide for a while and assess his situation, this much he knew.

*

Eventually, Doctor West drifted into consciousness the same way someone would dip into a pool – one frozen inch at a time. His head throbbed and there was blood on the back of it. He wobbled to his feet and reviewed the state of things.

The morgue was definitely a shambles.

He staggered over to the window and saw that the beast had smashed through it. Glass was everywhere.

"Mindless thing," he muttered.

It was time to leave this town.

END

Maturation

Part of a writing marathon at the H. P. Lovecraft Film Festival, "Maturation" is inspired by Caitlín's request for something futuristic, with nanotech.

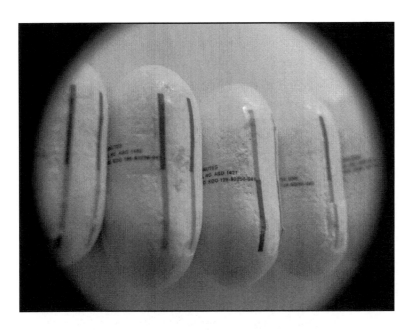

The room was cold.

"You could heat it up in here," Caitlín said. She wrapped her arms around herself, but it didn't seem to help.

"I'm sorry," Doctor Migliore said. "There was a mixup with the grant and we had to come over to the smaller offices in this wing." He shrugged. "Facilities hasn't quite figured out we're here yet, so the heat doesn't kick on until ten."

She shivered.

"Look," he told her, "we've been putting up with this for more than three weeks, so we've got some blankets. Here." From a cupboard behind the table, he withdrew a couple of blankets. Smallish things, dark blue.

"These are from airplanes."

He nodded. "Probably why they charge so much now," he said. "We stole all eight of their blankets."

Close Your Eyes – Tales from the Blinkspace

He stepped over to the computer to review her information. At least that's what it looked like, based on what she could see around his shoulders. A Post-It note was taped to the bottom of the monitor, reading "No Gaming!" She grinned. Networks.

"So, how you doing this morning?" he asked.

"I need coffee," she said. "Saturday is inappropriate for an eight a.m. appointment."

He nodded. Typed a few things. Turned around. "Dick!" he called.

An intern popped out.

"Could you get Caitlín some coffee, please?" he turned to her, quizzically.

"Just black," she said, "and hot, please."

"The good stuff from the Cat Lab, too, if Jane's not paying attention. Don't give her the stuff we drink. If she catches you, tell her it's for a subject."

"You got it!" and Dick vanished.

"Okay, just working through a few things on your intake form but while I'm doing that, if you have any questions at all, please feel free to ask."

Caitlín looked around. It wasn't a complicated setup, a fairly simple lab, but a bit on the low-rent side. The equipment was sparse, but still modern. Everything was clean, and that was a good sign. The lights didn't flicker.

"How long you been here?" she asked.

"Well, in this lab, been about three weeks, but here at the University, about four years. Been a real ride, though. No one likes Human Subjects Research around here." He shook his head. "It took us four applications to even get a hearing in front of the Board."

He squinted at something on the screen.

"You're not a student?"

"Is that a problem?"

"No, no, it's fine, I'm just not used to non-students participating in studies. Students are the ones always willing to do anything to their bodies to make a little beer money, is all." He looked quickly up at her. "Not that we're just doing 'anything,' mind you. It's that students, well…"

She smiled. "I understand. Not a student, but I have a lot more free time than I used to and I do miss being on campus, so I figured I'd try this. It sounded interesting."

"Oh, it is!" he said.

Close Your Eyes – Tales from the Blinkspace

"Although the forms weren't exactly super-clear," she said. "Something about immune system work?"

Dick came in, balancing a huge cup of coffee. "I hope this is enough," and handed it over.

Caitlín blew on it a bit and sipped. "Thanks, that's perfect."

Dick looked back up at the Doctor. "I'll be right outside the door if you need me," and once again vanished.

The Doctor looked at her cup. "I think he thought you were looking for a swimming hole."

"It's okay, I drink a lot of coffee when I'm not otherwise drinking or eating."

"Yeah, sorry about that. We kinda needed your system clean to get good readings."

She nodded. "So, immune system work?" she prodded.

"Right. Well, yeah, basically we're testing your immune system. It shouldn't be a huge thing – the whole process takes only about half an hour or so."

She raised an eyebrow. "And I have to come back when?"

"Oh, well, only if you have any troubles. The aftercare form'll have all that information. We do it here. Real quick."

He turned the monitor a bit so it faced her more.

A slide appeared, a microphotograph, of a smooth-surfaced ovoid, with a series of holes ringing it.

"This is ours," he said. "Basically, it's a kind of artificial blood cell, designed for a very specific purpose. Although it looks a little like a red blood cell, it's more like a white blood cell. With a cape."

She peered at the image. It slowly rotated.

"You made those?"

"Well, that's about as accurate a description as any. We grew them. Or rather, encouraged the components to grow together in just a certain way. They're a kind of maintenance machine, in the general sense, but these are specifically designed to hunt down a particular kind of tracer. In the long run, we're looking at these being a kind of regular injection, to help with someone's immunity."

"So you would, for example, be able to cure a disease."

"Or just protect from one, yes. Assuming we had the proper profile."

She looked up at him. "I've read stories…"

286

Close Your Eyes – Tales from the Blinkspace

He smiled. "We all have. Nope, these won't go haywire. No AI, no hidden intelligences, no secret desire to take over the world. They just fix things, keep everything moving along, and keep you healthy. These particular models have had most of that programming set aside, and they only have a life span of about forty minutes before they break down."

"Seems impractical," she said.

"It's still being tested. There's code for replication, and that's nearly half their programming, but again, we've clipped that away, so once they die, they just die and your body flushes them out. They're pretty much inert after that.

"What we're going to do is inject a sample of them into you, and then in five minutes, inject a collection of tracers. They're a small bit of organic material – harmless – but the maintenance machines are designed to find them and destroy them."

"How do you know if they work?" she asked.

"Each machine sends us a little report." He smiled and showed her a section of the screen, a narrow piece that was empty. "Each machine sends us its own signal, tells us what it's doing. It'll be kinda messy for a while, but it'll peter out as they start breaking down. We'll do a full analysis afterward, but this is just kind of a real-time review."

He entered a little more data, then checked his watch.

"Ready to start? Any more questions?"

She thought about it.

"No, I'm good. Let's get started."

He nodded.

The injection itself was painless.

A few more entries in the computer…

"Am I waiting for anything in particular?" she asked.

"No," the Doctor said. "At this stage, mostly what's happening is that the machines are just spreading through your system."

As if in response, the edge of the screen lit up.

"See," he said. "Little robot status reports."

Caitlín pointed at the screen. "What's that mean?"

One of the entries was in red text.

287

Close Your Eyes – Tales from the Blinkspace

"Oh, that's odd," he said. He peered more closely. "It looks as if some set of the machines has shut down. That's not supposed to happen."

He tapped a few keys.

Other lines turned red, and the previous red lines turned bright blue again.

"Okay, well, that's not happened in the other subjects, but I think it's probably fine…"

His voice trailed off.

"Doctor…?"

All the lights were back to blue. He turned to her.

"Everything should be fine, but for some reason, all the machines shut down and rebooted. Very peculiar."

"But that's okay, right?" asked Caitlín.

"Oh, it should be okay, just, it's never happened before. Normally, they kick right in, but this batch is acting differently."

Caitlín coughed. "Not bad, though?"

"Oh no, not bad. Probably better, in fact. Looks like the reboot opened the full code sequence."

He thought about it a moment, then shook his head.

"No, we're going to have to stop. We're not ready to test the full sequence. I'm sorry, Caitlín, but we're not going to complete the test."

She looked doubtful.

"Don't worry," he said. "It's not a big deal. I just send a halt signal and they all shut down. Instead of waiting forty minutes, they immediately become inert. It's like popping a breaker."

He tapped at the screen.

The reporting window flashed a couple of times and then all the signal lines switched to red.

The Doctor turned to her. "See, no problem. We'll keep you here maybe half an hour, if that's okay by you, just to keep an eye on–"

"Doctor, what's that mean?"

Caitlín pointed at the screen. All the report lines had switched back to blue.

She coughed again, a deeper cough.

288

Close Your Eyes – Tales from the Blinkspace

"That… that makes no sense," he said. He peered more closely at the feeds. "They're not supposed to do that at all. They've turned themselves back on."

A third coughing fit hit Caitlín and she doubled over. The Doctor turned to her.

"Dick, get in here!" he called out.

"Look up," he said to her. "Look up at me, Caitlín."

She looked up, and blinked. "It's bright," she said.

He looked into her eyes.

"That's not right," he said.

She shaded her eyes, then coughed again, shaking a bit.

"I'm… I'm getting really cold," she said.

The Doctor turned to the computer. "Dick, wrap her in blankets and call nine-one-one."

Blankets went around Caitlín as she started shivering. Doctor Migliore stared at the screen.

"They shouldn't be doing this. They've reset to their whole program. They're replicating and they're following their maintenance routine. But why…?" he turned to her. "Caitlín, have you been sick recently?" he asked.

She shook her head. "I've never been sick in my life," she said. "Not once."

"This makes no sense, then," he said.

"What's happening?" asked Dick.

"The machines are repairing what they think is some kind of damage or error," said the Doctor.

"Why is this… why am I like this?" asked Caitlín.

The Doctor looked at her again. "I don't know," he said. "Something's going on, the machines are doing what they're supposed to be doing, but it's not what we expected."

He looked into her eyes again. "I don't understand," he muttered.

She looked back at him and inhaled sharply, her nostrils flaring.

"Doctor," she said. "You smell… you smell…"

He held her by her shoulders, staring into her eyes. "What's going on?" he asked, partially of her, partially of himself.

Caitlín's head shifted, her eyes opened wide, and her pupils dilated.

Close Your Eyes – Tales from the Blinkspace

"Dick, go get me the—"

Her hand wrapped around his throat, stopping the words. He heard Dick gasp as well, and glanced over. Likewise, he was held in her other hand. Her fingers seemed longer, and felt like steel bands. Tight steel bands.

"I think I've figured it out," she whispered, and her voice was thick and wet. "Your machines are doing exactly what they're supposed to be doing. Fixing a mistake."

She licked her lips and her tongue was thin and black.

"…It's just a little ahead of schedule, though."

A thin nictitating membrane flickered over her eyes and she inhaled again.

"Ah, Doctor, you smell… delicious. Did you know that?" She stood up from the table. He hadn't quite remembered her being this tall. Her skin rippled iridescent and he heard a soft crackling from her as she kept straightening her back more, getting taller each time.

"Normally," she whispered, "We wait. It's best to mature with the rest of the family. But I'll be able to find them quickly enough. And won't they be delighted to find out how easy it is…"

She twisted each hand and both necks snapped.

The Doctor's mind slivered and fragmented, but his last thoughts were hearing her silvery wet voice.

"…how easy it is to hunt."

END

Close Your Eyes – Tales from the Blinkspace

A Progression of Eyes

More of a true story than you might think...

It all started with my camera.

My first camera was a 110 camera I won in grade school. I took many pictures with it.

A relative gave me a nearly toylike automatic 35mm, which I used until it broke.

By that time, I could afford to buy a shitty – but still tremendously better than what I had – 35mm SLR camera from a pawn shop. I used that camera for nearly twenty years before it disintegrated.

I subscribed to several different photography magazines, ever since I was a kid. I avidly read reviews, and took notes and planned my career as a professional photographer.

This went on until adulthood, whereupon I had two absolutely critical revelations.

The first was that I had absolutely no hope of ever being a professional photographer. First of all, I grew up poor as dirt. No matter how much I tried, neither my allowance or, later, my paycheck, ever came close enough to be able to afford those multi-thousand dollar cameras, those fancy chemicals, a house with a room I could devote to being a darkroom. Financially, I wasn't there. But even more importantly than that, I knew I'd never be a professional photographer because I seemed to be missing the Photographer Gene. I could never understand all the settings on a camera, all the f-

Close Your Eyes – Tales from the Blinkspace

stops and aperture settings. I was too impatient to understand the chemistry enough to develop my own pictures, and always went for the cheapest developer in town (which was K-Mart until that funky mail order place started up). I dutifully read the articles, but they practically seemed like a foreign language to me. Finally, I was pretty much ignorant of the subtleties of color. I wasn't colorblind per se, but when I looked at those glossy magazine pages with all their comparisons of this or that fancy film or fancy paper, they all looked exactly the same to me. I felt like a fly being asked to judge the difference between a Matisse and a Rembrandt. My abilities were about on par with the fly's, in that invariably, the best I could do was shrug and declare none of the candidates to be shit.

The second revelation, which ameliorated the first one quite a bit, was that I simply didn't care. I might not have the intellectual and perceptive acumen to tell the difference between Tri-X film and a banana leaf, but at least I was satisfied that the same lack of discrimination prevented me from feeling bad about it.

So, I took pictures. Hundreds of pictures. Probably thousands. Maybe one or two per roll I thought was neat, and every few rolls, I kicked out something that I really loved.

If this were a feel-good movie, this is the part where I would reveal that I was discovered by an agent, and the critics and public all agreed that my "out of the box" thinking was the sign of avant garde genius.

That did not happen, nor do I expect it to ever happen.

But I was having fun.

One of the important pieces about my first revelation was that it freed me of the need to be snooty about photography. When digital cameras came out, I was all over one of the first ones that came in cheap. I was still taking as many pictures, but now I could see it before I took it. I could adjust the settings and fiddle with it and get instant gratification.

This did not overly improve my picture taking, but it did result in a lot more pictures than before, when I had to wait for film to be developed to find out my focus was wonky.

Definitely thousands of pictures.

It's funny that I had to take thousands of pictures before I started noticing certain things.

As I've said, most of my pictures didn't turn out – attributable to all sorts of problems – but it was only after having that ability to review it instantly that I started seeing something that just didn't make sense.

I started seeing distortions.

Close Your Eyes – Tales from the Blinkspace

You know how once you buy a car, and suddenly you have the supernatural ability to see that same model all over town? I started looking back through my photo albums and loose pictures, and now that I've seen the distortions, I can't not see them.

In most of my pictures, there's distortion. Blurring, waving, wobbly lines.

I can't believe I never noticed it before now.

The distortions soon became the most amazing thing to me. I no longer cared about taking pictures of anything else.

I saw more of them in the city than anywhere else. When there were a lot of people out and about, I saw them. Now, sometimes when I was alone, there would be one in the distance, or one off in the periphery, but it was nothing compared to what I saw in groups and crowds. It was as if there was a whole second crowd of distortions.

One of the things in particular I realized, as I looked at my crowd photos, was that the distortions weren't random. They appeared in empty spaces, where there weren't any people. Oh, it would be a crowd, of course, but in that crowd, there would be a sort of gap or hole, and in the middle of that hole, a distortion appeared. At first, I figured that maybe there was something peculiar about that gap, something that made a distortion in the air happen. Eventually, however, I realized that wasn't the case. Eventually I realized that the people were avoiding those spots. The people were avoiding the distortions.

I started hunting distortions.

They were easy to find – every time I saw a crowd, I could look for one of those unusual gaps, take a picture, and sure enough, there was a distortion in it. A bit of wobbliness. Something not-quite right.

One day, I was at the waterfront. I was hunting distortions as usual, and was in the middle of a crowd. Camera to my face, I turned a slow circle, my back to the wharf railing. There were no gaps in the passing crowd, but I kept looking, just in case. Kept panning slowly.

I had nearly turned a full 180 when I saw it. Both the distortion and the gap. Right next to me. Less than a foot away.

I held my breath. I watched through the viewfinder, fascinated. I could actually see the distortion in the air, the faintest of shimmers. My eye watered, but I kept staring. As I watched, the distortion changed in tiny ways. As my eyes ate its shape, I felt my brain slowly accepting that this was a real thing, slowly filling in the gaps, The distortion started to look less like a simple distortion and more like a shape.

I felt a certain kind of madness creep down my neck.

It was definitely a shape. A shape that leaned on the railing, and looked out into the water, just as I often did when I wasn't hunting.

I adjusted a little more, and saw a little more.

My lungs were burning up – I had to breathe, but I couldn't make a sound. I couldn't move.

I watched the thing, and it completely ignored me, as much as it ignored all the other people who, without ever realizing why, stepped around it.

Finally, I couldn't stand it. As silently as I could, I exhaled.

It turned its head in the direction of the sound and looked at me. Not through me, not around me, but at me.

There are times, and I am willing to admit this, when human beings aren't the advanced life forms they like to pretend to be. There are times when we are exactly the same creatures who knelt at fires a half-million years ago, shaking a bag of bones to make the sun come up, to banish the shadows.

For me, that time was right then.

I couldn't take my eyes out of the viewfinder, but I stumbled backwards. Three steps. That should have been enough.

It turned fully and faced me.

I say it faced me, but then again, I don't know. I really don't. I think it faced me. I felt it face me.

It stepped toward me.

I was shaking terribly, and I have no idea how I kept the camera pressed to my face, but I did.

It took another step closer to me.

It reached out.

I screamed.

I wish I could report I was braver, or that I struck out at it, or that I did something other than scream and run, but I'm not an action hero, or anything else, for that matter. I screamed and I ran.

I ran as fast as I could – which wasn't as fast as I would have liked. I ran as far as I could – which wasn't as far as I would have liked. I ran until I couldn't run anymore, and then I took a breather and kept running.

My skin was crawling, my eyeballs burning, my hands shaking. I had long since looped my camera strap over my neck and shoulder, so at least I hadn't dropped my camera.

Close Your Eyes – Tales from the Blinkspace

At the corner of Columbia and Sixth, I leaned against a wall, panting desperately. I was out of breath, and my lips tasted like metal. My hands were shaking and the only thing my brain kept doing was repeating "No, no, no…" over and over like a broken toy.

After a few minutes, I calmed down enough that the shaking in my hands settled to a tremor.

I looked up and down the street. There were a few people out, walking, but nothing of note.

But still, my skin crawled.

I swore that I would not use the camera, that I would not look through the viewfinder, that I would not hold up that digital enhancement, but of course, the message had not completed its journey to my hands, who were already lifting the camera to my face.

In that case, then I would most certainly not look through the viewfinder. I would not try to see what else might be in this empty road. I would not open my eyes ever again to try and see what must have only been a heat wave, or a wind eddy. Thus, I was shocked to realize that I had, in fact, started looking down the street through my viewfinder.

I have, in my life, wished for many things. I've wished for a million dollars. I've wished for a new bike. I've wished for an "A" on a test. I would, without any shadow of a doubt, go back and not make any wish ever, if only the wish I made right then came true.

I wished I'd never looked through the viewfinder.

They filled the street. Like an army, they marched, a slow, deliberate, and maddening army. I could see them better. Still not reasonably well, but better. And, without a doubt, they could see me, because they all were walking toward me. Looking at me.

Then I realized it. I realized what was the issue. It was the camera. It had to be.

It started with the camera. It would end with the camera.

I left it on and lowered it. I saw them as their faces shifted downward, following it.

It was! It was the camera!

I set it on the ground and practically flew in the opposite direction, away from the madness filling the streets, away from the things that slipped through the air like breath.

At the corner, I turned and looked back. I saw the camera on the street, alone.

I saw the air around it shimmer and the distortions sliding around it, over it, reaching down with their ephemeral arms, reaching toward it.

Close Your Eyes – Tales from the Blinkspace

And I saw the camera shimmer, too, and then, as if it had suddenly forgotten it was a solid thing of this Earth, I saw it liquefy and splash open.

My hand stung, and I realized that in fear, I had shoved my knuckles into my mouth, and bitten them. I tasted blood. I whimpered.

And then I realized what I was seeing.

I was seeing them.

Whatever had happened in my brain was still in my brain. Was now a part of my brain.

I didn't need the camera any more. I didn't need anything. I could now see them, and I knew that I could never unsee them, that I could never pretend they weren't there, weren't all around us, moving and sliding between us. I stepped back, and my shoe knocked a bottle over.

They looked up.

At me.

My body turned to ice and fire at the same time and I rasped a breath and spun. I would run until I could run no more, and I would keep running. I would leave the city, and go where no one could find me. I would keep running until…

They were behind me, and I skidded to a halt.

I turned and the others were closer now.

I saw two old men talking across the street, as if this were any ordinary evening, and I knew they couldn't see what I could. They never would be able to.

I wasn't even sure they could see me anymore.

I opened my mouth to scream, but something flowed into it. Something that might have been an arm. Something that was cold as ice and wickedly malevolent. I couldn't close my mouth, and I felt it reach further.

I felt others wrap around me, from behind, and from the sides.

I felt them all surrounding me, and then, in the twisted ice of their arms and their faces that had no eyes, but stared into mine, I lost myself.

END

Blood of my Blood

A note found in a cabin deep in the woods of Oregon...

My dearest wife, always remember that my heart is yours forever. Always remember that.

I had hoped moving here would break my curse, but it only made things worse.

You often asked what horrors my past might have held to create such turmoil in my soul now. In some ways, this is the answer, and in other ways, I know it's not enough of an answer. For that, I'm sorry.

The voices that call me are the voices of my family. The nightmares that ripped me awake in the dark are the voices of my family.

Long before you and me, long before my father and grandfather, long before all of us, my family made an agreement with something dark. I don't know why. None of us know why. The reason is lost in time. But the commitment hasn't been.

Every son must go. Every son must change. Every son must become a thing of wings and teeth and hunger. We must travel across the darkness of eyeblinks and go into a shadow place and serve this beast forever.

But before we go, we must feed.

This is why I must leave now. I must leave while my mind is still human, while I can still control my feeding.

I know you understand.

Close Your Eyes – Tales from the Blinkspace

Please forgive me, my love.

Please forgive what I've done to you.

Please forgive what our son will do to you.

Always remember that my heart is yours forever.

END

The Publisher

Hellbender Media (Hellbender.net) offers rare and voracious entertainment for the reader who prefers the Unusual, including books, movies, games, and other fun things, as well as offering workshops, tutorials, and lots of interactivity with their fans.

Hellbender Media includes these and other strange products:

The DVD adaptation of one of the most amazing fantasy novels ever written.

A collection of bizarre short movies, composed entirely of 100% fun.

A 10-minute parody of the entire trilogy, hilariously told with... er, "puppets."

A short adaptation of one of Lovecraft's most intriguing tales.

The Author

Edward Martin III is a writer, an essayist, and an award-winning filmmaker from Portland, OR. He adapted and directed an animated adaptation of H. P. Lovecraft's *The Dream-Quest of Unknown Kadath*, produced *The Cosmic Horror Fun-Pak*, wrote and directed a 10-minute comprehensive period adaptation of *Lord of the Rings*, and is in deep post-production of *Flesh of my Flesh*, a ground-breaking independent zombie action movie. He's also in development or preproduction for several other feature films, and a handful of shorts.

Visit http://www.hellbender.net/ for more information.

Close Your Eyes – Tales from the Blinkspace

The Last Word

Writing the *Blinkspace* stories has been a remarkable journey. I never expected to make it through the whole year. I kept expecting that on some Thursday night (a new story was published every Friday for a year) I would completely crap out and the tap would just come up empty.

This almost happened several times.

On quite a few occasions, I'd be staring at a story that I'd been cobbling together. I'd stare and stare at it and actually think "No, I can't do this story – it's shit. "

The first time that happened, I panicked. Then I figured out the solution.

I'd lean back in my chair (which probably isn't as comfortable as I'd like it to be – or maybe I'm just getting old, who knows?) close my eyes and tell myself: "I get it. This isn't the story I'm *supposed* to write today. I'm cool with that. So, in that case, where is *this* week's story? " I'd just be quiet for a moment, let things wash over my brain.

And then it happened.

The story came.

In times like these, it was like watching a building explode in slow motion, in reverse. Many fragments would come together and then I'd see exactly the story I was supposed to write that week. I could tell that was the one.

And I wrote it.

Other times, I sat down thinking I was writing one story and as soon as my fingers started flying, the story would wrest itself away from me and travel in a direction I never anticipated. This, however, felt very natural.

What's really cool, what twists my brain up at the moment I'm writing this, is that I know I'm just touching the surface of the Blinkspace. I can already feel more stories.

I hope you enjoyed this trip, and I hope you enjoy the ones in the Future, too.

Wait-a-sec – this is sounding awfully woo-woo.

I'm not saying there's some kind of supernatural force at work, here.

But if there was, I would expect it to act exactly this way.

Made in the USA
Charleston, SC
12 January 2012